FORGET
WHAT
YOU
KNOW

CHRISTINA DODD

FORGET WHAT YOU KNOW

HQN

ISBN-13: 978-1-335-45384-6

Forget What You Know

HQN
22 Adelaide St. West, 41st Floor
Toronto, Ontario M5H 4E3, Canada
www.Harlequin.com

Printed in U.S.A.

For my in-laws, Tom and Lou,
who taught me a lot about a successful relationship on the day I walked in
and he was watching football on a muted TV while she read her book
and listened to show tunes on the record player.

As he said, "This way, I don't have to listen to the football commentators."

Thank you both for the great stories you told.

FORGET
WHAT
YOU
KNOW

1

A THOUSAND YEARS AGO, when the filthy, skinny miner tore the stone from the mud that cradled it for millennium and brought it to the surface, a sunbeam touched its craggy surface and in that instant, it blazed with the color of fresh blood. He had found a ruby, the largest and most magnificent ever forged in the fires of the earth. As he gazed in reverence, his son saw the interesting gemstone pulsing in the light, and driven by greed, he slit his father's throat and took the ruby for himself. Torn between the need to keep it as his prize, the desire to sell it for unimaginable riches and guilt for murdering the man who had given him life, he brooded over the unique stone…and fell into madness.

His wife imprisoned him in a miserable place among other madmen. To support her children, she searched his possessions. She found the stone and without hesitation, sold it to a wealthy merchant.

Seeking wisdom, the merchant took the ruby to the highest mountains and presented it to the holy man to serve him in his meditations. The holy man recognized that in its beauty, the gem held the potential to incite violence and so the holy man decreed the ruby should become the Heart of the Dragon.

This culture revered the dragon as a great laughing beast who with long claws patted his scaly belly and laughed with the voice of thunder. Artisans and craftsman carved black rock into a rough-hewn shape, and in its center they nestled the ruby. When they hesitated to shut the vibrant bloodred gem away from the light, the holy man assured them the ruby would take life and pulse in the dragon's chest. He ordered that the dragon's scales be plated in porcelain and painted with symbols of prosperity, wisdom, luck and community.

Perhaps the holy man foresaw the dragon's fate, for next he ordered two precious cat's-eye gems to be embedded in the dragon's face to serve as its eyes. When the light changed so did the color of the eyes, from greenish-yellow to purplish-red, and they would, he prayed, protect the dragon from harm.

That was the holy man's last command. One of the dragon's craftsmen killed the holy man and took the dragon to his cavern home. There he intended to crack open the dragon, retrieve the ruby and, with his newfound fortune, marry the woman he desired.

But the dragon ensnared him with its cat's-eye gaze and instead, the craftsman began a lifetime of work embellishing the dragon with precious metals. All his earnings were spent acquiring silver and especially gold. All his greatest skills were honed to plate first the dragon's chest and back, then its tail, four legs and many claws. When he had finished, he began again, placing gold beads across the dragon's breastplate, hiding the ruby heart behind more and more layers until the dragon was unbreakable. When the craftsman was sick and old, he stared into the cat's-eye gems, he heard the dragon's roar and saw the dragon wave an imperious claw—and the earth shook mightily.

The earthquake brought the mountain down, burying the aged man and trapping him with the Heart of the Dragon. For a thousand years, as flesh and bone turned to dust, the dragon and its ruby became, for most of the world, the stuff of myth…until a soldier, lost in the mountain tunnels, armed with a rifle, broke into what remained of the cavern. When he shone his flashlight into the dragon's eyes, he recognized what he had found. In his people, this legend lived and breathed. They called it the Dragon's Heart and he believed the cat's-eyes would see the way to the surface. They did, and when other men of his culture saw what he carried, he died in bloody battle against his kin.

Now the Dragon's Heart traveled among the wealthy and the poor, inciting love and violence, scholarly interest and bitter rivalry. It disappeared into private collections, was stolen, sold, passed from hand to hand by whatever means possible. Its teeth, horns and claws acquired glittering sapphires, amethysts, emeralds and diamonds. Jade of every color formed the scales along its spine. It was said that to disguise its worth, one collector dipped it in a smooth coating the color of rich mud, but left the eyes free, and he was killed for his audacity. Men and women pursued the Dragon's Heart until…it vanished.

Collectors hunted, made frauds, discarded them, killed and obsessed about the Dragon's Heart, never imagining the Dragon's Heart had disappeared into an unlikely suburban home in a small California town…

2

THE MEDIUM-HANDSOME AND perfectly coiffed news anchor droned on about the rising cost of living and how it was impacting the middle class and poor, then switched to,

> "You'll remember we brought you an exclusive interview with the woman who spearheaded the effort to have the almost-one-hundred-year-old Caballo Blanco Dam removed from the Caballo Salvaje River..."

"Stupid tree huggers," Bonnie Torbinson muttered. Since her husband died, she constantly kept the TV on. Before the stroke, when he could speak, he said the way she talked to herself was a clear indication of impending insanity. She figured talking to the television kept her sane. "Put the seaplanes out of business. No more docks. No more boats. No more waterskiing. All for a few migrant fish." She carried her lunch dishes from the dining room into the kitchen.

Living in the Torbinson Mansion, she had a housekeeping service once a week. Darrell had insisted on that. But she cooked for herself, and now as she loaded the dishwasher, she listened with half an ear to the noon news out of Santa Barbara.

"…As the water level behind the dam has slowly lowered, vehicles that plunged off Goldpan Highway at different times in its history have been revealed…"

"Dumb kids." That road had been constructed at the same time as the dam, and it clung high on the cliffs as it wound its way between the tiny town of Horseshoe Bend and Bonnie's own, larger town of Citation. Ever since it had been built, teens had considered it a rite of passage to drive like bats out of hell around its curves. Missed corners resulted in fiery head-on collisions and watery deaths. Her own son had assured her he never drove that route, and never drove while intoxicated, and then!

That ticket had cost her and Darrell dearly.

But it was only the one time.

Bonnie finished putting the glasses into the top rack, set the cycle and defiantly pushed Heat Dry. Normally she was environmentally conscious and let her dishes dry naturally, but if the tree huggers were going to take down all the dams, to hell with them, and to hell with the environment.

Jackie was a good boy, always had been. It was that thief, that Vadim Somova, who had got released from jail and on the same day broke into her house, took her son and her four-year-old granddaughter hostage, and stole that stupid statue Darrell brought back from one of his trips to Pakistan or Roughistan or whatever that place was. What did he call it?

The Dragon's Heart.

Bonnie slumped onto one of the cracked leather barstools. She hated Vadim Somova. Right from the start, that kid had been a bad influence on Jackie. And Vadim's family—a bunch of Russian hoodlums, every one of them. Right now, Somova's crime king brother lived in an estate on Lake Tahoe, living high like he was the Godfather or something.

It had been almost twenty-five years of waiting and hoping, but no one had ever found a trace of Jack or little Honor. She supposed Somova had killed them. Then Jackie's wife took the other little girl, Grace, and left town.

Cynthia was like a rabbit, scared all the time, watching Jack as if he was a mean boy. She watched Bonnie, too, and after Somova came to the house that day and got in the way…

No. That's not what happened. Somova came to the house and kidnapped Jack and Honor. That's what happened. Bonnie remembered now…

What had she been thinking about?

Oh. Cynthia. After Somova kidnapped Jackie and Honor, Cynthia had watched Bonnie, blamed Bonnie, and one day she took little Grace and disappeared, leaving Darrell and Bonnie alone.

Darrell had missed his granddaughters. He had mourned them. And he watched Bonnie, too, viewed her as if he blamed her. Hated her. Then he…

Bonnie sighed, exasperated with herself. It wasn't her fault. She was a mother who had done what needed to be done. She couldn't help if no one appreciated the depth of a mother's love.

Most of the time, Bonnie tried not to think about the truth of what happened that day, but… But since Darrell's death, she got so lonely—

The television went live to the lake, and Bonnie snapped to attention.

The on-the-scene reporter used her terse, this-is-a-terrible-and-interesting-turn-of-events voice:

"Yesterday afternoon, in the deepest part of the lake, below one of the few straight stretches on the road, a car was spotted from Brother Bear Overlook. Divers descended to find what they feared—a body—"

Bonnie got off the stool and paced toward the television.

"The male, who was strapped in the driver's seat, had been killed by a gunshot to the back of the head—"

"Who is it?" Bonnie asked.

"The body was recovered and identified, but that information will not be released until the family is notified."

The news anchor took over. "In other news—"
"Who is it?" Bonnie's voice rose. "Who is it? Who is it?"
A car pulled up outside.
She grabbed the screen and shook it. "Who is it?"
The TV broke free from the brackets, slipped out of her hands and landed on the tile floor. The frame twisted. The screen broke.
Bonnie stared at the wreckage at her feet.
And the doorbell rang.

3

"I WANT THE flowers for my granddaughter's wedding. She's in college, he's in college, they've got a baby on the way, they don't have any money and tulips are her favorite." The elderly woman, bent and frail, looked tearfully at the colorful swathe of drooping petals.

Zoey Phoenix overheard a wisp of the conversation and stopped behind a cart of hydrangeas.

"They'll be okay this afternoon," the flower vendor said.

Zoey sneaked a glance at the tulips and winced. *No, they won't.* Although she acquitted him of lying for profit. Mostly he looked horrified about the onset of an old lady in tears.

"But the wedding's tomorrow morning!" the woman wailed.

The vendor's tag gave his name as Angel of Sunnyvale Nursery, and he couldn't stand to lie that much. "Sorry, lady. No way will they last that long."

The bent woman looked around the vast floor of the famed San Francisco Flower Mart, 125,000 square feet of warehouse floor space, a profusion of color, a cacophony of sound, all overlaid by the rich, earthy scent of growing things. Roses (of course), poppies, chrysanthemums, lilies, lavender, lilacs. Eucalyptus, dusty miller, echeveria succulent, myrtle, sword fern. When arrivals came from all over the world, every flower was in season. Every flower except, today, tulips.

Angel observed the elderly woman's wistful sweep of the floor and said bluntly, "You're not going to find tulips anywhere else, either. First shipment of the year came in today from Washington. Tractor trailer's air-conditioning failed, and this heat took 'em down. Today we got a disaster on our hands. Tomorrow we'll be good."

"I can't come back. I just can't. The trip was…" She sagged. "Tomorrow I have to cook!"

Angel was a good guy. "You wanted three dozen pink tulips. I'll give you a dozen white hydrangeas and three dozen pink roses for the same price. Worth a lot more!"

The woman shook her head while tears leaked from her eyes. "I promised!"

What else could Zoey do? She stepped over to the cart, took a double fistful of tulips lying limp in a box and plunked them into an empty container. "They'll be fine if we get them in water." As she pulled her hand away, she ran her palms over the petals, then reached for another double handful of tulips and did the same thing.

"Hey, you, I've been in the business a long time." Angel was irritated and insulted. "I don't know if this bit of science is over your head, but putting dead flowers into tepid water never revives them."

"But…look at the blossoms," the woman said. "They do look better."

He looked, did a double take, rubbed his eyes and watched Zoey put another bunch of tulips into one of his containers. "What's in that water?" he muttered.

"Young lady, do you think these flowers will be good tomorrow for the luncheon I'm fixing those kids?" the old woman asked.

"I think they'll be good for another seven days," Zoey said firmly.

"Seven days? In this heat? Tulips can't last…" Angel gave up. "Sure, seven days. You revive dead flowers, I'm sure you can make 'em last seven days."

Zoey smiled at him.

His grumpiness slipped and he smiled back. "You can stay and work if you want. You've got a way about you."

"I need to help this lady get these flowers out to her car. But—" she picked up an armful of drooping tulips and hugged them, then handed them to him "—you've got the only good-looking tulips on the floor. That'll be worth something, won't it?"

"Sure will."

"How much do I owe you for the flowers?" the old lady asked tremulously.

Angel looked greedily at the beautiful, healthy tulips in her arms. He looked at the dewy fresh tulips he held. He looked at Zoey. "They were dead flowers, lady. They're free."

He watched the two women slowly walk out of the warehouse doors, then turned to the vendor beside him. "Was that Zoey?"

"Yes," Mario answered. "This your first time?"

"I never believed it before."

"You have to see it to appreciate it."

"Think she'd want a job selling flowers?"

"No. She's a breeder."

"Done anything worth mentioning?"

"She bred Dianthus Elanor." Mario indicated the stems lined with small, star-shaped, fragrant yellow flowers.

Angel did another double take. "You're shittin'?"

"Lately I heard she's been designing colorful carrots."

"Does the world need colorful carrots?"

"Does the world need Dianthus Elanor? I guess so, since every time I get those stems in, I sell out."

They watched Zoey come back through the doors minus the flowers. She met their eyes, smiled and lifted a hand in greeting, then wandered toward another aisle.

"Does she always smile like that?"

"The last couple of times I saw her...no. Got a divorce and that was hard on her. But it looks like she's back to normal."

"Who would be dumb enough to divorce her?"

"The way I heard it, she divorced him."

But Angel didn't get to hear why.

A wholesaler rushed up, pointed at the tulips, and the process of bargaining began.

4

ZOEY WANDERED DOWN THE AISLES, listening to the hum of commerce, absorbing the colors, the shapes, the scents and the joy the flowers brought everyone on the floor. She loved the exuberance of being with people she knew and understood so well. Local growers called out greetings, suggested she pull up a chair and bring them up-to-date, but she knew better—as soon as she stepped behind the counter, she'd be put to work.

She kept walking.

She'd come into San Francisco to visit her mother, or so she thought, but last night she woke at 2:00 a.m. to a pressing knowledge; right now she needed to be at the San Francisco Flower Mart. The early market was reserved for wholesalers, wedding planners and florists, and the urgency was left over from her days of working for Natasha Nakashima at Nakashima's Florist on Market Street.

Zoey had started work at fourteen. She'd been too young, she didn't receive a salary, but she didn't care; even at that age she already knew that her future lay in flowers, trees, vegetables, anything that came from a seed. She felt an affinity for living things—and they felt an affinity for her. She'd worked with Natasha for four years, spent many early mornings at the market before heading to school, and when she left for college, Natasha, the meanest woman ever to own a flower shop, cried bitterly.

Zoey earned a bachelor's degree in plant science, interned three summers in various breeding programs…and then she had made her mistake.

She fell in love.

She should have stuck with flowers. They were more communicative and less flashy.

"You! Zoey Phoenix!"

Speak of the devil. Natasha was headed straight down the aisle at her.

Zoey stopped and waited. Better not to meet her head-on; Natasha relished a good collision and a fierce fight. But when Zoey worked with Natasha, she'd learned a few tricks to handle all that aggression, and now she reached out and forcibly embraced her. "Natasha! What are you doing here at this hour?"

Natasha suffered the hug a second longer than Zoey expected, then shoved her back. "My nephew, the one who grows all the flowers—"

"The one in Healdsburg or the one in San Mateo?"

"Healdsburg. The idiot had surgery for a ruptured disc so I'm tending the farm while his wife, the delicate creature, sells from my shop." Natasha scowled.

"Is the delicate creature a failure?"

Natasha scowled harder. "No. She's good. People like her."

Zoey nodded. She could see that would irritate Natasha. "So you're in here selling his product."

Natasha's eyes narrowed.

Uh-oh.

Natasha grabbed Zoey's arm and shoved her toward the table with the sign for Rusakova's Nursery. "You'll help me now!"

Zoey knew better than to say *no*. That would never work.

Instead she glanced at her watch. "For thirty minutes. Then I'm headed back to Mom's."

"Your mother." Natasha shook her finger in Zoey's face. "She made my uncle pay big for his divorce. She's a cutthroat lawyer." She grinned. "I like that."

Zoey grinned back, sorted through the selection of flowers on top and under the table, and made a bouquet.

Natasha watched with satisfaction. "Good. You remember."

"How's everybody?" A hundred years ago, Natasha's ancestors had helped develop the California flower industry. Now her extended family lived up and down the length and breadth of the state, and they all remained dedicated to the flower business.

"Mostly good. Successful and making money." Which was how Natasha measured success. "Remember Fritz Nakashima?"

"The one in Watsonville who grows poinsettias?"

"He's gone off the rails, and it's *your* fault."

"My fault? I hardly know the guy!" Zoey had met him once at the shop and thought him a handsome, smug man, who thought well of himself for little reason.

"He found out you had created the Elanor and made a fortune. Fritz decided if you could do it, so could he."

"Well, sure. And when I have a free weekend, *I'm* going to write a book." In exasperation, because he wasn't the first to assume what she did was easy, she asked, "Does Fritz know I've got a bachelor's degree in plant sciences?"

"He figures he has flower breeding in his genes."

Zoey snapped, "In his ancestry, right, not his pants?"

Natasha cackled.

From the front entrance, the volume of voices rose.

"It's ten," Natasha said. "They've let the public in. We'll sell all the bouquets you make."

"This morning the guard didn't want me to come in. I don't have a badge. Then one grower after another recognized me, and the guard said, 'You're that Zoey,' and he waved me in. What does that mean?"

"That it's good to be a name of value."

Zoey sold her first bouquet, and gave Natasha the side-eye.

"What? Did you think I was the only one who noticed what you could do? With the flowers? With the plants?" Natasha briskly created a bouquet, smaller than Zoey's, but as always, with perfect color and balance. "People talk. If you don't want them to talk, you have to be more careful."

"Or never do it again."

"That would be best."

Zoey faced her straight on.

Natasha held up her hand in a stop sign. "I know. I encouraged you. But one way or another, they still burn witches."

"I am not a witch."

"Growing things listen to you. That is a gift, especially here in the market. It's worth money, and more important growers and florists could be…jealous." Natasha tapped her on her shoulder blade. "Always glance behind."

"I don't want to live like that."

Natasha held both palms up and let them rise and fall as if she was weighing Zoey's choices: quit, or glance.

If only it was easy to quit.

In disgust at Zoey's indecision, Natasha threw her hands into the air and changed the subject. "What have you been doing? Why have you never come to see me?"

As Zoey created bouquets and sold them, she settled into the role of flower seller. "I've been working with vegetables."

"Vegetables?" Natasha made it sound as if Zoey was acting in a porn movie. "Like tomatoes?"

"No, like carrots, radishes and rutabagas."

"People like tomatoes."

"Technically, tomatoes are a fruit."

Natasha grimaced. "What are you thinking, vegetables?"

"I like vegetables," Zoey said mildly. "I eat vegetables. Breeding them takes skill and patience."

Natasha snorted.

Zoey made another bouquet and sold it to an ecstatic buyer. "No, really. Breeding the unique colors and shapes that the restaurant industry worships is an art. After my divorce, root vegetables fit my mood. Nothing flighty or romantic about them—they're useful and hardy."

"If vegetables are so wonderful, why are you here?"

"This spring, something called to me." A return of Zoey's spirits lured her out of her workshop, away from her grow lights and her potting soils and out to roam the Big Sur hills around her home in Gothic, California. The call had come from the flowers; it was time to cup them in her hands, smell their wild scents, dream of a fresh blossom that would celebrate life.

After so many grief-stricken, lonely months, she was glad to be back to herself. She glanced up into the crowd. Another stone fell into place in the wall of her certainty.

A friend. She'd found an old friend. She finished her bouquet, handed it to Natasha and headed out around the table.

5

"SHASTA? SHASTA STRAKA?"

The willowy young woman swiveled to face Zoey. Her face lit up, and she rushed into a big hug. "Zoey? Zoey Damezas? Long time no see! Where have you been hiding?" She stepped back and viewed Zoey's face. "And what have you been doing to make you look so…"

Zoey waited.

"Thin?"

Zoey laughed. That word was better than some of the others Shasta might have chosen. "It's Zoey Phoenix again. Apparently a divorce will help with weight loss."

Shasta blinked, then rallied. "Every time I dump a guy, I eat my way into another ten pounds!"

"Then you haven't dumped anybody for a while, because you look great." Zoey meant it sincerely. Shasta was one of those women who other women didn't like, and they based their decision solely on her appearance. She was tall. She was graceful. She had wide brown eyes, dark arched brows and hair so black that in the sun it flashed with blue highlights. When they met in college, Zoey called her Snow White, which led to a shoving match, which Zoey lost. Zoey didn't care; she enjoyed seeing Shasta discomfited. It happened so seldom.

"Are you living in San Francisco?" Shasta asked.

"I'm here visiting Mama. Are you living here?"

"Are you kidding? I can't afford San Francisco. I'm an impoverished artist. I'm living in a rat-infested basement in Sunnyvale."

"Seriously?"

"I'm kidding. It's a perfectly vermin-free basement in Sunnyvale about a half a block from the old Westinghouse plant. Which is a Superfund site."

Uh-oh. "How is the art world treating you?"

"I'm living in a basement in Sunnyvale about a half a block from the old Westinghouse plant, which is a Superfund site," Shasta repeated, "and I'm working as a waitress at Big Moo's serving sundaes to three-year-olds."

"It sounds awful. What are you doing here?"

Shasta sighed, looked around and smiled. "I remembered coming here with you. It was such a lovely experience and I thought… I don't know, it seemed like the place I should be today."

"I'm glad you're here." Zoey tucked her hand onto Shasta's arm. "I can talk to you."

"About your divorce?"

"I don't know. I haven't been ready to…" Zoey didn't discuss the divorce. It still hurt too much. But Shasta had been there at the beginning, had been encouraging when everyone else said she and Luca were too different. Maybe it was time to talk. "Sure. What do you want to know?"

"I never thought you and Luca would get a divorce."

"You're the only one who thought that. His mother…"

Shasta acknowledged that with an emphatic nod. "Pretty sure you won the forever scariest mother-in-law award."

When Zoey thought of that scrawny old witch, she still shuddered. "Understatement."

They got to the end of one long row and Shasta headed around the corner to the next row, towing Zoey with her. "But I was there when you two fell in love. It was so hot, I got a tan sitting in the same room."

"Hot fire, cold ashes."

"Seriously? He looked at you like you painted the Sistine Chapel."

"He… Luca, he… You remember what he was like. Big and bold."

"Loud!"

"Right. He was everything a professional wrestler should be."

"Damned Luck."

"Yes." Damned Luck had been his stage name, and he'd lived up to the billing. "He was the luckiest man I ever met—until that last match. Even then, his self-confidence was so massive, he never worried. It made me want to shake him."

"Yeah, shaking him would have scared him. Maybe you could have slapped at him a little." Shasta was clearly sarcastic.

"All I had were my words, and he didn't listen. He said he was so close…"

"Close to what?"

"I don't know. A bonus? An award? Some glittery belt he could strut around the stage in?"

"Did you ask him?"

"No. By then I didn't care."

"So he didn't listen to you—and you didn't listen to him."

Zoey stopped, put her fists on her hips and faced Shasta. "Look! You're my friend. You can't take his side!"

"Sorry! Geez. Thought you'd want me to point out the obvious."

"No." And that was enough hashing over of her divorce. Foot traffic grumbled and flowed around them, making Zoey think of the small rainwater holding pond she'd created in Gothic, which gave her an idea. With a tug on the arm, she started them walking again. "Shasta, you would love Gothic."

"I... What?" Shasta blinked at her.

"Gothic. Down the coast. It's a great little town with seven hairpin turns. There's a castle at the top of the hill...very picturesque...except now the tower's being rebuilt and the scaffolding is kind of off-putting. Angelica Lindholm owns it. Do you know Angelica Lindholm?"

"I think so?" Shasta frowned in concentration. "My landlady watches her shows. Angelica cooks and gardens and cleans and... What has she got to do with Phantom?"

"Gothic," Zoey corrected. "That's her. We have some great restaurants and shops, and the graveyard is packed with celebrities—"

"Dead, I hope." Shasta's head whipped around and she pinned Zoey with her dark stare. "Isn't that town called City of Lost Souls?"

"Yes!" Zoey beamed.

"There's some legend about..."

Zoey recited, "On stormy nights, Gothic is said to disappear, and on its return it brings lost souls back from the dead."

"That's creepy. Why would you live there?"

"The legend's not creepy. It's romantic! Although on foggy nights, you can't see your hand in front of your face and it can be, um... Well, a couple of years ago there were these murderers who were hunting down this couple and one of them got killed."

"One of the couple?"

"No, one of the murderers. The other one is in prison." Zoey waved a dismissive hand. "But living in Gothic is so... Zen."

"Zen?" Shasta came to a screeching halt in the middle of the walkway. "Are you trying to talk me out of it?"

Zoey came to a stop with her. "I can always hear the sea, the waves, the seagulls, the storms blowing in and the silence of the fogs as they gather close... But listen, for you—Gothic is rife with artists. You could paint whatever you wanted. The cliffs, the waves, the dramatic clouds, the wind rippling through the grasses…"

"Flowers," Shasta said bitterly.

Zoey smiled. "When you paint flowers, they're alive. They almost tremble and grow."

"I don't want to spend my life painting flowers."

"In Gothic, you don't have to."

"I live in fear that's my fate."

"It's not your fate unless you deem it your fate. You're Shasta. You hasta be Shasta," Zoey teased.

"Shh!" Shasta put her hand over Zoey's mouth. Shasta's mother had told the tale of going into premature labor while hiking Mount Shasta, and Shasta had suffered teasing ever since. "No one knows that here. Don't you dare start it!"

She pushed her friend's hand away. "How is your mom?"

"She's slowing down a little."

"Not climbing every mountain anymore?"

"Not fording every stream." Shasta smiled crookedly. "It's the limp. She says it's an old gunshot wound, but I take that with a grain of salt."

"That does sound like one of her stories." Zoey smiled as she remembered the tales Genesis would tell. Each was a gem of peril and adventure, and Zoey didn't believe half of them. "I hate that she's not getting around as well. Every time I met Genesis, she seemed like a force of nature, a real West Coast kind of person."

"She is always charming."

Shasta wore a tight smile; maybe Genesis didn't approve of the basement in Sunnyvale. Which took Zoey back to her swiftly concocted scheme to bring Shasta to Gothic. "On my property, I have a shop where I breed flowers. There's a cot and an outside shower—nice, really—and there's no Superfund site anywhere near. If you like, you could help me. The Gothic Garden and

Flower Show is coming up—it is such a big deal for the community—and someone has to handle my part of the tour."

"Handle?" Shasta asked cautiously.

"Talk to the people. About flowers and vegetables and growing sustainably in fire-prone California. You know I hate that
stuff. Public speaking is even worse than—" Zoey searched for
a comparison.

"Your ex-mother-in-law?"

"Yes! Well, no. But yes."

"I could do that," Shasta acknowledged.

"You'd be great at it. Come and see if you like Gothic. When
I wandered in, I knew I was in the right place. I could breathe
again." Zoey spoke to the despair she could see in Shasta. "I
thought you might like to breathe."

6

IN THE ELEVATOR of her mother's condo building, Zoey cradled a bouquet in one arm, used her fob and pressed the button for the forty-second floor. As the elevator whisked up, she smiled at the wild assortment of blossoms that surrounded the sprays of forsythia. Not for her mother the well-organized, color-coordinated bouquets assembled by a florist; Morgayne Phoenix loved a wilderness of color, scents and shapes. Which seemed at odds with her personality: austere, straightforward, without a sentimental bone in her body.

The elevator opened into a sparsely decorated, elegant corridor, and Zoey took a left to one of the three condos that occupied this floor. Nobody needed that much space, certainly not a woman so determinedly single as her mother, but her mother liked the space, the view, the security and most of all, the knowledge that she'd created this kind of wealth for herself. Zoey didn't know who her father was or what he'd done to engender this kind of hard-eyed ambition in Morgayne Phoenix, but he must have been a real bastard.

Zoey knocked on the door, and when her mother didn't answer she dug out a key and let herself in. From inside the living room, she heard the television blaring.

Mama never watched TV in the daytime; she must be on some kind of video conference about her latest divorce case.

Zoey walked into the great room, the kitchen/living room combination, placed the flowers on the counter and waited for her mother to notice she had arrived.

But Morgayne faced the TV over the fireplace, her back to the kitchen, and watched. Watched so intently, she seemed to be—was—unaware of Zoey's presence. And she wasn't participating in a video conference; this was the local news.

Zoey dug around under the sink for a large vase, but she kept an eye on Morgayne. The way Mama stood, spine rigid, shoulders hunched, legs braced against the floor; it looked as if she was experiencing one of the area's occasional and perilous earthquakes. Which definitely wasn't happening.

Zoey filled the vase with water, lovingly placed the bouquet inside, and wondered what about this story had so captured her mother's attention.

As soon as the news story got to the end of the segment, Morgayne used the remote to take it back to the beginning, and began to watch again.

Zoey found herself enthralled by her mother's intensity. She walked to stand behind her.

The reporter stood in front of an old car being lifted by crane from…from its resting place at the bottom of a recently drained lake. A man's body had been found inside, in the driver's seat, shot in the back of the head. Okay. Sure. Interesting. A missing, priceless statue had been retrieved from the back seat. The cops stopped at a house to tell the man's mother—

Startled, Zoey blurted, "That looks like the house where Honey and I used to play!"

Morgayne jumped, hard, and swung around, arm up, as if fending off an attack.

Zoey lifted her hands, palms forward, and stepped back. "Sorry, Mama! I wasn't trying to scare you."

"No. No. I was watching the…" Mama glanced at the television, then at the remote she held. She seemed to require a moment to realize the connection between the TV and the remote, but when she did, she lifted it and killed the story. "Honey? You remember Honey?"

"Of course I remember Honey." Zoey grinned. "How could I forget my imaginary friend?"

"Your imaginary friend." Morgayne swallowed, brushed at her eyes and looked at her fingers as if startled to find them damp.

"Mama?" Zoey was alarmed. "Are you okay?"

Obviously she wasn't, but Morgayne forced a smile. "I was remembering…those years when you were so young. I'm proud of you. You're a wonderful adult, but I miss those mornings when you'd come out to the living room, snuggle against me in your jammers and whisper, 'Cheerios, Mommy, Cheerios.'"

Zoey put her arm around Morgayne's waist, leaned her head on Morgayne's shoulder and whispered, "Credit card, Mommy, credit card."

Morgayne laughed and gave her daughter a shove. "Use your own credit card! As cheaply as you live, you can afford whatever you want."

"I'm happy with the way I live," Zoey said mildly. "Gothic is quiet." She remembered the upcoming garden tour. "Usually. Interesting people—"

"Eccentric," her mother amended.

"Well, sure. A few great restaurants, an excellent grocery store. What else do I need?"

"You're twenty-eight, not a hundred. You need a nightlife! Dancing, music, friends, travel! At the least, a boyfriend."

"Thanks, no. Been there, done that."

Morgayne glanced toward the now-blank TV. "What's going on with Luca? Have you heard?"

"No." Why was her mother asking about Luca? How could Zoey go months without even thinking about him…mostly not thinking about him…only rarely thinking about him…and have two people mention him in one day?

"Is he still on the wrestling circuit?"

"I don't know." Zoey made it her business not to know.

"Well, he's not."

Then why did you ask? But Zoey didn't inquire; she thought that edge of hostility might reveal a little too much.

"He's the CFO of his sister Isabella's investment firm."

To hell with what she revealed. "Mother, why do you care?"

"Information is power." Morgayne walked toward the windows. "Since he joined the firm, their financial worth has made a significant leap upward. And they were doing fine before. Isabella is brilliant."

"They're all brilliant. Money bows to them. Before the decade is over, the Damezas family will own Manhattan. I told you, Mother. You just didn't listen."

"Yes. You did." Morgayne had a habit when she was thinking; she tapped her foot. She was tapping it now. "They take care of their own."

"Why are we talking about an episode better forgotten?"

Morgayne put her hand on her hip and gave up her marital philosophy. "Every person has the right to one early bad marriage."

"Is that what happened with you?" Zoey snapped.

"Yes. That's what happened with me. My husband—my first, my only—was not a nice man. We're lucky we got away from him."

Zoey stepped back in surprise and surveyed her mother.

Morgayne Phoenix was a handsome woman, in her midforties, determinedly fit, with a fluff of blond hair that framed her tanned face and brown eyes behind a pair of recently acquired glasses. Zoey often thought she looked like a sunflower, and certainly unwary legal opponents made the mistake of judging her by her appearance. But underneath that angelic exterior beat a ruthless heart; when Morgayne Phoenix took on a divorce, her opponent went down in flames. One element of her job, she said, was to rip a cheating man's balls out through his wallet. The other element was to secure safety and security for the wife and children who stood to lose so much by the dissolution of a union. And when she took on a case that involved abuse… the abuser suffered the full weight of the law. As a judge said, she was one scary lawyer.

But she never, ever mentioned Zoey's father. Zoey hadn't even known if her mother had married her father. "Is that why you've never married again?"

Morgayne touched her finger to her nose. "I learned my lesson. I'm too old to unlearn it." In a change of tone, she added, "Not to mention most men are scared of me, or can't handle my success, or if they actually convince me to go out to eat, I'm picking up the check."

"You are literally the meal ticket?"

"Exactly." Mama narrowed her eyes. "I suppose you want me to buy you dinner?"

"Yes, but at least I brought you flowers." Zoey grinned and gestured toward the counter.

"You're a wretched child, but I'm glad I have you. And your bouquets, which are always magnificent." Morgayne hugged her very tightly.

"Mama, is there anything you want to talk about?"

"No. Yes. Maybe." Morgayne looked into Zoey's eyes. "I miss your imaginary friend, Honey. I wish I knew where she was."

7

MORGAYNE PHOENIX WOULD never push her daughter out the door. She loved Zoey and treasured every moment spent with her. But the next morning, as she waved her goodbye, she breathed a sigh of relief and packed a small bag. She emailed instructions to her legal assistant Sally, climbed in her deep blue Miata and headed to the place she had hoped never to see again.

Citation, California.

To see the person she hoped never to meet again.

Her mother-in-law, Bonnie Torbinson. Because Jack Torbinson was dead. He was truly, absolutely dead with a bullet in his skull. The fish had plucked the flesh from his bones and he could never come back, never hurt her, never hurt Zoey, never again. She didn't have to be afraid anymore. She didn't have to glance over her shoulder for fear he was behind her. She was free. Zoey was safe.

And Morgayne had to return to Citation to find out the truth, all the truth, at last.

Once out of San Francisco and its suburbs, the drive took only a few hours. As she crossed the city limits, the old memories closed in. She was Cynthia Torbinson again, her life, her hopes, her family in ruins, destroyed by the man she'd married.

She opened her window and breathed the fresh air, let the warm breeze blow in her face.

No. She wasn't frightened, broken Cynthia Torbinson anymore. She was Morgayne Phoenix, a name she'd chosen for herself, a name that expressed her rise from the ashes. She didn't know how she was going to handle seeing Bonnie after so many years, but she knew she'd won a lot of divorce settlements for a lot of clients and she intended to use those methods to interrogate Bonnie. One way or another, she would find out everything that Bonnie knew about what really happened, and what she knew about the fate of her daughter, Honor… and Vadim.

She turned the corner into the cul-de-sac where Darrell and Bonnie Torbinson had lived ever since she could remember. In a street of big homes, theirs was the biggest, the tallest, with a four-car garage and the kind of yard only weekly visits from a gardening service could produce.

My God, how could it look the same? Shouldn't there be a stain on it, some indication of the horrors that had happened inside?

She parked in the lot by the greenbelt. Her father-in-law had believed the Dragon's Heart was valuable. Jack had believed it, too, and that had started the worst nightmare of her life, in Citation, when her name was still Cynthia. She leaned her head back on the seat rest and gave in to the memories…

Twenty-four years ago…

Cynthia hustled her four-year-old twin daughters down the street, begging them to hurry, promising them Grandpa would give them treats, and the poor babies were trying their best. Honor's legs were longer, but her arm was in a cast and Cynthia knew by the furrow between her brows she was in pain. If only Jack would let Cynthia have a car…

But he feared she'd leave him, and he was right.

She got a text and glanced at her phone.

Hurry up, bitch. You're going to make me mad.

He was always mad. Anytime he looked at her and the girls, he was mad. Jack Torbinson had envisioned himself as a playboy, a sex god, an actor. No, not an actor, a star! Not a husband, and never a father. But he was stuck in Citation, California, and it was all her fault. That's what he said, over and over. It was all her fault.

As if he hadn't chased her, declared his eternal love, promised her the best sex a woman could enjoy, said he would cherish her forever.

All lies. All lies.

Every day, she prayed for him to leave her, but the skinny little coward didn't dare leave his mommy and daddy. If he did that, he might have to face the world and find out she wasn't the cause of his limitations, he was. Sometimes, she thought that he knew it and that made him worse.

She coaxed, "Come on, Honor. Come on, Grace. Only a little bit farther." It used to be easier when she could carry them. But they were bigger now and the last time Jack had hit her, he knocked her down and kicked her spine, and the doctor told her not to pick up anything heavier than a gallon of milk. When he said it, he watched her while she fidgeted with her backpack straps, then asked, "Do you want to file a complaint?"

Her gaze flew to meet his. "Good God, no! He would…" She looked at her daughters, sitting so wide-eyed and still on their seats when they should have been giggling and squirming.

The doctor had worked in Citation his whole career. He knew without being told. "If you change your mind, I can help you."

Foolish man. If he did anything to harm her little Jackie, Bonnie Torbinson would run him out of town on a rail. He knew it, too, which is why he didn't insist on discussing it further.

Cynthia and her daughters turned the corner onto the cul-de-sac where

Jack's parents lived, the home Bonnie had created to raise her beloved only son. Only child.

And there he was, leaning against his muscle car, his Mustang, glancing at his phone and waiting like a volcano about to blow.

8

Today in Citation, Northern California

THROUGH THE CAR'S open window Morgayne heard a door slam hard.

She opened her eyes in reflexive alarm.

A man came out of the house, a good-sized guy with bulky shoulders, the kind who spent all his spare time in the gym lifting weights and sucking in his gut whenever a cute younger girl or guy walked past.

"I'll be damned," Morgayne murmured. "Mark Torbinson, the last remaining relative. Why were you visiting Bonnie?"

He scowled all the way to the car parked in the driveway, a silver Corvette. He squeezed into the driver's seat, slammed that door, too, and roared off, taking the corner at a speed that boded ill for any kid in the crosswalk.

Morgayne rolled up the window and got out of the car. "I suppose you were there because now you're Bonnie's heir, and it looks as if whatever Bonnie told you didn't make you happy. Interesting. The bitch won't be happy to see me, the long-lost daughter-in-law and now Jack's widow." She leaned a hand on the hood as the happy truth overwhelmed her again.

Jack Torbinson was dead, and Morgayne had hope once more.

"Let's see how much Bonnie will admit." Morgayne locked her door and headed to the Torbinsons' front porch. There on a table was a giant bottle of hand sanitizer, a stack of medical masks, a box of disposable nitrile gloves and a sign over the bell that said, "Sanitize. Mask Up. Put on Gloves. Don't Ring. Walk in." She'd hoped maturity and changes in her hair, makeup and confidence, and the addition of dark rimmed glasses, would save her from recognition. Now, as she followed the orders, she knew she might stand a chance to be anonymous. That could be a huge advantage. No messy hostility and hopefully more information.

Then she stood in the entry and looked for changes. She found none, except for an increasing shabbiness caused not by wear, but age. With only Bonnie in the house and no updates done, the place looked dated and tired.

A woman stuck her head out of the dining room. "Yes?"

Morgayne stared. Patrice Harris, one of Jack's degenerate buddies, here wearing beige slacks, a blue medical coat and an exasperated expression. "You're the…nurse?"

"Home care," Patrice said crisply. "Who are you?"

Either Patrice's early drug and alcohol days had killed enough brain cells, or Morgayne truly was unrecognizable.

The lie came easily. "I'm Adele from the church where Mrs. Torbinson worships. I'm here to console her about her loss."

"Right. She'll like that. She loves attention. It's not like she needs home care now. She's healthy as a horse. She just wants someone to wait on her. Go up. Tell her I'm fixing her lunch." From above, a bell rang. "Maybe you can keep her from ringing that damned—"

"I'll try." Morgayne climbed the stairs. Getting in was easier than she expected. Now to see if her mother-in-law bought into it.

As soon as she stepped across the threshold, Mrs. Torbinson placed the bell on her night table, crossed her arms over her chest and demanded, "Where's my lunch?"

Morgayne almost laughed. No recognition there. And why would there be? Bonnie was one of those people who scanned all the faces in a room, dismissed most as unimportant and spoke only to the people who could do something for her.

"Lunch is on its way." Morgayne kept her voice low and soothing. "Mrs. Torbinson, I'm Adele, the youth pastor at the Citation Lutheran Church. Pastor Burns sent me."

"Where is Pastor Burns?" Bonnie's frown had created well-used lines between her brows, and everything about her tone was accusatory.

"Lately he has asked the same question about you." Morgayne ladled on the guilt.

Thankfully, Bonnie's eyes shifted away.

So she hadn't been to church in a long time. Good guess, Morgayne. "Pastor's dealing with building the youth center to which you donated so generously." Morgayne knew Bonnie's idea of charity work was writing a check, not getting involved. "I'm here to ask if we can offer counseling after receiving the sad news about your son."

Tears leaked from Mrs. Torbinson's eyes. "My Jackie."

Morgayne wanted to vomit. Her Jackie had been a beast, and shooting and drowning was the least he deserved. "I understand it's been years, yet at the same time, his death is news to you."

"They found his body. My little Jackie was at the bottom of the lake. He was shot in the back of the head. I'd always hoped he was out there somewhere in the world. But when he didn't come home…"

Morgayne handed her a tissue.

Bonnie sniffled and wiped her eyes. "When Jack tied up that awful man, I was afraid—"

"Jack tied up Vadim Somova?" Was Bonnie finally admitting the truth? "The opposite was reported."

"No, I didn't… I'm confused. Of course Vadim tied up my poor boy."

Interesting. Bonnie had gained a lot of weight, but otherwise looked about the same. Yet that was a telling slip, one that implicated her beloved Jackie. Had time eroded that sharp and unpleasant steel-trap mind? "Vadim kidnapped your son and grandchild and stole a priceless antique."

"Not priceless."

"And it was insured." *Whoops. Not so sure of yourself, Morgayne.* "Wasn't it?"

"Yes." Bonnie reached for the controls of her hospital bed and raised the back a few degrees. "When is that Patrice going to bring my lunch? I'm hungry. She's lazy. I don't know why the doctor recommended her for the job."

Morgayne didn't give a damn about Patrice or Bonnie's lunch. "Surely you turned in the theft and took the settlement. Which means now that the Dragon's Heart is recovered, it's the property of the insurance company." She had just now realized that. All her focus was on discovering her daughter's fate.

"I never made a claim," Bonnie said.

"What? Why not?" Morgayne's mind clicked through the possibilities and came up with the only likely possibility; because if Bonnie had turned in a claim for such a large amount, someone from the insurance company might have investigated events and all Jack's transgressions and Bonnie's deceptions would have been revealed.

"It was only two hundred and fifty thousand dollars." Bonnie dismissed it with a wave of her pudgy hand. "That's not so much. We could afford to lose it."

Morgayne was a successful woman, and she worked with a lot of successful people, but nobody ever waved off a quarter of a million dollars. Bonnie's attitude was a confession in itself,

and Morgayne began to think how she could convince the police to investigate more closely. A few words in the right ears…
"It sounds like a lot of money to me. But I'm merely a youth minister."

"Right. So you don't know much about money."

Morgayne could have told Bonnie that the poor understood more about money than the rich. And after Morgayne had taken Zoey to the city, they had been poor for a very long time.

Querulously, Bonnie said, "The way Mark acts, you'd think that statue was priceless."

"Who's Mark, and what does he have to do with it?" Morgayne knew, of course, but she wanted to hear Bonnie's version.

"Mark Torbinson. Darrell's nephew. Forty years old, not married, no children, no responsibilities, all he does is exercise. He's worthless—and he's my heir. He just left."

"I saw him." With massive insincerity, Morgayne said, "Nice car. Perhaps you have fresh thoughts about the loss of your grandchildren?"

"Why would I have fresh thoughts about my grandchildren?" Bonnie asked sharply.

"Twin girls, four years old," Morgayne recited. "One disappeared with your son, one disappeared with your daughter-in-law. How difficult this must be for you, to be reminded of the children's fresh young faces and joyous laughter, and not knowing their fates." She took a chance and looked deep into Bonnie's gaze.

They were like a fish's eyes, cold and without comprehension. What did she expect from a woman devoid of normal feelings?

"Jack named the girls Grace and Honor. Traditional names. The one girl didn't even bother to keep the name he gave her." Bonnie's voice was hard and cold.

Wait. What? "You know about one of the girls? Where she is? What she's called?"

"Before he died, my husband traced my daughter-in-law and the child." Bonnie did not act as if that gave her pleasure or relief.

Morgayne couldn't believe it. Could *not* believe it. Bonnie had known where she was, where Zoey was, and she'd never bothered to contact them? "Your husband. I understood he had been incapacitated by a stroke." Belatedly she realized she should behave less like she knew all the truths and more like a youth pastor. "How wonderful that he recovered so—"

Bonnie interrupted. "That female physical therapist helped him learn the computer accessibility features and behind my back, they found Cynthia and Honor, where they were living, what names they were masquerading under. He would have contacted them, too, but I… He died before he was able to fulfill his dearest wish to bring them back into the family." Her eyes shifted from side to side.

Morgayne had never thought Bonnie could kill, but she'd raised a monster, she'd raised Jack, and Morgayne knew better than anyone the lengths Bonnie would go to protect him and his reputation. Darrell's death had been convenient, securing Jack's inheritance. Too bad Jack was dead. "Was the Dragon's Heart found with the body?"

"In the car with him."

"As I understand the story you related at the time of the theft and kidnapping, Vadim used the table runner to tie up Jack, put him, the dragon and the little girl into the car, and—"

Bonnie looked up sharply. "That's the truth!"

"Were Vadim or the child found?"

"No. Vadim got away." Bonnie rubbed her head. "You look like someone I used to know."

"I hear that all the time. They say I look like that actress, Renée Zellweger. Personally, I don't see it." Glibly, Morgayne waved that off. "You've contacted the other girl and her mother? They…don't wish to have a relationship with you?"

"Obviously they don't or they would have returned to the

place they belonged. If they'd wanted to have a relationship, they would have been here waiting for Jack to return." Bonnie's voice rose. "No loyalty, that's what it is. No sense of responsibility. He raised that girl up when he married her."

"Cynthia?"

"Yes. Cynthia!"

Morgayne was dumbfounded. Her parents were stiff-necked, pious and well-to-do. They'd refused to help Morgayne and her children, insisted Morgayne honor her wedding vows, and Morgayne didn't give a damn if she ever saw them again. But when she married Jack, she had hardly been a waif from the wrong side of the tracks.

Bonnie continued, "Jack gave the twins life. Their names. Everything!"

Black eyes. Broken bones.

"They never showed gratitude. They never loved him."

Insult your grandchildren when you know how badly Jack treated them… How dare you? Morgayne looked down at the oxygen tube that snaked across the floor. She looked at her foot and her shoe. She contemplated how easy it would be to press her foot on the tube… Probably the same way Bonnie offed her own husband. Morgayne tucked her shaking hands behind her back and took a calming breath. "Would you like me to intervene with them for you?"

"No, I… No, I took care of matters. I ordered a package pickup and sent the Dragon's Heart to Grace."

"What?" Bonnie had managed to shock Morgayne.

Zoey was going to receive the Dragon's Heart? Morgayne needed to talk to her at once, explain everything and make sure Zoey put the Dragon's Heart into a safe place ASAP, before the fortune hunters arrived on her doorstep. Before she was murdered for a statue she hadn't asked for and didn't want.

Bonnie viewed Morgayne shrewdly. "That's exactly how my nephew reacted, and with more reason than you. He's now heir to the Torbinson fortune. Seven million dollars and counting. That should keep him in gym memberships."

"That statue is worth more than—" Morgayne interrupted herself. A youth pastor wouldn't know about the Dragon's Heart, how it was sought by treasure hunters throughout the world. The only reason she knew was that her father-in-law had told her. Jack had known, too; that's why he stole it.

But while Morgayne was surprised that Bonnie was clueless about the Dragon's Heart's true value, she guessed that figured. Bonnie never listened to her husband; it was always about Jack. "Your nephew is a fortunate man," Morgayne said. "I hope he realizes that."

"He isn't fortunate until I die. As I told him! With the exception of my collapse brought on by…" Her voice wobbled. "By grief and the long slow heartbreak of losing my son—"

"Losing your whole family," Morgayne reminded her, and patted her hand forcefully. "You poor, poor dear."

Bonnie yanked her fingers away. "If there's one thing I learned in my internment in the hospital, it's that I'm basically healthy, especially for a woman of my age. I'm not dying any time soon."

Lady, you don't know how close you came today.

"Are you sure we've never met?" Bonnie raised the back of her bed so she was sitting straight up. "You really look familiar. Pull down your mask."

Morgayne stood. "You undoubtedly saw me last time you came to church. As soon as you're on your feet, I look forward to greeting you again."

Bonnie sucked in a breath to demand more loudly Morgayne pull down her mask.

Patrice knocked on the door. She wore a mask and gloves, and was holding a tray of steaming chicken soup and oyster crackers, a toasted cheese sandwich and a glass of wine.

"About time!" Bonnie snapped. "I'm weak with hunger. I need to eat!"

Patrice rolled her eyes at Morgayne, then cocked her head and stared as if she, too, thought Morgayne looked familiar.

"Bring that over here. Tuck my napkin under my chin!"

The way Bonnie gave orders, with contempt and without respect, reminded Morgayne she might not be the only person who had looked at the oxygen line and harbored lethal thoughts.

Patrice wrenched her attention back to Bonnie and Morgayne slipped out of the room, down the stairs and out the door. She hurried toward her car, desperate to get away from that place, that woman, the memories and the lies. Now she understood why Mark Torbinson had driven like a madman as he left the house.

He'd discovered that for years, Bonnie had known her granddaughter's location, and she didn't care enough to visit, call or touch base. Yet now that the Dragon's Heart had surfaced, she'd sent it to her. Why? What possible reason could she have for doing such a thing now, at this late date?

Morgayne thought she knew. Darrell Torbinson had despised his son. He and his nephew, Mark, had been close, and bonded over Darrell's collection of valuable artifacts. The real reason Bonnie had sent the Dragon's Heart to Zoey was to spite Mark, and she'd done it without a thought to the consequence this would have to her granddaughter.

Morgayne's hand trembled as she leaped in the Miata and told the onboard vehicle control system to call Zoey.

Zoey was on her way home to Gothic. There, if the treasure hunters hadn't already stolen it, she would find a package, and tucked in among the wrappings with the Dragon's Heart, she would find danger. Morgayne ripped off the gloves and the mask, and drove onto the street while the phone rang and rang…

Voice mail picked up.

Morgayne left a message. Cell service could be sketchy on the roads Zoey traveled. She could finish her investigation and if Zoey hadn't phoned yet, she'd start texting and calling in earnest. No reason for alarm…yet.

9

PATRICE FELT ALL kinds of sympathy for the woman from the church who had headed down the stairs and out of the house like the devil resided in this room. She longed to do the same. But she had to work for a living, gross work like helping Mrs. Torbinson bathe and change her nightgown while all the while Mrs. Torbinson insulted her for her incompetence. She wondered if Mrs. Torbinson ever thought someone who hated her might somehow take revenge, but such an idea apparently never crossed Mrs. Torbinson's mind. "Here's your lunch, Mrs. Torbinson." Patrice placed it over her patient's lap.

Mrs. Torbinson didn't fall on it like she usually did. Instead she sat staring straight ahead, moving her jaw like a cow chewing her cud. "I know that woman. I know that woman…" she muttered.

"I thought she looked familiar, too. Figured I'd seen her around town." Patrice went over to the double-hung window that faced the backyard, popped the lock and raised the pane.

Mrs. Torbinson whipped her head around and glared. "Shut that window, you! Are you trying to kill me?"

Lady, you shouldn't ask questions like that. "It's such a lovely day, I thought you'd like some fresh air."

"No. Shut the window. Fresh air will give me pneumonia."

Patrice gently lowered the pane.

"And lock it. A lock is a feeble defense against all the killers and rapists on the streets these days."

Patrice made a show of looking out. "Mrs. Torbinson, you're on the second floor."

"Can't be too careful. Killers and rapists," she repeated.

Patrice did not say, *No one wants to rape you.* She did make a show of clicking the lock.

Mrs. Torbinson went back to chewing her cud. "Where do I know her from?"

Back to that. "You probably remember her from church."

"No. From years ago…she's older now…" Mrs. Torbinson picked up her fork, took a bite of chicken and snapped her fingers. "That woman was my daughter-in-law."

Patrice's head snapped around. "Cynthia?"

Mrs. Torbinson looked over at Patrice. "I forgot. You knew Jack, didn't you?"

In the Biblical sense, a lot and often. "We went to high school together. We were friends." *We smoked so much weed together.*

"Then you can tell me. Wasn't that Cynthia?"

Patrice had been so intent on performing her role in today's drama, she'd hardly paid attention to the visitor. Now she concentrated, trying to bring up that face, to compare it to the proud prom queen in high school who had become Jack's bruised and cowering wife. "Yeah. Yeah, I think it was. Now that Jack's dead, Cynthia's a widow. Figured to come back and see what she could score." That made sense to Patrice.

"She came for information about the Dragon's Heart." Mrs. Torbinson laughed sourly. "She got what she came for. I told her where I sent it."

"Where?" Patrice didn't care, she simply wanted to keep Mrs.

Torbinson talking. She'd done some illegal stuff in her day, but she wasn't a thief, at least not the thief of a statue that would land her in jail for the rest of her days. She'd been to jail; she didn't like it.

"I sent it to my granddaughter." Mrs. Torbinson watched, and cackled when Patrice did a double take. "Yes, I'm not as stupid as you might like."

Patrice took that as a warning that maybe she didn't have Mrs. Torbinson completely buffaloed.

"Come away from that window!" Mrs. Torbinson snapped.

Patrice walked over to the bed and smoothed the covers. She would divert Mrs. Torbinson another way. "I didn't know you knew where your granddaughter was. The one that Cynthia took with her when she ran away, right? That's great. Nice of you to send the dragon to her. Is it really valuable?"

"Darrell always said it was. He said every treasure hunter in the world was after the Dragon's Heart. He said they'd do anything to get their hands on it." Mrs. Torbinson sneered. "Maybe so. It was ugly."

"I saw the news story. I was expecting more bling," Patrice admitted. "Now we know that Vadim is maybe out there, somewhere, with Cynthia's other little girl. Cynthia's probably looking for them."

"Why?"

When it came to emotions, Patrice knew she had her own issues, but this woman was cold to the bone. "Cynthia loved her kids, and she always had a thing for Vadim."

"What?" Mrs. Torbinson's voice cracked. "That little whore had a thing for Vadim Somova, the man who killed my son?"

Wow. Way to distract the old hag. Patrice continued to do caretaker-like things: fill the water pitcher, fluff the extra pillows, take Mrs. Torbinson's temperature with the digital thermometer. "I thought everybody knew. Vadim chased after Cynthia, which made Jack want her. After Vadim got shipped off to prison, Jack convinced Cynthia to elope and she came back pregnant." *Should she keep talking? Why not?* Mrs. Torbinson was staring straight ahead, shoveling food in her mouth, clearly in a frenzy. That made Patrice's job so much easier. She wandered back toward the window. "After the twins were born, Jack told me—" when he was so bombed he couldn't see straight "—he thought Vadim had knocked up Cynthia and she'd married him so her parents didn't disown her. You remember how holier-than-thou they always were." Still were, as far as Patrice knew.

"My poor baby boy," Mrs. Torbinson lamented, "carrying that burden all by himself. Why didn't he come to me?"

"Because he didn't like to admit he was a sucker." *For sure not to his mommy who thought he was a piece of perfection with buttercream frosting.*

"I would've handled it," Mrs. Torbinson pronounced, "and no one would ever have been the wiser."

Something about Mrs. Torbinson's expression sent a chill up Patrice's spine. She didn't know what that cruel woman would have done, but for the first time she understood exactly why Jack was such a son of a bitch. He'd suckled *vicious* right out of his mother's tit.

Patrice had done what she'd come to do. Now to get out. She backed toward the door. "Your temperature is a little elevated. I'll call the doctor's office and see what they advise. When you're done with your tray, ring and I'll come up and get it."

When she left the room, the window was unlocked and the pane slightly raised.

10

THE NARROW NACIMIENTO-FERGUSSON Road wound from Modesto over the Santa Lucia Mountains, then past Gothic and to the Pacific Coast Highway and the sea. Rated one of the most scenic in the world, the highway had recently opened after a lengthy closure due to fire and landslide and was clogged with every kind of vehicle. Zoey held tight to her patience and drove her red Mini Cooper at the stately pace set by the motor home driver who steadfastly refused to take a turnout and let the traffic pass. When she got to Howard's Ranch, she impulsively took the turn onto the gravel road that led to the old ranch house. Keeping an eye on her rearview mirror—she wanted no one to follow her—she took an immediate right onto a dirt track. A slow, pothole-filled half mile took her to a trailhead. She parked, got out and climbed the steep slope to the historical site José Howard himself had shown her not long after she'd arrived in Gothic, fresh from her divorce and still grieving.

"This—" José had taken off his cowboy hat and pointed at a rubble of broken and muddy adobe bricks "—is all that remains of a wayside cross built in the eighteenth century by the Spanish friars who walked north to convert the Indians. And this—" he pointed to a grassy mound covered with native flowers "—is the reason the cross was built here. This is a Native American mound."

"A grave mound?" she had asked.

"Maybe. Or maybe it's a place where Native Americans worshipped their gods. Or hid their valuables. It's been here my whole life and my father's life and my grandfather's life, and we have never disturbed it. We care for it." José proudly proclaimed himself to be a descendant of the area's Native Americans and of the Spanish and Mexican and American peoples who followed them. "The friars wanted to obliviate even the memory of Native customs, so they built the cross on top of the mound." He pointed at the bits of adobe bricks scattered at the base of the raised earth. "Yet somebody moved the cross off to the side."

"Or something moved it," she said.

He viewed her with consternation.

"I meant like an earthquake."

"Right! Right." He seemed relieved. "An earthquake could have toppled it, too."

Zoey knelt beside the mound and touched the flowers. "If you don't mind, I'll take photos."

"I don't mind. We don't tell outsiders about this spot, but when I saw you with your seeds and your soil testers, I knew you were one with the earth." He sounded satisfied. "Common flowers grow here, California poppies and lupin, but some I've never seen anywhere else."

"Maybe this mound holds forgotten flower seeds?" Zoey suggested.

"Maybe." He put his hat back on his head. "Come any time. When I'm grieved, it's a comforting spot to be."

Zoey hadn't realized the grizzled old rancher would see her mourning. But a lot of knowing was taking a moment to look, so she thanked him and for the last two years, she'd taken every moment she could spare to come this way and pay her respects to the crumbled remains of the wayside cross—and to the vibrant mound.

Today, as she had the first time, she knelt and examined the flowers. Every time she came, a different and colorful array had burst from the earth, and now the brilliant reds and warm golds held sway, warming her heart, nodding in the breeze as if to assure her she'd healed from the hurt of walking away from her marriage. She examined each plant, spoke to each blossom, exercised her memory and named the flowers she recognized and used her phone and ID app to identify the rare species. She used her Fiskars embroidery scissors to clip blossoms. Some, she thought, needed to be preserved, and some had potential to be crossbred to produce a new color or new shape. She slipped the blooms in the small paper bags she carried with her and stowed them in her backpack.

When she stood, the knees of her jeans were grass stained and she had dirt under her fingernails—and she was smiling. A butterfly fluttered past her nose, then dived into the mound to settle on a single flower that had begun to unfurl. Following its lead, she knelt again and examined the flower.

Silver green lacy leaves provided the perfect backdrop for the simple flower, a poppy with five violet-blue petals, splattered with crimson, and with a golden bull's-eye held aloft on a slender stalk. Vaguely she remembered seeing a picture of something like this, but where? She used her app, but the app as much as shrugged and said, "I dunno." She always carried her battered field manual with her; she opened it and researched this flower by color, kind, size. Nothing.

Closing her eyes, she rubbed her forehead, coaxing her brain…and slowly a picture formed, of a white page and a delicate drawing in a book titled, *Plantas de California*. The book was hand bound and carefully preserved, drawn by the hand of a nineteenth-century Spanish lady, a birthday gift from Luca. The detailed illustrations were exquisite, lightly colored and precise. An elegant cursive identified this blossom as *amapolas gracia de dios*.

Zoey's eyes snapped open.

No one had seen this flower for a hundred and fifty years. It was assumed to be extinct. If she was right, if this was that flower, she'd made the discovery of the century. If she could entice it to produce a seed, she would have helped save a glorious plant to gladden the hearts of whoever saw it. If it reproduced as did other California poppies, the flower would set a fruit, a slender dehiscent capsule, which would explosively open to spread its seeds across the landscape. Or in this case, in the bag where she would place it.

With a word of thanks, she brushed the butterfly aside. She cut three of the blossoms, taking care not to harm the plant, and placed them in a bag. She looked around and realized how much she loved this life, this place. And she walked with extra care back to her car, got in and drove back to the highway.

The parade of cars had passed on, giving Zoey a clear road and a smooth trip. She couldn't help it; she grinned as she turned onto the highway and took the first few curves. The day was California gorgeous, she was headed home, and if she was right, she'd made the flower breeder discovery of the century. Only one minor thing concerned her; her mother's odd distraction.

Yet she knew one thing for certain; her mother could take care of herself. And did. And welcomed no interference.

She drove out of a stretch of curves onto the straight stretch. The old live oaks reached for each other across the pavement. Light and shadow flickered over the car. She rolled her window down enough to inhale the scents of leaves and soil, warm asphalt and welcome.

When and if Morgayne deemed it necessary, she would confide in her daughter. In the meantime, Zoey made her plans to work with the flowers she had gathered. Her home's former owner had built a spacious shop with handcrafted cabinets, a large central island and lots of room for trays of soil and pots full of growing things. She had placed comfort mats in strategic spots on the concrete floor. Skylights brought in the sun and garage doors opened the view toward the sea and the land. She strained to get there and—

Zoey heard a squeal of tires. Out of the corner of her left eye, she glimpsed movement. There! To the left. Tall. Broad. Black and chrome. Coming right at her from the side!

No time to react.

Impact!

Glass exploded. Her window. The windshield.

Desperately, uselessly, she spun the wheel. No control. No control!

Metal collapsed and her car roared in agony.

Her door. Caved in.

Her hand broke against the steering wheel.

She screamed with agony.

Tires squealed on the asphalt. Hers? No. Yes. Maybe. Yes!

The smell of gasoline.

Fire. The car was on fire!

And the vehicle that had hit her continued to shove her Mini sideways toward the edge of the road. She glanced to the left.

A steel bar over a chrome grill. Headlights set high above the pavement. A powerful motor that roared in her ear, promising destruction.

The right side of Zoey's car toppled into the ditch.

She lifted her arms to protect her head.

The world turned upside down.

Right side up.

On the right. A tree. A tree... Collision!

More glass. Everything flying at her, clawing at her. Bleeding. She was bleeding.

Still the vehicle attacked, advanced. She was caught between it and the oak. Metal crumpled and moaned.

She moaned.

Everything broken. The car. Her nose. Her forehead. Her hand.

Someone was screaming.

Someone was gravely injured.

Someone was going to die.

Oh, God. I'm going to die.

11

MORGAYNE TOOK THE highway out of Citation toward the lookout where Jack Torbinson's car had flown off into the lake. She stopped at the Brother Bear Historical Overlook, got out of the car and took in the view. It was a beautiful day: clear skies, towering clouds, brooding green pines, jutting gray rocks and a road that clung to the canyon overlooking what a mere year ago had been a reservoir. The tree line marked the former shore. Below there was no growth, only rocks that barely held themselves in place in the canyon that plunged to the river. On the far side a series of cabins, luxury and otherwise, lined the former shore.

She thought about Jack, driving like a maniac along the road with Honor in the backseat and Vadim unconscious on the floor. And she remembered...

Twenty-four years ago...

Honor walked on, refusing to let Jack intimidate her. Maybe if she cowered...

But Cynthia couldn't ask her daughter to be less than she was, and anyway nothing appeased Jack when he was in one of his moods.

Grace stumbled when she saw him; he frightened her so much she got clumsy at the sight of the man.

Honor caught her sister, helped her stay on her feet and burst into tears.

Cynthia stopped and knelt beside her. "What's wrong, darling?"

Honor tried to stop crying. "I… I hurt m…my arm."

"I'm sorry, Honey." Grace looked miserable at her part in causing Honor's misery.

They shouldn't have to be brave, not when they were so young, Cynthia needed to learn from them. She glanced at Jack. She had to stop fearing the pain he inflicted. But what if she faced up to him? What if he killed her as he had threatened time and again? Who would care for her daughters then?

When they got close, Jack grabbed Cynthia by the upper arm, lifted her onto her toes and hustled her toward the door.

The girls followed.

Jack opened the door.

Honor was still crying softly.

He turned on her with his fist clenched.

She shrank back and tried to swallow her tears.

"Jack, stop," Cynthia said. "You broke her arm. Isn't that enough?"

"What do I care about that kid?" Jack was running hot; he'd been snorting coke again. "She looks like—"

Cynthia interrupted, "No, she doesn't. She looks like herself."

Jack looked at her, nostrils pinched, ready to strike.

"Don't you want to go in and see your mother?" She didn't know why they were here, why he thought it was so important they all show up and be present for…whatever he intended to do. But she knew how to distract him.

"Yes. My mother." His contempt for Bonnie could not have been more blatant. He pushed the door all the way open and gestured them in. He shoved Honor as she scurried past. The worst kind of bully—a

grown man picking on a little child. "Go in and see Grandpa," *he said.* "That old piece of broken—"

"Jack, they're children. You don't want them to repeat that. He supports us!"

Jack sneered, but shut up and headed into the depths of the house.

Cynthia ushered the twins into the study to see Darrell. The stroke that had felled him had turned him from a vital, upright gentleman with a shock of white hair into a skinny, stoop-shouldered, troubled shell, who couldn't stand without assistance. As usual, he sat in his recliner with his walker close at hand and invited the girls over. He smiled at them and when Jack shouted, "Cynthia!" *he waved her off.*

Cynthia went in search of Jack—it didn't do to keep him waiting—and found him in the trophy room, a room lined with lighted cases, glass shelves and all the collectables Darrell had gathered in his travels. He was talking to her mother-in-law, his brown eyes bright with a persuasive light.

Bonnie, of course, was listening as if Jack was reciting the gospel.

Cynthia saw her turn off the alarm for the case with the Dragon's Heart. "Don't do that!" *She hastened into the room.* "He'll—"

Jack pointed his finger at her.

She shut up.

Vadim Somova stepped through the door.

And for the first time in five long years, her heart beat with the rhythm of her hope—and her love.

Today...

Morgayne got back in her car and drove toward what had been the upper end of the lake, saw the sign for Beachside Estates and took a right onto the narrow road. Pines closed around her, and from here, she couldn't see cabins, she could only see driveways that slithered off and For Sale signs beside each one.

She drove until she reached a point where the trees parted and she was looking across at the Brother Bear Overlook and down toward a handsome home. She figured what the hell, pulled into the driveway, got out and hiked down to the cabin. She knocked on the door.

No answer.

Fine. Whoever owned the place wasn't here, and what they didn't know wouldn't hurt them.

She walked around and down, close to where the waterline had once been, and came to a sudden stop at a short metal fence. Beyond that was one of the docks she had seen from the other side, decrepit and thirsty for the water that would never return.

As she stood there, measuring the distance from the overlook to the river bottom, a middle-aged woman walked briskly toward her and called, "Be careful. It's not safe!"

"I can see that." Thankfully, Morgayne didn't recognize her. "I used to live in Citation, and ever since that story came out about the car that they pulled from the lake, I've been remembering this place and thinking…"

"Were you friends of Joanne and Katie?"

"Joanne and Katie Ness? Yes, I was, a long time ago."

"They're trying to sell the cabin. Of course. We all are. How stupid is this, all of us perched along a shore beside a lake that doesn't exist. I'm Emma." She offered her hand.

Morgayne shook it. "I'm Morgayne Phoenix. That story about the car, and the man who'd been shot, and the other man and the child who weren't in the car…"

"You came out to see if anyone saw anything."

"Yes." Morgayne looked across the lake. "It's haunting, isn't it?" She'd never meant anything so much. "I knew the family. I knew them…so well." To her horror, her voice trembled and she found herself wiping tears off her cheek. "If I knew what happened to… Do you think they lived?"

Emma made her decision. "Joanne and Katie rescued the man and the child."

"W…what?" Morgayne's knees gave way. She sank down onto the ground, put her head in her hands. She wanted, needed to ask all the questions, discover all the answers, but this news, coming after so many years, made her faint with joy, with hope, with wonder. Vadim and Honor had survived. They were alive. Somewhere, they were surely alive.

Emma knelt beside her. "This means a lot to you, huh?"

Morgayne nodded. Her fingers were wet with tears. She wanted to speak, but she knew if she did, she'd start crying in earnest.

Thankfully, Emma told the story without urging. "They told me about it years ago. That they were on the lake puttering along and fishing. They heard a gunshot, sounded like from the highway. They looked up in time to see a car fly off the overlook and go airborne. It landed where the water was deepest and sank."

Morgayne wiped her cheeks, raised her head, stared, wide-eyed and riveted.

"They cranked up the motor—it was a fishing boat, not a ski boat, so the motor was feeble—and they headed over to where the car went down. Nothing they could do, of course, but feel bad for whoever was inside..." Emma took a breath.

"And?"

"Someone popped to the surface."

"Alive? Really? Alive? How long were they under the water?"

"According to the girls, good long minutes. The man was holding a child. In a car seat!"

Morgayne covered her mouth in reactive horror.

"He swam for shore, towing the child, pulling her after him as swiftly as he could. The child was unconscious, blue with cold. Joanne and Katie revved up the motor, caught up as he was floundering with exhaustion. They couldn't get him into the boat without capsizing, but he insisted they bring the child in and take care of her. Joanne steered while Katie got the child—a little girl—out of the car seat and performed CPR. She came to life—small children have a better chance against hypothermia and drowning, but she was in desperate shape. The man clung to the side of the boat as long as he could and finally told them, insisted to them, that they take the child and leave him to die."

Morgayne found herself making a sound of distress.

"Yes, the way Joanne and Katie told it, it was awful. They tried to tell him to hang on, but he let go and sank. They got to shore, ran up to the house, wrapped the child in a blanket. The little girl was sobbing now. Joanne called emergency, but cell service is always sketchy over here, and it was worse then. Katie flipped on the TV, trying to entertain the child until they could get her in the car and to the hospital—and they saw the news story about Jack Torbinson, Vadim Somova, Honor Torbinson and the dragon statue. At that moment, Vadim Somova knocked on their screen door."

Morgayne froze in horror. "He'd heard what the news was saying?"

"Yes. But here's the thing." Emma developed a bitter half twist to her mouth. "Jack Torbinson had a reputation around these parts as a general little dick."

"I remember him." An understatement.

"He was a specific little dick to Joanne and Katie."

"Of course. They were lesbians. Jack prided himself on his—" Morgayne snapped her mouth shut. She'd already said too much.

Emma viewed her shrewdly. "Right. You do remember him. On the other hand, Joanne and Katie had just heard that Vadim was a juvenile delinquent and freshly released prisoner, and this reportedly dangerous felon stood dripping, blue with cold, staring at them through the screen door."

Morgayne's mind painted a vivid picture of her little girl and the man she loved, balanced on a knife's edge. "Nothing to stop him from opening the door, coming in and murdering them all."

"But on that lake, Joanne and Katie saw what they saw. They witnessed a man who, if he hadn't risked his life to bring that little girl up from the depths, could have shot to the surface of the lake, waded out and walked away."

"If he'd left the child to die." Morgayne was still leaking slow, incredulous tears.

"Right. When the little girl, little Honor, saw him at the door, she reached for him with both her hands. Joanne made her decision, walked over, unlatched the door and invited him in."

"Nice distinction."

"Important distinction. He and Honor spent the night. I don't know how, but he had Jack's wallet. Joanne and Katie gave him cash so he didn't have to use the credit cards. They let him drive their old car to get away—he promised to somehow return it—and two weeks later they received a new car to replace it."

"And?"

Emma lifted her hands and dropped them. "And I don't know. Isn't that enough?"

"That's great," Morgayne said fervently. "But is he alive? Is Honor alive? Where are they now?"

Emma concentrated on Morgayne. "I don't know. But I suspect you're going to do everything to find out."

"Yes. I am." Morgayne's phone rang. She pulled it out of her pocket; the call originated in her office. She answered, "Sally?"

"Morgayne, listen." Sally was using her *Soothe the Client* voice. "Listen, you have to be calm."

Morgayne's hand tightened. "Is it Zoey?"

"Yes. How did you—?"

"Is she dead?"

"No. No, but it's not good. She's… It's really not good. Let me give you the information I got from the police."

12

"WHEN I CAME up to pick up her lunch tray, she was dead." Patrice spoke to Citation Police Chief Jenny Coe, but she couldn't take her gaze off Mrs. Torbinson's body on the floor beside the bed. "She was fine when I left her. Maybe she had a heart attack."

"Didn't you say you removed the pillow from her face?" Officer Søren Van Dijk took photos of the scene.

"Yes," Patrice said, "but she could have—"

"There are signs of struggle. She kicked off the covers. Her nightgown is twisted." Officer Van Dijk indicated one of her hands. "She's got blood under her fingernails. Is that your blood?"

"No. No, look!" Patrice extended her arms. "I'm fine. I'll strip naked if you don't believe me. I've got no scratches. I'm not the one who did it!"

"So you admit this is a murder?" Officer Van Dijk asked.

"I don't know. I guess so." Patrice wasn't stupid. She had a record. She knew that record meant everybody would point all the fingers at her. "But how did... I mean, after I left her, I locked the front door. She had a thing about killers and rapists.

She wasn't confined to bed. She had a security camera in the kitchen. She spied on me to make sure I did what I was told. I'm telling the truth!"

"Her window was open," Chief Coe pointed out.

"Her bedroom's on the second floor. She asked for fresh air." Patrice looked off to the left. "What was the harm?" *Or rather, what had gone wrong?*

"Bonnie Torbinson was afraid of infection. With the masks and the gloves, that's obvious. Apparently she was also concerned about security." Chief Coe looked through her notes. "Someone turned off her security system."

"I did. I did every morning when I came to work. I mean… she had visitors sometimes." *Not often. No one liked her.* "I got tired of disarming that stupid alarm."

Van Dijk made a show of examining the windowsill and looking out the window. "It looks as if a small grappling hook pierced the sill and a rope marked the paint on the side of the house. Looks like you had an accomplice."

"Did Mrs. Torbinson have visitors today?" Chief Coe asked.

"Yes. Yes!" *Thank God, yes.* "Her nephew, Mark Torbinson, came in and when he left, he was angry."

"Hmm." Van Dijk seemed doubtful. "What makes you think he was angry?"

"After he talked to her, he stomped down the stairs and slammed the door." She was telling the truth, Patrice assured herself. Maybe someone else had seen him.

"Do you have his number?"

"Yes. He was her emergency contact." Patrice dug her phone out of her pocket, looked it up and showed Van Dijk, who noted it.

"Anyone else?" Chief Coe asked.

"Yes." When Patrice remembered who it was, how Cynthia had lied, she wanted to cheer. This would save her ass. "This lady showed up, said she was from Mrs. Torbinson's church.

She said her name was Adele. She talked to Mrs. Torbinson for about a half hour, then I took the lunch tray up and Mrs. Torbinson was troubled because she kept saying she knew that woman. Mrs. Torbinson figured it out—it was her daughter-in-law, Jack's wife, who disappeared after Jack did."

"Cynthia?" Chief Coe smiled fondly. "We were friends."

Doesn't that just figure? "Mrs. Torbinson said Cynthia wanted to know about the Dragon's Heart. Because it's worth a lot of money. So maybe it was her who…who offed her. I mean, lying about her identity and all that." For the first time, Patrice noticed Chief Coe wore a steely expression.

Chief Coe asked, "Where is the Dragon's Heart now?"

"Mrs. Torbinson said she sent it away."

"How?"

"Package pickup. I don't know which one."

"There should be a record on her computer," Van Dijk said. "What's her password?"

Patrice snorted. "Like she would tell me!"

Van Dijk stared at her, levelly. "We'll check the house for fingerprints."

"There won't be any. You saw. She made everyone wear nitrile gloves. Look, I've been caring for people in Citation for years, and—" Patrice had picked up a few things now and then "—nobody has ever died under suspicious circumstances."

"We'll scrape the killer's DNA out from under her fingernails." Patrice knew Van Dijk from before, from her wild days. He was accusing her now. "Why don't you tell us who your accomplice is?"

"I don't have an accomplice. I don't know who did it!" Patrice dabbed at the sweat on her forehead. "I'm telling you, I just…"

One of the other officers clomped up the stairs, came to the door of the bedroom and stared meaningfully at Van Dijk. Van Dijk spoke quietly with him, then came over and spoke quietly to Chief Coe, who asked, "Patrice, do we have permission to examine your purse?"

"What?" Patrice didn't know where this was going.

"It was sitting open on the table," Van Dijk said. "The officer glanced inside and saw a bank envelope on top. Looks like it's stuffed with cash. A hundred-dollar bill is peeking out."

Patrice knew she was in trouble. More trouble. "I was in the bathroom. I have to go sometime! I heard footsteps, the back door open and close... I guess someone came in and left."

"Left a bank envelope full of cash in your purse? Why would someone do that?" Van Dijk asked.

"Why didn't you mention the footsteps sooner?" Chief Coe asked.

Because I didn't know I'd been paid in a way that incriminated me in a goddamn murder.

In a friendly tone of voice, Chief Coe asked, "Why don't we start at the beginning? Who has been to see Bonnie Torbinson this morning? Why was her window open? Why do you have so much money in your purse?"

The one bribe I've taken in all these years, and I get caught. All my luck is bad... Then Patrice saw the way the police were viewing her, as if she was a murderer, and started talking. "Somebody called me. Voice was disguised. Maybe female? I'm not sure. Offered me money to leave the window open. I said no, no. I refused. But this person assured me they wanted to ask Mrs. Torbinson a few questions and she wouldn't be harmed..."

13

LIKE A CYMBAL'S CRASH, pain and fear brought Zoey to consciousness. She opened her eyes to see a strange room painted pale green, her mother asleep on a cot, and from the window a light shone so bright it hurt her eyes. Her heart pounded, her head ached, her body hurt, her hand was on fire. She lifted her left arm close to her face and saw two fingers fastened together and held to a splint with surgical tape. An IV tube was threaded into the vein at her elbow. A huge vase of colorful flowers sat on the table beside her.

Hospital. She was in a hospital.

As soon as the thought formed, the door swung open and a woman dressed in medical scrubs rushed in.

Her mother roused at once.

Both women looked at Zoey.

Morgayne burst into tears.

Zoey knew what that meant. She'd been badly hurt.

Would she recover?

Perhaps, but the way she felt, it was going to be a bitch.

Her mother went into the bathroom and splashed for a moment, then came back with a damp face and combed hair.

The nurse? doctor? came to Zoey's side and clicked a switch on the heart monitor. In that preternaturally calm voice medical people were trained to use, the woman asked, "How are you feeling?"

Zoey wanted to answer, but her mouth was so dry. She tried to wet her lips.

No spit.

Her mother picked up a glass, came to the other side of the bed and slipped a straw between Zoey's lips. "Sip."

Zoey sipped and swallowed. Even that hurt. "Pain."

The woman's name tag identified her as Nalini, RN. "On a scale of one to ten?"

"Ten." Her voice rasped in her throat.

"Where?" Nalini asked.

"Head." With her uninjured hand, Zoey touched her forehead. Gauze. Her head was wrapped in gauze. "Head."

"Can you tell me your name?" Nalini asked.

"You don't know my name?" Then Zoey realized—they were worried about brain damage. "Zoey Phoenix. I live in Gothic. I was going home. I found a flower…" She tried to sit up. The pain in her neck knocked her backward onto the pillow, but nothing could distract her. "My backpack! Where's my backpack?"

"I've got it, honey." Morgayne rubbed Zoey's other shoulder. "Calm down."

Zoey subsided. "I found a flower." In her mind she could still see it, perfect, blue with red splatters and lost for so many years. "Then I—" She tried to remember. Tears leaked from the corners of her eyes. "Then… I don't know."

"You're doing great," Nalini said. "Let's give you some pain reliever."

While Nalini prepared the injection, Zoey asked Morgayne, "What don't I know?"

"You were involved in a hit-and-run. The bastard pushed

you off the road. You've been unconscious for—" she glanced at her watch "—forty hours. You've got a concussion, two broken fingers, multiple contusions. Thank God you were wearing your seat belt."

Zoey stared at her mother's face, trying to absorb the words, but as the medication took effect, her understanding faded. The room faded. She fell asleep…and into a nightmare of smoke and murder, fire and fear.

14

PAIN AND FURY WOKE ZOEY. Even before she opened her eyes, she asked, "Don't you have anything that works better than this?" When she did open her eyes, the view was exactly the same, except Nalini was gone, and the person in the medical uniform wore a name tag that said Dr. Felsing.

He looked up at her mother. "She's doing well."

Zoey snarled at him.

"Zoey!" Morgayne sounded as if she couldn't believe her daughter's temper.

Dr. Felsing grinned. "Don't worry about it. Attitude is a sign of recovery." He pressed the call button, then leaned over Zoey. "Pain reliever's on the way. You'll feel better soon."

As he turned away, Zoey caught his arm. "How long do I have to stay here?" Because she had a flower that needed to be investigated and bred and every minute wasted meant a loss of viability.

"Two or three more days. When you were brought in, you were in ICU in serious condition."

"Whoever hit you and drove away deserves a death sentence," Morgayne said fiercely.

Dr. Felsing gave a nod. "You'll have to come back and have surgery on those fingers, but we couldn't do it while you were in a coma." After delivering that cheery news, he left.

"Just great." Zoey's whole hand felt inflamed, broken, swollen. "I need both hands to work."

"I know, honey." Morgayne's voice was conciliatory.

Which somehow made Zoey madder.

The pain reliever arrived, Name Tag Joséph administered it, and Zoey waited tensely, each moment an eternity, for it to take effect. "Mom, you said you have my backpack?"

"I do. And your wallet. The contents appear to be intact, so robbery was not the motive."

"That makes it all better." Light hurt her eyes.

"The police released your personal effects to me. Your cell phone…that's broken. I've got a new one for you. I'll make sure you get it when you're released from the hospital."

"I don't care about my phone. I only care about those flowers!" Zoey was nasty. She knew she was. But pain rasped at her patience. "Who's taking care of my plants?"

Morgayne brushed at her eyes and laughed a little. "I knew you would ask that, so I called Angelica Lindholm. She said her crew handled maintenance and they would continue until you return. I know she has a reputation as a ballbuster, but she seemed pleasant."

"That's because the Gothic Garden and Flower Show is coming up in a few weeks and my yard is one of the prime destinations."

"She mentioned that." Morgayne changed the subject. "Your car's totaled."

"How? What happened? I don't remember…" Zoey remembered the flower, then nothing. Fretfully she rubbed her forehead, touched the gauze, dropped her hand to her side.

"You were on the highway, driving home. Law enforcement

thinks some large vehicle—a pickup or a Humvee—fitted with a steel push bar came out of a driveway—"

"What driveway?"

"Neimeyers'."

That helped fix the location in Zoey's mind.

"The vehicle hit at a high rate of speed, T-boned you and pushed you off the road. There was a ditch and a slope, and your car rolled and might have kept rolling but it hit an oak."

Nothing about this sounded familiar. But— "Oh, no. Was there damage to the oak?"

Morgayne closed her eyes, took a breath and let it out. "You would worry about that. I didn't ask about the oak."

"Sorry, Mama." Zoey hadn't meant to upset her mother more. "Did the Neimeyers see what happened?"

"No. Their house sits far back from the highway, and they're hard of hearing."

The pain began to ease. "The driver just…left the scene? Left me to die?"

"Hit-and-run," Morgayne said again. "A vicious crime."

This wasn't fair. "Didn't *anybody* see something?"

"At the time of the collision, there were no other vehicles on-site. The people who found you were traveling east." Morgayne held Zoey's uninjured hand and rubbed it gently. "They said they heard the collision, so they were close, and they didn't meet an oncoming vehicle. Whoever it was, went west."

Bit by bit, Zoey relaxed. Her rage began to subside. She could take a breath without constriction. She noted another huge vase of colorful flowers beside her bed. Ever the florist-shop worker, she calculated the price.

Someone had spent a lot so she could be cheered when she woke.

Good. She deserved it.

Morgayne must have been watching anxiously, because now she said, "Dear, I have to tell you something."

"Okay."

"About who we were and who we are and why… I can't make excuses. I should have kept… But you have to understand I could find no trace of them."

Zoey's eyelids were drooping. "Mama, are you making sense?"

"No. Wait. I can finish a coherent sentence." Morgayne took a long breath, looked down at the floor, looked up at Zoey.

Zoey could have sworn she looked guilty. Had she ever seen her mother look guilty before?

"I got married when I was eighteen," Morgayne said. "I had to."

Zoey forced her eyelids open. Now, this was interesting, and complete news to her.

"The guy I married…he said he loved me. But I didn't trust him…mean reputation…the babies…"

Zoey was drifting, but that hooked her attention. "The babies?"

"…Suspicious. He wanted…abortion… No! … First time he hit me."

"Mama!" Some guy had had the guts to hit her mother? Her mother, the second-degree black belt?

"…You were okay, usually, but Jack thought Honor…"

Zoey woke up, widened her eyes, stared hard at her mother.

Morgayne paced across the floor as she did when she was preparing for a tough divorce case. "…Stole the dragon…"

Great. Now Zoey was hallucinating about a dragon.

"…Vadim… Honor…" Morgayne took Zoey's hand and squeezed it. "Do you understand?"

Zoey didn't, but clearly this was important to her mother. She could tell from Morgayne's tone, from the way she held her shoulders, by her frown and embarrassment. "Sure."

"I'll wrap this up so you can rest." Morgayne spoke more quickly. "…Never be safe as long as Jack was alive… Victim's guilt… Swore I would never again be a coward."

"You're not!" Zoey wasn't sure she was actually speaking the words.

"Really? Oh, good. I was afraid… I took you and left… I did look… Years… No sign of them…"

Zoey nodded.

"…Believed they were dead." Morgayne sounded sad. So sad.

Zoey wanted to hug her. But she couldn't lift her arms. She couldn't even lift her eyelids. The last thing she remembered was her mother's kiss and her whisper, "He'll protect you. Wish me luck," and something else so weird Zoey half roused…then inevitably surrendered to sleep.

Morgayne caressed her daughter's hair. Zoey had been wide-eyed and interested until a few moments ago, assuring her mother she understood. Then she slid down on the pillow, hard asleep. Had she comprehended? The secrets that had shaped her past? The danger to her caused by the Dragon's Heart? Why Morgayne needed to leave, to go seek her long-lost daughter and the man who had saved her and taken her to safety?

Security in this hospital was good, and Zoey would remain unharmed here. Leaning down, Morgayne kissed Zoey's forehead. "Be safe, my darling. Be careful." She had arranged that Zoey be guarded when she was released, and by the man who would sacrifice his life for her. Yet when Zoey realized who would be her nurse and bodyguard, Morgayne feared the explosion would light the sky on fire.

15

"MISS PHOENIX, YOUR RIDE IS HERE."

Zoey opened her eyes a slit and looked at nursing assistant Peter, his fingers grasping the handles of a wheelchair. She'd been dressed and waiting since breakfast, anxious to get out of the hospital. After the first hour, she decided sitting up was too ambitious and reclined on the bed.

Not that she wasn't a lot better. She was. But it had been a while since she'd exerted herself to such an extent. Stuff like lifting her arms to pull on a shirt turned out to be painful, sweaty work. Pulling on panties, then a skirt with an elastic waistband... Whew.

Peter helped her raise the head of the bed, then assisted her off the mattress and into the chair.

She thanked him, he handed her the written instructions from the doctor, assured her they'd been texted to her, also, and they headed to the elevator. She had prescriptions for pain reliever and a sleep aid, instructions on how to care for her broken fingers and what symptoms to take seriously—extreme headaches, loss of vision or consciousness...duh— and the doctor's telephone number with instructions to call ASAP for an appointment in four weeks' time.

They descended the four floors to the lobby, then Peter wheeled her out to the carport and made a call.

The air was dry and hot, even in the shade; during the twelve days Zoey had been hospitalized, summer had arrived in the Salinas Valley.

In moments, a black vehicle pulled up to the curb.

Peter checked the plates. "Here we are."

This didn't look like her mother's car. In fact, it looked like a car Morgayne would hire to take her to the airport if she was in a hurry: tough, anonymous, an expensive vehicle that loved the road. Maybe Mama had hired a driver. Or...

Peter set the brake on the wheelchair. "Front seat or back?"

Zoey's skin chilled, because the last person she had known who owned a car like that was—

"Front." She tugged her jacket over her shoulders.

Yet...no. What she was thinking was beyond unlikely. Her mother would never thrust Zoey into such an awkward—

Peter opened the door, put a hand under her arm and helped her inside.

A single glance told Zoey she'd been right to feel a chill.

Peter shut the door.

Zoey gave him a feeble wave, one that only slightly wrenched her shoulder, then turned to the driver. "Luca, do you have my backpack?"

16

LUCA DAMEZAS FACED HER, the woman who had dumped his family surname for her maiden name, who had dumped him because she didn't like his profession. His elbow rested on his seat back and he wore a carefully constructed no-expression expression. "Good to see you, too, Zoey." He reached in the back seat, grabbed the strap and handed her the bag.

Like a mother embracing a long-lost child, Zoey hugged it to her chest and closed her eyes in relief, then opened the side pocket and pulled out several crumpled paper bags.

He knew what those bags meant. He'd seen enough of them during their marriage. More of her flower breeding projects.

She opened one, two, three, then stopped. She must have found what she wanted, because she took a long breath, looked up toward the ceiling and breathed, "Thank you."

"You're welcome," he replied, although he knew she wasn't talking to him.

For the first time, she focused on him. Critically. As if he was an aphid devouring her rose leaves. "What are you doing here?"

He wanted to grin. But his grin would be a grimace.

All his life he'd been big, handsome, charming, his mother's joy and the center of his six sisters' affection. From the time he was eleven, schoolgirls had fluttered around him, and he liked it. Reveled in it. High school had been sports, one girlfriend after another and graduating valedictorian. Freshman year at college had been more of the same; he excelled at sports, women and study. His sisters laughed at him, told him he was due for a comeuppance.

He laughed back, so full of himself he thought he would never fall.

His mother warned him to be careful to find the right woman, because when he found love, he would love with all his heart.

He didn't laugh at his mother; no one laughed at Giuseppina Damezas, not to her face. But he waited until she was out of sight and rolled his eyes.

Then...there was Zoey Phoenix. She had been his assigned biology lab partner. She was cute with long brown hair crammed into a plastic clip at the back of her head, moss green glasses she repeatedly shoved up her nose and wide eyes that changed color when she blinked. First brown, then green, with flashes of gold... He was fascinated.

He stood there, aware of the covetous glances he was attracting, waiting for Zoey to notice him.

She didn't. Her attention had been on the flower she had taken apart to examine. Using tweezers, she placed pollen on a slide, stuck it under the microscope and put her head down to the eyepiece. Without lifting her head, she groped for her pencil. When she didn't find it, she snapped her fingers at him.

His chest deflated. He handed her her pencil, shoved a tablet under her hand and watched as she sketched the pollen in detail.

By the time she lifted her head, he'd pulled a stool over, perched on it and sat, chin in hand, watching her. "Shouldn't you be doing your work?" she asked. "I don't care how cute you are. I won't let you copy mine."

Cute. She thought he was cute. He could work with that, and he rolled out the phrase he'd been working on. "I hope someday you'll look at me the way you look at that flower."

She blinked at him. Repeatedly. Finally she said, "Is that a pickup line?"

He burst into laughter. "Obviously not a good one." He scooted his stool around beside her, pulled his microscope close and went to work. By the end of class he realized Zoey was an astute observer, a talented sketch artist, she loved everything to do with biology and flowers and she hadn't come to college to party or drink or (unfortunately) get laid. It took him a lot of concentrated attention to get her to look at him the way she looked at a flower, and even then he knew every snapdragon, dandelion and rhododendron ran a close second.

After three years of dating and three years of marriage, he didn't even want to laugh at his mother anymore. He had given Zoey his whole heart...and she had broken it.

Now Zoey was looking at him, not blankly as she had in biology or lovingly as she had during the marriage, but with irritation and maybe some alarm, and she repeated, "Luca, what are you doing here?"

I couldn't stay away any longer.

Someone honked behind them.

He glanced in the rearview mirror, gave the driver a wave, put the car in gear and drove out of the hospital compound. "Your mother asked me to come and care for you."

"My mother? My mother? My mother sent you?" Zoey put the accent on different words as if somehow that would help explain the inexplicable.

"Yes." He took a right onto the busy street and toward the turnoff for the Nacimiento-Fergusson Road.

"My mother hates you..." She glanced at him in alarm. "Where is my mother?"

"Damned if I know." Nor did he care. Not after that divorce handled so coolly and competently by Morgayne Phoenix. Even before she met him, she disliked him. Zoey was too young, she said. When he pointed out he was only a year older, she declared they were both too young. She never gave him a chance; right from the start was convinced a man of his build and his profession would have to be an abuser. After three years of marriage, he would have thought she'd learned better. Then to be treated like a criminal who had daily assaulted her daughter, to have his character dragged through the mud while Zoey cowered somewhere out of sight...

No. He didn't give a damn where Morgayne Phoenix had gone. He only wished she hadn't dragged him into the business of protecting Zoey. When he thought of someone deliberately trying to kill *his wife*, he did *not* want to roar in fury.

As if she read his mind, Zoey said, "I am not your wife."

"I am aware." *Tell that to my heart.*

"How is it possible that my mother asked you to come and care for me... *Care for me?* What does that even mean? If she couldn't be here, why...?" She put her hand on her chest, leaned back and, if he wasn't mistaken, hyperventilated.

It was a little early for that.

Luca pulled into a parking lot and parked under the PhoNow sign. Twisting around in his seat, he found a paper bag with the remains of his McDonald's breakfast. He dumped it out and handed the empty bag to her. "Cup that over your nose and mouth and breathe."

"I don't think I can..."

He put it over her face. "It should still smell like a bacon, egg and cheese biscuit. That'll cure what ails you."

She took a few quick breaths, then withered in her seat. "Better," she said.

"Sure?" He took the bag away. "Let me see you."

She got an expression on her face. Like she didn't want him to look.

Why, he didn't know. Last time she'd set eyes on him she'd

made her indifference clear. But never mind that he had six sisters, he didn't pretend to understand women. It was a whole different gender.

His fingertips hovered over her face; over the healing scabs where the glass had cut, the taped and bruised nose, the skin around her eyes that was no longer black, but a rainbow of purple and yellow and orange.

She sat very straight, shoulders down, chin up, and when he indicated she should turn her head, she did...but cautiously.

He knew what that meant. "How's the whiplash?"

"Lousy. It's all lousy." Her eyes filled with tears.

"I know, honey." He reached in the back seat, dug around in his bag and handed her a tissue. "Your mother said you were T-boned by a big vehicle and shoved into the ditch and left."

"I don't remember much. The panic. The pain. The noise. No control. The smoke."

"There was a fire?"

"I don't know." She took a long breath. "And the poor tree."

He couldn't help it. He grinned. "Of course you remember the poor tree." From the cooler in the back, he produced a cool, wet cloth and applied it to her forehead as if she was a Victorian maid in a faint. "Your mother called. In her own charming manner, she accused me of trying to kill you."

17

LUCA KEPT HIS touch light and impersonal, which was a testament to his self-control.

"Kill me?" Zoey's hand groped, took control of the wet cloth and smoothed it over her cheeks. "Why would she think...?"

"Because someone very determinedly ran you the hell off the road and left you to die. That *is* the definition of hit-and-run."

"The Nacimiento-Fergusson Road is fairly well traveled. Busy, even, at the right time of day. Anyone trying to kill me by running me off that road was stupid, because they were likely to get caught. It couldn't have been you." As an afterthought, she tacked on, "You're not stupid."

"How kind." And inaccurate. For the past two years, ever since the divorce, he'd been convinced he was nothing but a big lump of stupid. "Whoever it was didn't get caught, and you were off the road and down a slope. A few more feet you would have been out of sight and you could have bled to death." He glared at her taped nose, black eyes, and spared a special glare for her broken fingers. "Whoever came out of that driveway at that moment had planned the move carefully."

"You don't know that."

"However, regardless of the acrimoniousness of our divorce, I did not try to kill you." She'd already said she didn't believe it. But he had to say it anyway.

"No." She put her right hand, the hand with bruised knuckles and no broken bones, on his arm. "Luca, I know."

A wellspring of sarcasm rose from his gut, all of it unworthy of him. He didn't pick on people who were weaker. Not that he ever thought of Zoey as weaker; she had always been his match. But now…she was bruised, she was thin, she was pale, she couldn't meet his eyes, maybe because she was ashamed of how she'd treated him—he could only hope—but mostly, he thought, because the wreck, the pain, the bright headlight of death that had shown in her eyes had shaken her belief in her own invincibility.

He didn't understand her, but he understood that, at least.

"This whole thing has sent Mama off the deep end. Who would deliberately try to kill me?" Her voice cracked. "I'm a flower breeder."

"Yeah, I'm your assigned bodyguard. After Morgayne got over her hissy fit and agreed I wasn't a killer, she demanded I come for you on your release. I haven't heard from her since."

"In the last few days, she hasn't been to visit me. She hasn't called. I haven't been able to speak to her at all."

"That's not normal. Did she not tell you what she was doing?"

"I think so."

"You *think* so?" *What the hell?*

"I was in pain. They gave me drugs. She talked to me. Something about her honor."

"Her honor." *Had he heard her right?*

"And a dragon."

He couldn't help it. He laughed. "A *dragon*?"

She chuckled a little and clutched her side. "Maybe a wagon."

"Or flagon? With the dragon?" He quoted one of their favorite old movies.

She chuckled harder and groaned "Stop. Stop! It's true, it hurts to laugh."

"All right. All right. I know that feeling." But grinning so widely felt good. It was comfortable being silly with Zoey. She made him complete. Which was a damned shame since he was only here until Morgayne returned.

Zoey breathed deeply, carefully, then asked, "Do you not know anything about what has happened that sent her away?"

"She was vague. Something about her past and yours."

"She didn't think that something in our backgrounds were the reason I was hit, did she?"

"I don't know. I didn't question her." Although, not that that would be good, but probably better than what he feared.

"Regardless of what my mother thought, you didn't have to come to care for me."

Yes, I did. Because...but he couldn't tell her why. He couldn't explain that he might be the reason she had been hunted, hurt, almost killed. That had been the secret he'd kept from her for so long... "The trip's going to take a couple of hours. How about if I tilt your seat back, drive carefully, and you can relax."

"All I do is relax." She sounded cranky.

"Best thing for you." He cheerfully repeated the phrase she'd so often used on him. "Do you want something to eat first?"

Her eyes brightened. "Yes. I am so tired of hospital food!"

He thought he had recognized that particular kind of cranky; she was hungry. Good to know he could still read her. "Lupe's?"

"Yes! Please. Thank you. I haven't been since our honey—" She stopped.

"Our honeymoon." He looked into her eyes, compelling the memories. She was in bad shape, but a little squirming would do her good. Or at least—if she was squirming, it would do him good. "I'm surprised. We ate there every night after... well. After."

She kept her gaze fixed firmly on his chin. No eye contact for her!

"You loved their flour tortillas and the melted butter and refried beans." He kept talking, his voice smooth as the melted butter she loved. "Don't forget those chicken enchiladas and—"

"Stop." She put her hand on her skinny rib cage. "You're killing me!"

No, I'm not, although there were times when I thought you deserved it, and I'm not going to let someone else kill you. He put the car in gear, and in five minutes they were at the Lupe's drive-up window collecting the party pack of tacos, an order of chicken enchiladas, an extra order of refried beans, and of course the hot flour tortillas and melted butter.

He parked under a tree, distributed the food, and Zoey ate like a starving person. When she finally leaned back with a sigh, she said, "Save the leftovers. I've got nothing in the house for dinner."

"I ordered groceries from the Gothic General Store, so we're good." As talented as Zoey was in so many ways, she was a lousy cook.

She darted him a surprised glance. "How did you know about the General Store?"

"Your mother told me."

"Ah." She relaxed.

She didn't want to think he'd kept track of her, had researched her home, her town, her activities.

Well, he had. It was creepy and stalker-ish, but when she left him, he worried about her. He missed her. He obsessed about her. He wanted to go to where she was and demand she return to him. When she had convinced him of her indifference…everything in him howled in protest.

He stowed the food in the back seat, gave her a bottle of water, lowered her seat back and suggested, "Go to sleep. I'll wake you when we get there."

"I never sleep in the car," she said fretfully.

"I know." He got back on the road.

"Where are we going?" She should have thought of that sooner.

"Your place in Gothic. Apparently your mother thinks it's safe."

"That's nice." She was relaxing. "I thought she didn't like it."

"She said safe, not comfortable."

Her eyes closed. "At least no one will attempt to kill me there."

They might try, but they'll have to get through me first.

18

THE COLOR OF THE SUNLIGHT, the steady descent, the scent of home woke Zoey. Without looking, she knew they had passed the summit of the Santa Lucia Mountains and were now descending toward Gothic. She groped for the seat controls, raised herself into a sitting position and filled her soul with her first glimpse of the rolling hills and the endless vista of the Pacific Ocean.

"Awe-inspiring, isn't it?" Luca asked.

Moving with the caution engendered by discomfort, she turned to look at him.

Luca's father, Carmine Damezas, had lived in New York City in the garment district. In accordance with an archaic family custom, his mother, Giuseppina Bianca Aosta, had been brought from Italy to marry him. By the time Zoey came into the family, Carmine had died, probably from the exhaustion of living with a woman as difficult as his wife. That unlikely couple had brought seven children into existence, each more beautiful than the next, and Luca was their crowning achievement, their youngest, their only son, a man so strongly compelling in size and shape and...oh, those eyes.

His dark eyes made sexual creatures swoon. His eyelids drooped; he looked like a man who knew how to pleasure a woman into the wee hours of the night. That, coupled with his black hair and the curl that slid over his forehead and begged to be caressed, meant that he was voted prettiest wrestler in the world, beating out all the female wrestlers. He had said, "Looking at the plethora of gorgeous women wrestlers, it's obvious the voters look for something different than I do." In a business that loved the greasepaint and the shouts, his rare soft-spoken modesty had endeared him to many. Not all...but the ones who counted.

Sitting with him enclosed in a car was no time to remember that.

"Yes," she said. "Awe-inspiring. Would you stop at the next rest stop? I need to go."

"Thank God. Me, too. That supersized limeade might not have been a good idea."

He was so irritating...when he was right. "You could have stopped anytime."

"I didn't want to wake you."

"I wasn't sleeping that hard."

"You were drooling."

Horribly, completely irritating.

He pulled into the rest stop and parked. "Wait. I'll come and help you."

She wiped at her mouth and watched him sprint around the car.

She knew he sprinted not because he had to go so badly, but because he never walked when he could run. The man loved movement, he loved the physical exertions of life and he was good at everything he did. When they were married, when she wasn't admiring him, she wished he would fail at one thing. Just one.

Then he did.

Her heart broke.

She hated herself.

But she hated him more.

He opened the door, leaned down and slid an arm around her waist, waited while she transferred her legs to the outside, and hefted her up and out. She wobbled; he held her until she had her feet under her, then together they made their way to the accessible restroom. "I'll go in if you need me," he said.

"No." She was definite. "I was taking care of myself in the hospital." She stepped in, shut the door in his face, utilized the rails for support, used the facilities, decided he was right, supersized had been a bad idea, and stepped out about the time he dashed back to the door.

He put his arm around her, they walked to the car and before she sank into the seat, she paused to gaze at the view. She could see the Nacimiento-Fergusson Road winding toward the cutoff for Gothic. Near the top of the Gothic bypass a rocky ridge, Widow's Peak, overshadowed the town. Below that, she could see the Angelica Lindholm estate and the Tower, an edifice built by the Swedish silent-film star, Maeve Lindholm, who in the early 1930s had bought land and created the town to her specifications. Lined by buildings and homes, the bypass took wild hairpin turns as it lurched through town. At the far end of Gothic, when she squinted, she could see her own small house and shop sitting isolated from her neighbors. Beyond that, the vista was magnificent: summer-yellowed slopes, wave-battered sea stacks, the ocean's endless surges and the horizon that stretched to eternity.

Home. She'd come home to heal.

And she'd brought Luca.

Tears prickled her eyes. She blinked and hoped he hadn't seen them. She shouldn't care, but danger lurked in unbridled emotion. She knew she should not fling herself into his arms and cry. He'd been furious about the divorce, and hurt. For sure, he'd been incredulous. To have his wife, the woman he adored, tell him he had to quit wrestling—what was she thinking? He enjoyed wrestling. He was good at it. He made piles of money on endorsements. He enjoyed the comradery. He laid out all the pluses, and he said it as if she should comprehend and agree.

She comprehended, all right, but his laughter and casual dismissal of her plea led to the realization he didn't care what her reasons were, he would do what he wished. Their relationship did not hold up well to scrutiny.

She began to rethink their marriage, and then...then he got slammed to the mat.

As she stood by his hospital bed and watched him writhe with the agony of a ruptured disc, her heart broke for him. At the same time, she suffered that niggling bit of resentment. If he'd listened to her, he wouldn't be broken and she wouldn't be here, at his side, wishing futilely she could do something to help him. Even worse, she desperately wanted to say, *I told you so.*

She didn't understand why an intelligent, educated, successful man would risk his life for wrestling. For the fame? The glory? The adoration? He seemed completely able to brush all those ego fillers aside. She would have seen him all the way through recovery and stayed with him for their lifetimes, as she'd promised, but on the day she heard him ask his physical therapist how soon he could return to the ring...she walked. As she drove away, she called his mother and told her to come to fetch him.

Giuseppina didn't even wait until Zoey had finished her sentence before she snapped, "I knew you'd never last."

Depending on where Luca Damezas was in the process of detaching himself from the love, the marriage, the turmoil, the anguish, he would do one of two things: use any outburst from her as a reminder of how good they had been together—and they had been very good—or gently and with great finality set her away from him.

She didn't know which one she dreaded more. Better suck it up so she didn't have to find out.

"Out there, far out to sea…is that a fog?" He pointed. "Because if it is, that is the densest fog I've ever seen."

She saw it, too, a blue-gray fog that obscured the horizon. "I wonder which lost souls it will bring tonight?" she murmured.

She hadn't meant Luca to hear, but of course like every other extremely fit part of him, his hearing was excellent.

"Lost souls?" he asked. "Transported how? Where? What are you talking about?"

"In Gothic, there's a plaque on the Live Oak Restaurant and it says—" She looked at Luca. She thought of her first night in Gothic, how she had groped her way down the street, lost and unable to find her bed-and-breakfast, and drawn by the muffled sound of surf to the far end of town. There she had discovered the house and the shop that was now her home.

"Nothing," she said. "It's just a superstition."

Luca's eyes narrowed on her. "You used to trust me more than that."

19

AS LUCA AND Zoey drove past the ornate gateway that blocked the road to Angelica Lindholm's estate, the speed limit sign changed from a sedate forty miles an hour to a tedious twenty. Luca slowed, and Zoey rolled down her window to take a deep breath. From the corner of his eye, he saw her relax into the soft leather seat. He'd never seen her so at home.

What the hell was it with her? He'd been a lot of places, and wherever he hung his hat was home.

Zoey was so quintessentially a California girl, not the blonde, tanned beach girl, but someone whose roots went deep into the varied soils of California. He'd once asked her mother how long their family had lived in California, and where. Morgayne had said, "My family's lived in the state for generations."

"And her father's family?" he asked.

"Them, too." She'd turned her shoulder on him and walked away, and now he wondered whether it was her deliberate determination to ignore her past that called her away when Zoey needed help. He wondered, too, if she feared that past had almost killed Zoey on the Nacimiento-Fergusson Road. Something had scared her; when she called him, her voice had trembled with terror for her daughter. Of course he in turn announced he would be there. She wasn't the only one who had reasons for terror.

As he drove into Gothic, through the first of the torturous curves, he wondered if Zoey had realized what she'd done.

She had moved to a place that resembled *his* mother's ancestral home, a tiny coastal village on the Amalfi Coast. The main street, cutting back on itself again and again as it wound its way down the hill toward the ocean. The buildings which had been strengthened to withstand earthquakes, yet retained their early twentieth-century charm. The tiny 1930s Craftsman-style houses, the quaint shops that advertised local merchandise. The inviting restaurants where people sat at sidewalk tables eating, drinking and watching the traffic pass. If someone had, in an instant, set him down here, he would have wondered if they had landed somewhere in the Mediterranean.

As they passed the Live Oak Restaurant, Zoey waved at the customers seated at the outdoor tables. Luca would bet a discussion about the identity of her companion would spread through the town at lightning speed. At least, he hoped so. He wanted Gothic to know Zoey Phoenix's ex-husband had arrived. He wanted speculation and gossip. He wanted her to be uncomfortable.

He was a jackass.

He would admit that the occasional bright pink tour Jeep and the plethora of all-terrain vehicles parked here and there in no way resembled Italy, nor did the glittering window of Madame Rune's Psychic Readings and Bookshop. "Psychic?" he questioned.

"Gothic is reputed to be a navel of the universe, a place where the knowledge of all times swirl, and if a person is sensitive, even the future is revealed." As Zoey spoke, her voice was light, but she didn't mock the belief.

"You are kidding."

"There's Madame Rune right now standing with Sadie. Sadie's the petite one." Zoey indicated the exceptionally tall, exotically dressed and draped female who towered over the woman who stood in front of Sadie and Hartley's Rock and Mineral Emporium. "Madame Rune is renowned for her readings, and people come from everywhere for her glimpses of their futures."

"The hell you say." Luca looked more closely at Madame Rune. "They both look as if they're on the verge of tears," he observed.

Zoey tried to turn and look, grabbed the back of her head and groaned. "I don't know why they would be in tears..."

They took the second hairpin turn.

Zoey cried, "Oh, no!"

An ambulance sat in front of one of the houses, lights flashing, as EMTs loaded an elderly woman on a stretcher.

Luca saw Zoey's hand go to the door handle. "Wait!" he warned, and pulled off the road and onto the sidewalk.

As soon as he put the car in Park, Zoey was out the door and hurrying toward the ancient man, who leaned on a cane and watched desolately as the ambulance did a three-point turn and headed up Main Street toward the highway.

Luca backed up to the barbershop and parked in a space marked, For Customers Only. He got out, waved after Zoey and said, "My wife!" to the woman who watched him, her arms forbiddingly crossed over her chest.

Her eyebrows went up, she looked at Zoey and back at him, and nodded.

He ran after Zoey and caught up as she reached the elderly gentleman.

She put her arm through his. "Mr. Kulshan, are you all right?" she asked.

"Better than I deserve to be," he said in a trembling voice. "My old lady was supposed to call me to come down for lunch—"

"They live in separate houses," Zoey explained to Luca.

Which made no sense, but Luca nodded.

"She was late and I got tired of waiting, so I took a nap. But Irene wasn't being ornery for a change. She was getting the garden ready for Angelica Lindholm's stupid garden show, and she fell." The hand gripping the cane shook as much as his voice. "She couldn't get up. Her phone was on the porch. She managed to crawl over, up the stairs, and call me. I had my hearing aids out, so she called emergency. You know how long it takes them to get here."

"Thirty minutes at top speed," Zoey told Luca. "You've seen the road." She turned back to Mr. Kulshan. "Then what?"

"She called the restaurant because she was worried about me, and Ludwig came over with the key—"

"That's the waiter at the Live Oak," Zoey told Luca.

"—and woke me up." Mr. Kulshan clutched the material of his shirt, over his chest, over his heart. "I should have been the one who called a neighbor, but we had a fight and I thought that Irene… I should have known better. When she says she's going to do something, she does. She told me she was going to make me lunch. She would have if she could."

"What did the EMTs say about her condition?" Zoey asked.

"*She* said she was fine. *They* are taking her in for X-rays and observation. I think she broke something. She was hollering pretty good when they moved her." Mr. Kulshan wiped his eyes on his sleeve, then, as testy as any grandfather protecting his favorite child's reputation, he looked at Luca and demanded, "Who are you?"

"I'm Luca Damezas."

"You're a big specimen. Where'd you pick him up, Missy?" Mr. Kulshan looked hard at Zoey. "I heard you got banged up in a car wreck. Two weeks and that's as good as they could fix you?"

"I'm much better," she assured him.

"Hmph. Luca Damezas, where do you come in?"

Zoey interceded before Luca could answer. "He's a family friend. My mother asked him to come and care for me." She lied like a pro.

Mr. Kulshan looked Luca over—and that took a while. As if Luca wasn't standing right there, he replied, "Big bugger."

Luca decided to inject himself into the conversation. "I used to wrestle."

"Professionally?" Mr. Kulshan hiked himself a step closer. "A couple of years ago, we had a wrestler here in Gothic. Nuttier than a fruitcake."

Interesting. "Who?"

"Big John Hammer. Crazy John, we call him now."

"I met him once. Horrible man," Luca confirmed. "But you know, Mr. Kulshan, if I were a monster, Zoey's mother wouldn't have called me."

Mr. Kulshan nodded. "Right. Smart woman, that one. Like her daughter."

As they spoke, a fit woman in her fifties with carefully careless auburn hair came around the corner of Mrs. Kulshan's house.

Mr. Kulshan groaned.

Luca looked to Zoey for an explanation.

"Angelica Lindholm," Zoey said in an undertone. "She can rub people the wrong way. Mr. Kulshan especially."

A young, nondescript woman followed her, walking and speaking into her computer tablet. But she must have been watching, because when Angelica stopped, the young woman halted, ceased talking and focused her attention on Angelica.

"Zoey! My dear! Your mother told me you'd been in an accident!" Angelica stepped forward and embraced Zoey without quite touching.

Zoey looked surprised, as if that was as close as they'd ever been.

Angelica continued, "Orvin, Hudson and their crew have

faithfully cared for your greenhouse, your shop and your garden."

Zoey sagged with relief. "Bless them. I've been so worried!"

"No need. When you left, I did promise I'd make sure your
garden was tended," Angelica said crisply. "Although I never
imagined it would be for so long."

Luca began to understand Mr. Kulshan's antipathy.

"How do you feel?" Angelica asked. "Will you be able to
show your impressive gardening creations at the Gothic Garden and Flower Show?"

Luca diagnosed Angelica's tactics. First concern, then guilt
and now the demand for payoff.

"I always enjoy the show, so I'll do my best," Zoey said softly.
"But of course you wouldn't want me to overdo it after such a
debilitating injury."

Luca almost grinned. That was his Zoey. She claimed to have
nothing in common with his mother, but they were the same
in one important matter—they didn't take shit from anyone.

"Of course not. Your first concern must be your health." Angelica didn't sound insincere, exactly, more unconvinced. "Let
me know anything I can do to help you." She transferred her
attention to Luca. "Are you her nurse?"

"No, he's my—" Zoey stopped herself.

He offered his hand to Angelica. "In a manner of speaking.
I'm Luca Damezas."

She was one of those powerful women who knew how to
shake a man's hand. Her dry palm met his, equal to equal, she
shook and they separated. Nicely done. If he was to base his
opinion on a handshake, he would say he liked her.

Best to wait and see.

"I'm a family friend—" the claim tasted bitter on his tongue
"—and have agreed to stay with Zoey until she's feeling better."

"That's a tiny house for you and her. One bedroom. Where

are you going to sleep?" Trust Mr. Kulshan to go right to the heart of the situation.

As Zoey realized the logistics, trust her to look horrified and mortified.

Thanks, honey.

"When Zoey's mother called me," Luca said, "she assured me she would provide a bed in the shop."

Zoey sagged in relief.

Mr. Kulshan's gaze measured him from top to toe…again. "Better be a damned big bed."

"California queen," Luca assured him.

Mr. Kulshan cackled. "Anything less and you'll hang over on all sides."

"If there's anything the Angelica Lindholm family can do to assist in this situation, please feel free to contact us." Angelica summoned the young woman to her side. "This is Marjorie Mardesich, my new assistant. Marjorie, this is Zoey Phoenix, our local flower breeder, and Luca Damezas, who will be caring for her during her recovery. Zoey, Marjorie is your advocate."

Marjorie shook hands with them both. Her handshake was more of the squeeze and release type, as if she didn't want to touch in the first place.

"Angelica, what happened to your last assistant?" Zoey asked.

Mr. Kulshan snorted. "Same thing as happens to all her assistants. She made a run for it."

Angelica narrowed her eyes at him. "Thank you, Mr. Kulshan. In fact, I am exacting in my requirements and lately, my assistants have been…inadequate. On the other hand, Marjorie's been with me only a few days and has picked up the intricacies of my organization with exceptional speed."

Marjorie inclined her head. "I'm organized by nature."

She was so bland Luca didn't trust her—and he had become an untrusting bastard dominated by suspicion. His gaze shifted to Zoey. Who could blame him, with his wife standing bruised and broken beside him? Everyone assumed a man had rammed her with a huge vehicle, but why not a woman? One fact dominated his thoughts—someone had tried to kill her. The only question was…why?

Had her past caught up with her?

Or had his sins?

A car pulled up onto the sidewalk. A car door slammed.

Luca turned.

A young woman came around the front of the car.

He recognized her. *Shasta Straka.* My God, that was a blast from the past.

She waved and shrieked, "Zoey! I'm here!"

20

SHASTA RAN TOWARD THE GATE. She put her hand on the latch, saw Zoey's face and did a double take. "What happened to you? Zoey, what happened?"

Zoey couldn't contain her dismay. When she'd asked Shasta to come to Gothic, she had been healthy, happy, sure of herself, envisioning a new start for Shasta similar to the one she herself had fought for and enjoyed.

Then the hit-and-run, the injuries, the pain, her mother's disappearance and… Luca Damezas, back in her life. How could she, in the midst of physical and mental turmoil, do anything to help Shasta?

"Zoey?" Shasta stepped through the gate and paced toward her friend. "What happened to you?"

Zoey wasn't quite sure what to say. "Shasta…good to see you?"

Shasta looked from Luca to Zoey and back. "Are you two getting back together? Zoey, what happened to your face?"

"I was in a car wreck," Zoey said.

"No, we're not getting back together," Luca said.

Mr. Kulshan's hearing wasn't good, but he heard all that. "Zoey, I thought you said he was a family friend."

"She did, didn't she?" Luca grinned, utterly relaxed.

Shasta looked around at the group into which she'd blithely walked, and the bright hope on her face dimmed.

Zoey felt suddenly tired and sad. She had meant to be a friend to Shasta, to help her find a new and hopeful life. Now because even this small amount of effort had overtaxed her, and because Luca was a major disruption she would have to deal with, she didn't know what to do with her.

But Shasta was staring at Angelica. "Are you…?"

"Yes. We haven't met. I'm Angelica Lindholm." As Shasta introduced herself, Angelica assessed her from her gold flip-flops, up the light blue T-shirt dress and to the fashionably ragged cut of brown hair. "That's an extraordinary outfit. I love the…" She waved her hands up from the hem to indicate the profusion of blossoms that Shasta had painted on her material.

"Thank you. I—"

"You painted that, didn't you?" Angelica zeroed in on Shasta's face. "Are you an artist?"

"Yes. I—"

"Those flowers seem almost to breathe. Have you got your portfolio with you?"

"Yes, I—"

"Show it to me." Angelica's personality was forceful; she always knew what she wanted and went after it.

Shasta looked around as if bewildered. "Now? Here?"

"Yes. Here and now. I want to see it."

Shasta glanced at Zoey as if confounded, then scurried back through the gate to her car.

Angelica turned to her new assistant. "Get this young woman's name and information. She is exactly what I was looking for."

Shasta returned, clutching a narrow shoulder bag and a sheaf of drawings loosely contained in a large folder. "I've scanned my paintings into my tablet—"

"I want to see the originals." With a gesture, Angelica indicated that Shasta show her her work.

Shasta juggled the bag and portfolio, managed to pull out the first handful of drawings and hand them to Angelica.

Angelica sorted through them at lightning speed. While Shasta tried to call her attention to the landscapes, Angelica was nodding at the sketches of flowers and plants. "Yes, yes, the landscapes are fine, but discomfiting. These, though, are exactly what we need." She held two of the flower paintings.

"Need? I don't understand—"

"The annual Gothic Garden and Flower Show raises money for my California Golden Poppy Association, which devotes itself to resourcing water for fire-prone areas, and brings in much-needed cash for local businesses as they provide services for visitors. A good part of the income is created by selling posters and framed paintings of the flowers and gardens featured in the garden show. A year ago, I hired an artist for this year's show and he was unable to complete my vision." Angelica's eyes narrowed. "Now we're massively behind."

"Who was it?" Shasta asked.

"Bobbie Bobbert."

"Yeah." Shasta nodded sympathetically. "He's a fu...punker."

"Right. A punker. Is that a word?" Angelica clearly doubted that. "Your work is much better than his, and you're here, now! I assume because you're an artist, you're in need of work."

"Yes. But I came here to develop my landscapes and it sounds as if your proposal is for my plant work only."

"Your landscapes are perfectly...serviceable, if disagreeable. But these!" Angelica held the flower paintings in both hands. "Genius."

"I came to paint the sea, the land, the skies!"

"You can do that, too. In fact, you can do that and sell your paintings when the crowds show up. I'll make sure they're placed where they can get attention." She caught sight of Shasta's dismay. "With what I'll pay you in advances and commissions on any flower garden paintings, you'll be able to stay in Gothic to refine your landscapes. In fact, do you have a place to stay?"

Shasta looked at Zoey and Luca standing together. "I was going to look for somewhere…"

Angelica turned to Marjorie. "Send a text to my housekeeper to prepare the garden studio and adjoining bedroom for Shasta." She turned back to Shasta. "You'll stay with me. It will be more convenient for both of us."

Shasta looked around, helpless to hold back the raging tide that was Angelica.

"Marjorie!" Angelica snapped the name. "Show Shasta the figure I'm willing to pay for completing the work on time. Add a bonus of 25 percent because, Shasta, you'll have to devote yourself full-time to this project."

Marjorie tapped on the screen, brought up the figure and passed it to Shasta, then caught the tablet when it slipped through Shasta's abruptly weak fingers.

"That, um…" Shasta cleared her throat. "I can… Yes, I'll do it for that."

"I'm finicky," Angelica warned. "But I'm fair. Aren't I, Mr. Kulshan?"

Mr. Kulshan rumbled as if he had indigestion, then admitted, "Take the job, girl. You won't like her, but she'll pay you a bundle."

21

"MR. KULSHAN, LET ME help you up to the porch where you can sit down." Luca didn't wait for Mr. Kulshan's response; putting his arm around Mr. Kulshan's back, he half carried him onto Mrs. Kulshan's porch and lowered him into a seat. He spoke to Mr. Kulshan for a moment, then went into the house and returned with a glass of water and what looked like a small wrapped candy.

Zoey watched them with more affection that she would have liked; Luca had a way with old people, even ones as grumpy as Mr. Kulshan, and he had noticed Mr. Kulshan's weariness and taken action.

"Did he give him a butterscotch?" Angelica tsked disapprovingly. "The elderly should never tax their digestive system with sweets."

Luca arrived in time to hear her and delivered up his mother's favorite pronouncement. "It's too late for him to die young."

Angelica's expression made it clear she didn't quite get the joke. "Marjorie, send someone to help Mr. Kulshan back to his home and stock his refrigerator with meals."

Zoey muttered to Luca, "He's going to hate that. He hates her gracious lady routine."

As quietly, Luca answered, "I would, too."

"On Thursday at 2:00 p.m., the Gothic Garden and Flower Show committee is meeting in my conference room. I'll see you there, Zoey, and if you wish, you may bring your escort."

"She isn't allowed to drive, so yes, I'll be there." Luca shot Zoey a sharp look. "Shall we get you home?" In the same gesture he used with Mr. Kulshan, he put his arm around her back and helped her toward the car.

Way to make me feel old and feeble. "At least you could have brought me a butterscotch, too," she said.

"We've got to stop at the Gothic General Store to pick up the groceries." His voice smiled and he seemed more genial, less driven by anger and memory. "I'll get you one then. Maybe even two."

The Gothic General Store and its parking spaces occupied the outside of the lowest curve in the Gothic main street. Built of pine logs, its rich reddish-brown stain, green tile roof, broad windows and wide porch invited everyone to come in and browse, or sit and rock in one of the painted chairs. "Nice!" he said as he parked on the side of the pine log building. "Big."

"All of us who live in Gothic shop here, and there's nowhere else for the tourists to pick up a cooler and drinks for their day at the beach, so yes, big." Zoey looked at the store with affection. "I always thought the store looks like a rustic inn in a national park." She fumbled with the door handle. "I need to pick up my mail."

"I can do that."

"You can't. Inside there's an actual U.S. post office. You can't stroll up and tell them it's okay for you to pick it up. Everyone knows me, and they don't know you, and—"

"It wouldn't be legal for them to give it to me. Got it. Hang on." Luca dashed around the front of the car, opened her door and, with his hand under her arm, he helped her out.

Annoyed, she wanted to shake him off, say she could take care of herself, but she reminded herself she needed to save her strength. As soon as she got to her shop, she had seeds to plant, vegetables and flowers to care for. She let him assist her up the stairs, across the wide porch and into the store.

In Gothic, the General Store was exactly that—a grocery store, clothing store, store that featured local ceramics, jewelry, glasswork, art of all kinds. A candy store, a store packed with ready-made sandwiches and Angelica Lindholm–prepped gourmet meals to cook at home.

Luca looked around, observed the goods, turned to Zoey and said, "Angelica Lindholm really does own this town, doesn't she?"

"She does. Maeve Lindholm, the founder of Gothic, was her great-great-great-great—" Zoey hesitated "—grandmother. I think that's all the greats involved." She smiled at the young woman rolling down her sleeves as she hurried toward them. "Hi, Tamalyn. This is Luca Damezas. He's picking up our grocery order."

"Follow me and I'll pull together the last of the items." She beckoned.

Zoey gestured for him to follow Tamalyn and walked to the back of the store, where the post office had been marked off and secured. She rang the bell and a woman in her thirties, Jael Ramage, Gothic hometown girl, poked her head out of the back room.

"Hi, Jael. Could I get my mail?"

"Sure, Zoey. When I heard about your accident, I stuck it all in the same cubby."

Zoey wanted to snap that it hadn't been an accident.

But Jael had disappeared, and came out with a stack of papers and envelopes. "Bills and ads, mostly, although you did get a package. When we heard it was going to be a while before you got out of the hospital, Mrs. Kulshan took it so it wouldn't rattle around and get crushed. Which turned out to be a good thing, because a couple of nights ago, someone broke into the back room and rifled through the mail."

That was news. Other than a few fender benders and incidents with inebriated tourists, Gothic was crime-free. Or at least, it had been since Zoey moved there. "No! What was stolen?"

"As far as I could tell, nothing. And in case you're wondering, it's an automatic door lock, no way for it to be my fault." Jael was obviously sensitive about the subject. "I don't like to think someone's that good at picking locks."

"How weird, and yes, spooky." Zoey pressed a finger to her forehead, then winced and lowered her hand. "I wonder what I ordered?"

"Good-sized package. Something from Citation, California. Mrs. Kulshan and I figured it was one of your specialized plant heat lamps. Or some such."

"Maybe," Zoey said doubtfully. "Whatever. I can't get it from her now."

Jael leaned across the counter. "I heard what happened. Poor lady! She's too nice to suffer like that."

The two women nodded solemnly at each other.

Luca arrived with an insulated backpack slung over one shoulder and a heavy-duty grocery bag in the other.

At the sight of him, Jael jumped and stared. "You...you're Luca Damezas!"

Oh, no. Zoey wanted to slap her own forehead, but it hurt too much.

Luca smiled. "I am. Are you a wrestling fan?"

Zoey recognized the signs of Jael's burgeoning excitement.

"I'm *your* fan! And you're here, in Gothic, in the store, at the post office, talking to *me*."

Luca offered his hand. "It's always great to meet someone who appreciates the art."

Jael shook his hand. Shook it with both of hers. Shook it some more.

Luca had to put down the grocery bag to extract his fingers from her grasp.

"Could I have your autograph?" she asked.

"Next time I come in," he promised. "Right now I need to get Zoey home and off her feet."

Jael, who had previously been friendly, shot Zoey a glance that clearly labeled her as an intrusion and an annoyance. "Oh!" Her eyes gleamed, and she returned her attention to Luca. "How about the Damned Luck roar?"

When Luca was wrestling, he had made a name for himself by giving a beastly roar to stir up the crowd. "Maybe another time."

"I'm here whenever the post office is open," Jael said. "Come to me for all your mailing needs!"

"Thank you, I will." Luca picked up the backpack, took Zoey's arm and said in a clear, deep voice, "Come on, honey."

When they had walked out onto the porch and far out of earshot, Zoey said, "Good thing I need both hands for all this mail…honey…or I'd smack you."

"I'm sorry." He did sound sorry, at least. "That doesn't happen often anymore. You'd be amazed at how quickly people have forgotten me. Still, I wanted to make sure she understood you weren't my sister or my cousin." He held Zoey's arm as she hobbled down the stairs, opened her door and lowered her into her seat. Leaning in, he fastened her seat belt for her. "I know you're peeved, but I figure it's best to deflect any possible visits from a courting female, at least until you're able to care for yourself." Before she could answer, he shut the door.

By the time he put the bags in the trunk and got into the driver's seat, she was sorting her mail. She didn't look up, and she didn't challenge him. They both knew what could happen if Jael was a fervent fan. They'd dealt with those kinds of hopeful, delusional women and men before, yearning to bring their imagined soul mate bond to life and at the same time ignore his other relationships, family and romantic, as if they didn't exist. Sometimes letting fans know he had another commitment did fend them off. Theoretically, she understood. Emotionally, after two years of divorce, she did not want to be paired with him in that way.

He'd always had an uncanny ability to read her mind; he read it now, and in a massively irritated voice he said, "After you dumped me, my sisters decided to help me get over you and threw a variety of fabulous women my way to distract me. Beautiful. Rich. Foreign. Intelligent. You name it—they flung them at my head."

Her mouth tasted like envy felt. "I'll bet they didn't have to fling too hard."

"I wasn't cooperative."

She liked that more than she should.

He added, "At first."

And…she disliked that *way* more she should.

"After I lost my temper one time too often—"

"You lost your temper?" He had astonished her. Luca was one of the most easygoing people she knew. Among the shouting, blustering, scene-stealing business of wrestling, control of emotions was a prized possession and the greatest wrestlers, the ones who survived, did exactly that.

"When I was little, I was renowned for my tantrums, but my sisters trained me out of them. Two years ago I discovered that controlling your temper doesn't mean it's gone, merely lurking on the edges." His fingers flexed on the steering wheel. "Roxanna pointed out that *you'd* divorced *me*, so dating other women wasn't cheating, and Lamira pointed out that if I got laid, I wouldn't be such a mean bastard. But, as they say, the spirit was willing but the flesh was weak."

"What?"

"You figure it out."

Luca turned onto Zoey's property. "This your place?"

"Yes. Do you mean you couldn't—" Zoey was incredulous. Behind the legend of the wrestling master with the glorious body stood the man, Luca Damezas, who worshipped her body with his until she understood what it was to mate with a man. "Come on, Luca, you don't expect me to believe that."

"Believe what you like, but the truth is, I didn't care enough to bother." His voice got rough and, for Luca, almost censorious. "What about you? How's *your* dating life been?"

22

"NONE OF YOUR BUSINESS!"

"That either means there's been a lot of activity or none at all." He slowed to a halt in front of the tiny white-painted house.

"You don't know that!"

"I know you. I made a project of studying you." He turned, put his arm on the seat back and studied her now. "I'd say that considering you're in a small town where the dating field is limited, and because it took me a lot of concentrated attention to get you to even look at me, your love life is a barren wasteland."

A vivid, angry flush rose in her face and contrasted nicely with those bruises. "Do you want to give me the details of your love life and your unwilling flesh? No? Then time to change the subject!"

"Okay." He was satisfied with what he'd discovered. "Where should I park?"

"In the carport."

"A two-car garage and I have to park in the carport?"

"It's not a garage. It's my shop, and the garage doors are there to let in air and light."

"I should have known. You're headed there now, aren't you?"

"Yes." She clutched her backpack and its precious cargo ever closer. "I need to see what has happened with my plants, my seeds, my breeding projects!"

"Listen to me. I'll give you fifteen minutes. Then you're due in the house for dinner and bed."

She shot him a look of loathing.

He came around to her side of the car, opened her door and helped her out. "I'm here as your bodyguard in case someone did try to kill you—and you're not going to injure yourself on my watch." *Because I still care about you.*

"I'm fine," Zoey snapped.

But beneath that display of annoyance, Luca saw the indication of pain knit into her brow and the fine vibration of exhaustion in her hands. "I can tell. Go on now. Your fifteen minutes have begun." He watched her hobble toward the door of the shop, leaned against the car and took a moment to look around.

Nice property, located well below Gothic; its nearest neighbors were visible, but far up the road. Guessing by the style and a certain structural weariness, the house had been constructed in the early 1940s. Its wide front porch faced the Pacific Ocean, a mile away, and the constant breeze carried the restless scent of brine and faint rhythm of the waves.

By comparison, the shop was only a few years old, naturally stained cedar with a garage door on opposite walls to let the breeze through and the doorway, where Zoey tapped the keyboard of the electronic lock.

Looking down the slope from the house, he saw a garden of raised beds surrounded by deer fencing. Practical. There she could grow her experiments in full sun. In a hollow below that stood a roughly square rustic rock wall enclosure. Roses and wisteria climbed to the top and over and bloomed an invitation to enter. "Look at that," he whispered. "Look what you created on your own."

Early in their marriage, he'd seen her reading *The Secret Gar-*

den, a children's book his sisters had all read, and he asked about the story. Which opened a torrent of enthusiasm about a secret walled garden that served as a healer to broken souls who found their way in. She shoved the book into his hand and told him to read it. He had stalled as long as he could; he so did not want to read a book written for little girls.

When he finally picked it up…he loved it. The nasty little girl transformed by the garden, the mean little boy transformed by the garden, the lost soul of a father transformed by the garden…

The book gave Luca a glimpse into the world of plant magic that inspired Zoey's passion, and in turn, Luca was inspired. As a surprise, he'd built Zoey a stone walled garden on their family property in Upstate New York. He'd filled the beds with the best soil available, planted roses and constructed arbors…

That garden had been one of the many ways he'd sought to pin Zoey down until she could grow roots on his land. She had loved it, he knew, and loved him for surprising her, but she'd never felt at home there. Not even the garden had convinced her to stay.

The memory of her implacability made him wonder what he was really doing here. He leaned into the back seat to grab the grocery order from the Gothic General Store—and from inside the car, he heard the inhuman sound she made. He'd never heard such a cry from any living being—loss, agony, disbelief. He banged his head on the car doorframe, swiveled and raced toward the open shop.

He found Zoey standing wide-eyed and trembling in the middle of a jumble of overturned pots, scattered plants, dirt widely spread and hoses severed and spewing water.

In his most terrible voice, Luca asked, "Was the door unlocked when you walked in?"

Looking around at the destruction of her workspace, she nodded.

He hustled forward, took her by the elbow and walked her

back out the door. "You do not ever enter a place that should be locked and isn't. Someone could still be in there. Stay there. I'll be back." He entered the shop again.

Even with the broken grow lights, it was well lit; a profusion of skylights opened the space to sun. A scan of the building, more intensive than the first, revealed no one was there, but he opened the two garage doors and the addition of yet more sunlight somehow made the destruction more horrifying.

He exited to find Zoey walking toward him, staring and flexing the fingers of her right hand. "They're not dead yet," she said. "The plants. I can repot them now and—"

"No, you can't. It's a crime scene. We shouldn't have set foot inside." He glanced toward the house; the front door was ajar. "Did you go into the house?"

"No. Why?"

"Good. Because it's open. Someone could be in there. Get in the car. We're leaving."

She remained stubbornly in place. "If someone's trying to sabotage my work, they won't bother with the house." She started toward the gardens below the house. "But they would break into my sunlight garden!"

He caught her arm, swung her around and forcefully led her to the car. "You have to let that go for the moment. We don't know why this was done." As he thought of the possibilities, his blood ran cold. He got her into the seat, raced around to the driver's side. He backed up with a squeal of tires and before they hit the asphalt highway, he had autodialed 911 and made a concise report.

When he hung up, he glanced at her. "I can't let anything happen to you."

She nodded and relaxed. "I know."

Then, like an idiot, he ruined it. "Your mother would murder me."

23

THAT EVENING, WHEN Luca and Zoey had finished speaking with law enforcement, when law enforcement had taken photographs, counseled caution, promised to send a deputy past as often as possible, when Angelica Lindholm's gardening crew, led by head gardener Orvin Isaksen, had arrived on their plant rescue mission, performed their magic and gone, when the locksmith had replaced the broken lock with a temporary lock, Luca put Zoey to bed. He offered her a pill for pain and a glass of water.

She didn't take them. Instead she said, "Please, you have to check my sunlight garden and my walled garden."

"Angelica's gardeners said the locks were secure and had not been tampered with."

"They didn't go inside and look. Please, Luca. Take the keys. I need to know if my plants are alive and happy." She stared up at him with those wide, pleading, *I and I alone must protect the plant world* eyes.

He gave in. Of course he did. "All right, but you have to promise me you'll take your pain meds when I come back. And while I'm gone you'll stay in bed flat on your back and rest."

She frowned, disgruntled.

He warned, "I'm not going if you're going to hang out the window and watch me."

"All right!"

He tucked her under the worn hand-stitched quilt at the foot of the bed. "I'll lock the house behind me and keep an eye on it. Mostly to make sure the intruders don't return, but also— I'll see you."

"Why don't you believe me?"

"Because we're talking about your *plants*. You love them."

"They have feelings!"

"So do I. I'm worried about your safety and I'm worried about your health. Promise me on that seed you're so excited about that you won't get up."

She nodded and winced and nodded more carefully. "I promise."

"I'll be back as quickly as I can."

Guilt must have stirred in her, for she said, "Luca, I wouldn't ask... You've had a hard day, too. But once I have the seeds started in the shop, I transplant them into the sunlight garden. In this climate, they grow so well. Everything I've been working on for the past year is planted down there." She sounded fretful and at the same time apologetic.

"I know. I remember from before." *When you lived with me and we were happy.*

"And my walled garden is...well, you know that, too."

"Yes. I like that you copied the garden I'd made for you." He realized his tone had been crisp. "Where are the keys?"

"In the second desk drawer on the left at the back under a pile of papers marked, 'My manuscript.'"

He grinned crookedly. Of course she'd never put her garden keys in an obvious place like on a hook by the back door...where she kept her house keys. "Where is your whistle?"

She looked startled.

"You did keep that, didn't you?" When his own troubles

started, he studied the ways to keep Zoey, his sisters and his mother safe, and one of the simplest ideas was a loud whistle, the loudest on the market: easy to obtain, easy to use, definitely an attention-getter.

"Yes. For a woman living alone on the edge of the continent, it seemed like a good idea."

Thank God for that.

"But the whistle was on my key ring and those keys were lost in the wreck."

Because he wasn't a fool and didn't imagine he was invincible, especially when he was not on his guard, he had bought himself a whistle and put it on a chain. He dug into his bag and handed it over. "If you have any reason to think someone other than me is in the house, use it and I'll be here in a flash. You'll do that?"

"Yes, if you will just *go.*"

As he left the house, he locked the door behind him. Law enforcement had strongly suggested they leave exterior lights on to discourage any return of an intruder, so the porch and the shop were illuminated. Beyond that, the half-moon painted the world in stark black-and-white. The ground to the west sloped away from the house, and he thought if he tripped and fell off the porch, he would tumble all the way to the Pacific.

An exaggeration, of course, but above and to the east the Gothic lights shone with the highway winding like a dark ribbon through it, and beyond that, the occasional tree that dotted the landscape. He jogged down to the sunlight garden, circled it, hands brushing the deer fencing, which was intact. He went to the gate; it was locked and in the moonlight, the plants looked healthy, nestled into their raised planters.

Satisfied, he jogged down to the walled garden and circled it, searching for the wooden door he knew was here. He found it on the north wall, facing away from the highway and surrounded by an arbor of fragrant honeysuckle. Using his touch, he found the lock and inserted the key. He opened the door, anticipation humming in his veins, and stepped inside. At once, the sense and sounds of the world faded, leaving him encased in luxuriant nature. He saw at once the garden was untouched by intruders; flowers and vines grew in abundance. He thought he saw the opening to a maze and wisely decided not to investigate tonight. He needed to get back to Zoey and reassure her that all was well.

As soon as he stepped out from the sheltering wall, the wind blew in his face and the rumble of the ocean spoke in his ears. He locked the door and looked up toward the house. The area around Zoey's home had been cleared of any vegetation large enough for intruders to conceal themselves. Someone had recognized both the joy of living alone on the last flat spot on the west side of North America, and the danger.

He ran back, and as he climbed the steps to the porch, the rosemary hedge that grew at the edge of Zoey's front porch released its woody scent.

Zoey had indeed found herself a beautiful place in the world.

He called as he stepped inside, "It's me!" and entered the bedroom.

She reclined on the bed, her head on the pillow, one hand clutching the edge of the quilt and one clutching the whistle.

He sat on the edge of the bed, took the whistle out of her hand. He placed it on the nightstand and rubbed her fingers. "The gardens are secure and what plants I could see are well and undisturbed."

She relaxed with a sigh. "Thank you. I couldn't bear after all this if...if..."

"All is well," he said firmly, "but we need to talk."

"About what?"

"Your mother has disappeared and left no forwarding address. You were seriously injured by persons unknown. Your home has been searched and a piece of your life's work trashed. We know about your mother's honor and the flagon with the dragon, but that really doesn't tell us *why* any of these things are happening."

"They might be related to my past." She blinked at him. "But how? When my mom and I got to the Bay Area, I was four. Mom had a little savings and that kept us afloat while she worked and finished college and law school. When I was eleven, she passed the bar and after that...things got better. What about that would bring this kind of violence and destruction down on me? I wish I could remember what Mom said in the hospital, but I was hurt. I was drugged." She seemed to struggle with her thoughts. "I can't remember anything except, you know, the dragon and her honor."

"Maybe I can help. You got to the Bay Area...from where?" He'd always wanted to inquire, but she had been so patently uninterested.

"I don't know."

"You must have asked your mother about your father, about where you were born, all the stuff people use to define themselves."

"When I was young, I tried, but she always got tearful and I stopped." Zoey closed her eyes wearily. "Really, what difference does it make?"

"It makes a big difference if these attacks on you are related to your earliest years. Your memories of that part of your childhood are murky."

She opened her eyes, fixed them on him sternly. "Murky? Why would you say that?"

"One time—" Luca tried to see beneath that very adult facade she had concocted "—in a moment of weakness, you told me about the Mean Man."

"What did I say?" she asked warily.

No, she wasn't going to get away with that. He countered, "What do you recall?"

She closed her eyes. "It's confusing. I was little. Bits and jumbles. None of it makes sense."

"Tell me again."

The Mean Man didn't like Gracie. Whenever he was around he picked on her in little ways. Turned off her favorite TV shows. Pinched her arm, then made fun of her when she cried. Slapped her if she didn't stop. Whenever her mommy caught him, she stood up to him. But Gracie didn't like that, either, because when he slapped Mommy, he knocked her down. Mommy broke a tooth. Mommy had a black eye. Mommy couldn't wear shorts because she had bruises where he kicked her.

For Honey, it was always worse.

Later, when Mommy took Gracie away from the town, Gracie realized Honey was her imaginary friend. But in her memories, Honey was just like her: a little taller, a little smarter, a lot braver. When the Mean Man picked on Mommy, Honey yelled at him.

He knocked her into the wall.

When Honey finally opened her eyes, she told Gracie she was faking to scare the Mean Man. He was scared, too, because he yelled at them all, then slunk away and slammed the back door. Mommy gathered her girls and held them close for a long time, then they went to the Strict Lady's house and visited the Man Who Couldn't Stand Up.

"What else do you remember?" Luca asked.

"I don't remember anything else."

"Zoey..."

"Those pills knock me out." She turned onto her side. "I'm going to sleep now."

He sighed. His weight lifted off the mattress. He said, "I'll sleep in the living room. Call me if you need me."

That woke her enough to make her protest, "You're too big to sleep on that love seat. Go sleep in the shop. I've got the whistle around here—" she glanced around "—somewhere."

He handed it to her.

She clutched it.

"Tomorrow the security people will be here," he said. "Maybe once we've got cameras and alarms, I'll let you sleep alone."

She wanted to complain about his choice of words—what did he mean by *maybe*?—but then she was asleep.

Luca searched the house until he found the linen closet, which was also the pantry.

This house was in serious need of closets. In fact, it was in serious need of a second bedroom, a second bathroom, a living room with space for more than a love seat, a recliner, an end table with a lamp and a large screen TV on one wall. The kitchen had been remodeled, so there was that.

He pulled out a sheet, realized it was merely queen-sized and going to be huge on that feeble love seat excuse of a couch and at the same time small on his oversize frame. No matter, he couldn't leave Zoey alone in this house, not tonight, anyway. He'd asked her about her family, and from the way Morgayne had sounded, he knew she feared something in their past. But his greatest worry was that the peril that lurked in the shadows had to do with him, the wrestling and his aborted mission.

He tossed the sheet at the love seat and went to check on her.

Zoey was deeply asleep, huddled in fetal position, her brow furrowed. She twitched as if somewhere in her brain, someone was chasing her. He supposed, considering what she'd gone through in the last few weeks, her dreams would be both horrible and full of peril.

Leaning over her, he rubbed her back and murmured soft, nonsense words, hoping to reach her, and after a moment she took a long breath. She rolled back on the pillow, flung out an arm.

He slid his hand out from under her head and smiled to see her relaxed at last. He removed the whistle from her now-open palm and frowned at the bruises she still carried. Theoretically he knew she wasn't the most beautiful woman in the world, but when he watched her move, coaxed her warm smile, listened to her discuss flowers in a way that made him realize what a miracle each little seed would produce…he wanted to spend his life with her. Again.

When she left him, when he reached a point of resignation, he told himself it was better this way. She had nothing to do with him, ergo the menace that had stalked him would no longer stalk her.

Now this. This return of fear. He bent close to her, breathed the scent of her, felt the upsurge of deep male possession.

She opened her eyes.

He closed his. She would not like to see him leaning over her in the grip of such a deep, stirring, protective emotion.

She didn't seem to notice what he felt. She started talking as if he knew what had happened in her mind. "When Honey came home, she had bruises on her face and a cast on her arm."

He stroked Zoey's forehead. "Honey was your imaginary friend? Are you sure she was imaginary?"

"Yes… I can remember when I realized that Honey was gone forever. I was about six. I was desolate. I cried and cried, and Mommy explained that sometimes someone we love has to go away to be safe, and told me to forget her."

"Do you think Honey is safe?"

Zoey snapped to awareness. "I think she was my imaginary friend."

"Sure." He nodded. "Okay. Go to sleep, then."

She closed her eyes and immediately fell asleep. He wondered if she'd really been awake. Detaching his fingers from hers, he went out onto the front porch.

Funny. When Morgayne had called him, he'd wondered why she'd seemed so certain Zoey's accident had been no accident. But he'd been so knee-jerk horrified, so sure that somehow the accident had been related to his own situation, he hadn't really thought to ask. After listening to Zoey's vague memories, he realized it was time to ask Morgayne what she knew. So he dialed her number—and got sent right to voice mail.

Huh. Considering how worried Morgayne had been about Zoey's safety, it was odd that she had her phone turned off. Odd and troubling. But his mother and Zoey's mother had one thing in common; they were strong women who took care of themselves and didn't welcome well-meaning interference. So he put his niggling concern about Morgayne on the back burner, figured he'd speak with her tomorrow and dialed another number, one he had hoped never to call again. In a low voice, he explained today's events, listened to the response and said, "As soon as you can, send somebody."

24

Dima Somova's estate
On the shores of Lake Tahoe

MORGAYNE PHOENIX DIDN'T like to think of herself as being trapped in Dima Somova's Lake Tahoe home—but she hadn't seen her car or her cell phone for almost a week.

She had arrived at Dima's estate determined to find out what he knew about his brother's fate and the fate of her daughter. She'd been prepared to have a phalanx of guards turn her away. After all, Dima Somova was wealthy, secretive and rumored to be involved in more criminal activities than any one man could surely handle.

But in fact, when she pulled up to the unassuming wrought iron gate, punched the call button and stated her name and purpose, a woman's pleasant voice directed her to follow the signs for the office, the iron gate opened and she drove through.

Looking back, she wished she'd paid a little more attention to the ominous clang of the gate as it closed behind her. But she'd thrown the dice, and really, what were her choices? Finding that car in the lake, knowing Jack was dead, killed by a shot to the back of the head, that Vadim and Honor had made it to shore and were alive somewhere... She had to come. No one else could tell her where they were.

She'd been to Dima Somova's estate one other time.

In the years after she left Citation, when she could take the time away from study, she'd searched for any sign of Vadim and Honor. There had been nothing, and she was first afraid, then sure Jack had murdered them, and for far too many nights, she'd cried herself to sleep, convinced she couldn't do what she'd set out to do: free herself and Zoey from the horrors of Jack's shadow.

But through hard work and sacrifice, she passed the bar.

That very night she had a dream. Vadim and Honor came to her, spoke to her, reassured her they were alive and happy, and they told her not to worry. They promised all was well.

She wasn't a woman who believed in fate or precognition or contact from beyond, but that dream was so real that when she woke up she resolved to do what she'd been afraid to do: go to Dima Somova and demand the truth. Did he know what had happened to his brother—and her baby girl?

She arranged for Zoey to go camping with a trusted friend and drove to Dima's estate. He'd met with her at once. He had the coldest blue eyes she'd ever seen, even colder than Bonnie Torbinson's. He sat behind his massive desk and listened to her questions, bluntly told her he wasn't in contact with his brother and had no idea whether Vadim and Honor were alive. He pointed out, though, that if Vadim wanted to make contact with her, he would, and that was a cruel blow to her hopes. Then he sent her on her way.

She'd pulled over in the first rest stop on I-80 and sobbed in despair. She didn't for a second believe Dima Somova had no knowledge of his brother's whereabouts. He hadn't built this estate and created this network of people by not knowing *ev-*

erything. But what could she do? She didn't have the power to force him to reveal the information.

She pulled herself together, went back to San Francisco and became a divorce lawyer, driven by the need to help women receive justice in a divorce settlement. She'd helped a few men along the way, too.

Her reward had been that news story.

Jack was dead. The brute she'd married had died with a bullet through his skull, no doubt put there by Vadim. Jack had finally run into someone he couldn't bully, and he'd died for his mistake.

She was glad. She was free. At last she knew she was a widow.

Vadim and Honor weren't dead at the bottom of the lake, so were they alive somewhere in the world?

Hope reared its traitorous head.

Then she got the call that Zoey had been run off the road. She spent days in Zoey's room, talking to her, touching her, coaxing her, sleeping on a cot to waken and start it all again. In the dark hours of the night, she experienced the terror of a mother who had lost one child and could easily lose another. Her resolve strengthened. She would go to Dima Somova. She had found her strength and she knew how to seek out weaknesses and exert pressure, and he *would* tell her about Vadim and Honor. But he simply never showed up.

Once at the estate, she was invited to sit in a waiting room. After a couple of hours, the well-groomed woman who sat at the desk got a call. In a polite voice she suggested Morgayne would enjoy a meal by the pool. Morgayne said she wanted to meet with Dima now. The young woman announced he was out of town. While Morgayne sputtered, the young woman suggested that Morgayne would like to freshen up, and the meal would be served in thirty minutes.

Morgayne asked when Dima Somova would return.

The young woman denied any knowledge.

Morgayne said she'd leave the estate and return when he came back.

The young woman said no, Dima intended to speak with Morgayne…when he arrived from his travels.

Which left Morgayne feeling trapped and…well, if she insisted on leaving, would she ever be allowed back in?

Another woman, not so young, took Morgayne to a guesthouse with a living room, kitchen, bedroom, bath and a wraparound porch with a view of Lake Tahoe. There for days she stayed when she wasn't swimming in the pool, dining on the deck and visiting with Dima's all-American discreet 1960s wife, Jennifer, who apparently vetted all his visitors and decided who would be allowed an interview with the great man. When a suitcase arrived with her clothes, she wasted quite a few minutes wondering how someone from Dima's association had got into her condo to pack her clothes and send them on. She tried to figure out how long she was going to be stuck here and after weighing her options, asked Jennifer for the ability to communicate with her daughter Zoey. Jennifer regretfully denied that to her, yet as compensation she showed photos of Zoey and Luca, alive and well. Or rather, Luca was well and Zoey was alive.

Morgayne had no doubt she was stuck. When she made a move too far in any direction, she was intercepted and steered back to ground zero.

Today, finally, she sensed a change in the atmosphere, a bustle, a liveliness she took to mean Dima had returned.

Jennifer came to find her. She had a softness to her, a slight smile, and she said, "Dima will see you now."

"Does he know why I'm here?"

Jennifer's face lost the smile, and she looked almost stern. "Dima knows everything."

"As I suspected." Nothing got in Morgayne's way this time. She walked into Dima's office. He sat behind his desk. If anything, his blue eyes were more glacial than they had been fourteen years ago.

Morgayne seated herself without an invitation. "Look. I know you heard about them finding my husband at the bottom of that lake with his brains shot out. Good riddance. They didn't find Vadim or my daughter Honor. They're alive. I know they're alive, and I need to find them. Find Honor. Find out whether Vadim had kept her, raised her or put her up for adoption. I don't believe he would have abandoned my child in the woods. But that doesn't mean he would want to raise a small girl on his own. He had been just released from prison… You know that, of course." She was talking too much—she knew that—but all the thoughts she'd been trapped with for days were overflowing.

"Why didn't you come to me sooner?"

"What? I did come. Remember? More than, um, fourteen years ago."

He waved her to silence. "I mean—why didn't you come as soon as the car was discovered?"

"My other daughter, Zoey, was involved in a hit-and-run. She was badly hurt. Unconscious. Close to death."

"Yes." His eyes narrowed. "What a coincidence, to have that happen so soon after the discovery of the Dragon's Heart."

Thank God. Someone else with her thoughts. "Agreed." She leaned forward. "But why go after her?"

"She is the heir presumptive to the Dragon's Heart."

"I left Citation. All those years ago. I told no one where I was going, what I intended. No one followed us."

He cut her off with a sharp gesture. "Don't be foolish. Of course someone tracked you. No one vanishes off the face of the earth without a trace."

"Then where are Vadim and Honor? They vanished off the face of the earth. *Where are they?*"

"Let me make inquiries."

She wanted to say she knew he knew where his brother was.

Dima knows everything. But she didn't challenge him. "Okay!
Yes, thank you, that's what I hoped you would say." She stood.
"Now I need to go back to Zoey."

"No. You're safer here. I'll send someone to watch over her."

"I got her ex-husband to come and take care of her."

"Luca Damezas?"

Of course Dima knew him.

"I've met him."

Of course he'd met Luca.

"Good choice. Good man. Nevertheless, I'll send someone.
You will remain here. My wife has pleaded your case most elo-
quently. She's the reason I saw you. Her word is final, and she
would take it amiss if you were hurt."

"I'll take it amiss if my daughter is hurt!"

"I will send someone," he repeated again.

"And you'll let me know." She wasn't asking. She was telling.

"I'll send someone," he repeated with great finality and went
to work on the papers spread across his desk.

Morgayne had been dismissed. Most definitely dismissed.
She stood.

Without looking up, Dima said, "When you came all those
years ago, I suspected you were seeking confirmation of my
brother's existence to harm him."

She stopped in her tracks. "Why would I do that?"

"You harmed him before."

In a fury, she sprang toward the desk, slapped her hands flat
on the surface. When he looked up, she leaned so close her nose
almost touched his nose. "When?"

Nothing moved inside those cold blue eyes, not surprise, not
interest, certainly not fear. "When he fell in love with you in
high school."

Her palms itched to slap Dima. "I didn't harm him. I loved
him back."

"Did you?"

"All these years. So many years. Why would I lie?"

"As soon as Vadim was in prison, you married Jack Torbinson. He was a stud. He was a find."

"He was an abuser. He was a bully. Do you have any idea what my life was? What my daughters' lives were?"

He studied her, weighing her responses. "Tell me one good reason why I should help you."

She gave him two.

25

Twenty-five miles outside Tambov, Russia

VADIM'S RUSSIAN ASSISTANT came into the cave carrying Vadim's tool bag, Vadim's computer tablet, and wearing a concerned expression. "Flint, there's a message from your brother in Nevada."

Vadim rose from his squat before the electrical panel he was installing for the potato storage system. "My brother?" He stripped off his gloves and extended his hand.

Palchevskii handed over the tablet. "He flagged it as urgent."

"Really? What the hell?" He read the text:

Thought you'd be interested in this.

A video. A video from a television station. Dima had sent a video. Whatever it was, Vadim was interested; ever since he'd demanded out of the family business to raise Morgayne's daughter, Dima had effectively washed his hands, leaving Vadim to his fate.

What was so important that Dima contacted him?

Vadim looked up at the clearly fascinated Palchevskii. As far as Vadim knew, Palchevskii spoke only Russian, but in this country it was best to assume someone was always listening. Even if Palchevskii had already played the video, Vadim's reaction would be observed and analyzed. "I'll take this outside. You cut the pipe."

Palchevskii's face lit up. "I cut the pipe? Without you?"

"You've learned well. You can do it." Vadim watched Palchevskii pull the pipe cutter out of the bag, nodded and exited the cave. He waited a moment, then stuck his head back in. "Don't smoke in here."

Palchevskii sighed mightily and shoved his cigarettes back in his shirt pocket.

Vadim stepped over to his work truck and tapped the video's forward arrow. The network news report started, and it focused his attention as his brother knew it would.

The Caballo Blanco Dam…

A car retrieved from the bottom of the lake…

A man's body inside, shot in the back of the head…

Bonnie Torbinson on her doorstep, collapsed in a shocked heap.

Vadim watched the whole video. Twice. One clear thought floated through the turmoil of his mind. *Too bad that bitch Bonnie Torbinson hadn't died.* He looked around, over the fields, at the horizon, searching for equanimity, trying to think what would happen now, what the result would be from this turn of events.

He decided what he had to do. Now, how best to do it?

He returned to the cave, put his hand on Palchevskii's shoulder. "I'll be flying to the States."

"Now? To the United States? I know you're from there, but…"

Vadim watched Palchevskii, silently asking how he knew that.

"I…your Russian. It's very good, but your accent…" Palchevskii changed the subject. "But you are to finish this installation within the next week!"

"You will have to complete the project using your own

knowledge—and when you do, you'll be the lead on all future projects of this type. I'll leave the truck in front of my apartment and the keys in the grease can beside the stove. You can pick it all up tonight."

"You're giving me your truck? Your equipment?" Palchevskii was clearly floundering. "You're not coming back?"

"I doubt it. I'll be dead, or in prison, or I'll be exonerated and free to do what I want. What I want is—" Vadim smiled briefly "—probably wishful thinking, but it's kept me alive all these years." He smiled more broadly. "Remember, don't smoke. You'll blow up the cave, and yourself with it, and my truck and tools will do you no good."

Palchevskii fumbled with his cigarettes while looking at the electrical panel, then shoved them back in his pocket. "I will never again smoke near the electrical panel again."

"Goodbye." Vadim shook Palchevskii's hand, got in the truck, drove toward Tambov and never looked back.

26

ZOEY WOKE AT DAWN, opened her eyes, looked at the mess in her bedroom: drawers emptied, bookshelf overturned, linens tossed, and she moaned. Chaos reigned throughout the house, and the sheriff's question echoed in her mind.

Do you have anything of value that someone would be looking for?

Of course the answer was yes…but only in her shop, not in the house.

Having a care for her aches and pains, she got to her feet, looked down at herself and sighed. She still wore yesterday's clothes. She supposed if she was going to her shop to play in the dirt, yesterday's clothes were the right thing to wear.

Her backpack with its precious cargo leaned in the corner behind the lamp. She gathered it up, stepped around the piles of clothes and books, and made her way to the bathroom—also a wreck—then, spotting the whistle on the nightstand, she slipped the chain around her neck and walked into the living room.

There she found Luca, in his underwear, sprawled half on, half off her love seat. It was an understatement to say he did not fit. He looked like a puppet with its strings cut, disjointed and catawampus.

She lingered for a moment. She had forgotten how pretty he was. Or rather…she had convinced herself to forget how pretty he was.

Zoey wished she could say she was immune, but no. Perhaps if when they first met, he had ignored her… Instead he had smiled as if the sight of her gave him pleasure. He listened when she spoke, even when she was enthusing about flowers, and he respected her opinions. He laughed at her jokes, he catered to her tastes, he made her feel pretty and as if she'd fallen into a slightly blurry, colorful and sparkling cartoon. His square face and muscled chest provided a sense of solid dependability, while his powerful thighs and hips and butt made a woman wonder what she would see if she stripped him bare.

Worst of all, he had proved his intelligence and willingness to work hard.

How had he known the qualities that attracted her?

The problem was, he didn't know those qualities. He *possessed* those qualities. Strength, warmth, intelligence, a strong work ethic: that was who he was.

She'd made her choice. No time for regrets.

Knowing that he had a bed in her shop, a bed to fit him, and yet he chose to stick close to her as protection…that thought warmed, and yet, she shivered.

Most definitely no time for that.

As she tiptoed through her living room, she looked, as she had last night, at the disaster. To her casual eye, nothing seemed to be missing. The walls were not spray-painted, her cushions were not slashed. So if the object was not to vandalize an unoccupied home…why would someone upend her furniture? Was law enforcement right? Was someone looking for something? But what?

She eased her way onto her porch and shut the door behind her.

The wicker furniture had been shoved around, the pillows tossed, but again, no damage had been done.

She sank down on the step and took a moment to appreciate the day. The breeze off the ocean was sunny-morning cool, the sound of the waves sounded like the heartbeat of the earth. The view reminded her why she had chosen to settle here; the marriage of sea, earth and sky provided a peaceful frame to her hours.

Last night she had insisted that Luca check on her gardens; he had assured her the rows of gloriously colored flowers and green vegetables were untouched by greedy hands. Thank God for that.

Her shop occupied her real concern. The memory of the destruction made her hurry along the gravel path to the door. There she punched in the code and walked inside.

It wasn't bad. In fact, it was much better than yesterday. Orvin and his crew had cleaned the shop so thoroughly and organized so well she almost didn't recognize it. Her carefully composed soil had been collected and put in its boxes, her hoses were repaired and her grow lights had been replaced and restored to their original positions.

She took a long breath of relief.

It was as if yesterday had never occurred. Except…

Angelica's people had done a credible job of repotting and replacing her vegetable experiments: the barely begun, pink-fleshed fingerling potato she thought would be fun for home gardeners, the seedlings of the seriously purple carrot that grew too fast and split too easily. Sadly, root vegetables hated to be transplanted, so that batch of experiments was ruined.

On the other hand, the infant leafy plants looked limp but as if they might survive: the blue-eyed daisy surrounded by wildly fringed golden pedals—that would be a florist's favorite—and the daisy relative that produced an abundance of large, stiff-stemmed, white blooms, perfect for flower arrangements…except it gave off a smell of dog doo.

None of Zoey's projects were immediately successful; they

all needed work to reach perfection. But to unearth them as if they were unworthy and of no value! Who would be so vicious?

She sniffled. She loved her space. The primary pieces had already been installed when she moved in. A canvas cot folded into one wall and could be lowered for such time when she worked too long and was too pooped and filthy to go to the house. Cupboards and counters covered the walls. An island with cupboards beneath and a basalt countertop on top was her main workstation. She had procured four comfortably padded counter stools for her use. She'd found an antique table with fold-down leaves and two sturdy chairs and added them for the friends and business associates who sometimes visited. A rocking chair finished her decor, a place to rock and think when she needed an aimless moment.

She reached into a cupboard and brought out a new planting flat, eight inches by eight inches. She filled it with her home-made seed germinating soil—one part loam, one part peat moss, four parts garden compost mixed with a slow release fertilizer—and spread it evenly in the flat. Removing the bag with the poppy seeds, she carefully searched them out—they were so round, so black, so tiny! Yet powerful, miraculous. Add dirt, water and sunlight and they became a plant, a living thing that reproduced by blooming in glorious color. In that shining violet blue with red splatters on the petals with a glorious gold eye...

She placed the seeds on top of the soil, pressed them in, watered carefully and placed them in a sunny spot. Leaning close, she placed the flat of her hand on the soil and spoke. "Grow up. Grow strong. Reproduce. Make beauty." She heard a footstep behind her, and she jumped so hard and turned so fast her neck reminded her that two weeks ago she'd been broken between a tree and a car driven by a killer.

She groped for the whistle.

27

"I'M SORRY!" SHASTA stood just inside the doorway. "I didn't mean to startle you. I heard Angelica say she was going to send someone to check that your shop had been cleaned to her specifications, and I took the opportunity to flee."

Zoey put her hand on her chest to calm her racing heart. "Already? Not that I'm surprised. Angelica does wear on one."

"It's not her, exactly," Shasta admitted. "I've seen her only briefly."

"Come on in." Zoey lovingly patted the soil once more, then put water in the electric kettle. Her teapots ranged from the whimsical to the traditional, and she selected one in a soothing celadon green. She measured her tranquility herbal tea into it, then pointed at the stool next to the island counter. "What's wrong?"

Shasta seated herself. "Nothing. Really. I'm in a great bedroom situated next to a *glorious* artist's studio. The light and equipment are an artist's fantasy. I got there, she ordered one of her staff to unpack for me and told me to start painting right away. I did, and when I looked up, everything was arranged. At 6:30 p.m., Dela brought me dinner on a tray."

"You didn't have to put down the brush? And get distracted?" Zoey poured the boiling water into the pot, put the lid on it, put it on a tray with two miniature cups and brought it to the island. She seated herself. "It has to brew."

Shasta nodded and kept talking, almost breathless with the need to get it all out. "At nine thirty, Dela brought a cup of hot chocolate and orders I should go to bed to prepare for today's long hours. Then...then Dela got me up at 5:00 a.m.! She laid out my clothes, turned on my shower and took my breakfast order. I didn't think I was going to be allowed to escape that apartment, ever!"

"Then you ran for it?"

"Not exactly. At nine they announced my scheduled break, a walk in the gardens. Which, since I'd spent hours painting flowers...no garden for me." Shasta set her chin. "Her assistant was scheduled to check on you, so I told Marjorie that we were friends and I was worried about what happened here yesterday—"

Zoey tensed. "How did you hear about that?"

"Dela told me. From what I can tell, Angelica's staff hasn't enjoyed so many juicy tidbits in one day, ever. They're sorry about Mrs. Kulshan. They like the Kulshans, especially the fact that Mr. Kulshan gives Angelica shit all the time." Shasta cupped her forehead in her palm and chuckled. "They love that Mrs. Kulshan gives Mr. Kulshan shit all the time, too. In Angelica-World, everything is calm, polite and ordered, and nothing untoward is permitted. Except who's going to tell two old people they can't mouth off if they want to?"

Zoey relaxed. "Certainly not Angelica. So you grabbed an ATV and drove down?"

"As fast as I could."

"Shasta, I'm sorry." Zoey poured the tea into the cups, added a teaspoon of honey to each and pushed one toward Shasta. "I never foresaw this. Is Angelica's schedule destroying your artistic instincts?"

Shasta looked as if she was in pain. "Actually...with no distractions, I've completed two paintings. I don't have to cook or plan and...they're genius."

Zoey lifted her cup toward her mouth and paused. "The paintings are genius?"

"Brilliant. I've never done anything like them."

Zoey stared at her friend, her undisciplined, artistic friend, and cackled.

After a moment of affront, Shasta cackled, too. The two old roommates laughed hard, lying across the island, and when they hiccupped to a stop, Luca said from the doorway, "I haven't heard that for a while." Although he wore a wrinkled T-shirt, the same briefs he'd worn to sleep in, his hair stood on end, and he was breathing hard, he sounded good-humored.

Zoey scrutinized him. "You okay?"

"I woke up and realized you were gone, and after yesterday—"

"I didn't mean to scare you. You looked as if you hadn't slept well, so I tiptoed out. I took the whistle." She lifted the chain and showed him.

"Smart," he grunted.

Shasta looked between Zoey and Luca. "You didn't, um, sleep together?"

"If we'd slept together, we'd still be in bed," Luca snapped.

Which told Zoey how little and uncomfortably he'd slept.

"A tiny bit irritated," Shasta said out of the corner of her mouth.

Zoey ignored her and fetched another cup. "Here." She poured tea, stirred in honey and shoved it toward him.

"Thank you." He took it and frowned at the brew. "I think. Is this one of those weedy drinks you make?"

"Yes, dear." Damn, they had already fallen into those husband/wife routines.

He scowled. "Do you have real caffeine?"

"In the house. Drink this first—it will soothe your irritation. Then go make yourself a cup of Irish Breakfast."

"Irish Breakfast…tea? Thank God I ordered coffee from the Gothic General Store." He slugged down the small cup, placed it on the table and turned away. And turned back to Shasta. "I am not irritated!" He stalked out of the workshop.

Shasta was grinning. "He hasn't changed a bit. A crank until that first cup of coffee."

"Apparently. Tonight I'll convince him to sleep out here in his bed. He'll fit better, it'll be cooler and he can make his brew before I see him."

"How long will he be here?"

"Until my mom gets back from her trip."

"Where did she go?"

Zoey gave a one-shouldered shrug. "You know Mom. She's a free spirit."

"*Your* mom?" Shasta couldn't contain her surprise. "Did you confuse her with *my* mom?"

Zoey sipped her tea, letting the cool flower flavors of lavender and chamomile soothe her. Not even with Shasta would she admit, *Mom is afraid someone tried to kill me and Luca seems to agree.* Zoey didn't believe it; she didn't. Yet both her mother and Luca were sensible, down-to-earth people, and their conviction, combined with the destruction of her workshop, made her wary of, well, everyone.

Shasta glanced at her watch, grimaced and finished her tea. "Angelica has tracked me down. I'd better go back before she sends an official reprimand. I'll see you Thursday, right? At the pre–gardening show briefing?"

"I'll be there." With some sarcasm, Zoey added, "Can't wait."

28

AFTER SHASTA LEFT, Zoey placed her unharmed hand on the soil of the planting boxes, smoothed the surface, patted down the places that felt too loose, dug her fingers in the soil that had been mashed too firmly.

Luca stepped in the door with coffee mug in hand. "How are your plants feeling?"

He startled her, but this time she took care not to project fear to the already traumatized seedlings. "They're bruised. They're frightened. They don't understand."

"I don't understand, either. Who above the age of five gets their jollies out of dumping dirt on the floor?"

She looked at him.

"I know. A rival breeder." He held one hand palm up.

"Almost three weeks ago, I put in an appearance at the San Francisco Flower Show. I met florists. I met other breeders. Everywhere at the market was the Elanor dianthus, and possibly that reminded someone, or even a corporation, that I'm alive and capable of another breakthrough."

"I remember." He was irritable about being reminded. "Flower breeding saboteurs."

"Do you remember Natasha? Her nephew Fritz has decided to get into the business because it *must* be easier than growing flowers."

Luca snorted.

"There's money to be made, lots of it, and when I bred the Elanor, I made it." Awash in the sudden return of the old bitterness, she turned her face away from Luca.

She had done it for him. She'd bred Elanor for him. He'd been wrestling, he told her, for the money. He would quit when he had enough to go to grad school and spend the years studying. Then he could get a super safe job, support her and his mother.

She told him she didn't need to be supported. His mother told him she had everything she needed. But he was the youngest, and the only male, and the need to provide for his loved ones was bred into those Mediterranean genes.

Every night when he went into the ring, Zoey feared that he'd be hurt, killed, and all the magic in the world couldn't re-animate a dead plant...or a dead man. She looked down at her hand, pressing too hard and too angrily on the earth, and pulled it away in alarm. The plants didn't need that.

She gestured toward the loft. "What do you think of your space?"

He put down his mug, climbed the spiral stairs and examined the space over the carport. "Nice!" he called. "I like the skylights. I'll bet on a clear night, the stars are beautiful." He chuckled. "I'll bet the movers had a tough time getting the mattress up here. Where's the shower?"

She took some satisfaction in saying, "Outdoors."

He stuck his head over the rail and looked at her, eyes narrowed.

"It's the cedar structure beyond the shop. Trust me, when it's sunny it's better than inside in the claw-foot tub, and it's summer. It's almost always sunny. Except when the fog rolls in."

"Okay, sounds good." He came back down the stairs and took

the last four in a jump over the rail. "I've got to be careful up there or I'll hit my head on those slanted ceilings."

"I'm sure." She was not a petite female, but she never had a problem with that.

"I like this." He gestured around, then picked up his mug and cradled it in his palm. "I like the pale golden wood and the garage doors and the light. I imagine the plants do, too. Did you build it?"

"The former owner built it. He was a metal worker, created medieval swords and armor, and amazing pieces of art. Him and his wife visit occasionally. From South America. Which come to think about it, might be a good place to be." She took a breath and asked the question that had nagged at her since he had appeared to transport her to Gothic. "Does your mother know where you are?"

"Good Lord, no. If Ma knew I was here, she'd kill me." When speaking about his mother, he didn't even pretend courage.

"Don't be silly. She adores you, her only son. She'd kill *me*." Zoey wasn't being funny.

Neither was Luca. "Yeah… My mom…when you left, she was so mad."

"I know. She hunted me down and told me."

"You are kidding." He pulled over a stool and sat as if he needed the support.

"She came in thinking I had deliberately hurt you and figured out pretty fast I was as miserable as you were. That probably saved my life." Zoey wasn't kidding. Giuseppina was one scary women. "Although not my pride—she ripped my character to shreds. Also my morals. It wasn't until she started in on my mom's morals that she got an earful back."

He fought a grin. "I wish I'd been there to hear that. Did she back down?"

"Your mother? She doesn't know the meaning of backing down. *But* when I pointed out to Giuseppina that she's skinny, old and riddled with arthritis and if she said another word about my mom, she wouldn't get any older…she looked at me funny and put a sock in it."

"That was one of her complaints. She thought you were bloodless."

"One of her complaints?" Zoey's voice rose. "She *complained* to you about me?"

"She worried you would introduce a strain of quiet, unemotional, overly civilized people to our hot Italian bloodline." He laughed loud and long. "Mama didn't understand about you. She didn't realize that beneath that cool, overly composed exterior was a woman of molten passions and a passionate heart."

"You were the only person who ever saw that in me."

He looked at her with melted chocolate brown eyes that reminded her exactly what he, and he alone, knew. "Damned straight."

Nope! None of that! Time to skid away from that subject. "I figured the only reason your mom was even in the U.S. was some deal made with the Italian government to get her out of the country."

He thoughtfully pulled on his lower lip. "I was told it was a simple betrothal, but…possibly. You're afraid she'll show up here?"

"Yes! Aren't you?"

"No. You said it. I'm her only son, and my existence transcends my stupidity in loving you. Don't worry. I'll protect you."

"Protect me from your *mother*? You might as well try to stop the tide." She looked around in a panic. "I could go to my mom's condo. There's a concierge. I can instruct them I want to be strictly alone. I can have groceries brought in. I'll be safe. Why didn't my mother think of that?"

A smile played around his lips. "What about your plants?"

"They're not worth dying for!" She looked at the trays and trays of tiny plants, at the seeds waiting to be plunged into the earth, and her flurry collapsed. "I can't do it. I can't leave them." She glanced out into the sunshine. "I haven't even seen my gardens."

"Come on, then." He went to the wheeled cart that sat against the wall and pulled it over to her workstation. "What do you want to take down?"

She had designed the cart to transport her soil testing kits, her soil amenders, her seeds, her tools in carefully organized drawers. A padded seat on the top provided somewhere to sit when she planted her raised beds. Once the drawers had been pulled, she could lower the padding to the ground and kneel on it to save her knees while she weeded and dug. It was a miracle of organization, exactly what she needed—and Luca had taken her designs and made them a reality. He was a man who made good things happen.

She kept the cart loaded with the essentials, and after an absence of so many weeks, she would need additional fertilizer. Her gardens had been created to be self-sufficient, with rain collection and drip irrigation, but with summer underway the plants would be feeding heavily. She needed mulch and soil modifiers and whatever might be needed to fix a leak or clear a clogged hose.

By the time she was done, Luca was finishing up a phone call. "The security people will be here in two hours. They're doing a full site upgrade with digital locks, plenty of light and motion sensor alarms. Alerts will come in on your watch, your computer and on a panel in the house and the shop."

"What's this going to cost?"

"No more than what you won in our divorce settlement." He gestured impatiently. "What's it worth to you to be safe?"

"You're right. My plants will be safe, too." She pushed her cart out the door.

He removed it from her grip. "It's a steep descent. You keep yourself upright, I'll manage the cart."

A path through the waving grasses wound down from the

house and shop toward the secret garden. Zoey headed there first. Luca followed. A few twisted cypress trees broke the horizon, and beyond that stretched the eternal blue of the ocean and sky. She stopped once and stepped off the path and gestured widely. "Have you ever seen anything so glorious?"

He said, "Your view, and the sound of the ocean…they satisfy my soul."

She liked the sound of that.

"When we've cleaned up, can we go to the beach?" He loved the beach, the mountains, the forest, Christmas and family. He never complained about the sand, the thin oxygen, the pine needles, and only occasionally about his mother, sisters and mother-in-law. And never ever about his wife.

Being around him reminded her how much she liked the man. Time to distance herself. "You can go to the beach whenever you like," she said firmly.

His eager face fell.

She sighed. It was like kicking a puppy. A *mastiff* puppy. "After the Gothic Garden and Flower Show is over, I can go, too."

"I'm here to help." He sounded as firm as she did. "Your jobs are to recover and stay safe."

They stopped at the gate, where roses climbed and bees buzzed so joyously the garden seemed to have a voice.

He looked beyond and below at the tan boxes sitting among the grasses. "I didn't see those last night. You tend hives?"

"A beekeeper places her hives here, near the gardens where the bees can feed. She cares for them, harvests the honey, shares that with me and sells the rest, while I reap the benefits of their pollination."

"I love honey!" He used the key and threw open the door.

She stepped through and sighed in relief and delight.

The castle-gray stone walls framed the garden with security. She had created flower beds along the walls. At the back, blue delphinium and rosy foxglove mingled. Along the gravel paths, dianthus in clumps of red and pink wove their spicy scents into the aromas of earth and living plants.

"You did build a maze!" Luca plunged into the entrance framed by a wisteria arbor.

She followed him. "A little one. I wanted some intrigue in the garden."

"Where does it go? How do I get there?"

"Left hand on the hedge and on to the center."

She followed him as he plunged into the maze and followed it to the center where, around the grassy knoll, lavender blossomed in colors from white to purple.

"Perfect." He cast himself on the grass and gazed up at the dark blue sky and snowy white clouds.

She stood against the hedge and gazed at him. And remembered...

Zoey fell in love with Luca the day he took her to the Portland International Rose Test Garden. She'd been impatient to visit; they'd arrived at 6:30 a.m., wandered the paths, then found a bench beside a fountain. The warming effects of the early sun intensified the roses' fragrance. Beside them, a scarlet "Rita Dennis" rosebush bloomed; Luca cupped a blossom in the palm of his hand. In his deep voice, he spoke of the ruffled, frilly petals, so feminine, so graceful... With the fingers of his other hand he carefully spread those petals wide to show her the yellow stamens. The scent of the rose and the scent of Luca filled her head, and for the first time in her life she didn't care whether she toured every garden, sought out every plant, marveled at the variety of blossoms. All she wanted was for him to touch her like he touched that rose.

"Come on!" He extended a hand to her. "Take a moment. Your plants have missed you. They'll be happy to have you relax among them."

She wanted to tend her garden, but he was right. She walked over, took his hand and let him help her down to the ground. As she stretched out beside him, she did relax. She connected to the earth, absorbed the strength of the vines and the joy of

the flowers, and experienced the infusion of healing. "I feel better," she whispered.

He leaned on his elbow. "I knew you would." He smiled as
if the sight of her gave him pleasure.

Luxuriant scents filled the air, and she thought again of his
hand touching that rose...

Then, bless his heart, he said, "I never understood why you
were so worried when I wrestled. Until that last injury, I never
got more than a bruise."

29

ZOEY SURVEYED LUCA, reclining beside her, tall, strong, handsome, all smug confidence, all smooth competence. Why not tell him? He had quit wrestling. Maybe if she said the right words, he'd stay quit. Because even if they weren't together, she wanted him to be alive. She didn't want to live in a world that didn't contain Luca Damezas. "Having you wrestle was like being married to a cop. Every night when you put on that stupid costume and left for the ring, I was afraid you'd get hurt. Killed. But not for any good reason, like to serve and protect. For fame. For glory. For *money*."

"There was more to it than that."

"Yeah, right." She eased herself into a sitting position. Taking a breath, she told him what she'd never told him before. "I was there the night Tiny Andrew died in the ring."

Tiny Andrew's nickname was a joke in his own family. He towered above the tallest, huskiest wrestlers, both in proportions and in wins, and it was a rare fighter who could win a bout against him.

Luca sat up straight and fast. "No. No, you didn't come to

the bouts. I reserved a seat for you in front. Every night, there was a seat for you. You never came."

"The guys knew me, and they used to let me sneak in, stand in the back, watch you...wrestle. Then I left. Once I knew you weren't horribly hurt, I left."

"You told me you didn't want to watch. Not even on television."

"When you went on tour, I *needed* to watch the fight. But I didn't *want* to watch the fight." She turned away from him. "I always watched, and I always watched through my fingers."

"You saw Tiny Andrew...die?" He examined her face and saw...something. The reflection of fear, of grief. "You never told me." Luca was there, behind her, putting his arms around her. "Zoey..."

For one moment, it felt so right for him to hold her, comfort her. So deliberately she brought up the memories. "After the bout, they said Breaker Reed meant to flip Tiny onto his back, but he over rotated, and Tiny...all the way at the back of the arena, I heard his neck crack. All the way from the back..." As if it had just occurred, disbelief struck her. One moment, Tiny had been alive, fighting, laughing, spitting, yelling, and the next... "How does that happen?" she whispered.

"I was watching from the stars' box, and I'll never forget that sound, or the way he went...limp." Although Luca had had nothing to do with Tiny's death, he sounded wretched and guilty.

She didn't care about his sorrow. She jabbed him with her elbow. His hands loosened. "That's when I knew I had to earn enough to get you out of wrestling and into something safer. I believed you, you see, when you said you'd quit when we had enough for you to go to graduate school and me to have land for my flower projects."

"Really, it wasn't as simple as that." He spoke quietly, his gaze level.

"Not as simple as the plain fact you were so addicted to the adrenaline and the adulation you couldn't give it up when offered the chance? You want to explain it to me differently?" She'd been so proud of herself for finally setting aside the acrimony, and now after less than forty-eight hours with Luca, bitterness spread in her like an invasive species. "I don't know why I brought it up. I don't think any of these plants will be as wildly successful as Elanor—maybe the daisy, who knows? But someone's worried enough to tear up my workshop, and—"

That the wild flower I discovered has produced a seed.

"You should have told me about Tiny." His voice was getting quieter, as if he struggled with painful emotions.

"I told you when I told you the marriage was over."

"You did not."

"Not in so many words," she allowed. "I said that you deserved to be happy, and I deserved to be happy, and we would never be happy together."

"We're happy apart?"

"We can learn."

"When?" He put his hand flat on his chest. "It's been two years, and without you, it hurts to breathe. Sunshine hurts my eyes. Every joy is an agony because you're not there to share it with me."

She dismissed that with a wave of her hand. "That's all leftover from your injuries."

"My body is strong." He tapped his chest. "It's my soul that withers."

No other man of her acquaintance would say something like that. Admit their hurt, their vulnerability, and in poetic terms of life and death and pain. Terms she would use as a grower and breeder.

He wasn't done. "I used to want to love a woman. I believed that she—you—would be that person who all my life would fight with me and live with me and give me joy. That together we would grow strong. But this…this love hurts too much. I'm tired of being in pain. I wish I could stop loving you."

Two days and they had come full circle, back to the place where she loved him and he loved her—and they couldn't make it work.

Although perhaps they could try. He had finally quit wrestling. His family was faraway. Her mother didn't live here. They could try to work their way through the sticky morass of anger and anguish, maybe get counseling. Because he was right, pain hovered too close, waiting to seize her. He was within reach, and all she had to do was look into his eyes, touch his arm…

So she did. "Luca, perhaps we could—"

Under her hand, his muscles tightened. "Yes?"

She concentrated on him, on the words to make this right. "After all we had, alone is so—"

His cell phone rang.

She jumped.

He ignored it. "Alone is so…?"

Ring.

She fought against sanity's return. She wanted this love between them. They completed each other.

Ring.

But he was right. She had spent the last two years getting over him. Loving him hurt too much, and no matter what she imagined, they could never have been casual lovers. She removed her hand, looked away, back toward the maze. "Should you get that?"

It rang again. "Son of a bitch." He pulled his phone out of his pocket and glanced at the screen. "Damn it to hell. It's the security team. I *have* to get this." He answered. "Yes? You're here? In the driveway?" He sighed. "I'll be right there." He put his hands around her waist and boosted her to her feet. "Until security has been all over this place installing motion sensors and locks, I'm sure you'll agree it's best that you remain close enough to bring me running with a shout. Or a whistle."

To disagree would be foolish. "Yes, of course." But she didn't want to walk out of here at his side. They'd said so much, yet left out so much.

He stood and dusted off his butt.

Together they walked back through the maze, out the gate and up the hill.

"If the security team is here, I can give you this back." She lifted the chain with the whistle from around her neck and offered it to him.

"Keep it. Hang it in the shop. Use it if for any reason you feel threatened by anybody. I'd rather run to rescue you and find out we were mistaken than find you had been hurt or taken by someone we trust."

"Like who?"

"If we knew who tried to kill you with a Hummer and who trashed your shop and home, I could answer that question. Couldn't I?" His patience was clearly frayed.

"All right." She clutched the whistle tighter. "But if we're that worried, we'd better get one for the house, too, and one for you."

He stopped.

She took a few more steps and looked back at him.

He said, "I ordered this morning. I'd get a case of them if I thought they would keep you safe."

30

AS THE FESTIVAL gardeners and performers arrived, Angelica viewed the conference room with a critical eye.

Bottles of chilled Angelica Lindholm water.

Check.

Individual baskets of baked goods from her kitchen.

Check.

Tablets loaded with the Gothic Garden and Flower Show data.

Check.

Shasta Straka's matted painting, placed on an artist's display stand and covered with a black velvet cloth.

Check.

Marjorie had done a competent job of setting up the conference room, and she gave her a nod of approval.

Señor Alfonso arrived first, followed by Ludwig, who carried a paper bag that exuded the odors of fresh thyme, rosemary and basil. Freda Goodnight followed, carrying a stack of pamphlets with details about the Gothic Museum and Cemetery, which she distributed on the chairs. Zoey came next, her hand on the massive forearm of the massive Luca Damezas.

After meeting them in Mrs. Kulshan's yard, Angelica had

asked Marjorie to research Zoey's past with Luca Damezas, and the online research turned up a lot of info, some of it factual and some of it the kind of speculation she knew from bitter personal experience that celebrities suffered. Their mating and marriage had been some kind of cosmic weirdness, a matchup of a brawny man to a woman enchanted with delicate petals, blossoms and scents. As Angelica had scanned the printout, she said, "Divorce was inevitable, of course. There has to be a meeting of the minds as well as the bodies for a successful union."

"What about hearts?" Marjorie seemed honestly curious.

Angelica hesitated, then admitted, "I don't know. I dearly loved my son, but when it comes to a personal love relationship, I have no experience. Not that I wasn't willing, but after I'd created my empire and thought it was time… I discovered the man I adored had moved on."

"That's skanky!"

"In all fairness, he waited a long time, and he did warn me there was a time limit. He's educated, with a good job. He has traveled. He has a wife and children and now a grandchild. Of course, I sent a baby gift." With that, Angelica had said more than she ever had before.

Luca seated Zoey in the second seat, the third row, then left and returned with Mr. Kulshan. Mr. Kulshan leaned heavily on his walker and had Luca seat him in the front row. "Can't hear," he said loudly. "Gotta get close."

Luca took a seat on the end next to Zoey. There he could stretch out his legs, although he stood every few minutes as the Gothic master gardeners arrived and came to speak to Zoey and inquire after her health.

When Sadie and Hartley of Sadie and Hartley's Rock and Mineral Emporium arrived, everyone smiled. They were Gothic's unofficial hospitality couple. People visited them from around the world; Sadie's relatives, Hartley's relatives, geology students, friends… Somehow, everyone found their way to Sadie and Hartley's home and shop.

Madame Rune appeared, coins jingling, fringe flapping, holding a clear quartz crystal on a silver chain, which she delivered to Zoey with the advice to wear it for healing and protection.

Zoey promptly put it around her neck.

The Beards rolled in, a smiling couple who settled down next to Mr. Kulshan and gave him an update on the goat babies, showed him photos and promised that when Mrs. Kulshan returned from her hospital stay, they would bring a few of the kids to visit.

At precisely 2:00 p.m., Angelica summoned Orvin Isaksen, her head gardener, Shasta, the artist, and Thistle, the musician. While she moved to the podium, Orvin, Shasta and Thistle took seats in the front row. She began, "As you all know, I'm Angelica Lindholm. On Friday at 6:30 p.m., the festival will kick off with the traditional party in my garden. The honored guests will be offered light refreshments." She signaled the waitstaff, who came in with the sample appetizers and passed them along the rows. "The guests will board one of the two Gothic Surreys with the Fringe on Top—"

Mr. Kulshan said in his overly loud voice, "A fancy name for a fancy bus."

"—and do our twilight tour of the gardens." Angelica bent a stern gaze on Mr. Kulshan.

He crossed his arms and cackled.

"Our guests will be shown the gardens in order. The Live Oak Restaurant will show their herb garden and provide appetizers and recipes. Located behind Sadie and Hartley's Rock and Mineral Emporium is their Japanese garden with bridge over raked sand, with polished rocks and driftwood providing accent points." Angelica gestured to Sadie and Hartley. "Would you show them the sales piece?"

Sadie stood and held up a polished box that held a replica of the garden. "The Zen Garden is available in varying sizes and includes a small rake to create the wavelike furrows in the sand."

"That piece has been very popular in recent years," Angelica said. "Next is… Mr. Kulshan's German beer garden."

Silence fell. Everyone considered Mr. Kulshan.

He waved. "Not doing anything illegal!"

Angelica narrowed her eyes at him. "I hope not, sir. Next the visitors will visit Mrs. Kulshan's shade garden. Her yard surrounds a two-hundred-fifty-year-old oak and her colorful coleus, begonias and impatiens light up her yard. In Mrs. Kulshan's sad absence, Orvin has put the finishing touches on the display. Thank you, Orvin, for that and for your years of service!"

Without expression, Orvin lifted a broad callused hand.

Angelica found Orvin and his brother, Hudson, odd, elderly men with proper British accents they seldom used…because they seldom spoke. When they did, their words were gruff and unwelcoming. Yet they'd been her gardeners for twenty years.

She continued, "Freda will lead a tour of the Gothic cemetery and entertain our guests with colorful tales of Gothic's past, and next is Zoey's 'secret garden,' always a highlight of the tour, as are her herbal teas, which we market under the Angelica Lindholm line."

The applause this time was heartier and personal.

Sadie came to her feet. "Dear Zoey, we're so glad you're out of the hospital and your husband is here to help you."

"We're not married!" Horrified, Zoey confessed, "We're divorced. Luca has been kind enough to come and stay with me until, um, I've recovered enough to be on my own."

Sadie clasped her hands. "What a lovely man!" She beamed at him.

"I'm sleeping in the shop," Luca volunteered.

"Which is none of our business." Ruthlessly Angelica took command again. "The next stop on the tour is Madame Rune's brilliant crystal meditation garden displaying local artists' glassworks. The final garden is the Beards' garden and petting zoo, where the guests can purchase handmade goat milk caramels."

"And always do." Mrs. Beard couldn't be more smug.

"Then back here for supper and to listen to the folk music of Thistle!" Angelica gestured toward the musician, who picked up his guitar, strode to the stool and played one of his original melodies…

…which wasn't to Angelica's taste, but the light melodious strumming melded with the garden tour concept. On the other hand, Thistle himself *was* to her taste: in his forties with soulful dark eyes, a well-trimmed beard and fingers that caressed the strings and made her wonder…

Well, no, that would be massively inappropriate, but she could *wonder.*

He finished to applause, and Angelica said, "Thistle will perform three times a day in my garden. Once on Saturday and once on Sunday he'll ride the Gothic Surrey with the Fringe during our once-a-day *musical* gardening tour—which is filled up for the entire three days. On Saturday we'll host five tours, one an hour starting at 9:00 a.m. On Sunday, we'll host four tours starting at 10:00 a.m." She chopped the edge of her hand into her palm. "We will remain on schedule!"

"You're not going to get any argument out of us, Angelica," Madame Rune assured her. "By the time the last bus leaves, I'll be thoroughly tired of two things—explaining that no, I can't spontaneously go into a trance, and smiling."

Everyone laughed.

"Finally," Angelica said, "most of you are familiar with the trouble we've had getting art for this year's garden show, and at the last minute, Shasta Straka came to our rescue, proving that sometimes even I have to abandon preparation and put my hopes in prayer."

Laughter rippled through the room.

Angelica beamed. She so seldom tapped into everyday humor.

"Now we present the painting that will be this year's Gothic Garden and Flower Show poster." She moved over to the artist's display, gestured Shasta to join her, and together they lifted the cloth off the matted painting.

The audience gasped in surprise, then clapped enthusiastically.

Shasta had painted a single magnolia blossom, white against a light blue wash of Big Sur sky, and somehow with a few brushstrokes created a miracle of rich fragrance, tender joy and luxurious texture.

"Since her arrival three days ago," Angelica continued, "Shasta has worked tremendously hard. Choosing one from among her completed paintings proved difficult because each has its own special glories." She gestured to her waiting staff, who carried in three more of Shasta's paintings. All featured a single blossom, and each blossom trembled with saturated color that lifted the spirit.

The Gothic gardeners broke into a babble of congratulations.

In a commanding tone, Angelica said, "With that, we're done discussing the garden tour. My cook has laid out refreshments in the conservatory. There you can mingle with Thistle, Orvin and his gardening crew, and Shasta. I've brought in a distinguished art appraiser from San Francisco to look at her artwork and give us his opinion."

People stood, but Mrs. Beard loudly interrupted. "Angelica, every year we have the same problem. Guests get in their own cars and show up at the gardens and want a private guided tour. We've got goats, and people interrupt the milking, upset the nannies and agitate the kids. You promised that this year you were going to do something about it!"

"I've been waiting for someone to ask." Angelica wanted to pat her own back. "To encourage people to use the buses, when they get on the first time, they're handed a five-by-seven card with the official tour painting printed on it. Each time they get back on the bus, they get a stamp that specifically represents that garden, and when they have all eight garden stamps, they receive a passport to Gothic—and a free, full-size Gothic Garden and Flower Show poster!"

A profound silence fell over the room.

For a mere moment, Angelica felt anxious.

Then Sadie said, "That's genius!"

"I'll be damned, woman." With Luca's help, Mr. Kulshan got to his feet. "Every once in a while, you do get a good idea."

"Actually, I'm pretty sure she's the savviest person in the room," Madame Rune said.

Nods all around, and Angelica experienced an unusual warmth coming from the gathering. She understood she was possibly not good at understanding and developing human relations, although she didn't know why when she was so good at everything else. So moments when she felt like part of the human collective were rare and wonderful, and she savored this one.

And all the while, one person watched and listened, considered the possibility that Angelica might wise up, and what could be done to put her out of commission.

31

LUCA HELPED ZOEY to her feet and escorted her, hand placed lightly on her spine, into the conservatory. People watched and smiled, and she made a play of stopping at the first of Shasta's paintings and waiting until the others had walked past, headed toward the food table. In an undertone, she asked, "Why is the rumor going around that we're married?"

"I suppose someone who knows you knew the name of your husband and…" He stopped. A memory flashed, of him parking illegally at the barbershop, waving his hand after Zoey and announcing, *My wife*. "Oh, hell."

"What did you do?"

"I may have misspoken."

She lightly put her uninjured hand to her still-tender forehead.

"I'll explain," he said in irritation, "to everybody."

"It's too late. *Everybody* knows."

"If news travels that fast, my explanation will clear it up as quickly."

"What color is the sky in your world? Gossip doesn't work that way. The news that causes a furor travels at the speed of

light. The disentanglement of that news never quite occurs."
She muttered, "Especially since you're staying with me."

"It wasn't my choice to—" He cut himself off. She was right
about the gossip—people were looking, and getting louder wasn't
going to help. In what he considered a reasonable tone, he said,
"When they come down for the garden tour, I'll show them my
bed in the shop. That should untangle all the knots."

She closed her eyes and nodded. "Yes. That might help."

He didn't know which was more irritating, that she was unsure his method would work, or that she was so dismayed her
Gothic friends would think they were involved. "Some women
would be glad to be with me."

She opened her eyes and grinned. "I know, honey. I never
meant to insinuate you aren't a lovely hunk o' man."

He was irritated. *He was.* But when she teased him, she made
him amused at himself. "I have a fragile ego."

Now she laughed out loud. "Your ego is impermeable, the
result of being the adored only son and having six older sisters
who spoiled you rotten."

He took her arm and led her down the row of paintings. "*Rotten* is an exaggeration. I'm mildly decaying."

She laughed again, then stopped abruptly at one painting.
This one was not a flower, painted in all its delicate beauty, but
a landscape: the view of a calm blue ocean with sea stacks pro-
truding from the water, a silver beach tucked into a hollow of
land, and in the distance, golden cliffs lit by the setting sun. It
should have been beautiful, but—

Luca leaned close to Zoey's ear to say, "That's unsettling."

She nodded. Somehow the artist had taken a beautiful scene
and twisted it so that it was…corrupt. The perspective was off,
the balance was incorrect, the colors were harsh… She couldn't
quite put her finger on what exactly was wrong, but looking at
those works was like watching a train wreck. She couldn't look
away, but they made her vaguely ill.

He checked the signature. "It's definitely Shasta's work."

Zoey had known it was Shasta. When they'd been college roommates, she'd seen Shasta's landscapes, but it was only after first viewing the flower portraits that she realized how odious these works could be.

Shasta flitted up, eyes wide and shining. "Did you know Angelica brought in an art critic from San Francisco to assess my paintings? Lawrence Thorlacius!"

"That's marvelous." Zoey put her hand on Shasta's arm. "Your life has turned a corner!"

"After so many years of chasing two dreams, I finally see my path clearly." Shasta exhaled as if she was relieved, and impulsively hugged Zoey. "After I'd painted ten flower posters, Angelica let me do a landscape, and look! The art critic is not at all impressed with the flowers. He says those are for people who like pretty prints on their walls, but he's gushing about my landscapes."

Luca glanced around. Shasta's landscapes had been placed on stands throughout the conservatory. "Did he say why?"

"He said I portray the wild world as rightfully, mindfully hostile to all beings that walk, fly and crawl on the earth." Shasta looked at her own work and nodded. "He said that's a rare quality in a landscape artist, especially a female."

Zoey made a grumbling sound.

"No, Zoey, you know it's true. Women create softer, gentler, homier paintings."

"Which doesn't mean it's wrong!" Zoey could have ripped into a tirade about that.

But Shasta charged on. "Most artists draw the world as they *want* to see it, in glory and grandeur."

Sounding calm and interested, Luca asked, "You don't see glory and grandeur?"

"Yes, and enmity and the great and terrible desire to exterminate life." Shasta sounded so sure. "Have you ever been up in the mountains alone, seen the lonely stars, felt the bitter cold, heard the stone creaking and known that one small earth tremor could create a rockslide to bury you alive?"

"I've been in the mountains alone," Luca acknowledged. "When I look at the stars, I don't think of my own extermination, but of my own reach for eternity. It's a different perspective of the same thing."

Shasta looked at him as if he spoke an alien language.

Zoey looked at him as if he spoke a language only she understood.

"Angelica is signaling me to come and talk to Lawrence!" Shasta flitted away.

"The sad thing is," Luca said, "because of him, she's never going to paint pretty flowers again. What did she mean about pursuing two goals?"

"I don't know. I only knew about the successful painter one."

Madame Rune wandered over, scarves fluttering, and in her Julia Child voice said, "That young woman is going to be famous. One way or another, I see an extraordinary future."

"As a painter?" Luca clarified.

Madame Rune turned her head, focused on Luca and repeated, "One way or another."

32

ANGELICA TOUCHED LUCA on the shoulder. "I believe Mr. Kulshan is ready to leave."

Luca glanced at Mr. Kulshan. A few minutes before, the elderly man had been animatedly speaking to Thistle. Now he drooped in his seat and looked as if the commotion of so many people made his neck hurt.

"He misses Mrs. Kulshan," Angelica said.

"Yes. Zoey needs to go home also. She hasn't completely recovered." She was actually doing well, but he wanted to remind Angelica that she couldn't make more demands than Zoey's health would allow. "This will be the excuse I need to drag her away."

Angelica caught his arm. "If you get the chance to view Mr. Kulshan's garden, that would be greatly appreciated. He hasn't allowed anyone in his backyard in months, I don't see how he could do the work all by himself, and knowing Mr. Kulshan as I do—"

"Of course, Angelica, I'll see what I can do." He carefully did not promise to report to her, though.

Luca loaded Mr. Kulshan and Zoey into the car, drove out

to the highway and down Gothic's main street to park in front of his home.

"Too much fuss today. But I don't mind you two. Nice kids. You belong together. You ought to get two houses like me and the missus. Then you can be together and spend time apart." Mr. Kulshan started his slow preparation to exit the car. "Did Angelica tell you to check out my garden?"

"Yes," Luca and Zoey said at the same time. They exchanged wry glances.

"Come on." Luca helped him out of the car. He gripped the rails of his walker and led them around the walk on the side of the house to the backyard. A tarp covered his garden plot. He grinned at Luca. "Go ahead, son. Peel that back and take a look at my German beer garden."

Luca tossed the tarp aside and burst into laughter.

The garden had been neatly hoed into rows. Stuck in the soil and spaced along the rows at regular intervals were…beer bottles.

"All German," Mr. Kulshan said proudly. "Drank 'em myself. One a day for the past year. Then I'd trot out and stick them in the ground. Had to keep the ground cleaned of weeds, but used my hoe for that. Mrs. Kulshan knows, of course, and shakes her head at me…" Just like that, he stopped smiling and looked lonely.

"Mr. Kulshan, you've done it this time. Angelica will…" Zoey shook her head at him, too.

Mr. Kulshan pulled down the seat on his walker and lowered himself onto it. "Do you think she'll have a conniption fit? Because I can't keep a woman up all night anymore, but I like to think I can still give Angelica Lindholm a few sleepless hours."

"I'm sure Angelica will toss and turn." Zoey pressed her lips to his forehead. "Let's get you in the house where you can rest. You have to be in shape for Mrs. Kulshan's return."

"Two more days," Mr. Kulshan said. "Only two more days. Those doctors promised she's coming home on Saturday.

They're going to send a nurse, but I told 'em, I hate to leave my home, but I'll move in with her until she's better. She likes to keep track of me. She'll heal faster if I'm around." Thirty minutes later, the elderly man was asleep in his recliner, his remote control and his pills and a bottle of water on the table next to him.

Luca and Zoey stood and looked at him, bent and withered, and in love with his wife of seventy years.

"They made it work. When they couldn't live together, they figured it out," Zoey said, then wished she'd kept her mouth shut. Complicated and wrenching and emotional as this conversation could be, she didn't want to have it standing here in Mr. Kulshan's house, knowing she had to walk out, get in Luca's car and drive down Gothic's main street.

Too many eyes to see. Too much speculation to fuel.

"It sounds as if two houses worked well for a long time. When Mrs. Kulshan fell and he didn't know it, he recognized it was time for a modification. If a relationship is going to survive, it has to adjust as circumstances change." Luca wasn't worried about eyes and speculation. "Isn't that right?"

That last question sounded patronizing, was patronizing, demanding her agreement to something blatantly obvious. He was talking about Luca and Zoey, and she was talking about Luca and Zoey, and if they were going to speak in coded messages, she had one for him. "I heartily agree. That's compromise, and it involves compromise from *both* parties. Now—I need to stop at the Gothic General Store to pick up chicken manure." And she flounced outside, down the walk and out the gate.

She didn't even know she could flounce.

Luca followed her to the car, held her door, came around and got in the driver's seat.

She waited to hear his next volley, wanting to finish this now that they'd started, dreading the inevitable pain as they fought their way to agreement—or another, painful break.

Instead, as he pulled into traffic, he said, "We're putting chicken manure in my car?"

33

SO THEY WERE shelving the discussion until another time. Or forever. *Calm. Breathe.* Forever would be best. Yet the tiniest sorrow scratched at her heart. "Don't worry, it's bagged manure," she assured him. "Sanitized."

"Meaning it doesn't smell…much. I've been in the car with your chicken manure before. At least we can put it in the trunk, the weather is good and we can open the windows." A car turned onto the street directly in front of them.

Luca turned the wheel, slammed on his brakes and missed the vehicle by inches.

Zoey clutched at her seat belt. "He never even looked!"

The driver behind them honked furiously, yelled and gestured.

Luca lifted a calming hand. "It happens. That's why my drivers' training teacher had a placard that said, Never Drive Faster Than Your Guardian Angel Can Fly. Not that I listened when I was a kid…"

Zoey thought that at the least, he could have clutched the wheel too hard or screeched the tires. Instead he was always in control of himself and his vehicle, prepared for any eventuality, knew where he was going, and never got excited. It was reassuring and at the same time, so irritating.

"While I'm at the store, I'll pick up some gardening gloves," he said.

"You're going to garden?"

"You need help, don't you?"

"Probably." She looked at her broken, taped fingers and admitted grudgingly, "Yes, I do."

"My computer's set up, but I don't care what Lamira says, I refuse to work more than eight hours a day. I'm her brother, not a workhorse, and if you listen to her, everything's an emergency."

Zoey chuckled. "Working for your sister can't be easy. Especially not that sister. Lamira is *driven*."

"She wants me to open a branch office on the West Coast. I told her I'd have to discuss it with my headhunters first." He grinned. "That makes her insane." He gestured toward the Bendy Wendy's Yoga and Gym. "I checked out Bendy Wendy. As a trainer, she's good and she'll help me work out, but I can only do that so many hours of the day, too. Instead I'll shovel chicken shit and plant seeds." He smiled as he contemplated the idea of gardening. "It'll keep me out of trouble."

Zoey wasn't sure how she felt about these revelations. The violence she had faced and the possibility of deliberate ill intent was overwhelming. Living with him, having him care for her, opened so many doors she had intentionally slammed shut…but she had convinced herself having him with her was all right because it was temporary.

Now she learned he considered moving to the West Coast? If she objected, would that reveal too much? Not that he was asking her opinion, and the West Coast covered a lot of ground. He could be all the way down in San Diego or all the way up in Washington. Or Alaska! He could live in Alaska!

Him helping her in the garden was the least of her worries.

She glanced around, looking for a distraction—and found it

sitting in the window of Mrs. Santa's Gifts and Tea Shop. "Stop! Isn't that Ripley Rath?"

Luca slid the sedan into the tight parking spot with yet more of that irritating control, turned and looked. "It is. I wonder what's she doing here? How do you feel? Could we go in and say hello? After that genteel afternoon at the Tower, I could use a little roughing up." He caught sight of her expression and asked in surprise, "You don't like Ripley?"

"She didn't approve of me."

"Ripley doesn't approve of anyone who thinks football has four innings."

"I was joking!"

"She doesn't understand humor. She's one of the least subtle people I've ever met." He extended his hand to her. "Come on. If Ripley Rath can visit a girlie tearoom, you can spend a few minutes with the most famous female wrestler of all time."

"Who says she's the most famous female wrestler of all time?"

"She does."

A gust of laughter caught Zoey by surprise and hurt her ribs, so she let Luca help her out of the car and across the street.

Located in one of Gothic's earliest homes, the tearoom was painted white with red shutters and sky blue, green and red Craftsman-style trim. The gate of the white picket fence was open, decorated pots and wildly blooming red roses lined the walk to the door, and when they stepped into the waiting area, Zoey watched for Luca's reaction.

He blinked at the walls covered with framed Christmas prints, Christmas-themed ceramics, English porcelain Christmas-painted plates on decorative hangers. Santas decorated the light switches. Painted evergreen branches climbed the table legs and Christmas tree bulbs dotted the wallpaper. The waitstaff wore ruffled, rose-embroidered white aprons, mobcaps and red dresses.

His mouth quirked. "Way to get roughed up." Then, "My

sisters would love this. Especially Mina." When Winifred, the owner, hurried up to greet them, Luca said, "Mrs. Santa, I presume?"

Winifred dimpled and curtsied. "That's me." She transferred her attention. "Zoey, how are you? I heard about your accident. I'm sorry."

"Every day I'm feeling better, thank you."

"Having your husband here to help you must make a great deal of difference."

Zoey smiled tightly. "Ex-husband. Winifred, this is Luca Damezas."

He gestured toward Ripley. "We saw our friend in the window and we'd like to join her."

"I'll bring chairs. Will you be having a meal or tea?"

"Tea," Zoey told her. "And a plate of your excellent cheese crackers."

Winifred smiled in self-congratulation. "Angelica has been begging me for the recipe. When she is desperate enough to offer a bribe, we'll talk."

Luca took Zoey's arm and hurried her toward Ripley's table. "Ripley? What you doing in Gothic?"

Ripley had been concentrating very hard on her own plate of cheese crackers, and when she heard his voice she leaped to her feet and enveloped him in a hug. "Damned Luck! Here in Gothic. You are just the man I wanted to see."

"Here I am. What's up?"

Her gaze moved to Zoey. "Back together with the old wife?"

That wasn't hostile at all. "No. Luca is helping while I recover from an accident."

Ripley surveyed her as if she had just noticed the breaks and bruises. "Sure." She returned her attention to Luca, then looked again at Zoey. "Oh. Yeah. That explains a lot."

Winifred brought chairs, and Luca held one for Zoey, then pulled one up for himself. "What did you want to see me for?"

"Can't talk about it here." Ripley cupped her chin in her hand and fluttered her eyelashes at him. "Too many people."

Coquettish was not a good match for Ripley. "You traveled to Gothic specifically to see me? How did you even know I was here?"

She dropped the smirk and straightened up. "That I'm here is fortunate for you."

Zoey wanted to tell her to knock it off, Luca was off-limits, but—she couldn't do that, could she? He was on-limits to any woman who wanted to make a run at him, and apparently Ripley had decided to get in the race.

Winifred placed a steaming Santa teapot and two cups on the table and a Santa plate of cheese crackers between Luca and Zoey. "Would you like a warm-up on your tea?" she asked Ripley.

"Please. That would be great." She confided to Luca, "This place serves an herbal tea that is out of this world." She dribbled honey into her cup and stirred it vigorously.

Looking pleased, Winifred tucked her hands into her apron. "It's the blend Zoey developed for me."

"Really?" Ripley's tone conveyed disbelief.

"That is what I do," Zoey pointed out. "Work with herbs, flowers, plants."

"Yeah. I guess." Ripley held up a cracker. "Anyway, these are great."

Luca picked one up and crunched into it. His expression grew blissful. He ate another one. More bliss. Zoey hadn't seen him look so euphoric since the last time she…

Nope. Not the time or the place to think of that. There would *never* be a time or place to think of that.

"You've made a hit with Luca," she told Winifred.

"He's a big man. I'll get him his own plate." Winifred hurried away.

"Spoiled." Zoey took a cracker and said, "I told you, every woman in the world wants to spoil you rotten."

"What? All I did was like her crackers." He nibbled on one. "Butter. Flour. Cheddar, I think. A little cayenne. But what makes them so crunchy?"

"Are you asking me?" Zoey asked.

"No." He was emphatic. "Never." *Too emphatic.* "I wish my mother was here. She's good at figuring out recipes."

When Zoey thought of Giuseppina, the distance between New York and California didn't seem far enough. "Having your mother here would really be the blossom of this particular stink flower of a week."

"At least we'd have cheese crackers whenever we wanted." He grinned at her. "Ma might even make you chicken piccata."

"She only did that for my birthday, and my birthday's not for months."

"You know how much she liked to cook for you—you were so appreciative."

"She can really cook." Zoey missed that about her, anyway.

"She owes you for the past two years," he said.

"Let's not invite her, anyway." Sitting here with Ripley was awkward enough. She didn't need Giuseppina across the table from her, too.

He dropped the smile. "Doesn't matter. Her arthritis has gotten so bad, she doesn't travel unless necessary."

"Except to Italy."

"Not even to Italy. Not last year."

"Oh, no. Luca, I am sorry."

Giuseppina was in her early seventies, and had spent years battling the slow erosion of health and mobility, and losing, to rheumatoid arthritis. Ever since Zoey had first met Giuseppina, she'd walked with a cane.

But that did not mean Giuseppina Bianca Aosta Damezas would succumb to the use of a utilitarian cane; once a year she flew to the Amalfi Coast to visit relatives and to Rome to terrorize the Italian designers she patronized. She always came back smartly dressed with her thick, iron gray hair fashionably cut and carrying one of the massive leather purses she favored. If she had given up her annual trek, she was truly losing her battle with mobility.

"I'll send some of my tea back with you when you go," Zoey promised.

"Thank you. She would appreciate that." He looked around at the Christmas decorations as if seeking joy. "Last month Ma mentioned, oh so casually, that she missed the miracles you performed with your herbs."

Zoey's temper got the better of her. "She also said if I was better in bed, you'd have been happy to quit the circuit and stay home."

"Oh, Ma!" Luca groaned and groped for Zoey's hand. "She doesn't know what she was talking about. You're the best in bed."

Zoey wrestled her hand away. "I know." She wished she'd kept her mouth shut; no need to give Ripley, of all people, an insight into the disintegration of their marriage.

Ripley loudly cleared her throat. She scooted her chair closer to Luca and got his attention. "I was already here because on the Nacimiento Fergusson Road, there's a meditation camp, and they're hosting a course on mental toughness. After last week's bout, I could use all kinds of toughness."

"How are the injuries?" Luca asked.

Ripley rotated her shoulder. "Bruises, nothing more. I don't get badly hurt. It requires too much downtime."

"And your dad wouldn't like it."

Ripley seemed surprised at his observation. "I'm no longer guided by my father. After that bar fight a few years ago, he developed cognitive issues. He's been diagnosed with dementia. But even if he's not himself now, his old advice is still good."

"As long as it doesn't make you ignore a serious injury." Luca seemed to believe she would do just that. "Any important news from the circuit?"

"Don't you follow it *at all*?" Ripley asked in surprise. "Does it make you miss it too much?"

"Nope. At first I was too busy learning the ropes at my sister's firm. And… I was bitter about losing my wife over the sport."

"She didn't have to leave," Ripley snapped.

"Yes, she did." Zoey didn't mind sitting here like the third on a date, but when they started talking about her as if she wasn't there, she'd stick her two cents in.

Typically, Ripley glanced toward her and away, then charged on, filling Luca in on the gossip while Zoey nibbled the few cheese crackers that escaped Luca and sipped tea. When her phone rang, it rang loudly, interrupting the genteel buzz of conversation in the tearoom. With an apologetic smile, she dug it out of her pocket, quieted the ring and glanced at the caller ID. In profound relief, she reported, "It's my mom's office. I'll take it outside." Leaping to her feet, she hurried toward the door, and was almost knocked over by a woman of about Ripley's height.

"Excuse me," Zoey said in automatic courtesy.

At the same time, the woman said, "Watch where you're going!"

Startled, Zoey looked up into her hostile face. She looked like Ripley, if Ripley had gained weight in her waist and belly, if Ripley tanned too much and moisturized too little, if Ripley dyed her hair yellow-blond and teased it into early sixties–style big hair.

Zoey saw the woman's gaze sweep her bruised face and broken hand. "Looks like you came out second in an ass-kicking contest." Then…she laughed!

The phone rang again, and Zoey didn't care about anything but talking to her mother. As she crossed the threshold, she said, "Mom! Where have you been?"

34

"**IT'S NOT YOUR MOM**," the voice said in Zoey's ear. "It's Sally, and I need to talk to your mother!"

Sally was Morgayne's assistant, a normally even-tempered woman who handled everything with aplomb. Now she sounded frazzled, and Zoey used her soothing voice. "I don't know where she is. I thought you—"

"The Durant divorce is exploding in massive piles of shit, and she's not answering her phone!"

"I know. She told me she might not be in touch… I think she said that…" Zoey rubbed her forehead. "I was on painkillers. The memory's vague. Didn't she appoint another lawyer to work with Mrs. Durant?"

"Yes, but that lawyer wasn't prepared to deal with a murder!"

"Mr. Durant killed Mrs. Durant?"

"Turn that around!"

"That's not good." Not even Luca and Zoey had considered murder. Not seriously, anyway.

"There's so much money involved! They got into a fight about who got custody of their cat—and she killed him." Sally sounded exasperated with the antics of the very rich. "Now Mrs. Durant wants the best to handle her case. She wants your mother and your mother has vanished."

"Did you explain my mother's a divorce lawyer, not a defense lawyer?"

"She's not listening to me. I'm *just* the legal assistant with a bachelor's degree in legal studies." Sally spaced her words precisely. "She would listen to your mother!"

"Did you send somebody to Mom's condo to make sure she's not there?"

"The housekeepers were there. They hadn't seen your mother. Neither had the doorman or the facilities manager."

"I'll call her again, but—Sally, did Mom ever talk about a dragon?"

"A what?"

Immediately Zoey felt stupid. "The stuff I remember is so random. Something about a dragon, and her honor, and my father hitting her—"

"That would explain her choice of career. The part about your father, not the dragon and her honor." Sally sighed. "I'll try to find someone else who will satisfy Mrs. Durant. In the meantime, search for your mom and I'll do the same." She sounded more worried than exasperated. "You don't suppose she's run into trouble?"

"If she has, I feel sorry for the trouble," Zoey assured her, but when she hung up she called her mother's cell and let it ring until voice mail picked up, and left an urgent message.

Zoey took a fortifying breath and re-entered the tearoom, and found Luca leaning over Ripley and talking rapidly. Winifred was running to the table holding a wet washcloth, which she pressed to Ripley's face. The big woman, the blowsy blonde, watched with her hands on her hips.

Zoey pushed her way in. "What's wrong?"

Winifred thrust pills at Ripley. "Here's the pills you asked for. Swallow them fast!"

Luca handed Ripley a glass of water and leaned close until she swallowed it.

Winifred turned to Zoey. "She's got a bee allergy and she put honey in her tea."

Zoey got a glimpse of Ripley's fiercely resentful face. "Stupid weakness," she mumbled through swollen lips.

"Have you called an ambulance?" Zoey asked.

"My assistant is here." Ripley gestured to Blowsy. "Yolanda will take me to a doc."

"I don't suppose you could wait while I had some tea." Yolanda sounded hostile and self-pitying.

"No, she can't," Luca answered.

Yolanda looked him over and smiled appreciatively. "Luca, good to see you." She feigned a punch.

He caught her before she could land it.

She viewed his grip on her wrist. "You always were a nice guy. Miss you in the ring! Wish you'd come back. Having you quit was bad for the sport."

"The sport doesn't need any one person." Luca was matter-of-fact. "It survives on its own ability to entertain."

Yolanda wasn't in shape for the sport, but more and more Zoey was sure that at one time, she had to have been a wrestler.

Meanwhile, Ripley pressed the wet rag to her face. She was almost weeping. She lurched to her feet.

"Weak, weak, weak." Yolanda took her arm and yanked as if rough handling would keep Ripley erect.

Everyone in the restaurant watched as they got into the car at the curb.

Zoey turned to Luca. "That's quite an allergic reaction. I wish I had my bag of herbs with me. I could have brewed her a cup of tea that would have relieved some of her symptoms."

"*You* can wring all the good stuff out of the leaves." He comprehended and appreciated her ability to care for plants in a way no other person on earth had ever done.

She inclined her head. "Yes. Even with dried herbs I can… coax them. But what I don't understand is—why would Ripley put honey in her tea if she knew—"

"She said it had never happened before." Luca pulled out his wallet, paid for the tea and crackers, and guided Zoey out and back to the street.

"Her assistant looks familiar."

"Bleached hair, out of shape, looks like five miles of bad road. She's familiar, all right."

Luca's description surprised her. He wasn't usually so harsh. Then Zoey recalled that laugh at the sight of her bruises. "She's kind of a bitch, too."

"Definitely a bitch and a washed-up wrestler. Yolanda Beecher, won every bout one year. After that, it was all downhill. Lots of celebrations, not enough training, kept getting hurt, self-medicating with drugs and booze, driving under the influence. Got arrested enough times to spend time in prison. Been in and out of rehab. It was kind of Ripley to hire her." He helped Zoey into the car, came around and got in. "Yolanda is a good part of the reason Ripley is so cavalier about her own safety. You saw. Yolanda shames her for every injury. Eggs her on when she should rest and recuperate."

"All wrestlers sport such an overwhelming body type." Zoey could still picture them leaving arm in arm. "But with Yolanda and Ripley it's more than that. They do truly resemble each other. Are they cousins?"

Luca gave her a sideways glance. "Yes. And half sisters."

"You are kidding." She knew he wasn't.

"Ripley's father, the old bastard, married Ripley's mother, then while she was pregnant with Ripley, slept with her mother's sister."

"It's a soap opera!" A horrible soap opera. "Ripley's father got beat up in a bar fight and that led to dementia—"

"Couldn't happen to a nicer guy."

Luca's flat delivery surprised her.

"He's a bully. Big guy. Always wanted a son but couldn't stop slapping on his wife long enough to let her carry one." For Luca, who took such care to never use his strength anywhere but onstage, that behavior was inexcusable. "I feel sorry for his caretakers. I imagine they're good at ducking."

"Ripley has issues." *Such* issues. "I suppose I get the mental strength of believing you can't get hurt, but that thing about not having allergies…"

"That's her father all the way. I only met him a few times, but he bragged his solution to her getting injured was to use his fists on her."

"My God!" For the first time, Zoey felt sympathy for Ripley. "She never saw the wrong in that?"

"Ripley's not well-liked on the circuit because if someone does get hurt, they're dead to her. It's like she's afraid she can catch whatever they've got."

"Did she do that with you?"

"I assume." He shrugged. "I was dealing with other issues, like physical therapy and divorce. I didn't notice Ripley's absence."

"She's friendly enough now." *Too friendly.*

"Yes." He drummed his fingers on the steering wheel. "While you were on the phone, she urged me to get back in the sport."

"Are you tempted?" She shouldn't care—but she did.

"No. Then she said that was good, because she knew something I didn't, and she winked at me." He frowned. "I *think* she might have been flirting with me."

"I think that's a good possibility." Especially with that chin in the hand/big eyelash flutter.

"If she was, she isn't good at it. Anyway, she wants to meet privately." He didn't ask if Zoey approved.

Not asking for approval was fair. She supposed. He didn't owe her anything. She didn't owe him anything. *That* they both needed to remember.

"We've got to pick up your chicken manure at the Gothic General Store." He parked, ran up the stairs and into the store.

She leaned back and closed her eyes. Since she'd arrived home, dealt with the break-in, planted her seeds and tended her garden, she had felt herself growing well, gaining strength from her connection to the earth and to growing things. Today had reminded her it hadn't been so long since she'd been out of the hospital, and her exhaustion had a lowering effect on her spirits.

The trunk opened and slammed, the driver's door opened, Luca slid into the seat and started the car.

She tried to look alert and not at all despondent.

He drove past the General Store and parked at the spot with the best viewpoint—looking out over the top of the Gothic cemetery, around at the hills and over the wide blue Pacific. He turned to her and offered her a package.

"What's this?" She unwrapped it and found a pair of gardening gloves, size medium. So not his. "Thank you?"

"Try them on." He took one and slid it onto her right hand.

She held up her left hand, with its brace that held her two middle fingers together. "The other one's not going to work."

He took the remaining glove and ever-so-carefully slid it on. "The first time we were here, I talked to Angelica, told her I wanted the fingers altered to fit around the brace."

Zoey lifted her hand, turned it back and forth, examined it in wonder.

"She jumped right on it, found somebody to do the work. It turned out well, don't you think?"

Zoey looked up into his pleased brown eyes. "Luca," she faltered, and she was reminded of their good times, those magic moments when they first fell in love, the settled times when they sat together and read books, the passionate times when they touched and tasted and loved. "Thank you. You are so kind."

He brushed that aside. "I know you. You'd forget about your injuries, dig in the earth and get an infection. You'll wear it?"

"I promise." She heard herself; she'd said that before, her solemn vow when they had married. The church decorated with flowers from all her grower friends, him in a dark suit looking awestruck and proud, their mothers weeping, his sisters grinning…and *I promise* said from the bottom of her heart. Did he remember?

Of course, he did. His eyes turned sad and bitter. He turned away, started the car and drove to her home, helped her inside and left her alone to nap before dinner.

She did. But painful memories and the ache of lost love invaded her dreams, and when she woke, the afternoon sun slanted in the room, hurting her eyes and mocking her with brassy light that illuminated all the heartaches that loomed again before them.

35

ZOEY GAVE UP ON HER NAP, changed into her work clothes, collected her new gloves—she smiled when she looked at them— and walked out on the porch. There she found Luca speaking on his phone in a terse voice quite unlike his usual easy delivery. When he saw her, he turned away and concluded his phone call.

"You don't have to do that. I was going out to the shop." She started toward the steps.

Luca followed and caught her arm. "If I could have a minute…well, probably more than a minute… I need to tell you something."

His tone warned her. "That I'm not going to like."

"That you're going to *hate*."

That she was going to hate? Oh, no. Zoey sank into the cushioned wicker porch swing. She didn't want confirmation of an affair with Ripley. That's what it had to be. Right? She couldn't imagine anything else would keep him on the wrestling circuit when his mother, his sisters and his wife pleaded with him to stop. An affair shouldn't matter: they were divorced, she had detached herself from their relationship, she was happy without him…

But she knew, *she knew*, she had seriously overestimated her detachment.

"While I was on the circuit," he told her. "I started getting letters."

Love letters, she supposed. "Letters? Or emails?"

"Letters. That was what got my attention." He sat next to her, faced her, his face serious and intent. "Actual, typed on a piece of paper, sent through the USPS letters. With a stamp."

"Whoa." This conversation had headed off in a different direction than she expected.

"At first I thought some grandmother had developed an obsession with wrestling, which was fine, except my mom's a grandmother and she uses email."

"To great effect." After the divorce, Giuseppina had written a scathing letter forbidding Zoey to ever enter the Damezas domain again. By domain, she meant all of New York City, New York state and possibly all of Italy.

But not the point. "What did the letters say?"

"At first they were nice. Love your style, keep up the good work kind of thing. I was flattered. I kept them."

Zoey still wasn't sure where this was going.

"Which, it turned out, was good." Luca's mouth was grim. "Because slowly the tone changed."

Zoey went on alert. "Changed to what?"

"Grandma became a coach. She critiqued my bouts, and when I lost to Boomer Burger, she told me to stop fooling around and get serious about the sport."

"That's still not—"

"She began to make veiled threats."

"What kind of threats?" Zoey paced out her words. She was confused. This was what had distracted him from their marriage? This was what consumed his interest to the point she imagined…well, every bad thing a wife could imagine?

"This woman said if I had less distractions in my life, I would fulfill my potential to be the greatest wrestler of all time."

"You were very good. If one liked that kind of competition." That involved possible mutilation and death.

"Not good enough, according to my grandma-critic. She told me being the best wrestler of all time was my new goal."

Tiny shivers began to work themselves up Zoey's spine. "That's creepy," she muttered.

"I gathered the letters and examined them. I hadn't paid any attention to the postmarks—why would I? I was convinced it was some elderly housebound woman—and discovered she had mailed each letter from wherever the bouts took place."

"She was following the circuit." Zoey's relief at knowing he hadn't cheated darkened and shriveled like paper catching flame. This was worse. He had a stalker. A stalker with purpose and the money to follow and watch him.

"Multistate postmarks. But I thought it couldn't be... It seemed so dramatic..." He looked at his hands as if he could see blood on them. "Then Brad was killed."

"Brad? Your manager, Brad?" Of course his manager Brad. "No, he got hit by a—" The truth blindsided her.

"By a cement truck," Luca finished for her.

"He'd been drinking. Doing drugs." Brad had loathed Zoey, and she heartily returned the favor. He had encouraged Luca in his wrestling career and done everything in his power to break up their marriage. But Luca had been loyal to him and grieved when he was killed.

"Hit-and-run. The cement truck was stolen. A man was seen behind the wheel. A man who matched the description of Brad's drinking companion of that evening."

Zoey nodded, her mind awhirl with new concepts. The idea that Brad had been murdered brought his death to a new level of horror—and explained so much about Luca's ready response to Morgayne's summons, and his insistence he be her constant companion. He saw the parallel between Brad's death by vehicle and the attempt on her life, and he didn't want to be responsible for Zoey's death. Which was noble and right, and rather deflating.

Luca continued, "That's when I took the letters to the FBI."

She calmed her imagination. "Worrisome letters received across a multistate region. Definitely work for the FBI. What did they say?"

"That my she was a he."

"They *knew* this person?"

"He's a serial killer they had yet to find and identify."

Zoey tried to ask, *What?* But she couldn't form the word, make a sound.

"I was so fixated on the belief that the author was an elderly woman, I couldn't wrap my mind around the change of age and gender. But in the profiling department, they told me with very few exceptions, serial killers are male, and in this case, the killer's a sports enthusiast." Luca sounded matter-of-fact, telling this story he knew well. "This guy, they call him the Coach, finds a sports figure he admires and stalks him—or her."

"Wrestling."

"Not just wrestling. Different sports, different sports figures. There's a pattern. He begins by sending fan letters, but the tone darkens. The part about the goal—being the greatest batter in baseball, or the greatest quarterback in football, or the greatest goalie in soccer—is the point at which the murders start."

"That's crazy!" She heard what she said and backtracked. "Yes, of course it's crazy. We're talking serial killer here."

He put his hand over hers, smoothed her skin with his thumb. "It also makes sense in a horrible way."

She could tell Luca felt sorry for her, hearing this, learning this. "The killer eliminates distractions that get in the way of being the greatest? He kills people around them? Their friends? Other athletes?"

"Yes."

Over the edge. "Family?"

"And life partners," he confirmed.

Although it explained so much. "Brad. Your mother. Your sisters. And…me." She put her broken hand on her chest, felt her increasing heartbeat, and realized how close that beat had come to being extinguished.

"Most definitely you. In subsequent letters, you were mentioned as the current primary deterrent to my goal."

"After Brad, you mean?"

"He was blamed because he wasn't coaching me well. And you…"

"Me because I wanted you to stop wrestling?" Her voice rose. "How did this person *know* that?"

"Zoey, *everybody* knew that." He was clearly exasperated. "You weren't quiet about it. Then after the Elanor dianthus became a hit, the media decided you didn't come to the matches because you were too busy chasing fame and fortune of your own."

She came to her feet. "I bred that flower so you would quit."

"I know. I know." He tried to pacify her.

"You think the person who ran me off the road is your stalker."

"The Coach. It's a real possibility."

"One I couldn't have imagined. Because you kept me in ignorance."

"On the advice of the FBI," he assured her.

Like that made a peat pot bit of difference. She pointed a shaking finger at him. "I don't give a *shit* what the FBI advised."

Luca's eyebrows raised at her vehemence.

Yeah, asshole, I caught you by surprise. "After I left, you quit wrestling because I was no longer living in the family home under your protection. *This* is why you came back to watch over me."

"Your mother begged me. It was the right thing to do. I would have felt guilty if I had refused."

Rage, red and bold and rising, lifted her on a red tide. *Guilt?*

Almost without pause—almost!—he said, "I love you, you were hurt and I was afraid you were going to die before I had the chance to tell you again."

She stormed down the steps. Did she want to hide? Go to work? Run away and not come back until Luca was gone and she could be alone?

He followed, arguing, "If I'd told you, you would have demanded I stop and my contact at the FBI said I was the best equipped to catch—"

She swung around and advanced toward him. "Yes, I would have demanded you stop. I tried to demand you quit wrestling, for the sake of *you*, for fear you would have been crippled or blinded, die of a brain hemorrhage or lie in a bed in a never-ending coma. As other wrestlers have."

"Not many."

"Not many is too many! I wanted you to be with me, alive and well." She gestured widely. "I wanted travel, children, a life together in our own home, all the things you said you wanted. Now you tell me you couldn't abandon your part as bait for some maniacal killer!" She shook her finger under his nose. "You're the most selfish, vainglorious man I've ever met."

At last, he caught fire. "Maybe I am. Maybe I only wanted to catch the Coach so I could bask in praise. Or maybe I was intent on doing the right thing. Which of those people did you fall in love with? Which of them did you admire enough to set aside your reluctance and marry?"

36

ZOEY DIDN'T WANT to address *that* issue when she was enjoying such a ride on her tsunami of righteous red-hot anger. She
shouted, "I'm going to tell your mother!" Where that had come
from, she didn't know.

But it derailed *Luca's* rage. He calmed, squinted and scratched
the back of his neck. "I wish you wouldn't."

"I'll bet you don't." She stalked away again. She paced back
toward him. "You didn't tell me. You didn't tell her. Do your
sisters know?"

"Of course not."

"Because *they* would have told your mother, too." She headed
toward her shop. That was the best place for her right now,
among the plants that had lifted her for the past two years.
But she didn't stop talking. "As if the wrestling wasn't enough
to worry about, you took part in a manhunt. You could have
been killed, and then..." She stopped in the open garage door,
gripped the trim with her right hand and covered her face with
her left. To her horror, her fury became sobbing. Loud, hard,
ugly sobbing. She'd never done that before, not even when he

was hurt, not even when she'd made the decision to divorce, not even when it was final and she was all alone.

Not even when her imaginary friend had disappeared forever...

This final piece of the puzzle was too much. All of it, every bit of her life was in shreds. Her husband had hurt her, scared her, disregarded her. Her mother had left; would she ever return, or was she now like Honey, nothing but a torn and painful memory? Her own work had been wantonly destroyed, her home invaded, nowhere was safe and the garden show loomed.

And Luca, damn him, Luca tried to take her in his arms.

She turned and as hard as she could, she hit him in the chest.

The bastard winced, wrapped his arms over hers to contain them and pulled her into him.

"I'm gonna...snot all over your...shirt!" she shouted.

"I don't see how you could miss." He took her arm and walked her into the shop and toward the tissues. He pulled one after another out of the box and shoved the wad into her hand.

She wiped her eyes, blew her nose, dropped the tissues and punched him again. It didn't seem to be hurting him much, but it did make her feel better.

He picked her up, sat in the rocker, put her in his lap and rocked her.

She fought, then collapsed onto his chest and muttered, "You bastard."

"Yeah, yeah." He leaned into her and inhaled slowly, deeply, as if the scent of her fed some well-hidden need.

She could feel tension ooze from him.

He shoved another handful of tissues into her hand. "Blow your nose."

She did. Loudly.

He took the tissues away, dropped them beside the chair and kissed her, the kind of kiss that he'd first used to seduce her. Gentle, warm, seeking, as if all his life, he'd waited for this kiss.

She groped for all the previous emotions: disbelief, rage, sorrow. But those had all dissipated, leaving her empty. Affection filled the space within her, and passion, and most of all, an incredulous relief that they were back where they belonged, in each other's arms. This was good. This was right. This was what they'd been headed toward from the moment on the hospital curb when she saw him beside her in the car seat.

She pulled away. "I need to wash my face."

He wiped her cheeks. "You're beautiful." He leaned back and looked. "Maybe not as radiant as usual. I'll wash it for you." But first he gently pressed her head onto his shoulder, pressed his lips to her forehead and rocked her. "I do love you. I'm sorry I've put you in danger. I promise you I was only trying to do the right thing."

"I know." She put her arms around his neck and looked into his eyes. "Luca..."

Then, from the wide-open doorway, a cranky old lady's voice said, "It looks as if I got here in the nick of time."

37

SLOWLY, LUCA AND ZOEY PARTED. Reluctantly, they turned their heads toward the shape silhouetted against the light. Swiftly, the horror of this moment swept away all warmth and need.

She glanced at her watch. Yes, there was a notice that someone had crossed her property line. Probably Luca had a similar notice, but that small vibration had been lost in the fury, the conflict, the passion.

Luca said, "Mother, how did you track me down?"

"Do you think I disregarded the whereabouts of your ex-wife?" Giuseppina Damezas was a short, scrawny woman with a dark basilisk gaze, a hooked nose, stooped shoulders and that olive wood cane topped with a black crystal doorknob.

Probably it wasn't a doorknob, but to Zoey it looked like one, one of the cool antique doorknobs that irresistibly drew the eye and warned all but the most obtuse that Giuseppina was a woman who could hold her own against every force of nature and rule her world according to her wishes.

"Hello, Zoey, always a pleasure." Giuseppina could not have been more sarcastic.

Zoey slid off Luca's lap and stood on wobbly legs.

Luca supported her with one hand under her elbow, but he didn't get to his feet. Zoey diagnosed a still-raging erection, and was grateful for his discretion.

"Good to see you, too, Giuseppina." Also good to know she could speak coherently when her brain was so clogged with hormones she couldn't think. "What brings you to Gothic?"

"I came to visit my dear ex-daughter-in-law." Giuseppina's smile contained an edge. "It's been so long since we've had a chance to catch up."

They stood on Zoey's property in Zoey's shop, and she saw no reason to take attitude from Giuseppina. "What a coincidence that Luca is here, too."

"Isn't it?" Giuseppina pointed her cane at one of the chairs. "May I? It was a long flight and a long drive."

As Giuseppina no doubt intended, Zoey felt chagrin at having ignored Giuseppina's exhaustion. After all, it was one thing to stand up for yourself; it was another to allow someone to goad her to callousness. "Please. Sit."

"I don't suppose you have any of that marvelous tea you used to make me? It relieves the pain in my joints…it's better than those expensive drugs the doctors recommend." Giuseppina had a way of performing the role of pitiful old lady when it suited her.

On her worst days, Giuseppina was never pitiful.

But she was in pain. Zoey didn't have a doubt. "I'll prep your tea." Opening the upper cupboards, she pulled out the herbs.

"I would love that." Giuseppina grasped the head of her cane and used all her strength to lower herself onto the chair. "I've missed your herbs."

So I heard, but after everything you said to me, I thought you'd dance every day I was gone.

Luca must have recovered, because he came to his feet. "Ma, how did you get here? To Gothic?"

"I flew into San Francisco, hired a driver and he drove me down California Route 1. Beautiful!"

Zoey puffed with pride.

Giuseppina continued, "It reminds me of Amalfi Coast."

Luca chuckled. "I thought that, too."

"What? No, it's completely different!" Zoey did not appreciate having her lovely home compared to…to Giuseppina's lovely home in Italy. She filled the electric pot with water and with unnecessary force shoved the plug in the wall.

"The driver dropped me at the end of the driveway. My luggage is up there. Luca, you need to get it."

Luca, the chickenshit coward, abandoned Zoey to the tender mercies of his mother.

Fine. Zoey wanted to start this off on the right foot. Her teapots ranged from the whimsical to the traditional, and she selected a teapot appropriate for Giuseppina—a buff black ceramic with polished red and orange flames.

Subtle, Zoey.

She rummaged in her cupboard, found the appropriate tea and measured it into the strainer. Cupping the strainer in her palm, she willed the herbs to release their potency, for Giuseppina needed the strength to leave for her hotel. "Where are you staying?"

"I won't take up much room, dear."

Passive-aggressive much? "I don't have any spare room." Zoey placed the strainer into the pot. "As you can easily see, I own a one-bedroom house."

"A humble home is a welcoming home." Giuseppina looked out the open garage door toward Zoey's beloved refuge. "In my Italian village such a house is a mark of wealth."

"In California, too. Have you seen the real estate prices here?"

"Yes. I've looked. You've done very well with the—"

Zoey waited for her to complain about the divorce settlement.

"—money you made with your Elanor dianthus." Giuseppina had gleaming white teeth, and she showed them all when she smiled.

"But that house means I can't house overnight guests." Zoey flung out an arm toward the loft. "Luca is sleeping in the shop."

At the mention of Luca, Giuseppina's tone changed. "As long as Luca is in California, I will stay to protect him."

"From me?" Zoey gestured at herself. "*Me?* I'm not going to attack him, I promise!" The water came to a boil. She filled the pot, placed it on the island and pushed it toward the center to steep.

"From himself. I can sleep on this cot." Giuseppina stood, made her way to the fold-down cot, lowered it and pressed one hand on the stretched canvas. "The doctor said I should sleep on a firm mattress. This will be good for my spine."

Zoey thought of Giuseppina resting on the unyielding surface, going outside to the toilet, going outside to shower, and with a whimper, she surrendered. Like there had ever been another possible outcome. "You can have my bedroom. In the house. I'll take the cot. In the shop."

"No." Giuseppina waggled her crooked index finger. "No. Not while my son is out here. That's worse."

Luca arrived laden with two large suitcases. "My God, Ma, how long do you intend to stay in Gothic?"

"Not just in Gothic, Luca," Zoey said. "Here!"

"Here, where?" He looked around. He observed the cot pulled down from the wall. "Ma, you can't sleep on that. You wouldn't be able to stand tomorrow. Didn't you get a room in town?"

Was he oblivious? "She's sleeping in my bed in the house."

He dropped a suitcase with a thump. "Zoey, forget it. I am not giving up my bed in the loft to you!"

So much for reconciliation and tenderness. "I'm not asking you to!"

When Giuseppina was displeased she would give you what her family called The Look. More than once, when Giuseppina gave Zoey The Look, Zoey wondered if those eyes were really dark brown or if she was staring right into the devil's wicked soul. She gave Zoey The Look now. "It doesn't matter. I'm not leaving you two out here together."

"We're not together." Zoey ground out the words.

Giuseppina pointed at the rocking chair. "I saw!"

"That was a temporary aberration!" *It was. It was!*

Luca remained the calm, stolid bulwark he had always been. "Zoey's right, Ma, you cannot sleep on that cot. You'll be laid up."

Giuseppina gave *him* The Look.

But she didn't stand a chance, for Luca displayed a cunning ability to manage his mother. "If you're laid up, you won't be able to cook for us."

Giuseppina froze, then melted as she always did for her boy. "That would be a shame."

"You do remember I can't cook," Zoey added.

"Yes." Giuseppina's dark eyes looked her over critically.

Zoey deemed the tea had steeped long enough, poured it into a travel cup—a less-than-subtle gesture—attached the lid and handed it to Giuseppina. "All the more reason for you to get a room in an inn where you can get a good meal. I'll call the Live Oak."

"I've already tried the Live Oak. Also all the bed-and-breakfasts in town." Giuseppina reached into her massive bag. She pulled out a small flashlight, a metal multitool, a plastic bag filled with miniature servings of ketchup and mayonnaise, some crumpled tissues, a pack of batteries and what looked like a Las Vegas game chip. She deposited them on the counter.

"Nothing's changed, I see," Zoey said. At any given moment, Giuseppina had always been able to produce whatever was needed from that bag of hers.

She located her cell phone and pointed it at Zoey. "Look. You can check my history. The town flower show starts tomorrow night. There's no room."

Desperation enveloped Zoey.

"Honey, I can't fix this." Luca sounded sympathetic.

"We'll call your driver back," Zoey said to Giuseppina. "We'll find you someplace in Monterey."

"I *am* staying in Gothic. But I have a solution." Giuseppina waggled that finger between the two of them. "You solemnly swear you won't have sex in here. No sex! No kissing! No hugging! *No sex!*"

"I can gladly promise that." Right now, Zoey would promise anything to get Giuseppina away from her.

"Me, too. Really. Gladly." Luca didn't have to be so emphatic. In that irritating, patient tone he used when his women folk got fractious, he said, "Listen, Ma, Zoey and I had a moment. That's all. We have a past. I didn't come here to make love to her. I came to make sure she's—" He stopped.

Giuseppina gestured for him to continue.

"To make sure she's safe until her mother returns from the wild adventure on which she's embarked."

Giuseppina sighed and in a disparaging tone said, "Her mother."

Immediately enraged, Zoey turned on Luca. "I'll call Angelica. She'll find her a spot somewhere in that mansion."

"You do that." He took Giuseppina's arm and turned her toward the doors. "One way or another, it doesn't matter, Ma. You can trust nothing will happen. I'm here briefly until Zoey feels better. We've given our word. You can go sleep in the house and I will be safe from Zoey and any of her unruly passions."

Zoey prepared to blast him.

He stared at her with hard wordless meaning.

She let out her breath and smiled toothily. "I'll do my best to resist."

"Hmm." Giuseppina considered them both again. She walked

outside. She looked back. She looked forward and walked across the yard toward the house. Slowly. So slowly. She showed the crippling effects of hours of travel; the woman who wished to move at a bracing pace could only creep toward her bed.

Luca sighed sadly. He walked after her, spoke until she smiled up at him, helped her up the stairs and into the house.

This was one of the reasons Zoey had loved him. She had no family beyond Morgayne, and Luca's fierce devotion to his mom and siblings moved her heart. With a sigh that echoed his, she picked up the two suitcases—my God, had the woman packed rocks in here?—and trudged toward the house.

Her phone rang. She put down the suitcases, pulled her phone out of her pocket, looked at it and frowned.

Natasha Nakashima. What the hell was Natasha Nakashima calling for? Had she not dealt with enough querulous, bossy women today? Which was not fair to Natasha, but Zoey wasn't in the mood to be fair.

She answered with a snap. "What's up, Natasha?"

Natasha snapped back. "Have you heard from my nephew, Fritz?"

"Your nephew...?"

"Fritz! Has he visited you?"

Zoey blinked. "The nephew with the poinsettias in Watsonville?"

"Yes! Him!"

"I haven't seen him." Was everything today oddly disorienting? "Why would I?"

"Remember? He wants to do what you do, develop a new flower, get rich, never have to work again. He lost his property and his poinsettias. He deserved it—he's spent so much time bragging he hasn't worked a day." Natasha's voice hit a high note. "My sister called, frantic. He's disappeared!"

"I...no, Natasha. He hasn't put in an appearance. But there are a lot of people converging on Gothic." Like my former mother-in-law. "Maybe, um…"

"If he shows, call me. In the meantime, I'll tell my sister her son is spoiled and I don't care what happens to him!"

"That will help."

Natasha didn't catch the sarcasm. "I work for a living. My parents work for a living. My siblings, my relatives, everyone works for a living. In flowers! We're happy, we're successful! Fritz needs to work, too!" Just like that, her voice returned to normal. "How are you? I heard you got smashed up."

"I'm good." Zoey looked at her two broken fingers taped together and held with a brace. "Better, anyway. Who told you?"

"We sent flowers to the hospital. The San Francisco flower people. We wanted you to heal." Natasha was brusque, but she cared. "Did you see them?"

Zoey remembered the vase in the hospital and she smiled at the receiver. "I did. Thank you. Thank you to everyone. They made me happy."

"Good. You get better and come home to visit." Natasha's voice changed again. "If you see my nephew, kick his ass all the way back to Watsonville!" Just like that, she hung up.

Zoey chuckled. Natasha was a character and Zoey loved her, but she hoped Fritz kept his distance. She was ill-equipped to deal with an egotistical flower grower who had lost his livelihood, and right now, her own family matters were difficult enough. She didn't need to worry about Natasha's.

Picking up the suitcases, Zoey brought them inside and placed them in the bedroom. She changed the towels while Luca changed the sheets, promised Giuseppina she would *not* cook dinner and left Luca to help his mother slowly, painfully recline on the bed.

She went out on the porch, soaked in the peace and glory of the view and waited. When he stepped outside, she asked the question that needed to be asked. "Why did you tell me now?"

38

"ABOUT THE COACH? AH." Luca flung himself on a wicker chair and sighed. "The FBI assured me they had contacted a retired agent to monitor the situation, search for the still-un-recovered vehicle that almost killed you and help us as needed. He was supposed to be bringing his wife to the Gothic Garden and Flower Show and watch for suspects."

Zoey whipped around to face him. "And...?"

"His wife got suspicious, looked at the messages on his phone and pulled him off the project."

Zoey couldn't help it. She snorted. "I wish I'd had that kind of influence on you."

Luca took a breath, held it as if fighting to keep the words in and let it out.

She didn't know if she was disappointed or not, if she'd been picking a fight to get the issues out in the open. All she knew for sure was he had nobly resisted and they were back with the pressing issue of life...and death. "What will the FBI do?"

"The agency is contacting someone they believe can disappear into the background to ask if...this person—"

"Who is it?"

"I don't know, Zoey." He sounded reasonable, thoughtful. "I suspect they've found another retired agent and they don't tell you who they are. I mean, think about it. They're retired, but somewhere out there is a scary criminal who has reason to hate them, or who wants a notch on their belt."

"Makes sense." She considered people who already lived in Gothic. She couldn't put her finger on anyone she thought would be former FBI, although she supposed there was no actual FBI type of person. A tourist, then, someone from out of town. "Our help is anyone past a certain age with an uncertain past. Or someone who's been injured and is on disability. Or anybody we don't suspect."

"That covers it."

She had to say it. Grudgingly, perhaps, but still. "Thank you for…telling me about the serial killer. I'll be on the lookout for suspicious characters. Although I guess that's the problem. If he was a suspicious character, he wouldn't be a successful killer. Like the FBI agent, he blends into the background."

"Also right." Luca leaned forward and his dark eyes were even darker with intensity. "Zoey, I want you to know—it's not all vainglory that led me to this task. The FBI has collected information about the killings. The Coach is not an assassin who murders from afar. He's never shot anyone. He's never thrown a knife. He's a hands-on killer, a strong man capable of breaking a spine with his bare hands. He murders women. He murders children. He's inventive, and he's killed more than one skilled athlete who thought he was prepared for an ambush."

She did understand. "Because of your size and your sport, you're uniquely suited to defeat him."

"Yes."

"When you were hurt, laid out in the hospital, you were in danger."

"You and my family were under skilled surveillance."

"I wasn't asking about *me*. I was asking about *you*. Because you were helpless." Even now, the memory of his suffering in-furiated her.

"Yes, a watch was set over me, too. When you left, you went to stay with your mother. I tried to see you and she wouldn't let me. I lurked outside, waiting for you to come out. I wanted to talk. You never came out."

"No." She had been in hiding from him and the world. But she'd never quite managed to hide from herself, from her doubts and her heartache.

"With the security in Morgayne's building and the possibil-ity of an attack, that was the best thing you could have done. When you announced the divorce, it was deemed you were no longer in danger. But to cement your safety, I announced my retirement."

"Why would that cement my safety?"

"The Coach is focused. One athlete at a time. The thought was, he would consider me a failure and eliminate me."

She felt ill. Luca had worn defiance like a cloak, taunting the Coach to draw attention from his mother, his sisters, his wife. "Was there no attempt?"

"You may have heard I went to Italy." He smiled crookedly. "A few words to my relatives and I was safe. Even if the Coach had appeared in town, I was safe. You don't screw with an Ital-ian family."

"Good. Good." She looked toward the Pacific, toward the horizon, seeking a place where a killer didn't stalk them, where their problems didn't haunt them…where they didn't hurt each other. "Do we have any ideas who it is? Any at all?"

"The profilers at the FBI haven't figured it out." His mouth quirked. "But we have more motivation than they do."

The vista of the ocean, grassy rolling hills dotted with live oaks, a mature olive grove that could provide cover and the road stretching before and behind them like an arrow pointing them out to a sinister observer. "In other words, if you want to stay alive and see your flowers bloom, Zoey, pay attention."

Luca put his hand on her shoulder and pulled her close. "Exactly."

And if I want to see this man I love stay alive to see my flowers bloom, I need to be alert at all times.

She slipped from his grasp and collected the three seat cushions off the wicker furniture.

"What are you doing?" he asked.

"Making my bed in the shop." She ran down the steps, stopped and swiveled to face him. "One thing doesn't make sense. Why was I attacked *now*? Why has it all started up again *now*?"

"Oh." He looked guilty.

"What did you do?"

"I may have let Lamira announce the firm was opening an office on the West Coast, in San Francisco, and I would be in charge."

"You said she was thinking about it! You said you had to talk to your headhunters!"

"I'm sorry about the announcement, because it made you a target once more, and within a week you were gravely hurt." He walked to the top of the stairs, turned, and she recognized that determined expression. "But the Coach was right. In moving to San Francisco, I had a single goal; to get closer to you, Zoey. It's not over yet. I love you, I want to be with you and I have to try again."

She watched him walk into the house, and she breathed. Just breathed. The breeze off the Pacific carried the scents of salt and freedom. The sunlight warmed her skin. The soil below her feet fed her strength. But Luca challenged her, changed her, connected her to life and love.

She'd lost that once; she knew the bitter acrid taste of loneliness. Now, once again, he lodged within her, a vital element that transformed her from a solitary woman who stood alone on the face of the earth to a shared being: LucaandZoey, ZoeyandLuca.

Suffering, in turmoil, she stayed outside working until she got a text message to come in for dinner. She washed up in the shop and walked toward the house. The fog gathered in wisps around her and she spoke to it acerbically. "Giuseppina Damezas is the opposite of a lost soul. She damn well knows what she wants and how to get it." She referred to the Gothic legend, of course, and of course the fog paid her no heed and gathered closer.

She walked into the kitchen to find the table set with candles, Luca draining the pasta and Giuseppina finishing the lemon-caper sauce for the chicken piccata.

As Zoey stood in the door and blinked away tears, Giuseppina said, "Shut the door. You're letting in the fog, and it's time for your first, lost-past-time birthday dinner."

39

THAT NIGHT, ZOEY woke heart pounding, throat scratchy, covered in sweat. She sat up on her cot and switched on the shop's overhead light—and caught Luca halfway down the stairs in his boxer shorts and holding a pistol. She stared at him, stared at the pistol, wiped the tears from the corners of her eyes and gasped, "What? Why?"

"What happened?" His voice was low and terrible.

"I just... I just..."

"You gave the most inhuman yell. What happened?"

"Nightmare. I had a nightmare."

He sat on the step as if his knees had gone out from under him. He took a long breath and looked up at her. "Let me get my clothes on and you can tell me about it."

She didn't want to remember it, and she was sure she didn't want to tell him about it.

But he must have had his clothes laid out, because he was back in two minutes in a T-shirt and shorts, carrying his shoes and socks. He glanced at her, wet a washcloth at the sink, wrung it out and put it on the back of her neck. Pulling a chair up to her bedside, he said, "Tell me."

"It probably doesn't mean anything."

"I slept with you for years. I've never heard you make that sound before, and if nothing else, it means you're terrified."

She hesitated, then nodded.

"Look, Zoey." He leaned his elbows on his knees and looked into her eyes. "A lot of things are happening. Most of them are difficult. It's not surprising your subconscious has woven a story to explain events."

"I'm afraid…" she said in a low voice. "I'm afraid that's not the explanation."

"What is the explanation?"

"I'm afraid… I suspect this is a memory."

He sat up straight. "Tell me."

Honey and Gracie were playing on the stairs. Jumping up one tread at a time. Laughing. Shrieking. Having fun. Honey made everything more fun. Honey knew what Gracie was thinking, and Gracie knew what Honey was thinking. They had always been together, and they would always be together. Always.

They were almost to the top when a door banged open. The Mean Man's bedroom door. They froze, clutching each other's hands.

Heavy footsteps stomped to the top of the stairs.

Gracie looked up in terror.

The Mean Man's blond hair stuck out from his head. His blue eyes looked like pits in his skull. His T-shirt and shorts were wrinkled and stained, and even from two steps down, Gracie could smell his particular odor of whiskey, cigarettes and cruelty. He didn't say anything, he just lifted his foot…and kicked Honey down the stairs.

Honey thumped and thumped. To Gracie, it seemed the house shook each time Honey struck a step. Honey didn't make a sound—until she did. She hit the banister. She flung out her arm to protect her head. Her arm twisted behind her at an impossible angle, and she screamed. And screamed.

So loud. So terrible. Such agony.

Gracie glanced up at the Mean Man. His red-rimmed eyes flamed, his face contorted. She knew she looked into the mouth of hell. He ran down the first three steps.

Gracie flinched—and he saw her.

He swung at her with his big, clenched fists.

She grabbed a baluster in each hand, grabbed them so tight her hands hurt, and cowered, eyes closed, waiting for the Mean Man to get her, too.

The back door swung wide and Mommy ran in. She crooned to Honey.

"No, Honey. Don't cry, Honey…"

She yelled at the Mean Man.

"What have you done this time? Can't I walk to the mailbox without you trying to kill my children?"

The Mean Man yelled back at Mommy. He yelled at Gracie. He especially yelled at Honey, cursing her with the really bad words, telling her to shut up or he'd give her something to cry about.

Mommy got out her phone, pointed at him and told him to get out before the police arrived.

The Mean Man stomped back into his bedroom and slammed the door.

Gracie didn't dare cry, but she trembled. She shook. She stared at the backs of her hands where the tendons stood out white from her skin.

A long time later, people came and cared for Honey, and Mommy came to sit beside Gracie on the stairs. She spoke softly to her and tried to convince her to let go of the balustrade.

Gracie hunched her shoulders and shook her head.

Mommy promised she wouldn't let the Mean Man hurt Honey anymore.

Gracie wanted to believe her, just like she wanted to let go of the balustrade. But even when she tried, she couldn't. She couldn't feel her fingers. Mommy had to pry her loose, and when Gracie looked, her palm and still-curled fingers were stark white, and pressed into the skin were bluish lines from the balustrade's raised ridges.

★ ★ ★

Luca took Zoey's hand and rubbed it, and her fingertips tingled. She'd been clenching them so hard… He said, "Honey was your sister."

"I don't know. I guess." She tried to express the inexpressible. "In my mind, there's always someone else out there, who's a part of me, and yet in real life, I've never met her."

"Tomorrow we're calling your mother."

"I agree. Because there's more to this than I understand, and I need to find out the truth."

He leaned down, pulled on his footwear and tied his shoes.

"What are you doing?"

"I'm going for a walk."

She started to scramble out of bed. "I'll go with you."

"No." He put his hand on her shoulder. "No. Whoever pushed you off the road could have been, almost certainly was, the Coach. But his profile doesn't include break-ins like the one we experienced here. Your subconscious keeps pointing us in a different direction. We're missing something. I want to look around, and I need to think—and that's not possible when you're with me in the starlight." He kissed her, a comforting kiss that somehow irritated rather than reassured. "Go back to sleep. No nightmares this time. No memories. We're figuring it out." He strode out the door.

She watched, then stood up and tore the cushions and covers off her bed. "That's all very well for you to say. You're sleeping on a wide, firm mattress." She remade the cot again. "If I'm having nightmares, it's because I'm massively uncomfortable. And if I'm recovering memories…"

What further revelations lurked in the depths of her mind?

40

THE NEXT MORNING Zoey got up with the sun, showered outside in the chilly air, got dressed in work clothes and called her mother.

Morgayne's phone rang, and then went to voice mail, but the message wasn't the usual mechanical voice announcing her number and suggesting the caller leave a message. This time Morgayne herself said, "I'm currently unavailable, but I will be back in the office on Monday."

This was Friday.

"All right," Zoey said. That was definite enough.

The message continued, "If this is Zoey…don't worry, honey. I'm safe. You be safe, too. If you haven't already, put that dragon somewhere that it can't be easily accessed. As you must have guessed, things are happening. I'll be with you soon and I'll explain everything." The message finished and then…nothing.

Zoey stared at her phone in her hand.

Luca watched her as he came down the stairs from the loft, wearing a pair of shorts, holding his shirt and a pair of flip-flops, and frowning. "What?"

She told him about the message. "I'm supposed to put the dragon somewhere 'it can't be easily accessed.'"

"The dragon again. I thought it might be metaphorical, but—"

"It sounds as if it's a real thing."

"Yes. You're supposed to have a dragon of some kind." He contemplated Zoey for a few moments. "Did your mother sound as if she was under duress?"

"No. She sounded…excited."

"How long has she been gone?"

"A week."

"And she told you where she was going, but you don't quite remember. Her honor and the flagon with the dragon."

"It's not funny. Luca, I'm concerned."

"I'm not laughing," he pointed out.

"When she called you and asked you to care for me, why didn't you question her? Why didn't you ask why?" She already knew the answer. "Because you thought it had to do with the Coach."

"I still consider that the best possibility. Come on." He pulled on his shirt and started out the door. "Let's go eat breakfast."

"I'll eat out here." Because if she couldn't talk to her mother, she didn't want to talk to his. She rounded on him. "That's another thing. What's with your mother making me a birthday dinner?"

"She loves to feed people. You love to eat."

Zoey got out a bowl and spoon and put them on the counter with her whole grain cereal. "She's confusing. Does she like me? Does she not like me?"

"You'll have to ask her, but once she got over her rage about you divorcing me, well…" He spread his hands. "Ma's pretty devout."

"What does that mean? Are you saying she doesn't accept

the divorce?" Zoey realized her voice was rising. "After all she said to me?"

"Pretty sure she was in a rage when she was raking you across the coals." He glanced out the door. "Anyway, if you want to know what she's thinking, ask her. She *will* tell you."

Zoey flinched when she remembered the last time Giuseppina had told her what she was thinking. "No!"

"Aren't women supposed to be better at communication than men? Because you're pretty bad at it. That's something for me to remember going forward." He greeted Giuseppina as she walked through the open garage door into the shop. "Morning, Ma!"

She carried her voluminous Italian leather bag over her skinny left arm and gripped the knob of her gnarled cane with her right hand. She leaned heavily on the support. "Good morning, Zoey dear, did you sleep well out here—" her gaze zeroed in on the cot's rumpled blankets "—on your cot?"

"Very well. I hope you had a good sleep in *my* bed." Pleasant tone, but possibly Zoey needed to work on her hospitable feelings.

"I've had a cup of your tea and am moving more easily. Are you coming in for breakfast?"

"No." Zoey gestured at waiting bowl and spoon. "I thought I'd just—"

Giuseppina interrupted. "I got up early and made my fresh English muffins for eggs Benedict. Fried Canadian bacon, spinach, coddled eggs, and of course my hollandaise sauce."

Zoey's stomach growled.

"Isn't this evening the first tour of the flower show? You're going to need your strength." Giuseppina put her hand on Luca's arm. "Help me back in the house, son. Now that breakfast is done and I've got lunch prepared, I need to start on dinner. I'm planning shrimp and three-cheese grits. Yesterday I had my driver stop at the vegetable stand beside the road. I couldn't resist the heirloom tomatoes, so for a side, a nice caprese salad."

As they left the shop, Luca grinned back at Zoey.

"That's what you had in your suitcases?" Zoey muttered. "Tomatoes?"

Giuseppina's voice floated back. "Are you coming, Zoey?"

"Yes, Giuseppina." Zoey trudged after them. For a woman who had told Zoey she was dead to the Damezas family, she was doing an awfully good job of tempting Zoey back into the fold.

41

WITH MARJORIE AT ATTENTION, Angelica ran down the checklist of launch day final preparations for the garden show. "The Gothic Garden and Flower Show passports are here, at the starting point of all tours." She spoke firmly, as if that would make drop-ins impossible when she knew darned good and well drop-ins were inevitable.

"Good." Marjorie nodded approval.

"Both of the Gothic surreys are in perfect running order."

"Right."

"The stamps for the passports have been distributed to the master gardeners, and the colored ink pads with the color coding for each tour. Although—" Angelica looked over her Angelica Lindholm–brand readers at Marjorie "—they'll never get that right."

Marjorie said bracingly, "You have to give them more credit."

"Mr. Kulshan will get them wrong on purpose."

"Well." Marjorie grimaced. "Yes."

"When the guests convene here, I'll speak about tonight's musical launch and explain that their contribution in the form of their tickets and any additional they wish to donate will go to resourcing water for fire-prone areas and preserving native plant habitat."

Marjorie handed her a script.

Angelica scanned it. "Very good. An assistant who can write in my voice is priceless. Now, for the last thing on today's list. Mrs. Kulshan had rented one of her bedrooms for the festival to a South American couple. Mr. Kulshan has agreed the agreement should be met, but someone must prepare the house, stay in the house and make sure no harm is done by a renter."

"You want me to go survey the situation, make sure the spare bedroom closet and drawers are empty, and let housekeeping know they should send someone down to clean." Marjorie prepared to go.

"No." Angelica stood. "I'm going to do it."

Clearly startled, Marjorie stammered, "B…but you're Angelica Lindholm! You're too important to spend your time on such a trivial matter!"

Angelica appreciated Marjorie's spot-on appraisal of the situation. "That's true. But I hired such an efficient assistant, I can now trust the preparations for the festival will continue in my absence."

Marjorie beamed and relaxed. "Of course, Angelica. Thank you for your trust."

"I spoke with Mr. Kulshan today. If all goes well, Mrs. Kulshan will come home, to Mr. Kulshan's, with a nurse." Angelica collected her stack of fold-up boxes. "She's an elderly woman who's been in her home for many years. I want to take this opportunity to assess what needs to be done to allow her to stay in that home as long as possible."

"Oh." Marjorie looked at Angelica as if she'd never seen her before.

Angelica knew why. "I do have a heart, you know."

"I won't tell anybody… Do you need someone to stay in the

house during the festival? To make sure the guests don't smoke? Steal? Act irresponsibly?"

"I've already arranged for one of my crustiest gardeners to spend the night."

"Orvin Isaksen?" Marjorie was clearly horrified.

"Worse than that." Angelica pulled a long face. "Hudson Isaksen."

"Ohhh. The other brother. I've met him. In the garden. He, um, seemed to consider it an affront that I wanted a cut bouquet for your table."

"Both he and his brother have been with me for twenty years, are totally reliable, and with the Gothic Garden and Flower Show Hudson will be working all hours so he won't have time to insult Mrs. Kulshan's guests. He'll eat his meals here or on the job and do no more than sleep in the house." Angelica knew she was reassuring herself. "That will assure nothing untoward can happen."

"I wouldn't put a foot out of line if I thought the displeasure of Hudson could come down on my head," Marjorie assured her.

"Thank you for that support. That's exactly as I hoped. I'll take an ATV, complete the job, then come back as soon as I can. I have everything scheduled, but of course, the unexpected always occurs, the garden show starts soon and we're on the clock!" In a characteristic gesture, she chopped the side of her hand into her palm.

"Understood, Angelica. Take your time. I'll keep the ball rolling."

Angelica stepped out of her home, took a deep breath of fresh air and allowed herself a rare moment of pleasure in her surroundings. Of course she meditated every day in her conservatory; meditation was good for concentration and blood pressure. Of course she worked out daily; exercise sharpened the mind, reduced inflammation and helped control weight gain. But she couldn't remember the last time she had, spur-of-the-moment,

left her duties in the hands of someone else, no matter how responsible, and escaped.

Not that she was doing something without purpose. For a long
time, she'd been wanting to offer her assistance to Mr. and Mrs.
Kulshan. Mrs. Kulshan's fall provided the excuse she needed.
But to drive down Gothic's winding main street and really see
how her village was doing…that was a rare treat.

Even in the last day, the traffic had increased, both cars and
pedestrians, and she drove carefully, observing the rhythm of
the town, the shops that were busiest and the restaurants that
already had people waiting in lines outside.

All the original houses built in the original rush of building in the late 1930s and early 1940s were tiny. Mrs. Kulshan's
floor plan included two bedrooms, one bath, a tiny living space
and kitchen, and a back porch. Crocheted doilies spread lace
under the lamps and black-and-white family photos decorated
the walls. There were lists, too, on every surface, an old woman's way of organizing her life and memory.

1. Fertilize the begonias and the impatiens.

2. Hire Justin to spade manure into the garden.

3. When Zoey returns, deliver the package.

The package? Oh, dear. Mrs. Kulshan had fallen before Zoey's
return. Angelica would keep an eye out for a package meant for
Zoey and handle the matter.

In the second bedroom, where the guests would sleep, she
placed the folding boxes beside the dresser and opened the first
drawer. The scent of *old* filled Angelica's head. Old treasures, old
photos, old bits and pieces of a life sliding toward a close. It felt
sacrilegious, cleaning out the crocheted tablecloth and starched
linen napkins, yellowed pillowcases with beautiful embroidered
edges, a stack of official-looking papers and the old photos of two
young, happy people she realized were the Kulshans. She noted
that the drawers were lined with yellowing paper newspapers

and spent too many minutes reading the stories and chuckling at the ads from the 1960s, '70s and '80s.

When she'd finished the dresser, she headed into the tiny, dark walk-in closet and wasted several moments fumbling on the wall for the light switch. Finally her eyes adjusted enough to see the chain dangling from the light fixture. She pulled it, the bulb came on—and there on a side shelf, a large, battered, torn USPS cardboard box sat, addressed to Zoey Phoenix.

It had been mailed from Citation, California, and one side of the lid had separated from the body of the box. Curious, she peered into the hole—and a glittering golden eye stared back at her. She jumped backward—and bumped into somebody behind her.

She whirled, realized who it was, put her hand to her chest and in relief said, "Oh, it's you. Did you come down to—*What are you doing?*" She tried to duck the shovel as it swung at the side of her head, but it was too late. The metal rang like a bell against her skull. The impact knocked her sideways; she slid down the wall, fighting to slow her descent. Her bottom hit the floor and—she was out.

The gardener put down the shovel and leaned down to pick up Angelica's shoulders and drag her unconscious body farther into the closet.

From the doorway, someone said, "That wasn't very smart."

Orvin whirled. Said, "No!" And died with a bullet in his chest.

The Someone walked into the closet and pointed the pistol at the unconscious Angelica.

The front door slammed open. Voices shouted. The house was small. The Someone cursed at the noise, holstered the gun—and escaped out the back.

42

"PSST! ZOEY!"

Zoey looked up from her as yet unsprouted *amapolas gracia de dios* seeds. She had been crooning to them, describing their blue petals splashed with red, their vibrant yellow eyes, their feathery gray-green foliage. Yet they remained stubbornly unresponsive and she feared the time she'd spent in the hospital had destroyed their viability, and who knew when or if she would once again find the long-lost plant? "Hi, Shasta. I didn't hear you coming." She glanced at her watch. "In fact, you didn't set off the perimeter alarm. I wonder what's wrong with it?"

"I was wandering around looking for my next scene to paint." Shasta scuttled into the shop. "I probably skipped over it somehow."

Zoey didn't think it worked that way, but she was glad for the distraction Shasta offered. "What's wrong? Are you hiding from something?"

"I heard your mother-in-law arrived." Shasta pressed her back to the wall. "You know she never liked me."

"I don't think it was specifically *you*. I think it was anyone who was a friend of mine."

"Maybe. Anyway, that is one scary woman. When she looked at me, I always thought she saw all the way into my corrupt soul." Shasta shivered.

Zoey chuckled. "She's not that bad." Of course, her opinion had been influenced by today's celebration of Giuseppina's cooking, breakfast and lunch, and she looked forward to tonight's feast. "How's it going up there at the Tower?"

In an ominous voice, Shasta said, "Didn't you hear?"

That did not sound good. "Hear what?"

"Angelica was in a frenzy to prepare for the tour—"

"Of course."

"She took a few minutes to go down to Mrs. Kulshan's to fix it up for the lodgers who are arriving tonight, and she was attacked in the bedroom closet!"

"Attacked? Here? In Gothic?" Zoey was shocked, incredulous. "How? Why?"

"Apparently Orvin Isaksen followed her into the house."

"Orvin? The *gardener*?"

"Yes. Then he followed her into the closet, and he hit her with a shovel. Knocked her out!" Shasta hoisted herself up on one of the counter stools. "Before he could do more, guess what happened?"

Zoey still hadn't absorbed the bare facts. "Orvin had the nerve to hit Angelica? In the head? With a shovel?"

"Then somebody shot Orvin. Through the heart. Killed him!"

Zoey scrambled to catch up. "What...? Why...?" Did this have something to do with Luca's serial killer? She couldn't see the connection, but maybe... "Did they catch the killer?"

"No! Whoever it was ran out the back door and jumped the fence either onto the street or into someone else's yard."

Luca wandered in from the house. "Hi, Shasta. I saw you sneaking across the fields. What's up?"

"Listen to this!" Zoey waved an arm at Shasta.

Shasta recounted the story while Luca and Zoey exchanged glances.

Luca shook his head at Zoey; he didn't believe this had anything to do with the Coach. Taking over the questioning, he asked, "What do the police say? Are there fingerprints? Does anyone know Orvin's motivation?"

"The police are baffled. No prints." Shasta wiggled her fingers at them. "No official motivation that anyone can guess. Angelica's in the hospital."

"When does she come home?" Luca asked.

"Tomorrow," Shasta answered. "Apparently she has a broken jaw, bruising, one eye swollen shut."

"The Gothic Garden and Flower Show has to go on without Angelica?" Zoey staggered backward. Not that she didn't believe it could be done; knowing Angelica, she had a backup plan for every contingency. But Zoey still couldn't comprehend that anyone, especially someone who knew her, would clobber Angelica.

"I don't know for sure—" Shasta leaned forward "—but do you think she found something in the closet? Why would Orvin hit Angelica, and then someone kill Orvin unless they wanted something? Something of value?"

"In Mrs. Kulshan's closet?" Zoey asked incredulously.

Shasta deflated. "I suppose not. It doesn't seem likely, does it? Does it?"

"*Was* anything found?" Zoey got a vibration on her watch.

So did Luca, apparently. "The parameter sensors *are* apparently working." He stepped outside. "The Gothic Garden and Flower Show surrey is here."

"I don't know," Shasta said. "All anybody talks about is the shocking attack on Angelica."

"Naturally." Luca nodded. "Zoey, do you want me to stay and help with the tour? If you're uncomfortable, you know I'm glad to."

"It's okay." Zoey figuratively pulled up her big girl panties. "I can do it." She heard the sound of the motor, heard Thistle finish up his song and a light smattering of applause.

"I am out of here," Shasta declared. "That musician is weird."

"Weird? How?" Luca asked.

"He acts like he's looking for something. Watches everybody. Makes me uncomfortable." Shasta looked out the back door, then slipped away.

Zoey had begun to think the world had run mad. Luca stalked by a serial killer called the Coach, a serial killer who possibly had tried to kill her in a hit-and-run? Angelica attacked by her gardener who was shot dead in Mrs. Kulshan's closet? The festival musician watching everybody? Shasta acting jittery and almost excited about the attacks in Mrs. Kulshan's closet?

Zoey stepped outside and watched the tourists descend from the Gothic Garden and Flower Show surrey, eighteen women and men of various ages wearing differing expressions of boredom or enjoyment.

Compared to the threat of violence and death, leading a tour would be simple.

She noticed Thistle, and Shasta was right; he watched the tourists with far too much interest. She shivered and amended her thought.

Leading a tour was simple if no killer hid behind the mask of a guest, a musician, a bus driver...or a friend.

43

ZOEY SHOOK OFF her sense of unfriendly eyes that watched her, and stepped forward to meet the festival group. "Welcome to the Zoey Phoenix flower breeder portion of the tour. I'm Zoey Phoenix, the breeder of the Elanor dianthus." She showed them a stalk of the dianthus culled from Angelica's garden. "If you've bought a bouquet in the last few years, you're probably familiar with the Elanor. I'll guide you through my workshop and my garden area, and at the end of the tour, you'll have the opportunity to enjoy a glass of one of the iced herbal teas I developed for Angelica Lindholm's organic line of foods."

One guy smirked. "Is there a lot of money in herbal teas?"

Zoey looked him over. Broad shouldered, trim waist, handsome in a superior aging businessman sort of way. *He* was why Zoey didn't like public speaking.

The woman with him laughed nervously. "Darling, you can't ask that." To Zoey, she said, "You know husbands."

Zoey answered seriously, as if she didn't catch the snottiness. "There's more money in breeding flowers, but Angelica asked if she could market the blends, and of course I was honored."

The guy wasn't smart enough to quit. "Oo, did you make enough to paint the house your husband bought you?"

"Clifford!" He'd now thoroughly humiliated his wife.

He didn't care. "Gloria," he mimicked her, then glanced toward the shop and snapped his head back to stare.

Luca stood in the doorway, hands on hips.

She gestured him toward the group. He'd offered to take the group. He was good at this stuff. Let Luca deal with Clifford. She had no doubt he'd be good at it.

He strode toward them in that kind of big man strut he'd perfected while in wrestling, the walk he used to intimidate the other fighters.

Clifford did a double take, and when Luca was close enough, he asked, "Aren't you that wrestler—?"

"Yes, and, man, I had to come over and say—I heard what you said. I understand how tough it is when you realize you're in the presence of an incredibly successful woman. Women like Zoey Phoenix do batter a guy's ego. But I want you to know, I admire you for bringing your wife to the Gothic Garden and Flower Show anyway. That's the kind of thing that separates the men from the boys." Luca offered his hand. "Put 'er there."

Clifford stood wide-eyed and frozen. He wasn't quite sure if he'd been called pussy-whipped. He knew he'd been called a loser who was intimidated by successful women. He also knew if he took issue with Luca's insults, he could be squashed like a bug. He put his hand in Luca's, shook it and hastily withdrew it. He did not look at the other people on the tour, so he missed the smothered grins. But he knew they were there.

"While my ex-wife mixes your herbal teas, I'll take over the tour." He pointed around at the group. "Did all of you fill out your forms on the bus? Have you turned them in? Herbal teas have ingredients like lavender and chamomile that can cause reactions to sensitive individuals, and we don't want that!"

People dug cards out of pockets, backpacks and purses and handed them to him.

He passed them to Zoey and as the group walked away, she heard him say, "After the divorce she bought the house and the property with the money she made on the Elanor. As you can see by her breaks and bruises, she was T-boned by a Hummer, hit-and-run, and she's still fragile." Luca looked down at Clifford. "I'm here to take care of the little woman. She crooks her finger and, as we men do, I come running."

This time, Clifford saw the grins, but he kept quiet because… that squashed like a bug thing.

Yet somehow, by the time Luca brought the tour back from the gardens to the workshop for their tea, Clifford was Luca's best friend and even went so far as to compliment Zoey on her tea.

She stamped their passports with the proper color ink pad and stood with Luca to wave them goodbye.

Their part of the Gothic Garden and Flower Show launch day was over.

Time for shrimp and three-cheese grits with caprese salad.

44

AS SOON AS Giuseppina finished watching the ten o'clock news, she turned the TV off. "I'm going to bed," she announced. "So should you, Zoey, if you've got a dozen garden show tours tomorrow."

Zoey wanted to groan at the thought. "Only five. And four on Sunday. I'll be done by three. Because we will remain on schedule!" She chopped the edge of her hand in her palm in a pretty good imitation of Angelica.

"I can take over when Zoey wants me to." Luca grinned at her. "I have more experience handling the hecklers."

"Garden show hecklers." Giuseppina snorted. She pointed at Zoey. "You can brush your teeth in here. Luca can use the bathroom outside. There's no reason for more intimacy than necessary."

"Nothing happened last night," Zoey said.

Giuseppina intoned, "One night down out of all the rest of your lives."

Zoey and Luca paused in the act of standing up.

Zoey supposed Giuseppina didn't realize what she'd said, but she'd made it sound as if they would forever be battling unbridled desire. Every night. Night after night. "Okay!" She didn't dare meet Luca's gaze. "I'll be out in a quickie! I mean, not a…" She vacated the living room.

When she came back out, Giuseppina was on the bed in a comfortable-looking pair of pajamas, reading a book, a historical romance if the cover was anything to go by. "I've read that!" Zoey said.

"I got it off your shelf." Giuseppina marked her place with her finger and leveled a look on Zoey. "Where do you suppose this writer learned how to write so much sex?"

"I don't know." Zoey edged toward the door. She didn't want to discuss sex with Giuseppina. Not now. Not ever. "The bathroom's all yours!"

Giuseppina was apparently oblivious. "I remember when Luca's father and I were newly married. We did it everywhere. On the stairs, on the coffee table, on the kitchen counters…"

Horror-stricken, Zoey froze in place. *I've chopped vegetables on those counters!*

"The first time we visited Italy, we slept on a bed with an iron frame. We broke it." Giuseppina chuckled. "Carmine had to take it to the welder to get it fixed. The men laughed at him. The women… I had to guard him. You never met him, but Carmine was a big man like Luca, very vigorous. Like Luca, I suppose?"

Was Zoey supposed to agree or deny?

"You knew there was a reason we had seven children, of course."

Zoey nodded. Barely.

"I do miss Carmine. When you're used to a man in your bed, it is a sad loss when he's gone."

Zoey choked out something like, "Good night," and fled. She met Luca coming out of the shower. "Your mother!" she gasped, and followed him into the shop.

"Now what'd she do?"

"She told me about your father and their sex life."

He started toward the stairs. "Please don't tell me."

She flung out an arm. "What is wrong with that woman? Is she tormenting us because we promised not to have sex? Does she get actual joy out of seeing us suffer?"

Luca stopped, turned around and strolled toward her wearing a smile and a pair of boxer shorts. "Are you suffering because we can't have sex?"

"No." She was not going to back away, and he was delusional if he thought he could intimidate her.

"Because I am. Suffering."

Not intimidation. Temptation.

"Ever since I picked you up at the hospital, I've felt guilty because you were in such dire shape, probably because of my involvement with that serial killer case." Luca stopped so close his toes touched her toes. "My mind understands I can't touch you except to help you, and my body wants to bang your brains out."

"My brains are fine where they are." His chest, always a magnificently muscled acre of masculine beauty, was right in front of her nose. The heat rose off him and carried his scent to her nose. A scent she was sure he'd deliberately imbued with massive amounts of pheromones.

Two could play that game. She didn't have to suffer alone, damn it! She put her nose on his breastbone and took a long, slow sniff. And with her tongue took one dainty lick.

All that male bravado collapsed. He grabbed her shoulders, placed her at arm's length. "We promised Ma we wouldn't—"

The familiar, spicy, sexual taste of him lingered in her mouth. "Wouldn't what?"

"Have sex in here."

Held out like this, the intoxicating scent of him faded, but not her body's knowledge she was ready, and he was ready, and they were starving. She whispered, "What were we thinking?"

"We were thinking sex between us was a bad idea."

"Because it was so good?"

"Yes!"

They gazed at each other, memories of warm, sweet, fragrant nights, of a rosebud stroked along an inner thigh, followed by lips, lingered before them like ghosts of passionate nights past.

He removed his hands with great deliberation and moved toward the door.

"What are you doing?"

"I'm going for a walk."

"Again? You're barefoot!" And mostly naked.

"I'll step carefully." He strode out. It was definitely a stride, long legs making fast work of the distance between her and the door.

"Yeah?" she yelled. "I'm going for a walk, too." She was hot, irritated and horny. She watched Luca's dim figure hurry downhill on the path to the secret garden. A brief electronic flash of light as he put his finger on the lock and opened the gate, and he was inside.

She wanted to smile, and she wanted to cry, to see him take refuge in the place she'd made to give her succor from the memories of him. Taking a pillow and a blanket off her stupid, narrow cot, she flung it over her arm and headed out into the night.

There was no moon, only stars in a black night sky, the scents of growing things and night-blooming flowers, and the faint, far roaring of the Pacific Ocean.

She had only one place to be. In the secret garden with Luca.

45

LUCA LOVED ZOEY.

Luca loved sex.

Luca loved sex with Zoey.

He made his way through the maze through the cavern of night to the center of the garden, stood on the spot in the lawn where his bare feet crushed the grass and he could look up and see into the center of the universe—and he opened his arms wide and gave the Damned Luck Roar.

This Roar was compounded of frustration, desire, irritation and fear that he had somehow failed to protect his wife from the focused malice of the Coach. This house, this shop, this property was safe; he'd done everything in his power to make it so. But the Coach was still at large and gaining strength from his continued success. When Luca was gone from her world, Zoey would walk to the store or visit her mother and she would be exposed to danger, and Luca would never be free of his terror and his guilt. If he could, he would love her, sleep with her, watch over her, never let her out of his—

He heard a rustle as someone came through the hedge and swung around, fists up, to face... Zoey.

She stood there in the starlight, a practical shadow with a pillow in one hand, a blanket flung over her arm.

"You followed me." He was not happy. How could he be, when he loved her, wanted her, and knew that if he claimed her again, a maniacal killer would end her life?

"Of course I followed you." She spread the blanket on the ground. "We promised your mother we would not have sex in my shop. We did not, in fact, promise we never would have sex again."

He had to take a stand. "We're betraying the promise in the details." He was taking a stupid stand.

"If she didn't want us to have sex anywhere but in the shop, she should have been more specific. Luca..." Zoey stepped close to him, put her hand on his cheek and leaned into his body. "We face a world of danger, where a crazed killer would take our lives for no more reason than a physical contest filled with artificial rules. Luca, we face death tonight. We face death tomorrow. There's never been a time when death hasn't stalked us. This is all there is. You and me, skin against skin, body against body." Her hands slid in slow possession around his waist. "Tomorrow is a day of gardens, of tourists, of your mother and my mother and daylight and worry. Tonight is a moment out of time. Luca, we never have to speak of this again, but tonight, let's be together."

She was right. They had this moment, and possibly never another.

"No one can see us," she whispered. "We are alone in a locked garden."

"Then let's see what we remember about each other." He picked her up and placed her on the blanket. "Let's make new memories."

46

ZOEY HOPPED OUT of the outdoor shower, dried herself and donned her favorite sundress with bright flowers on a black background and a pair of comfortable sneakers. She debated going into the house for breakfast. After last night, the idea of meeting Giuseppina face-to-face was daunting. Not that it mattered; Giuseppina lived in Zoey's house. Sooner or later they had to run into each other. If only Giuseppina didn't have such a keen intuition about what her children were up to. Or perhaps it was how successfully she raised the specter of guilt about events that were—should be—none of her business. After all, Zoey and Luca had stuck to their promise. No lovemaking in the shop. Nope. They hadn't been even close to the shop.

Zoey headed for the house, where Luca had gone to give Giuseppina whatever help she needed.

Starlight and moonlight, crushed grass and the nighttime scents of gardenias and wisteria.

She swerved toward the shop, broke out the box of dry cereal and the almond milk, ate a bowl and put the dishes in the sink. She filled the kettle, plugged it in, and while her tea was brewing, she donned her gardening apron and went again to check on her seeds. She talked to them, coaxed them, praised them, patted the earth around them. When she got to the still-empty tray where she'd planted her one precious poppy seed, she took a fortifying breath, lifted the plastic lid and looked for any hint of green.

Nothing. Still nothing.

If this seed didn't germinate soon, she would have to admit defeat. It wasn't fair. She'd spent so much time in the hospital while the life in those seeds had faded. She so wanted this plant to have a chance at life. Yes, the beautiful color and shape would sweep the flower world as a bestseller, and Zoey Phoenix would be the proud breeder.

She liked the attention, she admitted that. But for her, there was something more; the desperate desire to help return vibrant life to a plant driven nearly to extinction by man, by climate change, by pollution, perhaps by the sad knowledge of other passings. If this plant grew and flourished, the world would be a brighter place.

Leaning down, she breathed on the soil, placed her palm over the slight mound that marked the place where the seed nestled. Putting in all her joy of the night before and all her hope for the days ahead, she whispered, "Come into the light. Feel the sun, breathe the air, lift your leaves. Thrust your roots deep. Then open a blossom and feel the earth rejoice!"

She closed her eyes and imagined that seed stirring in the soil, rising, reaching, breaking the surface...

She felt a movement against her palm, the slightest kiss of pleasure, and jumped back in surprise.

The plant was there, miniature, gray-green, stem bent, then popping erect, thrusting its first leaves up, then more fernlike foliage. It was in a hurry to make up for lost time. "You darling!" She beamed, adjusted the flat so it could stay in the sun longer. "What about you other two?" she said to the other seeds. "Do you want to be outdone by your sister?"

Another plant popped up. And the other.

Zoey's throat closed in emotion. "Wonderful," she whispered. "You're wonderful," and she caressed the plants with a light touch. Going to the other plants, she told them about the revival of an old flower made new, knew they would exalt in their new friends. She watered, fertilized, smiled and hummed.

It had been a very good night followed by a very good morning. She didn't want to give Luca all the credit...but surely his dedication to giving her pleasure had provided fertility to a seed balanced between life and death...

Zoey got a notification on her watch that someone had crossed onto her property. She frowned. She didn't expect the first garden tour for another hour.

She popped out the door and saw a silver Corvette parked in front of the house and a tall, well-muscled guy hefting himself out of the driver's seat. She sighed. Sure. Ripley Rath was here; why not more of Luca's wrestling friends?

Zoey stripped off her gloves and went over to meet him. "Hi there," she called. "I'm over here!"

The man turned away from the porch and walked toward her. When they got close, he said, "I'm Mark Torbinson." He watched as if waiting to see if she knew the name.

She didn't recognize him. "You're a wrestler."

"No. Not at all. I'm... Mark Torbinson."

That probably meant he was a news reporter from San Francisco or LA, someone Angelica had scrounged up to cover the festival and bring in the tourists. She'd done it in previous years, and when it came to flowers, Zoey was the star. She didn't mind doing her part to spread the word, so she gestured him down toward the sunlight garden where her most obvious experiments thrived. Or not. "I'm Zoey Phoenix. You probably know I'm a flower breeder, and my part of the Gothic Garden and Flower Show is to explain to the public how that works and display a few of my trials and successes."

"Oh." He looked blank. "Yes, I looked you up online."

"Good, you did your research." That helped. Having to explain her job from the ground up was exasperating. "My most obvious success was the development of the Elanor dianthus which if you've bought a bouquet lately, you've probably noted as a backdrop for the flashier flowers. From the time I got the idea until I had a viable specimen took four years."

"Wow, that's a long time." He seemed to be warming to the subject.

"That was fast for someone working on their own. Most new flowers are developed by large corporations with lots of researchers and huge budgets."

"How did you do it alone?"

"A good part of flower breeding is having a feel for what will work in the first place and what's possible to replicate repeatedly. The process involves well-kept records and some long nights." And why not? Luca had been gone nights, anyway. "For the last two years, I've been breeding vegetables. Not nearly as flashy but gardeners do love their purple carrots and pink potatoes!"

For the first time, he smiled. "I'm a big fan of coleslaw. Have you thought of breeding a cabbage that's both purple and green?"

She stared at him, struck by the idea. "No, but that's an interesting challenge. Wait a minute." She pulled a stack of sticky notes from her apron pocket and scribbled it down, then stuck it in the other pocket. "It doesn't do to depend on my memory. When I get really involved with one process, everything else flies out of my brain." They reached the sunlit garden and she gave him a brief overview of the plants growing there, pulled a carrot for him and cleaned it off, handed it over, then began the brisk task of sending him on his way.

He interrupted her. "Do you know who I am?"

"Mark Torbinson."

"Yes, but—do you know what I'm doing here?"

"Reporting?"

"No. Didn't you get a package—?"

Luca came running out the door of the house and down toward them.

47

ZOEY PROMPTLY FORGOT MARK TORBINSON. "What is it?" she asked Luca.

"Hi," Luca said to the guy who seemed obsessed with everybody knowing his name. "Listen, I've got to talk to my wife for a minute."

"I'm not your…" She gave up. He wasn't being a jerk; he didn't even notice that he'd said it. "What is it?"

"I got a message to meet my contact at the tearoom in a half hour."

His FBI contact, he meant. "About time." Which was unfair, but really. They needed to know who was in their corner, and if any progress had been made finding the killer here in Gothic.

"I know. He's got something to tell me." He gave her the meaningful face. "About certain events."

"Oh-kay." Zoey was still in the dark, but if Luca thought it was important that he should go, he should go. "Security system is on and, except for Shasta, very effective."

"I'm calling the firm about that today. No one should be able to sneak through the perimeter, not unless they can hack the system and I can't believe an artist can do *that*."

"Shasta is good with computers, but why would she bother? I'm pretty sure she's not the Coach."

"No." But he frowned.

"Will you take the ATV?"

"I'll run, get some exercise and get there sooner than trying to drive through festival traffic and find a place to park. You'll be careful? Keep an eye out?" For the first time, he sized up the man standing in the background. "Who did you say you were?"

"Mark Torbinson." Mark had taken to enunciating clearly.

Luca studied him. "I've seen you at the gym."

"Yes!" Mark seemed pleased to be recognized for whatever reason.

Luca pulled Zoey close and spoke into her ear. "He seems harmless, but you know how to call security."

"I do."

Luca took the opportunity to kiss her on the mouth, and when he pulled back, she smiled in bemusement. "You really need to work on your confidence."

He smiled back. "Is it lacking?"

"Nothing's lacking, as you well know."

They heard a sigh as Mark Torbinson headed up the path to his car.

"Who did you say that was?" Luca asked.

"Not sure. I assumed he was a reporter." Now she felt foolish about giving him her professional flower breeder routine.

"I'll find out what he wanted." Luca caught up with him, spoke for a minute.

Mark got in the Corvette, made a U-turn and hit the highway headed toward town.

Luca spoke into his watch, gave her a wave and ran uphill through the grass headed to the tearoom.

Zoey got the text:

He says he needs to speak with you about a package that was sent from Citation, California. Did you get one?

She texted back:

No. Last I heard Mrs. Kulshan has it.

Bad luck. He seemed pretty intent about it. Suppose it's the dragon?

"Huh." She replied,

That makes sense. What has this Mark guy got to do with it, though?

Don't know. Mrs. Kulshan'll be home today. We'll find stuff out then.

Zoey hoped so. Not only was she now incredibly curious, but if she was to judge by Mark Torbinson's behavior, the package was important. Because it was a dragon?

She grinned as she hiked up to her shop. At least she would always remember his name.

Then she promptly forgot it. All that mattered as she hurried inside was the knowledge those three seeds had sprouted and she had taken the giant first step to recreating a lost floral treasure.

48

A LIGHT KNOCK on the wide-open garage door turned Zoey from her delight in her plants to face the entrance, and Ripley strolled into the shop, dabbing her forehead with a white work-out towel. When she saw Zoey, she looked disappointed and sounded annoyed. "Hi, is Luca around?"

Zoey smiled warmly. Today she was feeling charitable to everyone, even Ripley Rath, who treated her so dismissively. "He went into town to meet someone."

"You're kidding. Now?" Ripley looked around as if Zoey had hidden him somewhere. "I got a message to meet him here."

Zoey lifted her hands to indicate she knew nothing of that. "I'm surprised you didn't pass each other on the road."

"I cut across country to get here." Ripley looked around. "Are you sure he's not around somewhere?"

That tone of accusation irked Zoey, and she snapped, "What do you think, that I'm hiding him? Luca? Have you seen how big he is?"

Ripley rounded on Zoey with a mixture of emotions in her eyes like Zoey had never seen, and she was suddenly aware that Ripley stood six feet tall with a female weight lifter's physique and the swift reflexes necessary to succeed in women's wrestling. While Zoey…well, Zoey was healthy and strong, used to digging in the soil and walking miles over the hills in search of rare plants, but she wasn't a fighter, had in fact turned her back so firmly on fighting she refused to think about any kind of violence at all.

Zoey also remembered the warning Luca had given her about someone who had taken a fancy to him as a wrestler, had decided he would be the world's best wrestler if stripped of all distractions like a wife, friends and family, and the FBI believed that the profile fit a serial killer, well-known for his sports enthusiasm. Whoever the killer was, he routinely followed the pattern of murder of family and friends and finally of the sports figure himself.

The FBI believed the killer was male. Luca had concurred. The witness who saw the cement truck hit-and-run believed the driver was male. The vehicle that ran Zoey off the road had been a Hummer, usually a man's vehicle. Most important—most serial killers were male.

Ripley Rath most definitely was not male. Tall, yes, fit, yes, but feminine in her dress, manner, sexuality. She liked men and men liked her. But… Yeah, but.

Ripley said, "You really ought to let Luca go back to wrestling."

"Me? I've got nothing to do with it." Zoey opened a drawer, selected a pair of small, sharp pruning shears and placed them on the counter. "He didn't quit until I divorced him."

"He didn't have the heart for it anymore. I don't think he cared about anything. I ran into him once in New York. We had lunch. I made a pass." Ripley bared her teeth. "First time in my life I've ever been rejected."

"Oh." Zoey knew she'd fumbled that answer.

"Are you glad to hear that?"

"No. I wish he had found another life without me." If he

had, maybe she wouldn't hurt at the idea of him refusing all offers. She had been so bruised from the last year of their marriage she'd only thought of herself, but now, seeing him here, she wanted him to be happy.

"He only ever cared about you." Ripley sounded resentful.

For Luca to be happy, he needed Zoey.

"Now you're back together." More resentful.

Zoey decided it seemed a good time to shape a few of the plants that had been repotted after the shop was vandalized. "Why do you say that?"

"Because you are. It's obvious. You get hurt. He rushes to your side."

Zoey picked up the shears and made a few random clips. "My mother asked him."

"He stays with you. Sleeps with you."

How did she know? "We have not slept together." A knee-jerk denial—and the truth; what they'd done in the garden was not sleep.

"I don't believe that. Since he's arrived here, he looks happy."

"Because he's about to—" *Shut up, Zoey.*

Was Luca's serial killer standing before her?

No, because Luca said the FBI had profiled the killer as male.

Yet remembering Luca's story of Ripley's upbringing, recalling Ripley's own wildly illogical rejection of her own injuries and allergies…it seemed likely that this woman was disturbed.

Disturbed enough to kill? To kill repeatedly?

Zoey glanced at the whistle she'd hung on a hook behind the sink.

She glanced at Ripley.

Their eyes met.

Ripley was watching her too intently.

"What's wrong?" Ripley asked. "You look funny."

Zoey must be wearing her suspicions on her face.

What if the FBI profiler was wrong this time? Was Ripley

actually an obsessed killer? Did she suspect Zoey was onto her? Zoey made up her mind. She turned her back to Ripley—a daring move, to Zoey's mind—slipped her clippers into her apron, then rummaged in the upper cupboard. "I promised to make tea for my mother-in-law to ease her pain." Which wasn't a lie. She had a standing order to make tea for Giuseppina.

This time she chose her red-lacquered dragon teapot with its wild grin, long claws and thrashing scaled tail that formed the handle. Luca had given it to her in college, and the dragon made her smile. The wild beast spoke to her about courage. She needed that courage.

She placed it on the island in front of Ripley, then moved back and forth as she lined up her tins of herbs and dried fruits. "You can have some tea if you wish."

Ripley lit up. "I'd like that. Not that I'm in pain—" she rotated her shoulder "—but…"

Zoey hastily improvised. "My herbal tea also helps rebuild tissue and strengthen muscle."

"Yes. Strengthen." Ripley spread her fingers and looked at the palms of her hands as if assessing their strength.

Zoey looked, too, and thought how easily this woman could snap her neck with those large hands.

Don't think about that. "Fresh rose hips work better than dried, the fresher the better. I'm going out to harvest. Do you want to come along?"

"Where?"

Zoey hung a basket over her arm. "The secret garden."

Ripley lit up. "Like the book, right? You did pattern your garden after the children's book?"

Zoey started toward the door. "I did, yes."

"I loved that book. I read it at the library."

Zoey halted in surprise. "At the library? Really?"

"I read a lot of stuff at the library until someone told my father." Abruptly, Ripley's eyes turned hot and resentful, and she oozed hostility. "Let's see this secret garden of yours."

49

LUCA STEPPED INTO Mrs. Santa's Gifts and packed-to-the-gills Tea Shop and looked around.

What the hell kind of FBI contact would want to meet in a tearoom? *Unless it was a female.*

He wanted to slap his own forehead.

Of course it was a female. He'd been looking for a man and if his sisters and his wife knew that, they would join together to hurt him with a curling iron.

He wouldn't tell them.

Winifred first told him the wait for a table was eighty minutes, then realized what a good advertisement he would be seated in the front window, and in a few minutes he found himself squashed into a lady-sized chair blissfully enjoying a pot of tea and a plate of cheese crackers. He kept looking around for his contact, but although almost everyone smiled warmly at him and a few of the wrestling-fan-type tourists asked for his autograph, no one gave him any indication they wanted to speak to him personally. He'd been there a half hour when he summoned Winifred over and asked, "Have there been any messages for me?"

"I don't think so, but let me check with the elves." Moments later, she came hurrying back with one of the waitresses on her heels. "Winky didn't have a message for *you*, but—" She gestured at Winky to speak.

"Ripley Rath was here waiting for someone—I didn't know who—when she got a message to join you down at Zoey's workshop."

He stood up so fast he knocked the chair into the neighboring table. "Sorry," he said to the lady behind him, and asked Winky, "When was that?"

"I don't know. We've been so busy. I've been run off my feet, but she waved me over and told me she had to leave and could I get her her ticket? I did and it was probably...forty-five minutes ago?"

"Okay, thanks." He started to dig for his wallet.

But he must have clearly communicated his horror, because Winifred put her hand on his arm. "Don't worry about it. You can square with me next time you're in."

"Thanks again." He sprinted out the door and down the street.

Winky started cleaning his table. "You told me never to let a customer go without paying."

"He's good for it." Winifred gestured over the next customer. "Anyway, I've got him by the cheese crackers."

50

HEARING THE HOSTILITY in Ripley's voice, Zoey's breath caught. Yes, she had a plan. Was it a good one? No. It stank like rotting potatoes. But she didn't have another idea to save herself, so might as well act her part whole-heartedly. "Let's go, then." She started out the door.

Ripley caught up with her at once. "I thought your secret garden was locked."

How do you know that, Ripley? "It is. The lock opens with my fingerprint."

"Really?" For Ripley, this was obviously new technology. "Any of your fingerprints?"

"Just one." *You'll have to cut them all off and try them one by one.* Zoey stopped.

Ripley ran into the back of her, knocked her forward, grabbed her before she fell. "Sorry. Don't stop so fast in front of me!"

"Don't follow so closely," Zoey answered.

"You steady?" Ripley asked.

No one was going to cut off her fingers…the killer was not noted for mutilating his victims, merely eliminating them… If one was going to generalize, not mutilating would seem like a feminine characteristic. She scolded herself for imagining the most gruesome scenario possible. But how could she not when Ripley was big enough to knock her off her feet, fast enough to catch her, strong enough to hold her? "I'm fine," she said and, when Ripley still held her, said, "Thank you." Ripley released her, and once more Zoey started walking down the path toward the garden.

Ripley fell in beside her.

Zoey needed to concentrate on a positive outcome. She might not have Ripley's physical gifts, but she had a walled garden with a door and automatic lock. All she had to do was convince Ripley to wander inside. With Ripley's fond remembrances of the Secret Garden, she thought that might be possible, and Ripley would be held at least long enough for Zoey to call 911.

Zoey stopped again and groped in her apron pocket. She had her clippers, but she'd left her phone on the island in the shop.

Ripley stopped, too. "What's wrong now?"

"I...forgot something."

"Need me to go after it? My legs are longer than yours. I'm a lot faster."

"I know." That was part of Zoey's problem. All the guile in the world wouldn't work if she couldn't get out of that garden fast enough. As for letting Ripley get her hands on Zoey's phone...no, no, no. Zoey might never get it back. "It's fine. Not important. I forgot my...trowel." She walked again.

As if she was pointing out a personal attribute, Ripley said, "I wasn't following too close this time."

Was Ripley trying to make conversation? Or was she trying to distract Zoey from the way she moved her hands, first opened, then lightly balled into fists, then open again like someone practicing a killing hold?

Zoey had more than one option. If this didn't work, she would try the tea. And like Ripley, she should make conversation as if it was normal to think she was about to die. In a chipper voice that would have felt right for a nutritional video, she said, "Rose hips are high in vitamin C, but most is lost in the drying process, and they're often used for osteoarthritis. Not that it's ever been scientifically proved to be effective."

"Mrs. Damezas seems to think it works."

Zoey strode down the hill through the tall grass. The scent of the ocean gave her strength and courage. "Perhaps for her it's psychosomatic."

"Do you believe that?"

"I believe if it works, it works." Zoey smiled as the old memory surfaced. "But when I first gave it to her, she was determined that it wouldn't. She didn't like me much."

"Does she now?" Ripley's voice was neutral.

"No. Not... I don't know." Zoey pointed to the beehives positioned between the two gardens. "The bees pollinate my flowering plants. Since you're allergic, you'll want to avoid being stung. Stay away from the flowers like Old Blush and Crimson Glory." She pointed at the antique roses, climbing up the inside wall and draping over to soften the outer stones. "They are prolific rose hips producers, and very attractive to bees."

They reached the garden door.

"Don't climb them," Zoey added for emphasis.

"I can safely promise that." Ripley was fervent.

We'll see. Zoey swiftly and she hoped secretively touched the lock with her left index finger. The lock clicked and she pushed the door open. "After you." She gestured Ripley inside.

Ripley walked through the gate and into the garden. She gave a satisfying gasp. "This is...fabulous. Just as I imagined it when I was reading."

No softening, Zoey. This is your one chance to escape a horrible death.

Without drawing breath, Ripley continued, "How much ground do you have here?"

Zoey lingered in the doorway and made a show of searching

along the woody rose canes that had already borne a flower and now drooped with small round orange rose hips. "Not quite an acre." She clipped one, two, three and dropped them into her basket.

As Ripley wandered farther inside, she spread her arms as if embracing the space. "It feels so much larger."

Unwillingly, Zoey warmed to Ripley. "I designed it to be a wilderness of flowers."

"It's so fragrant." Ripley found the path and walked toward the hedge. "Is that a maze?"

"It is." Keeping an eye on Ripley, Zoey clipped haphazardly at the rose hips.

"I've heard there's always a secret to a maze." Ripley disappeared behind the hedge.

Zoey dropped the clippers into the basket and started to step out of the garden.

But Ripley popped back out, her eyes bright with anticipation. "What's the secret of this one?"

Zoey had to tell the big lie. "Keep your right hand on the hedge and you'll reach the other door."

Ripley put her hand on the hedge and took a few steps, enough to disappear into the maze. "Another door?" she called.

"A secret door." Zoey kept her voice low. She felt as if she was betraying Ripley. *Face it, Zoey, simply because Ripley is thrilled about your garden, doesn't mean she isn't the serial killer.*

"A secret door for a secret garden." Ripley sounded delighted, and farther away, deeper into the maze. "I love the fragrances. This feels so wild and… Zoey, where are you? Are you coming?"

The last question was directed back at the start of the maze.

In a calm, firm voice, Zoey said, "Ripley, if you're not the killer, I apologize, but I have to save myself."

"What? No!" Ripley sounded as if she was plunging out of the maze and back toward the entrance. "Zoey, listen, it's not me. I'm the contact the FBI sent to protect you!"

"I don't believe you." Zoey stepped outside and slammed the door. The lock clicked, and she sagged against the oak panels. In a lower voice, she said, "I wish I did, but I don't."

"Shit. Shit! Where's the wall? Where's the door? I was just there." Ripley sounded as frantic as Zoey felt. She raised her voice. "I'm not the killer. Zoey, think! I couldn't have hit you with the Hummer. I was fighting that day! I won my bout. Look on your phone. I was in Cincinnati!"

Zoey ran toward her shop picking up speed with every step. "I'll look, all right. Right after I call 911."

The garage doors were down.

When she and Ripley walked out, Zoey would have sworn one had been raised. Maybe she was wrong. Or maybe—hopeful thought—Luca was back. But whatever, her phone was on the stand and she was taking the most direct route to catch the killer and keep Luca safe. And Giuseppina. And Luca's sisters. And by God, herself.

She slammed through the door and into the shop. She blinked at the shadows and leaped around the island and toward the sink and the stand that held her phone.

The phone was gone.

It had been there, she knew it had and—

From the corner of her eyes, she saw a movement. She screamed, turned and scrambled backward.

Yolanda. It was Ripley's cousin Yolanda, dressed in workout clothes and running shoes, sweatshirt tied around her waist. She was holding Zoey's phone.

Zoey put her hand on her chest over her racing heart. "You scared me," she accused. "Give me that thing. I need to call 911. And Luca. And—" She saw the bright yellow whistle on the counter, and for good measure, she picked it up and gave it a good hard blast.

Yolanda flinched and covered her ears. "What'd you do that for?"

"I've locked Ripley Rath in the garden."

"You locked my cousin in your garden?"

"Yes, but she's strong and determined, and sooner or later, probably sooner, she's going to scale the wall. I'll get help however I can get it." Giuseppina knew what that whistle meant. She would call Luca and the cops. "Now give me the phone and—"

Yolanda put Zoey's phone on the edge of the island. "Congratulations. You did what I could not. You neutralized my dear sister Ripley." She said *sister* as if it was a curse word, hit the phone with her fist, flipped it into the air and when it landed on the floor, smashed it beneath her heel. And smiled. "This is a lot more personal than mashing you and your car into a tree, and I promise, this time I won't leave until I've reduced you to nothing but a bloody, mangled carcass. That'll make Luca pay attention!"

As Zoey stared at the remnants of her phone, she knew she had made a mistake. A terrible, fatal mistake.

51

HOW TO FIX THIS?

She had to. Luca was gone, seeking his FBI contact…who Zoey had locked in the garden. She glanced at the clock on the wall. If the first garden tour was running on schedule, and she felt sure it was, the first surrey had just left Angelica's. She had forty-five minutes before the tourists arrived and found the scene of bloody carnage. Because this person, this Yolanda, would like to kill them all, all of the people who had a connection to Luca: first his wife, then his mother, then his FBI contact. The only person who could save Giuseppina, old and alone in the house, was Zoey. So…she would.

But what to do?

Her heartbeat went from rapid to galloping. Who knew standing still scared was worse than running scared?

She removed the basket from her arm, upended it and spilled the rose hips and gardening shears onto the countertop by the sink. She contemplated the shears. But no. Even supposing she could manage to stab Yolanda with them, they were too small to put a dent in that tall, muscled, efficient fighter. Still pondering, she cupped her hand around the rose hips and swept them into a little pile. She told Ripley she was going to make tea with them…

Her gaze turned back toward Yolanda, who stood motionless across the island, watching her with a cold enjoyment. "You know why I'm here, don't you?" Yolanda asked.

Zoey's gaze fell on the red dragon teapot, and at the canisters of dried herbs and fruits she had arranged beside it. She had intended to use bee-pollinated flowers and fruits to trigger an allergy attack in Ripley. With mothers who were sisters and the same father, the two women's DNAs were as entwined as two rosebushes on an arbor. This might work, and besides—what other plan did Zoey have?

"I think so," Zoey said. "Yolanda, you admire Luca's wrestling skills."

"He's the best in the business." Yolanda had the cold eyes of a snake. "Or he was, until you."

Zoey filled her teakettle, plugged it in and started it. "I'm making myself a cup of herbal tea. Would you like some?"

"Why are you doing that?" The woman was smart enough to be suspicious.

Zoey used her fingers to dribble dried minced peaches, lavender buds, chamomile flowers and cinnamon into the teapot's strainer. "You're making me nervous, so I thought a cup of chamomile and lavender tea would calm my nerves."

"I don't need to calm *my* nerves." Yolanda rotated her shoulders, her neck, as wrestlers did before they went into action.

Alienate her. Bad move. Go at it a different way, Zoey. "In your business, nerves are a hindrance, aren't they?"

"Nerves are a waste of time," Yolanda said truculently. "I *like* that moment when I step on stage, the crowd cheers and jeers, and I get to prove myself once again to those bunch of judgmental cretins."

"Luca doesn't wrestle anymore."

"He will. I can save him from this downward spiral." Yolanda's eyes glowed with a zealot's fervor.

"How will you do that?" Like Zoey didn't know the answer.

"I'll take away the distractions, help him focus once more."

Hoping for an allergy attack wasn't enough. Zoey had to do something more. She didn't know what, but definitely *more*. She took at stab at psychology. She slid a cup and saucer toward Yolanda, then slid it back. "Actually, it's probably best that you don't indulge in herbal tea."

"What do you mean?"

"For highly allergic individuals, herbal teas are a minefield."

Yolanda grabbed at the saucer and brought it to a place in front of her and across the island from Zoey. "I'm not highly allergic!"

"No, of course not. I didn't mean to insinuate there's anything sensitive about you." Zoey filled her sugar bowl with cubes and added her pair of tiny tongs. "You're very strong, but your cousin has a bee allergy—"

Yolanda laughed. "Yeah, when she was four she fell in a hive. So many stings and you should have seen her swell!"

Zoey had the suspicion Ripley might have been helped into that hive. "That explains why she's allergic to anything pollinated by bees. Flowers, stone fruits, and of course—" she got out her bear honey pot "—honey."

"That's my cousin, not me."

Zoey collected her small pitcher and filled it with almond milk. "Allergies run in families."

Yolanda waved off Zoey's warning with a sweep of her big, broad hands.

Zoey's eyes hurt from staring at those hands and imagining them killing people.

Killing other people.

Killing her.

Opening her locked cupboard, she removed the precious foxglove seeds she'd been developing in a glorious new flower color. She held the seeds between her palms and concentrated her energy, urging the seeds to release their poison. When she felt a response, she regretfully tossed them into the teapot basket. She poured the boiling water over the mix of herbs, spices, blossoms and seeds, filling the pot to the brim. "That should calm my nerves." She lifted the pot and gestured toward the cups. "If you're sure?"

"Come on! I'm thirsty!"

Zoey poured the two cups full. "Don't feel as if you should use honey as a sweetener just because I am." She added her honey and stirred while maintaining visual contact. "I won't judge you if you use sugar."

Yolanda added a generous dollop of honey and stirred vigorously. "You know, I'm wondering…"

Zoey picked up her cup and took a sip of her brew, then set her cup down. "Wondering what?"

"If you're trying to poison me." Yolanda looked at Zoey's cup.

Zoey managed surprise, and then quizzical amusement. "If you're in doubt, toss it in the sink. But I'm drinking mine. I really like the suggestion of peach and cinnamon I get from the brew. It's like pie in a cup." Actually, she already felt an unnatural buzz in her lips.

The poison in foxglove was digoxin, a cardiac glycoside used in heart medicines, and dangerous if ingested by mistake. Symptoms included nausea, headache, blurred vision, skin irritation and of course, slowed heartbeat. Zoey assured herself it was too soon for her to have any symptoms. But she blinked as she tried to focus on Yolanda. She needed to see her opponent…

Yolanda picked up her cup and took a slug. "You don't understand who I am, do you?"

"Of course I do. Why do you think you made me nervous?"

Yolanda put her cup down with a bit of a slam. "I've killed people."

"Multiple sports. Families and athletes. You hit me with the Hummer, pushed me into the tree, almost killed me."

"I thought you were dead or I would have never backed away." Yolanda was clearly disgusted with herself.

"Where did you hide the Hummer?"

"It's in an abandoned, bramble-covered barn. I stashed it and ran over the hills to Ripley's silly ass meditation center to—" Yolanda used air quotes "—discuss my cousin's requirements for her upcoming stay. Thanks to me, the people in charge detested Ripley before she even arrived."

"You plan so far ahead." Zoey placed her elbows on the island, but they hit harder than she expected and she felt the impact all the way up to her shoulder blades and down to the tips of her fingers, especially in the broken joints.

Yolanda pointed her thumb at her chest. "Successful serial killer."

Zoey kept talking. "You've never been caught or even suspected because the FBI thinks you're a man. Did you know that?"

"They're idiots."

"Yes." Time to challenge Yolanda to drink again. "What do you think of my herbal tea? You are right. You don't seem to be suffering any complications from an allergic reaction." Zoey lifted the cup to her lips. This time she barely wet her lips. Yes, convincing Yolanda to poison herself by demonstrating the brew was harmless could save Zoey's life. But killing herself in the process canceled that success, and if her vision was blurred, maybe Yolanda wouldn't notice Zoey's lack of enthusiasm.

"I'm having no reaction. Tastes great, too!" Yolanda slurped when she drank. "I love sports. I can always pick a winner, but sometimes…every time…they insist on spoiling themselves."

"Spoiling themselves?" The foxglove headache hit Zoey as hard as the Hummer had hit her car. "What do you mean?" Her tongue felt awkward. Was she forming the words?

Apparently so, because Yolanda said, "They have families. They get married. They have children. They love their mothers and fathers. When they should be concentrating on their game!" This time Yolanda drained her cup without thought or caution.

Zoey's reaction was gaining strength. Her heart began to slow. She glanced at Yolanda. Why wasn't she reacting, if not to the allergens, then to the foxglove?

Because her body mass was larger, of course. She outweighed Zoey by at least fifty pounds. Reaching over, Zoey picked up the teapot and refilled the cups. She took a sip and almost threw up—which reminded her what she should do next. Going to her drawer, she rummaged around, found her little bottle of ipecac and placed it in the sink out of sight.

"I never meant to handle a wrestling champion. I knew how dangerous it was to get close to my own sport. The FBI completely missed the connection between the first three athletes I coached. But could I depend on them not to notice my connection to wrestling?"

"The other athletes were in different sports?"

"Baseball. Hockey. Oh, and when Ripley and I toured Australia, I fell in love with Aussie football and coached one of the ruckmen. He really had it together. Didn't care about his family or friends, only cared about football." Yolanda puffed up in indignation.

Zoey looked more closely. Or maybe she was reacting to the peaches, the lavender, the honey.

"I hated to lose him," Yolanda said prosaically, "but I couldn't stick around."

Zoey didn't understand. Maybe it was the poison. Or maybe this didn't make sense. "How's he doing without you?"

"Didn't you hear what I said? I couldn't let him do it on his own. Before I left the country, I had to kill him." Yolanda sounded matter-of-fact, as if that was logical.

Zoey was horrified. So once Yolanda picked out a champion,

win or lose, there was no escape. Yolanda meant to kill Giuseppina, all Luca's sisters and Zoey. But inevitably, she would kill Luca, too, and she was tall and strong, and with the element of surprise on her side, she would succeed.

Yolanda's face flushed; she was sweating.

Yes. Her cheeks had puffed, making her squint. She was reacting to the allergens and the poison! Maybe, just maybe, the combination would bring her down. Zoey had to keep her distracted. "You said you never meant to handle a wrestling champion."

"Because I knew someone in the FBI might figure it out if I got too close to my home ground." She scratched at her arms. "Why have I got a rash?"

"Did Ripley have a rash when she reacted to the honey?"

"No."

"Then you're okay." Zoey tossed that off with a fair amount of insouciance, which was pretty good for someone who was afraid she was going to die of a self-induced poisoning before Yolanda could murder her. "Why Luca? What about Luca made you break your own rule?"

"My God, Luca." Yolanda clasped her hands at her chest. "With the right coaching, he could have won every bout. I *had* to tell him how to improve. It was my destiny. You understand that, right?"

"Right. So you wrote him letters."

"I instructed him!"

"But...?"

"He lost focus. Because of his mother. Because of his sisters." Yolanda aimed her attention at Zoey. "Mostly because of you. You who...did something to me. I feel sick. I feel dizzy." In a lightning-fast move, she vaulted the island, grabbed Zoey by her hair and shoved her against the counter beside the sink and shouted, "What did you feed me?"

52

THE PAIN IN Zoey's scalp helped to clear her vision. "What do you mean?"

"My heart's pounding." Yolanda glared into Zoey's face. "I'm seeing yellow halos around the lights."

Yolanda towered over Zoey, teeth bared, eyes bloodshot, cheeks mottled. She blinked hard as if trying to clear her vision. In another few minutes, the poison would take hold and Yolanda would go down.

But that wouldn't save Zoey. In another few minutes, she would be in a coma. In another few minutes... Zoey wanted to cry, to beg Yolanda to release her. But that wasn't the way to handle Yolanda. Instead she said, "I told you you might react to the tea. You wouldn't listen."

"I don't have an allergy. I'm not weak. *I'm not like Ripley.*"

"You're swelling," Zoey assured her and pointed toward the mirror above the sink. "Look. You definitely have an allergy." An allergy compounded by the foxglove.

Yolanda tightened her fist in Zoey's hair and meticulously grasped Zoey's jaw with her other hand. "I'm going to break your neck. It's faster than you deserve—you deserve to die a slow, horrible death for what you've done to Luca and me—but whatever you fed me…" She shook her head like a wet dog and muttered, "I don't have time." Her hands clenched.

Zoey only had one weapon. Lifting her left hand, she rammed her two broken, splinted fingers in Yolanda's eye.

Yolanda shrieked, released Zoey, staggered back with her hands over her face.

The impact jolted Zoey's poor abused fingers and she fought back the pain that seared her nerves all the way to her brain. She dropped to the ground, tried to stand and run, staggered as adrenaline and foxglove combined to destroy her nervous system.

Yolanda looked up. A bloody tear ran down her cheek. She gazed up at Zoey, and a demon stared out of those red-rimmed eyes. In a guttural voice, she said, "I'm going to make you sorry." She looked around, saw the pruning shears and grasped them by the handles. She lifted them before her face, turned them, admired them with her eyes. "So petite. Most people wouldn't know how to kill someone with these. But I know."

Zoey tried to sprint around the island. She barely kept her footing.

Yolanda grabbed her arm, swung her around, pushed her up against the counter again and pressed the clippers up under Zoey's chin. She opened them slowly. "This is going to hurt," she promised.

The door swung all the way open. It slapped the wall behind it.

Yolanda jumped.

Zoey hoped.

Giuseppina said in her bossiest voice, "Get away from my daughter-in-law."

Yolanda surveyed Giuseppina's skinny, emaciated, black-clad figure.

From the corners of her eyes, Zoey looked at her mother-in-law. She had a valiant heart, but no chance against a brute like Yolanda. "Ma, please go away," she said.

Giuseppina paid no heed to Zoey's plea. She pointed a crooked, arthritic, old finger at Yolanda. "You! The big girl! I'll tell you one more time. Get away from my daughter-in-law."

Yolanda took a firmer hold on Zoey's squirming body and grinned. "What are you going to do, Granny? Hit me with your bag?"

"No." Giuseppina pulled a small caliber pistol out of her large leather purse. "I'm going to shoot you."

53

YOLANDA HAD ONE moment to realize she was fucked.

The pistol blasted.

Yolanda screamed. Dropped the shears. Staggered away. Fell in a heap and writhed on the floor.

"Kids nowadays." Giuseppina hobbled over and placed the pistol on the island. "No respect. You all right, honey?"

Zoey stood gasping, holding her throat with one hand, holding the countertop with the other. She tried to speak, but could only croak.

Giuseppina moved faster than Zoey ever remembered. In a moment Zoey was seated on a barstool with a cool, wet cloth against her forehead, held there by a crooning Giuseppina, who at the same time dialed 911 on her own cell phone. When the dispatcher answered, she told Yolanda to shut up or she'd shoot her again.

Yolanda did shut up.

Zoey thought the dispatcher heard the threat and informed law enforcement before Giuseppina finished the sentence. She smiled.

Giuseppina filled the dispatcher in on the details in a clear, firm voice, then hung up. "Law enforcement is sending a helicopter." She leaned close to Zoey and in a low voice said, "Getting older doesn't necessarily mean wisdom. Daughter, I wish you to know that even the elderly—like me—can say the wrong thing, do the wrong thing, hurt the wrong person."

Zoey blinked and thought she must be suffering from a foxglove-induced hallucination. It almost sounded as if Giuseppina was apologizing for being such a battle-ax.

"I thought you were too much like your plants, part of another world of fluttering blossoms and green growth. I thought my son needed an earthy woman, and forgot that seeds germinated in the soil and thrust their roots deep to grow strong." Giuseppina's dark brown eyes gave Zoey The Look, but it wasn't the, *Damn you to hell* Look. This was possessive, more like the, *You are one of mine* and *Let's start again* Look. "You will breed good sons."

Incensed, Zoey tried to say something. Something rude. But her throat ached, her voice still didn't work and all she could do was croak incoherent words of indignation.

Giuseppina grinned at her. The damned woman had reset their relationship. Zoey was now her daughter and Giuseppina could happily treat her as she did her other daughters, prodding and poking while at the same time defending her against outsiders.

Zoey relaxed. She guessed it beat the alternative, especially since today, the alternative was Death by Yolanda.

Heavy, running footsteps sounded from outside.

Giuseppina pointed the gun at the open door with a steady hand.

Ripley raced into the shop, skidded to a stop, took in the scene: Yolanda bleeding on the ground, Zoey's waxy-pale face, Giuseppina's still and deadly face. And the pistol aimed at her heart.

Zoey gently placed her hand on Giuseppina's wrist and pushed it down.

Giuseppina didn't take her gaze away from Ripley. "She's okay?" she asked Zoey.

"Yes," Zoey assured her. "She's okay."

Ripley sighed in relief, then turned to her sister/cousin and exclaimed in disgust, "Really, Yolanda. You? All along, you? What did you intend to do if you were caught? Place the blame on me? I'm not Papa. It won't work. Law enforcement needs evidence!"

"There's evidence you were in on it!" Yolanda said viciously. "I made sure of that."

Giuseppina pointed the knob of her cane at her. "I told you to shut up. All I will allow you to do now is bleed. Warning, Missy! I can make you bleed more!"

Yolanda froze.

Zoey thought Yolanda wasn't afraid of anyone in the world… except Giuseppina. Deservedly so.

With a dismissive flick of her fingers, Ripley turned her back on her cousin and said to Zoey, "Those roses are a bitch to climb and those bees—"

Ripley was, Zoey realized, scratched by thorns and swelling from multiple stings on her face, throat and hands. That was the only thing that could have made her struggle out of Giuseppina's grip and off the stool. "She's going to die if I don't," she told Giuseppina in her raspy, wobbly voice.

Giuseppina muttered imprecations in Italian and eased herself onto a chair.

Zoey used her fingernail to flip the stingers out of Ripley's skin. "Any more?" she asked Ripley repeatedly. "Any more?" She dragged her over to the sink and told her to wash the stings with soap and water. While Ripley was doing that, Zoey started her electric kettle again. She rummaged through her cupboards, popped the lids on her herb containers, mixed calendula, willow, stinging nettle and witch hazel with honey to make a thick paste.

Ripley watched and in a raspy voice asked, "Honey? Are you trying to kill me off because I didn't get here early enough?"

Zoey cupped the glass in her hands and coaxed the plants to

release their helpful chemicals. "It'll help until the ambulance gets here."

"For her!" Ripley pointed at Yolanda, who was whimpering, clutching her hip, scooting around on the floor.

"The big baby," Giuseppina said with scorn. "She's not going to bleed *to death*, more's the shame. I used to be a better shot."

Zoey gave her mother-in-law a look. "You saved me. I owe you."

"Don't be a jackass. You're family. You owe me nothing." Giuseppina cackled. "Besides, if she dies, it's because you fixed her one of your brews. Back in Italy, I knew a woman like you. Scary. Dangerous. I'm glad you're on my side." She scrutinized Zoey from head to toe. "You look better. Not as ill. Did you heal yourself?"

Zoey realized she had. Just as she had urged the foxglove to release its poison and take over Yolanda's body, once the crisis was over she had given the foxglove permission to lessen the poisons in her own body. She didn't know how; it was all instinct. She nodded to Giuseppina. "I am better."

"Good." Giuseppina slid a glance at Yolanda. "You must have pulled the poison from her, too. She's not as swollen. No matter. The bullet'll keep her down." But she watched Yolanda's writhings with suspicion.

"Ripley, you're the one who needs to have an open airway until the EMTs can give you an adrenaline injector." Zoey slathered the ointment on the stings on Ripley's face and throat. "Why didn't they give you one after your last reaction?"

"They gave me a prescription."

Zoey gestured impatiently. "Where is it?"

"I didn't get it filled."

Zoey forgot her throat hurt and shouted at Ripley. She got in her face and shouted loud and long. She told Ripley people cared about her and that Ripley owed her fans and her friends a long and healthy life.

Ripley tried to interrupt several times.

Zoey told her to shut up and kept shouting. When she finally wound down, more from loss of voice than fading indignation, Ripley was sitting, quiet and subdued, rubbing the ointment into the stings Zoey hadn't seen. "This really does make them feel better," she said. And, "Does this mean we're friends?"

In Ripley's eyes, Zoey saw something she'd never taken the time to see before: loneliness. "Of course we're friends." She knew better than to follow that up with a hug or more kind words; Ripley didn't know how to handle affection. "You're still going to have to go to the hospital."

"I don't want to go."

"Then you should have got an adrenaline injector and you should carry it with you always!"

"I don't want to carry a—"

"I don't want to try to pull you back from the verge of death every time you climb a rosebush, either! Sucks to be you, you big whiner!" From the look on Ripley's face, Zoey thought she might have overdone it this time. She hoped Giuseppina wouldn't have to shoot Ripley, too, when Luca burst through the door.

He took a look around, assessed the scene and collapsed against the door, gasping. "Ran...all...the way...from...the tea shop... Passed the garden tour...almost here..."

"Running downhill." Yolanda came up on one elbow. "If you were mine, you'd be in prime shape!" She pulled a pistol from beneath her and aimed at Luca.

Before Zoey could draw breath to scream, Giuseppina shot Yolanda. Again.

The pistol flew out of Yolanda's grip. She flopped backward bleeding from the arm.

"That's better," Giuseppina said in satisfaction. "Practice makes perfect. I'm getting my old aim back."

54

LUCA MET THE surrey as it pulled into the yard and herded the tourists past the shop and toward the gardens. They returned to the surrey in time to see two ambulances and two law enforcement vehicles, alive with lights and sirens, turn into the yard. They wanted to stay and ogle, but Deputy Dave insisted they move on to the next stop.

Luca called up to the Tower, spoke to Marjorie and informed her of the change. She put him on speakerphone and let him repeat it for the newly arrived from the hospital Angelica Lindholm.

Angelica mumbled something.

"I didn't understand that," he said.

"She's had her jaw wired shut," Marjorie told him. "She said, 'Can't this town have one festival or tour without murder and mayhem?'"

"Gothic is simply living up to its well-advertised reputation as a center of mystical energy," he answered. "Surely you didn't think the tourists really came to look at the gardens?" He hung up, satisfied he'd given Angelica something to think about other than the pain of a shovel to the face.

The EMTs loaded Yolanda into an ambulance first, giving priority to the person with two gunshot wounds, possible anaphylactic shock and foxglove poisoning. By the time they got to Ripley, she was having trouble breathing and she underwent treatment and transportation without protest.

All the while, law enforcement interviewed Zoey, Giuseppina and Luca for their versions of the events. Deputy Dave, the officer who handled most cases occurring in Gothic, did most of the questioning. His recurring question was… "Mrs. Damezas, are you sure you shot the victim twice?"

"Victim?" Giuseppina snorted. "She's no victim. She's a cold-blooded killer."

"It's true," Zoey said. "She tried to kill me."

"By poisoning you with foxglove?" Deputy Dave was clearly trying to sort the events in his mind.

"No, no. I poisoned her to save my own life." Zoey pressed a hand to her stomach. "I still don't feel well."

"You poisoned yourself, too?" Deputy Dave clarified.

"I had to, to get her to drink the tea." Zoey didn't think it was smart to mention she'd heightened the poison in the seeds, then cured herself. That would sound crazier than drinking poison in the first place. "I have a natural immunity."

"Right. We'll assume most of the damage to Yolanda was done by the two gunshots." Deputy Dave turned back to Giuseppina. "Mrs. Damezas, I understand why you shot the alleged cold-blooded killer the first time. You walked into the shop and she had overcome Zoey Phoenix, who you call your daughter-in-law, and was threatening her with pruning shears held under her throat."

"That's right." Giuseppina nodded.

"Why did you shoot the second time?"

"When I shot her the first time, I missed."

"You missed?"

"I hit her in the hip. I meant to hit her in the chest."

"I see."

"She fell down, screamed and cried." Giuseppina gloated. "Served her right."

Luca interjected, "Yolanda is a serial killer who specializes in eliminating the families of sports figures."

"The hell you say," Deputy Dave said, startled. "How do you know that?"

"Because of my wrestling, I was involved in the search for the killer."

Giuseppina pivoted toward her son. "The hell you say."

Luca shut his mouth with a snap.

Zoey realized what had just happened. Her big ol' ex-husband had confessed to his mother that he had, without telling her, put himself in peril. Crossing her arms, Zoey leaned back. If it was possible for unholy glee to heal a woman, she'd been handed a full cup.

"You were never in danger," Luca assured his mother.

"Me?" Giuseppina pointed toward the bloodstained spot on the floor where Yolanda had fallen. "*I* can take care of myself. I brought down the killer. I'm not worried about *me*. I want to know if you deliberately set yourself up as bait to trap a serial killer."

"I wouldn't call it bait—"

"Is that why you wouldn't quit wrestling? Because you were putting yourself in danger?" Giuseppina's voice rose with each word.

Deputy Dave turned to Zoey and gestured a question. *What is going on?*

She grinned at him and waited for Giuseppina to break into Italian. Which she did. Then to punch her son. Which she did, several times.

Luca answered in apologetic Italian and deftly defended himself, since Giuseppina was short enough to cause damage to sensitive body parts—while he glared at Zoey.

When Zoey thought Luca's punishment was substantial enough, she said, "I'm sure Deputy Dave needs to get on with his inquiry so he can write his report. Maybe you two could wrap it up?"

Giuseppina pointed her finger at Luca and said a rapid spate of words in Italian. Zoey didn't know enough Italian to translate, but the tone conveyed anger, contempt and the incredulous disbelief that her son could be so stupid.

Zoey was completely satisfied.

Almost completely satisfied. "The trouble, Giuseppina, is that this man is always going to do the hard thing. He's always going to do the right thing. That's what you taught him to do."

Luca began to look pleased with himself.

Giuseppina scowled. "You approve of his heroics?"

"No. I yelled at him more than you did, and all in English."

With a sigh, Luca collapsed onto a stool.

"But knowing him," Zoey continued, "knowing he's always going to do the right thing, even when it's difficult—that's the man I fell in love with."

Luca took a quick breath.

"That's why I love him now." At last Zoey was satisfied. She looked over at Luca and discovered him staring at her like the last cheese cracker on a Santa plate.

"Do you?" He purred with pleasure and somehow moved so quickly and so close he surrounded her with his arms, his scent, his heat.

55

DEPUTY DAVE PICKED up the conversation with Giuseppina exactly where they'd left off. "Tell me why you shot the victim a second time."

"Killer," Giuseppina insisted. "That beast is a killer. Things were happening. I took care of Zoey, Ripley ran in, Zoey took care of Ripley and something about Yolanda attracted my attention. She was conscious, but wiggling around. Concentrating on something, fishing around underneath her sweatshirt."

"The one tied around her waist?"

"Right. I didn't like the look in her eyes. She knew she was caught, but she wanted to bring us all down. I knew men like that in Italy. Mean to the bone." Giuseppina pointed her crooked finger at Deputy Dave. "You know."

He nodded. "I'm in law enforcement, ma'am."

"Zoey was shouting at Ripley, Luca ran in—and Yolanda aimed the SIG P365 she'd managed to pull from her hip pocket. She aimed at Luca. At my son!" Giuseppina shrugged. "I shot her again. But I only shot her once more!"

Luca interrupted, "I've spoken to my contact at the FBI. He's on his way to the hospital to arrest Yolanda. Do you want to check in with him? It's Manuel Ortiz."

"That's the FBI serial killer guy." Deputy Dave pulled his phone out of his jacket and hit a few buttons. "I'd better talk to him."

Luca turned to Zoey and his mother. "You...women!" He engulfed them in a massive hug.

Zoey didn't know exactly how to react to being held so closely with Giuseppina. Then, with a sigh, she gave in and relaxed. It had been one hell of an afternoon.

"Your wife, she's pretty sharp." Giuseppina's voice was muffled by Luca's embrace.

"She's not my wife," Luca said.

"After last night? You could have fooled me," Giuseppina said sharply.

Zoey looked in horror at Luca.

Giuseppina pulled away. "I'm going up to the house to lie down. All this excitement isn't good for my heart. Tell *him* he can come to find me if he has more questions." She indicated Deputy Dave and hobbled toward the door.

Zoey started after her.

Luca caught her arm. "Let her go. If she wanted help, she'd ask for it."

Zoey waited until Giuseppina had left the building to whisper, "What did she mean by that? *You could have fooled me?* The moon was dark last night."

"Yes." He paused for a significant moment. "Ma always said she could see in the dark."

Zoey turned on him and glared.

"What?" He spread his hands wide. "We're adults. You don't care what my mother thinks, do you?"

Zoey stalked away.

He watched her, and he wore a half smile.

"Excuse me, Miss Phoenix," Deputy Dave called. "Don't disappear. We have to finish with your statement."

Tamalyn from the Gothic General Store rode up on her bicycle, two loaded grocery bags in the storage basket. Sticking her head in the shop, she looked around, said, "Wow." Then focused on Luca. "I've got a grocery delivery for Mrs. Damezas."

"In the house," Luca told her.

She nodded and headed toward the porch.

"Tamalyn's being nosy," Zoey said to Luca. "There's not usually much excitement in this town."

"You'd be surprised," Deputy Dave said to them both.

By the time they were done, it was late afternoon, Luca had led five garden tours, a good number of curious Gothics had wandered down to check out the action, and all the words had been said. Deputy Dave told them Yolanda had been treated for her injuries and allergic reaction, then put under arrest for attempted murder with other charges pending. Ripley had been treated, also, and kept for observation.

Luca had heard every word of Zoey's ordeal and kept taking her hand, hugging her, staring at her as if memorizing her face and muttering, "This ought to do it."

What that meant, Zoey didn't know. She only knew she was exhausted and no longer cared whether Giuseppina knew they'd had sex. Fighting off Yolanda and the foxglove poisoning had taken its toll. She wanted to eat and sleep, and not necessarily in that order. As Deputy Dave drove away, Luca got her to her feet and steered her toward the house. Inside, she found herself ushered into a chair at the kitchen table and served Giuseppina's *Zuppa di Pesce e Frutti di Mare*, a Mediterranean fish stew Giuseppina made on special occasions. Which explained the earlier grocery delivery.

Zoey sipped the rich tomato broth, ate the shellfish and the cod and dipped the crusty bread, and when she was finished, Giuseppina ushered her into the bedroom with instructions to sleep. Zoey halted at the door of the bedroom she hadn't done more than visit since Giuseppina's arrival. "Where will you sleep?"

"In my son's bed in the shop."

"Where's he going to sleep?"

"I'll manage." Luca's voice was soothing.

Zoey had visions of Luca overflowing the cot in the shop or overflowing the love seat in the living room. But his problem. She went through the rituals, brushed her teeth, washed her face, dragged out a nightgown and fell onto the mattress with a groan.

At the creak of the bed, Luca turned to his mother. "So, Ma, what do you say? After today, do you realize Zoey has enough courage and passion to breed a grandchild for you? A child of blood, fire and flowers?"

"Do you need my approval?"

"I never did."

Giuseppina nodded. "Then go sleep with your wife. Tonight she'll need you."

56

THE MORNING AFTER, Zoey had a foxglove hangover and she did not have the power to cure herself of that. She winced when Luca got out of bed. The mattress rippled, the floorboards creaked. The blinds rattled as he opened them. The window screeched as he lifted it. The damp smell of fog, earth and ocean rolled into the room. Luca gleefully announced the fog was thinning and it promised to be a sunny, bright day.

"No," she moaned.

"My love, get up. It is morning!"

Had she ever appreciated his robust cheerfulness? If she had, she couldn't imagine why. Right now, she wanted to throw up.

He forcefully helped her come to her feet and pull on a robe. She dragged herself to the breakfast table and gagged at the sight of the warm liquid green concoction Giuseppina set before her. Giuseppina insisted Zoey drink it, and by God, when she was done, she felt 1,000 percent better.

As she placed the empty glass on the table before her, she sighed in relief.

"Is that more like it?" Luca looked between his mother and Zoey, and he smiled.

"Yes." She put her palms on the table and hoisted herself up. "I'm not the only herbalist at this table."

"It's an ancient recipe," Giuseppina said. "I learned it from the witch in my village. If you want, I'll teach it to you."

"Yes, please."

"Shower, get dressed, go out to your workshop." Giuseppina made slow shooing gestures with her arthritis-warped hands. "Luca will help me clean the kitchen."

"Sure, Ma. What else are male children good for?" When Giuseppina swung her cane at him, Luca fended it off and picked up the dirty dishes from the table as efficiently as a butler. "Gotta take care of the womenfolk," he announced, and loaded the dishwasher.

"Nothing excites a woman like the sight of a man doing household chores," Zoey said.

He faced her, and his mouth curled in a half smile. "As you know, I'm fully domesticated."

Zoey stood, her feet glued to the linoleum, her heart matching the slow, strong rhythm of Luca's heart. Damn him for reminding her how much he excited her...in every way.

Turning away, she wandered into the shower in her own bathroom. When she stepped out, her second favorite sundress, an above-the-knee floral pattern, hung on the hook on the back of the door. She wondered if Giuseppina had brought it in, searched for the underwear that would go with it, realized there was none and recognized Luca's hand. Now that the danger was over, he was back to his old self.

As she fetched panties from her drawer and a pair of silver flip-flops from her closet, she contemplated what had been accomplished.

Between her and Giuseppina, they had neutralized the serial killer who would have taken out Luca. Them, too, but mostly Luca. On the personal front, Giuseppina had prepared food for Zoey, not merely last night when they all participated, but today also. Her green hangover medicine was a well-guarded secret, and she'd offered to share her recipe. Zoey did not underestimate the importance of that development.

Most important, Zoey and Luca were inching their way toward a relationship. She didn't dare call it a marriage, but first the moonlit garden. Then last night when she slept in his arms and every time she woke from a nightmare that smelled like fire, madness and death, he'd been there to murmur soothing words that eased her back into sleep.

Someday she would do the same for him, for she knew no matter how hearty he seemed, the last years of threat, trouble and fear had taken their toll on him, and he would need her as much as she needed him.

When she wandered back into the kitchen, Luca was ordering his mother to rest on the couch while he got things ready for the next meal.

She took in the scene, the stubborn woman facing off with her loving son, and when Luca jerked his head, she reached into the kitchen cupboard, got out her tin of the herbs that would ease Giuseppina's pain, then tiptoed outside. Perhaps Giuseppina had finally accepted her as a daughter-in-law, but she would not appreciate a witness to her weariness and suffering.

The morning sun played a golden peekaboo with the eerie curls of fog as the Pacific Ocean called it home. Pale cool tendrils wrapped around the shop and damp wisps drifted along the ground. Sound seemed muffled; she could hear only the constant pounding of the surf on the shore. This hushed hour reminded Zoey of the legend inscribed into the plaque at the Live Oak: *On stormy nights, Gothic is said to disappear, and on its return it brings lost souls back from the dead.*

"I wonder what lost souls wandered back last night?" Zoey murmured, then shook off the otherworldly sense of being between the hours. Perhaps, after all, she was still dealing with the effects of the poison.

To clear her mind, she opened both garage doors to let in the morning air, emptied the teakettle, put the herbs away, mopped up the bloodstains, erased all signs of the serial killer wrestling debacle. It was a new day.

At 10:30 a.m., right on time, the first garden show surrey arrived. Bright-eyed tourists descended the steps, and with renewed confidence, Zoey conducted the first tour. Not surprisingly, the tourists had heard of yesterday's incident. When she deflected their questions by asking, "Do I look as if I've been poisoned?" she got general laughter.

One tourist spoke up. "No, but you do look a little bruised."

"That's from my car accident a few weeks ago."

"Gothic is a tough place to live!" the tourist announced.

She steered the conversation back to flowers.

Luca appeared to conduct the next tour. She liked to be with him so she walked along. He held her hand. She smiled. The tourists got their passport stamps and left happy. As they waved, Luca said, "Only one tour to go and the Gothic Garden and Flower Show is a wrap!"

"Other than your serial killer, it's been smooth sailing." She said it without an ounce of irony, but when he laughed, she supposed he had a point.

"I'm going to go check on Ma, but I'll keep an eye out for any arrivals. You know, in case *today's* serial killer shows up." He walked out of the shop grinning.

"Smartass," she muttered. In the shop, she wrote up her notes on the effects of the foxglove, adjusted the flats of seedlings to get better light, turned her attention to the tiny plants of *amapolas gracia de dios*. In her mind's eye, she could see these three poppies opening their blossoms, showing off their blue petals, the splashes of red, the bright yellow eye...

A mail truck drove up and parked beside the shop. Jael hopped out, holding a large, battered box and, spotting Zoey, came into the shop.

"What's up?" Zoey was focused, coaxing her poppies to grow taller, stronger. She glanced toward Jael.

Jael wore vibrant spandex workout pants that skimmed her hips and a workout top that pushed her boobs up under her chin. The outfit was not flattering, but...oh, dear. She was clearly on the hunt. Poor Luca was in deep trouble.

At the last moment, Zoey changed her wicked cackle into a cough. Good God, she was turning into her mother-in-law.

"I heard you had a fuss here yesterday," Jael said.

A fuss? Is that what you call attempted murder, two shots fired, and two people transported to the hospital, including a suspected serial killer?

"Is Luca okay?" Jael asked.

"He's fine. He missed most of it." *Except for the part where he got yelled at by his mother and I declared love and he declared love. But no point in telling Jael all that. How could Jael be a thorn in Luca's side if she believed that?*

Not that she would. When it came to Luca, hope sprang eternal.

Zoey sighed. She'd have to put up with that for as long as wrestling fame shadowed Luca.

"Is he around?" Jael scrutinized the shop as if he could be hiding somewhere in the wide-open space.

"In the house." *I'd pay good money to see you go up and meet his mother.* "I'm fine, too, thanks for asking."

"That's nice," Jael said vaguely, staring out the open doors, straining to see a movement behind the living room windows. "Remember that package I gave to Mrs. Kulshan to give to you?"

"I do."

Jael held out the roughly treated cardboard box. "The police found it in Mrs. Kulshan's closet."

Zoey took the package in both hands. The weight startled her. Was this the size and heft of a dragon? "*That* closet? Where Angelica was attacked?"

"The very one. Do you think Angelica shot Orvin?"

The question startled Zoey. "Not unless she could do it, get rid of the gun and be unconscious the whole time. Is that the gossip?"

"With the festival ongoing, Angelica mostly out of action and her head gardener shot dead, Gothics are pretty wound up. Some of the tourists are scared." Jael reflected, "Although some are excited, too. Who do you think shot him?"

"Who discovered him?"

"Thistle."

"The musician? I mean, you can never say never, but surely he's not the shooter. He's so… Peter, Paul and Mary." Hastily, Zoey added, "Not in a bad way."

Jael giggled.

"Someone did kill Orvin, though, at close range, and escaped." Remembering her mother's warning to stash the dragon and be safe, Zoey said, "Scary."

"It's weird how nothing ever happens in this town. Now you got crunched and vandalized, the post office is broken into, Orvin's dead and no suspects." With the typical attitude of a hometown girl, Jael said, "Must have been a tourist."

"Sure. Must have been." Zoey was a lot more cynical about that. Everyone hid depths and desires, and in the right circumstances, everyone was capable of murder. Her mother-in-law, for instance. She grinned at the memory of Giuseppina cursing because she failed to shoot Yolanda through the heart. She placed the package on the island, noted one end was torn open.

"Here." Jael handed her a utility knife off her belt. "After everything that happened, I'm curious about this package."

Zoey sliced along the top taped seam and the other side, and spread the box open.

From the froth of crumpled brown paper, a gold jewel of an eye winked at her.

57

STARTLED, ZOEY LEANED BACK.

"What is it?" Jael asked.

"Something the fog carried in, perhaps." Zoey slid the packing paper off the box until she could reach around the statue and lift it out. She placed it on the island. "It's the dragon."

"It looks like it was dipped in licorice," Jael said.

"Or as if it's extracting itself from the stone that contains it." Zoey stepped back and smiled. "This isn't a European man-eating dragon, but one from the Far East, all thunderous laughter and sharp teeth and claws—and look at that tail!"

"Look at those eyes." Jael leaned into them as if mesmerized.

Zoey put a hand on her arm.

Jael seemed to wake. She settled back. "In the box. There's a note."

Zoey plucked a sheet of paper from among the wads of paper.

"What does it say?" Jael asked.

"Yes, what does it say?" Like a superhero made flesh, Luca stepped out of a shred of clinging fog and through the door.

In that instant, Jael forgot the package, the letter, the dragon and most definitely Zoey. "Mr. Damezas, I was hoping to see you again! I hoped you might come by the post office."

He paid only the slightest attention to her. "I don't have anything to mail." He walked forward, all his focus on Zoey. "Zoey, what does it say?"

She glanced at the handwritten note and the signature at the bottom of the page. "It's from my grandmother." She looked up at Luca. "My grandmother?"

"Everyone has a grandmother," Luca replied. "Two, in fact. You simply didn't know yours."

"Her name is Bonnie Torbinson." Zoey was still in a daze.

Jael typed on her phone, then announced, "Bonnie Torbinson of Citation, California, is recently deceased. Died under mysterious circumstances."

Zoey reeled backward. "My grandmother is dead?"

"Easy come, easy go," Jael said.

Luca and Zoey flinched away from her.

"You said you never knew her. How much mourning can there be?" Now that she had their attention, Jael bumped her hip between them. "Mr. Damezas, I heard that you and Zoey are divorced, and I was wondering—would you like to come to dinner? I make a mean lasagna, and I know that's your favorite. I read all about you online."

Luca picked up the package, walked around her and placed it on the other side of Zoey. He fished a smaller envelope out from among the wrapping paper and handed it to her.

Zoey read the note thoroughly. "My grandmother says I'm heir to the Dragon's Heart. Which I believe is this piece of art... and the dragon my mother warned me about."

"We're getting closer to your past," Luca said.

She tapped the paper. "Torbinson. Torbinson." She frowned, then lit up.

Jael said, "Mr. Damezas, if you'd rather have spaghetti and

meatballs or some other Italian dish, I can learn to make that, too."

"No! Thank you! I'm not coming to your house for dinner." Luca took a breath, calmed his annoyance and made a great effort to be firm, but polite. "Zoey and I are still a couple."

Jael huffed in disbelief.

"What do I have to do to make you go away?" Luca asked.

"If you'd give the Damned Luck roar of battle, that would make my day."

Which was not an answer, and both Luca and Zoey knew it.

Jael clasped her hands at her chest. "Please."

Luca sighed. "I don't do that anymore."

"Don't worry about her, Luca." Zoey looked up at him with amazement. "Mark Torbinson. That's who he is. He's a relative. More than merely Mom—I've got a relative!"

"Makes sense. He knew about this package." Luca stroked the statue. "The eyes are compelling, but this black stuff seems to be a coating of some kind." One of the edges crumbled in his hand. "Look. Underneath it glitters. Porcelain or some such. I wonder if it's valuable?"

Jael typed on her phone again. "This says the Dragon's Heart was found a month ago in a submerged car when Caballo Salvaje Lake was drained and it's…wow. It's worth some money. A lot of money." She doubtfully viewed the statue. "Except for the eyes, it's not very attractive."

"I wonder why *Mark* didn't deliver it?" Zoey asked.

"You're right, it seems odd to have it come by mail when he could have delivered it." Luca adjusted the position of the dragon to sit in the center of the island. "But families are complicated."

Zoey nodded. "Oh, yeah."

"You're thinking about my family, aren't you?" Luca asked. She nodded again.

"I think you're about to find out how complicated your own family can be." Luca sounded incredibly pleased.

Zoey read the note again. "My grandmother says my grand-father brought the dragon back from his travels. She said my father gave his life for it."

"What does that mean?" Luca said.

A woman's voice spoke from the open door. "It means Zoey inherited the legendary Dragon's Heart, and she's free to give it to her dear friend, Shasta Straka."

58

LUCA AND ZOEY swiveled to face the open garage door.

Silhouetted against the light, Shasta stood, eyes narrowed, automatic pistol held in both hands and pointed at them. She seemed at home with the weapon, a warrior princess in a video game.

Zoey was dumbfounded. "Shasta? What are you doing?"

Shasta sidled sideways until her back was against the wall.

Oblivious, Jael continued skimming her phone. "The news story says in the car with the dragon was a man's body. He'd been shot in back of the head."

"That must have been my father. I wonder who shot him and pushed him into the lake?" Zoey looked sideways at Shasta and that big pistol held so competently in her hands.

Jael glanced at Shasta. "No, not her. He was long dead." She shoved her phone in her hip pocket and puffed up her chest. "Mr. Damezas, really, I know you're a man of strength and honor, and you feel great need to be loyal to your first love. But if you would look around—"

"WTH?" Luca asked incredulously. He gestured at Shasta. "Jael, do you see what's going on here?"

Jael stared at Shasta as if she was a spectator at a wrestling match. "That's not a real gun, is it?"

"Yes!" Zoey had began to doubt Jael's ability to assess a situation, *any* situation.

Jael gave a sneer and walked toward the door.

"Wrong time, wrong place." Shasta gestured with her pistol, indicating Jael should return. "You're not leaving here until I'm long gone."

Luca and Zoey exchanged a long look that expressed a determination and belief they could somehow distract and dissuade Shasta from this mad course.

"You are kidding." Jael still didn't seem to get it, and she sounded outraged.

Shasta's eyes narrowed; her gaze leveled in a killing stare. "If you're lucky."

Jael's knees gave out and she sank to the floor.

Zoey sighed. "Luca, Jael is *your* fault."

He faced her. "My fault? *I* told her we were involved. *You're* the one who divorced me so she could read it online!"

Shasta swung her pistol between the three of them and shouted, "Look! Put the dragon in the box and bring it to me. You don't need to imagine, Zoey, that I'm really your dumb airy arty college roommate who wouldn't harm a flea."

"The dragon's eyes are compelling," Zoey acknowledged. "But why this particular statue above all else?"

"The heart! The ruby embedded in the body." Shasta stared at the Dragon's Heart and breathed as if she was in the throes of orgasm.

Luca stepped sideways.

At once, her pistol pointed at him. "Don't, I beg you. Don't play the hero. Zoey loves you so much, without you she'd die of grief. And Zoey is my best friend, so I'd have to shoot her so you could die together."

Luca halted and stood tense, waiting.

Zoey bounced on the balls of her feet. She wanted to run at Shasta, tear the weapon from her hands, slap her until she returned to reason.

But this Shasta was frighteningly calm, not at all the kind of inspired artist Zoey had known. The sense of unreality was falling away, replaced by a creeping fear. "You're threatening to kill me. How can you claim we're best friends?"

"You're the best friend I ever had," Shasta said flatly.

"That's a sad statement!" Had Zoey survived yesterday's murderer to be killed today by Shasta Straka? Would Luca die because Zoey hadn't seen the rot at the base of Shasta's soul?

"I suppose it is." Shasta didn't look sad. She looked triumphant and cruelly pleased. "Nothing you know about me is the truth."

"I met your mother. I know she's your mother because you look like her." In triumph, Zoey pointed out, "That's the truth."

"Yes, Genesis is my mother." Shasta sounded as bitter as lemon peel. "My mother, the world-renowned thief and an obsessed con artist who, along with a lot of other people, has spent her life scouring the world for the Dragon's Heart. She found it with my father in Tajikistan in Central Asia, in a cave in the mountains. He was a teenager, the last of his family who had been charged with preserving the Dragon's Heart from harm. She had sex with him and figured he was so blindsided by the glory of her body he wouldn't notice when she tried to steal the dragon. Instead, he'd already sent the dragon to the U.S. with a collector—"

"My grandfather." Zoey picked up the letter. She consulted it while the paper trembled in her grip. "Darrell Torbinson."

"Right. My father gave the Dragon's Heart to Darrell Torbinson because he believed Darrell when he said he would do everything to protect the heart from the hunters who sought it for its jewels. Genesis intended to hunt Darrell down." Shasta sneered. "My father shot her in the hip—"

"*That's* why she limps?" Zoey's head spun.

"My father was good with an artist's paintbrush and good with a gun, and he taught me everything he knew." Clearly a threat.

Zoey was still having trouble comprehending this still-faced shooter was the whimsical artist she'd known for years.

Luca apparently wasn't having trouble. Or maybe he was stalling, for he invited, "Go on with your story."

"As her occupation, my mother acquired things. Beautiful things. Antique things. From the time I can remember, from the time I could toddle, she taught me to *want* to acquire them, and *how* to acquire them."

"She was a thief."

Zoey thought Luca had succinctly summed it up.

"A small word for what she was. She dazzled, she sparkled, she distracted and she took. Sometimes the victims screamed for revenge, but usually...they bragged they'd had their encounter with the elusive Genesis. She stole from the wealthy who were thieves themselves. But her passion was for the Dragon's Heart." The truth spilled from Shasta as if it had been too long contained. "When she was well enough to escape, she couldn't because she was pregnant. With me."

"She *didn't* have you in California on Mount Shasta." Everything Zoey knew about Shasta was a lie?

"It was Tajikistan, it was winter, and the snow piled up higher than the sky. My mother gave birth, not that she had a choice, and nursed me, and—"

"And found to my amazement I had breastfed a viper." Genesis Straka had come from nowhere to stand beside Shasta, her much-smaller pistol touching her daughter's temple.

59

LUCA AND ZOEY looked at each other. Where had she come from? How had these people appeared at the precise moment Zoey had received the package containing the Dragon's Heart? Had they been observing so carefully?

Shasta's hand never trembled. She kept her pistol pointed at Luca and Zoey, but her eyes slid sideways toward Genesis. "Mother, what an unpleasant surprise."

"I would imagine. After all I've done for you, and you found the Dragon's Heart and didn't tell me? Ungrateful spawn!"

Shasta took fire. "All you've done for me? You did nothing for me! You abandoned me and my father!"

As the argument grew hot, Luca shoved Zoey behind him.

Zoey shoved back. "No, Luca, Shasta's right. We both live, or we both die."

Genesis and Shasta paid no attention, caught up in their own battle. "I taught you to love the Dragon's Heart, to seek the Dragon's Heart!"

"You left and you never returned. When I was eleven, the clan fighting got so bad Father had to take me to the U.S. Embassy and tell them I was an American child he'd found, the child of missionaries."

"Missionaries." Genesis snorted, then picked up the thread. "I'm the one who taught you English so they believed that stupid story."

"You taught me because you couldn't speak Tajik worth a damn."

"I speak a lot of languages," Genesis said testily. "Just not that one."

"I came to the United States. I lived with my foster parents and I *fit in*." Shasta spoke to Luca and Zoey. "I got a scholarship to the liberal arts college to refine my painting—and this monster showed up at the last minute and told me I had to go to the same *science* specialized college as Zoey Phoenix because *Zoey* was the granddaughter of Darrell Torbinson and his heir. I had to become Zoey's best friend in case she came into possession of the heart."

"You didn't *have* to do it," Genesis said. "You could have refused, gone on to your art classes, become the greatest painter in the world and still live in a basement in Sunnyvale. Because being an artist is more than talent and discipline, it's luck, marketing and virtuosity, and you don't have any of them!"

For the first time, Shasta faced her mother full-on. "I do!"

"If you truly believed that, you'd have told me to go to hell."

The two women faced off, pistols pointed, ready to take each other out.

"You…you…you…" Zoey stammered with a combination of shock and pain. "You became my roommate because I might inherit…"

"Yes." Shasta's voice was flat and cold. "Because you might inherit the Dragon's Heart." To Genesis, she said, "Although I never figured out how you knew Zoey was the heir."

"I'm good at what I do." Genesis's smile was as cold as Shasta's eyes.

"Yes, you are, and I should have suspected you were in the neighborhood when Orvin was killed."

"Orvin's dead? Orvin Isaksen?" Genesis sounded shocked. "That crafty old bastard is—"

"Like you didn't know!" Shasta said.

"I didn't kill Orvin."

The two women viewed each other with poisonous suspicion, afraid to take their eyes off each other. At the same time, they slowly separated, like gunfighters pacing off for a shoot-out.

Zoey and Luca exchanged horrified glances. Shasta and Genesis were going to kill each other.

As if he couldn't help himself, Luca spoke up. "A murder is a felony. A mother-daughter murder is an act of evil."

He might never have spoken.

"Listen! I deserve to know!" Zoey shouted. "What *is* the Dragon's Heart?"

Both women turned to gape at Zoey.

"I just received it," Zoey said. "My grandmother didn't explain what it is. I'd ask her in person, but she's been murdered, too."

Genesis shrugged one shoulder. "I used to be more patient."

"Mother, really? You killed her grandmother?" Shasta did not so much ask the question as assume the answer.

"Of course. I needed the information and she wasn't cooperative."

Zoey heard Luca breathe out a long, slow, "Shit."

She agreed with him. Two shooters, one who had recently killed, and she was pretty sure when this was over, only one person would remain standing—and it wouldn't be her or Luca.

"Mother, you're aging badly. That hip. The bags under your eyes. The wrinkles under your chin." As all daughters do, Shasta knew her mother's weaknesses and took aim at them with words. "You're running out of time. Why not leave this to me?"

Genesis flushed with rage.

They held those pistols as if itching to fire them at each other. Or at anybody who interfered with their frenzied desire.

Zoey was afraid for herself, afraid for the woman who had been her friend, afraid to see more bloodshed. More than anything, she was afraid Luca would try to do the right thing; to save her, he'd take a bullet and die. No matter what she said, how she objected, he would always be a hero.

She didn't know how to stop this; all she could do was try to stall until help arrived. Her fingers trembled as she gestured at the statue on the island. "As far as I can see, it's nothing more than this tar-dipped dragon with, well yes, fascinating eyes that change color. But there's nothing else interesting about it."

A man's voice spoke from the doorway. "The Dragon's Heart is a legend, a living piece of antiquity with the greatest ruby of all time beating in its chest." Angelica's gardener Hudson Isaksen did not hold a pistol; he held an Uzi cradled in one arm, and he pointed it at Genesis and Shasta.

60

ZOEY'S BLOOD CHILLED. Her broken fingers ached with the cold of icy fear.

Again Luca moved closer, putting himself between her and the new arrival. "Do you have any kind of weapon?" he asked softly.

Why was he asking? He knew the answer! "I'm a flower breeder," she whispered. "I have clippers! And…and foxglove!"

Too many weapons, pointed at each other, easily aimed at Luca and Zoey. Too many people willing to kill for an artifact that until a half hour ago, she hadn't known existed. She needed to demand answers, to buy time. But her throat constricted with fear.

"Hudson, how good to see you…and of course your big gun." Genesis cast a glance at his grubby gardening pants and oozed sarcasm. "It's been a long time."

That surprised Zoey enough to let words escape. "You *know* him?"

"Who do you think he is?" Genesis smirked at Zoey.

"He's Angelica's grumpy gardener." Whatever else he was, Zoey knew that.

"The girl's right." Hudson glared at Zoey and Luca. "What's

also right is that I've sought the Dragon's Heart my whole life. So of course Ginny knows me."

"Hudson, how do you fit in?" Luca asked. "I understood you've worked here for years."

"Years and years of dull labor while Orvin and I waited…" His crusty, rheumy eyes kept the shop and everyone in it under constant surveillance. "We were wealthy brothers from a good Norfolk family destined for boring respectability. But from the moment we heard about the Dragon's Heart, we were determined to find it. We ran away, spent years tracking the dragon." His grin was withered by sun and greed. "In Tajikistan, we heard that the dragon had flown far away. We tracked it to Central California—and lost it."

"By then they were so old," Genesis interjected, "they were too decrepit to continue."

"Too smart," Hudson corrected. "We strategized. We knew the dragon would eventually make its way to a wealthy person's home. We sought employment in a place where the staff changed quickly and gossip flowed among the servants—Angelica Lindholm's stronghold. Once the dragon reared its noble head, we knew we'd hear the rumor." Hudson laughed a dry cackle. "What an evening that was when the news announced that the dragon had surfaced. We called and talked to a Citation policeman. We used our stuffy English accents, and that chump told us the dragon had come to us here. Here! God bless it, it found us! We searched the post office—"

"It was you!" Jael said.

Hudson leveled his Uzi at her.

She hid her head and huddled on the floor.

Zoey had to interrupt; as annoyingly persistent as Jael was in her wrestling fandom, she didn't deserve to die. "You or Orvin broke into my shop and house!"

"Not me," Hudson said. "We didn't have to break in. We

were the gardeners in charge of caring for your plants until your return. We had keys."

"I'm the one who searched," Shasta said.

Hurt and aggrieved, Zoey asked, "Why? Why would you destroy my plantings? You know what they mean to me!"

"I thought the dragon would be in the house. By the time I got out here, I was running out of time and getting frustrated." Shasta was almost amused. "Sorry, Zoey, but if that's the worst that happens to you, be grateful."

To quiet and comfort her, Luca twined his fingers with Zoey's and spoke to the treasure-crazed group of gunmen. "The Dragon's Heart had disappeared into Mrs. Kulshan's closet. Isn't that right?"

Hudson transferred his still, cold gaze to him. "Orvin heard that at Angelica's Gothic Garden and Flower Show briefing. The backstabbing wanker didn't tell me. He said he was headed down to Mrs. Kulshan's to clean up for the garden show. I recognized the greed in his voice, and I followed him."

"You killed him?" Zoey could not believe it. "You killed your own brother over a statue?"

"It's worth killing anyone for." Genesis's twisted, avaricious smile resembled Hudson's. "It's worth killing everyone for."

"Orvin would have done the same for me." Hudson nodded with sanguine surety.

The three dragon hunters glowered meaningfully at each other—and failed to notice the silver Corvette that drove past and parked.

Zoey looked at Luca.

Luca closed his eyes as if he couldn't believe another person could possibly step through that door, then opened them. "If the dragon is worth killing anyone for, why didn't you shoot Angelica?"

"I would have. She'd seen Orvin. She'd seen what was in the box. Smart damned woman, she would've made the connection. But the gunshot brought people running. I couldn't even grab the dragon." His voice trembled as if he wanted to cry. "I jumped the fence and—"

Mark Torbinson stepped in the door. "Hello there! Remember me?"

Zoey frantically shook her head at him. "No. Go away."

Genesis, Shasta and Hudson didn't change expressions and kept their muzzles steady and in place: Shasta aimed at Zoey and Luca, Genesis aimed at Shasta, and Hudson's machine gun pointed midway between.

Mark froze, then with an expression of appalled surprise, Mark focused on Genesis and blurted, "You're Uncle Darrell's nurse!"

Hudson whipped around and pointed his Uzi at Mark.

Shasta flattened herself against the wall.

Mark leaped back outside and out of sight.

Genesis seized her opportunity and shot Hudson in his ribs. He fell to his knees.

Shasta moved her automatic pistol in a wide, erratic arc between Genesis and Hudson.

One thought propelled Zoey. *Protect Luca!* Zoey launched herself at him.

At the same time, from a standing position, Luca sprang into the air and toward Zoey. He kicked out with one leg; his foot made contact with the Dragon's Heart. He hit it with a solid thunk.

The three obsessed dragon hunters screamed.

The dragon lurched off the counter.

Luca grabbed Zoey, rolled in midair and they smacked the floor. His body provided a cushion, but the landing knocked the air out of her—and him—and all the parts of her body that had suffered when her car had been rammed blasted her with pain. Red specks swam before her eyes. Her ears rang—but still she heard the sound of the statue shattering on impact with the concrete floor.

61

"ARE YOU OKAY?" Luca pushed her hair off her forehead with a tender hand. "Zoey, are you hurt?"

He sounded so anxious Zoey fought back the agonizing wave, got her breath and nodded. She moved her lips, but no sound escaped. *We're alive.*

Luca put his finger to his lips. Gently he put her aside and sat up, head cocked, as he listened.

They waited, tense, fearful, for more gunshots.

Instead they heard the sound of scrambling and disjointed phrases. "Where is it?"

"It's not here."

"It's here."

"You took it."

"You've been right beside me all the time!"

"Found a cat's-eye."

"To hell with a cat's-eye. Where's the ruby?"

Gingerly, Zoey moved to crouch beside him.

They should hide. But where? In a cupboard? With firearms in the hands of those maniacs, nowhere was safe.

Although the maniacs weren't shooting. They were muttering, sobbing, grunting.

"It's not going well." Luca crept forward. "Now's our chance to get out and—" He peered around edge of the island.

Zoey crept after him and peered, too.

The dragon had shattered into chunks and particles and what looked like a swathe of glittering sand, and spread itself across the floor in a wide path.

Shasta and Genesis had holstered their weapons. Hudson had placed his on the floor. They crawled around, looking under the stools, the toe kick on the cupboards, scrutinizing the area as if the Dragon's Heart ruby had willfully hidden from them.

Hudson whimpered while he crawled, holding his side with one hand while blood oozed between his fingers.

Genesis kept touching her chest over her heart as if she thought the ruby would respond to its beat.

Zoey locked gazes with Shasta. Shock dilated Shasta's pupils, her eyes looked like slick black ice and she seemed unable to recognize another human being. She pushed mounds of sand into her palms, then poured them out slowly as if expecting the ruby to reform from the glitter. Finally, she sat back on her heels and in a choked voice said, "It's not here."

"It's got to be here," Hudson said. "I've waited all these years for it to come to me. It's got to be—"

"This isn't the real Dragon's Heart statue. It's a phony." Genesis's voice grew guttural with rage. "That Tajik lied to me. He lied to me, the mother of his child!"

Shasta swung around, hands up as if she wanted to strangle Genesis. "Don't start that, Mother. Why wouldn't he lie?"

Genesis stood awkwardly because of her hip and stalked toward the entrance. "I'm going back to Tajikistan, and if that artistic turd is still alive, I'll torture him until he reveals where—"

Shasta looked up at the ceiling. "Helicopters!" She looked out the door. "Law enforcement!"

"The bulls!" Hudson spat on the pile of sand he'd collected in his hand, then threw it aside.

Genesis removed her pistol from her holster, set the safety, placed it under a chair and raced out the door.

Shasta did the same with her pistol and followed.

Hudson knelt, cursing, trying to stand. Finally he dragged himself to one of the chairs against the wall and used it to heft himself to his feet. He shuffled over to the Uzi and tried to bend enough to pick it up.

The chop of the helicopter blades grew louder.

He groaned in pain, then half ran, half dragged himself outside and out of sight.

Luca and Zoey were suddenly, completely, thankfully alone.

Luca stood, looked around as if he couldn't believe it. "They're gone."

"I know." Zoey felt as if she'd consumed another dose of foxglove: light-headed, trembling and aching in every joint.

He offered his hand to Zoey. "You okay?"

She put her good, unbroken hand in his. "I'm going to feel that fall later, but right now... I'm sort of buzzed. Because we're alive. How about you?"

He hoisted her to her feet. "Buzzed, too, like after a good wrestling match. We should be okay. Two things wrestling taught me—how to launch myself from a standing position, and how to fall."

"And how to kick a statue off the island to distract the bad guys. Yay, wrestling." Zoey held out her clenched fist.

He bumped it, then pulled her into his embrace.

She didn't know whether she leaned against him or collapsed against him, but right now, this was the right place to be. "Who called the cops?" she wondered out loud.

Behind them, a man cleared his throat. "I did." Mark was back inside the shop and looking smug. "My name is—"

"Mark Torbinson," Luca and Zoey said in unison.

62

"THAT'S RIGHT!" MARK indicated the machine gun on the floor. "Probably shouldn't leave that lying around."

Zoey pushed the box of latex gloves toward Luca. He pulled on a pair and picked up the weapon. She opened her locked cupboard and moved her seed boxes aside, and he placed the Uzi inside. He returned for the two pistols and placed them inside, too, then turned the key and put it in his pocket.

Overhead, a helicopter swooped low and a loudspeaker commanded someone to remain still. Apparently they didn't, because shots were fired and the helicopter swooped away.

"I expected Gothic to be a quiet town," Mark said.

"Usually it is," Zoey assured him.

Another helicopter hovered overhead, and the loudspeaker announced, "Please do not enter that driveway. This is a crime scene. Do not enter the driveway!"

Shouting ensued.

Luca stepped over to the door, looked and thumped his head against the sill. "It's the Gothic Garden and Flower Show surrey. There are two women and a man leaning out of the windows, waving their passports at the helicopter and giving the police hell." He looked at her. "They want their stamps."

Zoey couldn't help it. She giggled. "What should we do?"

"Give me the stamp pad and the stamp and let me see if I can sweet-talk them into skipping this part of the tour." Luca took them from her. "You call up to the Tower and explain to Marjorie what's going on and that this group needs refreshments and extra attention."

"Right." Luca headed out toward the surrey.

Zoey called the Tower. Marjorie answered and again put Angelica on speakerphone. Zoey heard a muffled voice in the background, and Marjorie translated, "She wondered why police helicopters were circling the area, but knowing you, she suspected the reason would be another crime scene."

"Knowing me?" Zoey was incredulous.

"She says of course we'll appease the guests, but in the future, would it be possible for you to space your crises further apart, and not during what should be a gardening oasis of calm?" Marjorie added apologetically, "Angelica's a little perturbed at being sidelined and has been sharper than usual." The voice in the background got louder, and Marjorie spoke away from the phone. "I simply know it's not Zoey's fault!" Then into the phone. "Later, Zoey. It's time for Angelica's pain pill." She hung up.

Zoey stared at the phone in her hand. It wasn't her fault that her friend Shasta had been no friend, that Shasta's mother was a renowned thief and the woman who had killed Bonnie Torbinson, that Hudson had traveled the world in search of the Dragon's Heart and murdered his own brother. Heck, *Angelica* had hired the Isaksen brothers. She needed to shoulder part of the responsibility.

Luca arrived back in the shop, took one look at Zoey, took the phone and placed it on the counter with the stamp and pad. "Two of the helicopters have set down, one toward the Pacific

Coast Highway and one toward town. From what I was able to observe, they've captured Genesis and Hudson."

"Good!" Zoey wasn't in the mood to be charitable.

Luca continued, "The other helicopter has moved south."

"Shasta's younger and perhaps more likely to evade capture." To Mark, Zoey said, "You're my...cousin?"

"Your father's cousin. My second cousin. My mom was Darrell Torbinson's sister. Darrell Torbinson was—"

"My grandfather." She got out the broom, and swept the remains of the Dragon's Heart into a dustpan.

"Correct." Mark watched as she leaned down and extracted the two cat's-eye gems from the debris.

"When I realized your package had finally been located and the local USPS gal was delivering it, I followed her down. I thought I'd wait until you opened it and try again to tell you who I was and who they were—" Mark waved a vague hand toward the door where the Dragon's Heart hunters had disappeared "—and why you were receiving—"

"A fake treasure?" Luca asked.

Mark laughed. "Yes."

"You knew it was fake?" Zoey leaned the broom against the trash can and put the dustpan in the corner out of the way.

"Yes. It's a pretty good story."

"I'll bet it is." She showed the two men the gleaming gems that filled the palm of her hand, looked around for somewhere to place them, figured they must be fakes, too. "Okay if I keep these as mementos?" she asked Mark.

"Yes. They belong to you." In a voice weighted with meaning, he said, "You are the true heir to the Dragon's Heart."

She kicked at the sand on the floor. "Yeah...thanks." She slid the stones into her pockets, one on the right, one on the left, filled her hot water pot and plugged it in. She got out three cups. "Tell me your story, Mark. We're alive. We've got all the time in the world."

Luca gestured at the stools around the island. "Please, sit down and tell us."

Mark sat, then looked startled as Jael crawled out from underneath the cramped sink cabinet looking scared and crumpled.

Zoey sighed and got another cup. She'd forgotten Jael. So had Luca. Probably a deliberate subconscious slip on their parts.

Outside, they heard a vehicle headed up the driveway toward the house. A gray SUV drove up and slammed on its brakes. Two people piled out.

From the other side of the vehicle, Giuseppina shouted at them.

The driver, a tall, gangly loose-limbed man, went around to her.

The woman ran toward the shop.

Zoey's heart leaped, and she rushed into the yard and met Morgayne with her arms wide. "Mom! Oh, Mom, where have you been?"

63

MORGAYNE HUGGED HER HARD, looked at her face, then hugged her again, more gently this time. "You won't believe this. I've been imprisoned in a billionaire's mansion at Lake Tahoe."

"Billionaire's mansion. Lake Tahoe. Sure. After the last few days, I'd say that sounds about right." Zoey led her mother toward the shop. "I figured it had to be something for you to disappear."

"You do remember what I told you before I left?" Morgayne asked.

"When I was in the hospital? It's vague. I was pretty out of it." Although seeing her mother now, more of the bits and pieces begun to surface.

"I was afraid of that. But I thought I'd be able to call and explain...well, things didn't quite work out as planned." Morgayne saw Luca standing in the doorway and offered her hand. "You kept her safe. Thank you!"

"I didn't keep her safe." Luca shook heartily. "She's good at keeping herself safe, and me, too."

Morgayne beamed. "She is marvelous, isn't she?"

"Yes, ma'am. She really is." Luca took Zoey's hand and pulled her close to his side.

Morgayne nodded. "Yes, I thought that might happen." She glanced back at her driver, who was now speaking placatingly to Giuseppina. She lowered her voice. "What is *she* doing here?"

"Saving my life, Mom. No, really."

"That damned dragon." Morgayne sighed. "Fine. I'll try to be nice to her."

"No, the Dragon's Heart was today. She saved my life yesterday." Zoey laughed at Morgayne's horror.

She might have sounded slightly hysterical, because Luca said, "We all need to sit down." He ushered Morgayne and Zoey into the shop.

"Cynthia?" Mark stood beside his stool.

She blinked at him. "Mark? I never imagined I'd see you here, although I shouldn't be surprised." She looked around. "Is the Dragon's Heart here?"

Zoey pointed at the dustpan.

"Oh," Morgayne said. "It never was attractive anyway. I couldn't figure out what all the fuss was about."

"Mark's going to tell us. He says I'm the true heir to the Dragon's Heart." Zoey laughed a little.

"That is no small thing," Mark said as Giuseppina's scolding voice got closer and closer.

She came through the door scowling, the strange guy following close on her heels. She pointed at Morgayne. "You and your boyfriend almost ran me over!"

"We never even came close. Good to see you again, Giuseppina." Morgayne offered her hand.

Zoey tensed. Sure, Giuseppina had saved her from death and even been nice to her, but she wasn't sure her seventy-four-year-old ex-mother-in-law wouldn't spit in her forty-six-year-old mother's palm.

But Giuseppina examined Morgayne from head to toe, then

looked back at the man behind her. She looked at Zoey as if seeing something she'd never seen before and nodded. "Oh." She took Morgayne's hand. "I'm glad you're here. Zoey has been worried. Won't you introduce me to your friend?"

Morgayne blushed. Her mother actually blushed, which made Zoey look hard at the unknown man.

He was in his forties, darkly tanned and the lines set in his face proved he was not a man who often smiled. He dressed like a laborer in jeans, work boots and a brown denim button-up shirt. His dark hair was sprinkled with iron gray, and his startling blue eyes watched Morgayne with more fondness than any man had ever dared show her...that Zoey knew of, anyway.

He came at once toward Giuseppina as Morgayne said, "Giuseppina Damezas, this is Vadim Somova. He's a friend of mine from long ago."

"It is good to meet you at last." Giuseppina smiled with such pleasant charm, Zoey looked at Luca to see if he had figured out these undercurrents.

He lifted his eyebrows at her, then came forward to be introduced, too.

Zoey followed, of course, and he took her hand between his two callused palms. "I met you many years ago in Citation and—"

Morgayne cleared her throat. "Not yet," she murmured.

Zoey looked between them, trying to understand.

The sound of the police helicopter faded as it traveled farther south.

Mark extended his hand to Vadim. "I don't need an introduction. How are you doing? What have you been up to?"

Vadim released Zoey and shook Mark's hand, and in his rough, slightly accented voice he said, "Working. Electrical. In Russia. I returned as soon as my brother told me about..." He made a small circle with his fingers.

"You're not worried that the police will arrest you?" Mark asked. "About Jack?"

"They will. They must," Vadim said. "But I will be exonerated."

Morgayne moved close to his side. "I have excellent connections with criminal lawyers."

"Of course my brother does also," Vadim added.

Police sirens sounded in the distance, coming closer.

"I'm so confused," Zoey said to Luca.

He seated himself on a counter stool at the island. "Not even a glimmer? Those nightmares about the Mean Man, Honey, the stairway?"

"Maybe a glimmer," she acknowledged. "More of an impossible hope, really. Do you suppose that Honey is—"

A man stepped through the open garage door holding a large pistol at arm's length.

"Oh. My. God." Zoey couldn't believe it. "Another one?" It took her a moment, but she identified him. "You're Fritz Nakashima." Natasha Nakashima's nephew, the one who had decided to get rich by emulating Zoey and developing a popular flower for florists. "What are you doing here?"

He looked around at the small crowd, at Vadim, Morgayne, Mark, Giuseppina, Jael and Luca, and finally zeroed in on Zoey. "Give me your latest and greatest development."

Fritz wasn't like Shasta, Genesis and Hudson. His pistol didn't look like an extension of his arm. It looked like an uncomfortable appendage.

Zoey didn't like his tone. "Development?"

"Your plant! Your next plant! The one that's going to make you rich! Give it to me!" Fritz swung his pistol wildly.

No one looked impressed, and Zoey was about fed up with people stepping into her shop and demanding she hand over what was rightfully hers. "Give it to who? You? *You?* Do you know how fast law enforcement are going to grab you?"

For the first time, Fritz seemed to hear the sirens coming closer. "The cops? You called the cops? No, I want that flower. I told Aunt Natasha I'd succeed, and I will!"

"Not succeed. Steal!" Zoey thought about her precious baby plants, her *amapolas gracia de dios*, which she had found, worried about, tended, hoped to bring back from extinction, and her temper snapped. "I wouldn't give you a lukewarm pot of steeped foxglove!"

But hers wasn't the only temper that snapped.

Luca slapped his palms to the surface of the island. He rose to his full height. He opened his mouth—and he roared. An inarticulate, massive and threatening sound of absolute fury, the roar of the wrestler Damned Luck.

Fritz's hand shook. He knelt. Placed the pistol on the floor. Fled out the door.

Jael stood, staring at Luca as he subsided onto his stool. "Thank you," she whispered, and fainted dead away.

64

GIUSEPPINA GESTURED. "**CARRY** that woman out and put her in her mail truck."

"With pleasure." Luca had never meant anything so much in his life. He and Vadim picked Jael up by her hands and feet and hauled her out the door. They placed her on the driver's side seat.

She conveniently roused in time to reach for Luca.

Vadim blocked her.

The two men returned to the shop dusting their hands.

Jael roared away, her exhaust sputtering with indignation.

Giuseppina lifted her hand toward the ceiling. "What's with the police helicopters? What did I miss today?"

A babble of words assaulted her.

Giuseppina gestured for silence, and she got it. "Let's go sit on the porch, be comfortable and talk while the police round up today's set of villains." She leaned on her cane and hobbled out the door. "Every day more excitement. I may never want to leave!"

Zoey whimpered softly.

Luca didn't laugh out loud, but he knew whatever weariness had plagued his mother earlier had vanished. She was in her element with a crowd to feed, guaranteed entertainment and the chance to aggravate her daughter-in-law.

The chopping of the helicopter blades slowed as it landed somewhere nearby.

Deputy Dave stuck his head into the shop. "We have three suspects in custody and just nabbed another guy who ran out of here. Should we retain him?"

"Yes." Zoey said. "That bastard held us at gunpoint!"

"Right you are." Deputy Dave took a note. "Are there more? Less? Are we done for the moment? Should I arrest the head of the Gothic post office or give her CPR?"

Deputy Dave, Luca noted, was getting testy.

"Tell her to go back to work," Zoey snarled. "I'm going to open a bottle of wine."

Luca caught up with her as she passed his mother in the yard. "I'll help."

In the kitchen, she got out two bottles of wine.

"Five bottles." He arranged a cheese and charcuterie platter.

Startled, she protested, "There's only six of us."

"There's a lot to be said and it'll be thirsty work." He dug around in the tiny pantry and found the loaf of sourdough and the loaf of rye his mother had had delivered. He held them in his hands. "It's like she knew what was going to happen."

"Your mother's not a witch," she protested.

He dropped the bread on the table. "No, but my wife is."

Laughing, she tried to fend him off. But she didn't try too hard and before long he was holding her against the wall, kissing her deeply, warmly, breathlessly. "Tonight," he said, "we'll go to my bed in the loft in the shop, where there's room and quiet and you and I'll ask—are you a good witch or a bad witch?"

"When I'm with you, I'm a bad witch. A very very bad witch."

He growled like a big, warm, passionate bear. "I know you are."

When they finally came out carrying wine bottles and glasses, a pitcher of water, appetizers and paper plates, the family had distributed themselves around the porch: Morgayne and Vadim sat side by side in two dining room chairs, Mark perched on the railing and Giuseppina sat in the throne-like wicker chair.

They were watching as, out in the yard, Deputy Dave and the other law enforcement took statements from Shasta, Genesis and Hudson. And Fritz, who looked scared spitless, as he deserved to be.

When the three dragon hunters and the one flower kidnapper had been handcuffed and put into police cruisers, Deputy Dave returned to stand at the foot of the porch. "There have been conflicting reports of what happened today. Very conflicting reports. None of this seems to be related to yesterday's incident."

Giuseppina cackled drily.

"But the business about the dragon all sounds like the biggest load of crap I've ever heard in my days as an officer, and I've heard some incredible bullshit." Deputy Dave took a breath. "By any chance, are there any firearms I should recover?"

"Right." Luca dug the key out of his pocket and handed it to Deputy Dave, then walked with him to the shop.

When Deputy Dave came out, he wore gloves and carried all the weaponry the four intruders had packed in, including Fritz's barely used pistol.

Luca climbed the stairs to the porch.

Deputy Dave stood with one foot on the bottom step and one foot on the ground. "While I suspect the weapons will yield sufficient fingerprints to exonerate everyone here, I'll be back in the morning to get statements. No one is to leave the area. I trust you can all promise that?"

Everyone held a plate of food and a glass of wine, and they nodded agreeably.

He glanced up the road. "Better open another bottle of wine. Someone's coming."

"Not another Gothic Garden and Flower Show surrey?" Zoey barely contained her horror.

He looked at her wearily. "No, this is merely a car." With a wave of farewell, he got in his patrol car and drove away.

"Who could it be? Everybody's here," Zoey joked.

"Or in jail," Giuseppina joked back at her. "My daughters have been threatening to come and rescue you. Maybe it's them."

"That would be nice," Zoey said absently, then realized her lack of tact and hastily added, "Probably a tourist headed for the beach. Although—" she glanced toward the Pacific "—that fog is hanging out there, waiting to roll back in." She noticed how oddly Morgayne and Vadim viewed her, and Mark and especially Luca. *What?*

The anonymous gray car slowed at the driveway, then turned in. The gravel crunched under the tires. The driver pulled in behind Mark's Corvette and parked.

As the car door opened, Zoey sensed a change in the world, a return to a belonging of so long ago...

She stood. She walked to the head of the stairs. She stared at the young woman stepping out of the car.

Tall, sturdy, blonde, the woman viewed her with dark eyes that saw right through to her soul.

Zoey knew her. For the first time in twenty-four years, she looked into the face of her sister. Her heart overflowed with a special joy she thought had vanished from the world.

Her sister. Her twin. "Honey. Honey!"

65

ZOEY RAN DOWN THE STEPS.

Honey ran toward her. "Gracie!"

The two women opened their arms to each other and moved into an embrace, an embrace so familiar they might have shared it in the womb.

"Honey." Zoey tightened her grip. "Honey!"

Honey hugged her so hard, the years apart became nothing but a wisp of memory. "Gracie! Gracie, listen." Honey looked her in the eyes. "I'm Honor."

"I know. I really do. I'm Zoey."

"I know that, too."

In unison, the two women said, "But you can call me whatever you like."

They laughed and embraced and laughed, put their heads on each other's shoulders, and wiped each other's tears with their bare palms.

Zoey had to know. "Did you remember me? I mean, really remember me?"

"No. I had memories, but they were so faraway and so different from the life I was leading, I thought I must be remembering a movie. Sometimes I cried at night because I felt as if I'd lost a part of me, and when I was awake, I told myself you were my—"

"Imaginary friend," Zoey finished with her.

Again they stared at each other, remembering the childhood faces, comparing them to the sisters they were today.

From the side, Morgayne spoke. "Honor? Gracie?" Her voice quavered. "My babies?"

They lifted their heads.

She stood a few feet away, as if hesitant to intrude, as if unsure of her welcome.

Honor caught her breath. "Mommy?"

Zoey stepped back.

Honor and Morgayne rushed into each other's arms. Morgayne took Honor's face in her hands, looked and looked, searching out the changes, seeking the similarities.

Zoey watched, wiped the joyful tears that ran down her face and watched some more.

In unison, Morgayne and Honor turned to her, embraced her, and after so many years, they were a family circle again.

But not a whole family. Not yet.

A man's footsteps crunched on the gravel.

Honor squealed, "Daddy!" tore herself away and ran to Vadim. They hugged, murmured loving words, and with their arms around each other, they turned to Morgayne and Zoey. "This is my dad." Honor's every word was weighed with significance. "This is the man who pulled me from the lake and saved my life."

"The lake?" Zoey was finally starting to put the pieces together. "You and Vadim were in the car that went into Caballo Salvaje Lake?" She opened her arms to Vadim. "You saved my sister?"

His thin, lined, serious face lightened. "Yes."

Zoey threw her arms around him. "Thank you!"

He broke into a smile, changing all the lines in his face, accentuating the kindness and courage she now knew he embodied. He hugged her back, not tightly as he had hugged Honor, but tentatively as if unsure of her, her bruises and this development. Then he held out his hand to Morgayne. "Come on. Let's go hear Mark's story and tell our own."

Zoey checked with Honor.

Honor mouthed, "They have a story?"

Zoey lifted her shoulders, slid her arm around her sister's waist, and they made their way to the stairs and onto the porch.

Luca stood there, waiting to be introduced, and when Zoey had performed the ritual, he said, "What do you know? Gothic's legendary fog brought back your imaginary friend."

66

HONOR AND ZOEY sat on the porch swing. They held hands while Luca brought them a small side table for their wine and their plates. As he refilled the glasses, he took charge. "Mark is going to explain about the Dragon's Heart."

"Absolutely. It's a story I've been wanting to tell." Mark leaned against the porch post. "Darrell Torbinson was my uncle. My dad died when I was two. Mom was a math teacher and we did okay, but compared to the Torbinsons, we had nothing. We didn't visit very often—Uncle Darrell was out of the country most of the time—but when he was home, Mom would take me over. She'd talk to Uncle Darrell and I was left to the tender mercies of my older cousin."

"Jack." Bitter nuance tinged Morgayne's voice. "My one and only husband."

Luca saw Zoey and Honor exchange horrified glances.

"Our father?" Zoey mouthed to Honor.

Honor shook her head in dismay.

"Yes, Jack," Mark agreed. "I can't remember a time when I wasn't afraid of him. When I was little, he pinched me, hit me, then made fun of me when I cried."

"He sounds like a great gentleman." Giuseppina could deliver sarcasm like a jellyfish delivered poison.

"He was a nasty bully. Aunt Bonnie thought he hung the moon, but once Uncle Darrell had his stroke and stayed home, he figured out what his son was. By then I was in high school, Jack was married and had the kids, and I could go over and visit Uncle Darrell without Jack's interference. Also—" Mark grinned evilly "—the summer after my junior year, I grew. I grew taller than Jack. Broader than Jack. He didn't realize what had happened—maybe he thought all that early intimidation would have a permanent effect—but he should have looked up before he slapped my face, because I took him out with an undercut to the jaw. He flew backward…" Mark stopped talking and smiled. And smiled. Then he noticed the others watching him. "Sorry. I love that memory."

Laughter rippled across the porch.

"I wish I'd seen that," Morgayne said softly.

"He was so surprised," Mark told her. "Anyway, one day Uncle Darrell called me to come and visit, and when I got there he was alone and gloating. He pointed out the Dragon's Heart in his showcase. I wasn't too impressed."

The stress of almost losing Zoey—again—had faded, and Luca had thought things through. "It was a fake. The fake that got broken in the shop."

Zoey had been thinking, too. "Where's the real Dragon's Heart?"

Mark grinned. "Uncle Darrell had that one, too, and he showed it to me. The real Dragon's Heart is…so beautiful. Covered in gold, crusted in jewels."

"I never saw that." Morgayne was surprised and alight with pleasure. "I'm so glad Darrell pulled one over on that lousy, worthless…" She trailed off as if there wasn't enough miserable adjectives in the English language.

"Uncle Darrell kept it hidden. My God." Mark sighed with

delight. "I'll never forget seeing that thing for the first time. I fell in love. I didn't know if the myth is true and the world's most magnificent ruby beats in its chest, but the way that dragon looked at me, I believed it did." He roused from his reverie. "The eyes are the same on both statues, though. Really good gems."

With a look of consternation, Zoey slipped her hands in her pockets.

"The fake was compelling enough to fool even—" Mark jerked his thumb toward the highway "—those thieves. Uncle Darrell gave me the original, said it was my graduation present."

"What did you say to him?" Giuseppina asked.

"I was seventeen," Mark answered. "I said thank you."

Giuseppina laughed. "Good boy."

Luca noted the way everyone on the porch was listening: wide-eyed, enthralled, eating steadily, the way adventure movie watchers eat popcorn.

He passed the tray of appetizers.

Everyone helped themselves to seconds.

Mark poured himself a glass of ice water, then hopped back on the porch railing and sipped as he continued, "I took the dragon home. My mom said no, I couldn't accept such an expensive gift, and she and I took it back." Mark looked around. "In a box under a bunch of graded math tests which we figured Jack would avoid at all costs."

"Ha!" Morgayne exclaimed.

Zoey and Honor glanced at each other, then Zoey stared meaningfully at Luca and indicated he should bring the last wicker chair next to her.

Everyone seemed settled, so Luca decided she was right. It was time to fill a plate for himself, sit down and listen to every last titillating, tantalizing snippet. He brought the chair and settled it beside Zoey, got his plate, sat and balanced it on his knee. Leaning close, she put her forehead against his shoulder as if she needed a moment of support.

Honor observed with penetrating interest.

He hoped he could win her approval. These women were not identical twins, yet they looked like sisters. Honor was taller, Zoey was more intense, but they shared their skin tone and eye color and a dreamy, otherworldly quality that set them apart. Remembering how sincerely Zoey mourned the loss of her imaginary friend and seemed, even when she thought it impossible, to be looking for her, he knew Honor would be a part of their lives always.

Mark said, "Uncle Darrell was determined that I should have the dragon. Aunt Bonnie held the purse strings, always had, and he explained she wasn't going to pay for my college education, but this dragon would more than do it. He also explained his son was a viper and Aunt Bonnie was…undeserving, that when he died they would inherit a fortune. They didn't appreciate the antiquities he'd collected and they'd sell them for the cash. He wanted me to have the Dragon's Heart because I appreciated it, and I needed it. Mom said it belonged to the twins. Uncle Darrell said he would provide for them in different ways. At the time I thought that was okay, but now I know the Dragon's Heart should belong to Honor and Grace."

"If you sold it to pay for your college education, why are we still discussing it?" Luca thought he knew the answer.

So, apparently, did Zoey. "It's not as easy as that, is it, Mark?"

"No, it's not that easy. Once Uncle Darrell gave me the Dragon's Heart, the real one, he set about finding a buyer for me. He had to do it surreptitiously; if Bonnie had ever found out, she would have had him declared incompetent. While Uncle Darrell was engaged with that, Jack got himself into the biggest trouble of his life. We didn't know it at the time, but he got caught with his pecker in the…" Mark stopped talking, looked at Giuseppina and decided to change his way of expressing himself. "Jack was discovered in a state of undress with Gavin Sidorova's underage daughter."

"Is *that* what happened?" Morgayne nodded. "Figures."

Vadim coughed. "Bad move!"

"Who's this Sidorova character?" Giuseppina demanded.

"Friend of my brother," Vadim said. "One of the powers on the West Coast. Not a guy you want to get crossways with, especially about his little girl."

"Jack had to go on the run, and he had to go fast, and I would have been glad about that," Mark said, "but for what happened next."

Zoey stirred restlessly. "Mom, in all this, I don't understand. Why did you marry some guy as awful as Jack Torbinson?"

"Oh." Morgayne chuckled sadly and looked down at her hands folded in her lap. "I was pregnant…and the father of my child had just been sent to prison."

67

VADIM STOOD SO abruptly his chair toppled over backward. "Me? I'm the father of—" He swept an arm toward Zoey and Honor.

Morgayne stood, too, and said to Vadim, "Did that not occur to you?"

"We were careful!" he shouted. Then he rubbed his face. "It should've occurred to me. But my brother said…he made it sound as if you…and I knew you deserved better than me. When I got out, I wasn't even going to come back to Citation, but I couldn't keep away. I told myself I needed to see you to prove to myself that you were happy."

"That didn't work out well."

Zoey leaned forward. "Jack Torbinson is not my biological father?"

"Our biological father," Honor corrected.

"Our biological father," Zoey echoed.

"No." Morgayne could not have been more definite.

Honor looked at Zoey, did a thumbs-up and mouthed, *I knew it.*

Zoey sighed in relief. "Mom, you have to tell me how this all happened."

"Sure," Morgayne said readily. "I was the rich bitch in town."

Vadim leaped in. "You were never a bitch."

"Prom queen. Traditional parents who wanted me to grow up to be a housewife and mother. I would have done it, too, but I kept running into this guy." Morgayne pointed at Vadim.

He transformed himself with a grin. "I put myself in her way. She was so pristine. Clean. Pretty. She smelled good, like vanilla and cinnamon—"

Zoey knew what he meant. "She makes snickerdoodles when I ask."

Vadim nodded at her. "She smiled at everyone. She was nice to everyone. Even to me, and I was...my family was involved in every bit of theft and extortion in Northern California. With my older brother Dima in charge, we were expanding our range." He looked at Morgayne in a way that made Zoey want to cover her eyes. "I wanted to nail her."

Morgayne laughed. "I should have been horrified, but he was so rough, so genuine—"

"I genuinely wanted to nail you."

"—that I fell in love." She stopped smiling. "Which was stupid, because when Jack Torbinson got wind of it, he decided he wanted me. The Torbinsons were the important family in Citation, and Jack was a spoiled ratbag, used to getting his way."

"You fell in love with Vadim." Zoey wiggled her fingers questioningly. "How did he feel about you?"

"Every time I saw her, I felt as if I was running through a field of sunflowers in slow motion." Vadim's delivery was droll, but he was dead serious. "Meanwhile Dima did *not* approve of our entanglement, as he called it, and decided to induct me into the family business. I was to pick up stolen goods and transport them to Nevada. I got caught before the exchange was complete. Went to jail, got out on bail, went to trial, was sentenced to five years. I was a lousy thief."

"Or your brother set you up," Morgayne said.

Vadim nodded slowly. "Possible. The night before I was to be transported, I did a Romeo and climbed the tree outside Cynthia's bedroom and—"

"Like Juliet, I opened my window and welcomed him in."

"She pledged to love me forever."

"We made love." She sounded breathless, as if the memory took her back to the trembling edge of womanhood. Then her stance, her voice, her attitude changed to rock-hard affront. "After two weeks in prison, he wrote and told me he was no good, would never be any good, and to go on with my life."

Vadim turned on her. "I did not!"

"You did, too!"

"No, I—" He paused, caught by the hook of truth.

Morgayne gasped. "That son of a bitch Jack!"

"Or that interfering pain in the ass Dima." Vadim's voice ground like glass.

Morgayne leaned into his arms. He put his cheek against her and held her.

"Damned interfering people managing our lives. Look at the pain they caused." Morgayne looked up at him. "Could have been my parents, too."

"That occurred to me, too. Mostly, I'm so glad to know you didn't dump me as soon as I was out of town."

"No! I never would have… But once I found out I was pregnant, I didn't have a choice. My parents had raised me in the church. I had always tried to be the daughter they demanded… and now I was going to have a baby." Morgayne rubbed her forehead as if urging her mind to release the memories. "I couldn't face their displeasure, and honestly, I wasn't sure they wouldn't turn me out in the snow, figuratively speaking. So I ran away with Jack to Reno and got married."

Vadim's sad blue eyes grew haunted.

Morgayne stood, straight-backed and alone. "Jack was so…he thought he was such a stud, getting me pregnant on our honeymoon. I started showing right away and one of his cronies must have said something, because all of a sudden he was suspicious. And mean. He wanted me to abort and when I refused, that was the first time he hit me." Vadim reached for her, but she waved him away. "No. Let me tell this. When the ultrasound showed twins, he got conceited again. Then he read the results that said they were conceived before our marriage and all hell broke loose. And never stopped. The girls were fraternal twins: different sizes, different looks. Jack decided Honor looked like Vadim. He abused us all, but he particularly focused on Honor." She stopped. Stared into the past. And breathed. "I tried to leave him. My parents wouldn't help. My father-in-law had had a stroke. My mother-in-law threatened me. She said if I left Jack, she'd make sure I lost custody of my daughters." She looked around at them, in the now, proud and determined. "That's why I became a divorce lawyer. No woman who came to me ever succumbed to intimidation like that, or the shame that follows." This time when Vadim offered his hand, she took it.

Vadim took up his part of the story. "When I was released, I came back to Citation. Dima told me I was a fool, that Cynthia had forgotten me as soon as I left town, but I had to see for myself. I spotted her on the street. Somehow, no one had told me about the girls. I would have turned around and left, but… Honor's arm was in a cast. Cynthia's face was bruised. I waited for Cynthia to spot me, but she was hustling the girls along, glancing at her phone every few minutes, and they all had the pinched, pale expressions of the minor-offender prisoners I'd met. I followed them."

"Is that how you showed up? By accident?" Morgayne's voice rose. "Because you spotted us on the street?" But she didn't pull her hand away from his.

"I may have made some inquiries about how to find you," Vadim allowed. "I followed Cynthia and the girls to the Torbinson home, and there was Jack standing beside that penis-extender of a Mustang. He grabbed Cynthia by the arm and hustled her inside. Honor was crying. He turned on her and she shrank back. After that, I had a pretty good idea what was going on."

"You didn't know the girls were yours. You didn't know someone had lied to separate us. You didn't have to come in," Morgayne said.

"I thought hard before I did. From my perspective, you hadn't hung around pining after me for long. But something was wrong. I knew the kind of guy Jack was, so I knocked on the door."

Luca spoke up. "What you're saying, sir, is that you're a hero."

"No. No. I didn't have a choice. Cynthia was the love of my life, and I wanted her to be happy. Even if it was with Jack, I wanted her to be happy."

Hero, Zoey mouthed to Honor and Luca.

"The housekeeper recognized me as a friend of Jack's and let me in. I followed the sounds, found the twins sitting with their grandfather. The old man was trying to coax them to tell him what was wrong, what had happened to Honor's arm. I think he intended to do something about his son. Then I heard raised voices." He indicated Morgayne. "Hers I recognized, and I was transported back to that field of flowers."

Laughter rippled along the porch.

And hushed as soon as he spoke again. "I went in the dining room—long table, lots of lighted display cabinets filled with, my God, statues and gems and glasswork and ancient texts. One cabinet in the center held only a few items, and one was a black Asian dragon with compelling eyes."

"The Dragon's Heart." Honor sounded as enthralled as Zoey looked.

Vadim nodded to her. "Cynthia was arguing. Mrs. Torbinson was turning off the alarm. Jack told Cynthia to shut up, and he helped himself to the dragon. Mr. Torbinson arrived on his walker, summed up the situation, said a few impolite words about his son and his wife, and collapsed."

"He'd had a second stroke," Morgayne told them.

"Cynthia leaped to call 911. Jack knocked her backward and headed out the door."

"Vadim stopped him." Morgayne and Vadim were completing the story together.

"Jack pulled a pistol out of the inside pocket of his tough guy leather jacket." Vadim got a quirk in his cheek. "I'd been in prison long enough, I figured I could take it away before anyone was hurt—"

Morgayne interrupted, "Bonnie used a priceless vase to knock him cold."

"*That* I didn't see coming," Vadim conceded.

"She held the pistol on me while Jack tied Vadim up and put him in the Mustang. When that son of a bitch decided to take Honor, I leaped at him and he punched me right between the eyes. I went down and—" Morgayne's breath caught "—I couldn't get up. I struggled. Then... I was unconscious."

Vadim picked up his part of the story. "When I came to, I was tied up, sprawled in the back seat of Jack's Mustang. Jack was gunning it, taking curves at ninety miles an hour, knocking me from side to side—and Honor was in her car seat, crying softly. The dragon was tucked next to the car seat."

"My poor baby," Morgayne whispered, and gazed at Honor as if trying to memorize her face.

"I stayed low, got the binding off. Honor was watching. She was so scared, but not of me. It was Jack who terrified her, and I was determined not to let him hurt her again. I indicated to Honor she should throw the dragon into the front seat. She tried. She was only four. It was big. She was little. Her arm was in a cast." Vadim's words tumbled from him. "But seeing the dragon tossed got Jack's attention. He screamed at her. She tried again, and he reached back to slap her."

Even though he knew the results, Luca was riveted, frozen with anticipation. Beside him, Zoey was breathing fast, and beside her, Honor, who had lived through it, sat with her fist on her lips as if trying to contain a scream.

"I caught his arm. The car skidded sideways around the curve. I grabbed him by the back of the neck. His jacket was flapping, wide-open. I took the pistol out of his inner pocket. I shot him in the back of the head. The car careened off the road into a scenic overlook, flew into the deepest part of the lake and sank. I freed the car seat and retrieved Jack's wallet and…we lived." He wrapped it up with a minimum of drama.

Tears trickled down Morgayne's cheeks. "You kept our baby even though you didn't know she was yours."

"Of course she was mine. She clung to me, called me Daddy." Vadim leaned around to look at Honor, and he wore his affection in every glance and movement. "She was the one good thing in my life. Dima wasn't too happy, but he got us out of the country, helped me get training. He's not all bad, my brother."

Giuseppina settled back in her chair. "I'm too old for this kind of excitement." She fanned herself with a paper plate.

Luca thought of what his mother had done the previous day: saved Zoey by shooting a serial killer twice, taken care of his darling, fed her and insisted she sleep in his arms all through the night. *Too old?* Giuseppina was a marvel.

"What about you, Mom?" Zoey asked. "Why did *we* leave Citation?"

Morgayne gave a puff of frustration. "My mother-in-law lied about everything. The theft and the kidnapping she laid at Vadim's door, and everyone believed her. That second stroke incapacitated Darrell. He couldn't speak, he couldn't tell the truth. But he could hate her, and he did. She didn't care. She'd saved the reputation of her worthless son. I realized that as long as

Jack was out there and Bonnie was his cheerleader, Grace and I would never be safe. I took what money I could scrape up by selling Jack's possessions. I told Grace to forget all she knew, we moved to San Francisco to start anew…and every day I lived in terror of the day Jack would return to destroy our lives again."

Fog drifted through the yard and distributed the silence that fell over the group.

Morgayne sighed, then shook herself as if throwing off the old fears forever. Turning to Mark, she said, "So you see, it's kind of you to say my children are the true heirs to the Dragon's Heart, but they aren't related to you—or Jack."

68

MARK GRINNED. THEN HE LAUGHED. He laughed so hard he held his ribs as if they hurt. "That…is…the best…revenge on… Jack. Even better than…punching him silly." He calmed, but he still wore a big grin. "His kids weren't his, the dragon he stole was a fake and the real Dragon's Heart went to his despised cousin. Me." He looked around the porch. "Zoey, show them the cat's-eye stones."

Zoey put down her plate and dug the gems out of her pockets. She held them out toward him.

"Those are alexandrite," Mark explained, "the most precious of the gems known as cat's-eye, and the only valuable part of the fake dragon. Depending on the light, they change from yellowish-green to purplish-red. One gem each for Honor and Grace. It won't make up for all the trouble the Dragon's Heart has caused in your lives, but they're said to protect from the evil eye. After all this, celestial protection seems like a good idea."

The twins bent their heads over the stones, turned them and marveled.

"I'll help you choose which gem you get." Taking the stones,

Morgayne put them behind her back, shuffled them around and said, "Pick an arm."

The twins stared at their mother, looked at each other and both said, "Didn't you used to do that when we had to choose?"

"Yep." Morgayne grinned at them. "You do remember something."

They groaned and each picked an arm. Morgayne handed over the stones.

"The cat's-eyes are virtually identical." Mark sounded confused. "Why would you—"

Morgayne kissed Zoey and Honey on their foreheads, then seated herself next to Vadim again. "They're sisters. It saves squabbling."

"I did much the same with my daughters, only I didn't have enough arms." Giuseppina nodded her approval. "Mark, my hearing isn't what it once was."

Zoey exchanged glances with Luca. They both knew her hearing was excellent. On occasion, too damned good.

"I thought you said the Dragon's Heart was sold to pay for your education." Giuseppina leaned toward him as if to catch every word.

From the nods around the porch, that question had lingered in everyone's minds.

"No." Mark smirked. "I said Uncle Darrell *intended* to sell the Dragon's Heart to pay for my education. But after the second stroke, he couldn't walk. He didn't have full use of his hands. He lost his ability to speak. For me, at seventeen, it was horrifying. One day after Jack and Honor had disappeared, supposedly kidnapped by Vadim, I visited Uncle Darrell in rehab." Mark's eyes glowed with the kind of obsession only a true dragon worshipper could convey. "A stranger sat beside his bed, a man from Tajikistan."

Zoey gasped in shock. "Shasta's father!"

"The man who sold your uncle the Dragon's Heart?" Luca clarified.

"Yes, but… Mehrded sold Uncle the dragon for a minimal fee. At the time, his country was in turmoil, he'd been warned a dangerous thief had tracked down the Dragon's Heart—"

"Shasta's mother, Genesis." Zoey filled the gap for Honey and anyone else who might not have been privy to the whole tale.

"—and his intention was to protect the dragon, for opportunists would destroy the statue to get to the ruby heart."

Luca exchanged glances with Zoey. They remembered the frantic fortune hunters, sifting through the broken shards of the dragon, searching…searching… "The ruby was all they were after," Luca said. "That was all they cared about."

"Uncle Darrell knew that," Mark said, "and he vowed to always guard the integrity of the piece. When Mehrded visited Uncle Darrell in the care facility, his circumstances had changed. He was now famed as an artist and had the resources to keep the dragon safe. Before the second stroke, Uncle Darrell had intended to return the Dragon's Heart to him for enough money to put me through college."

In a wondering voice, Honor asked, "Did your uncle realize what the Dragon's Heart was worth?"

"Yes, but Uncle thought the dragon should return home, to Tajikistan, where Mehrded and his family had long been its guardians and would, in all honor, continue to be."

"Wow," Zoey said.

"Just wow," Honor agreed.

"Not everyone who knows the truth of the Dragon's Heart is corrupt," Mark said. "But—Uncle Darrell's private nurse was."

Zoey remembered Mark's outburst when he stepped into the shop. "Genesis!"

"Yes, seeing her clears up things I never understood, like why Mehrded never showed up for the exchange and how Uncle Darrell managed to trace Gracie's whereabouts and, I think, how a sudden heart attack killed him." Mark looked both sad and distressed. "Although it could have been Aunt Bonnie, too."

"Why bother with Darrell when it was known Jack had taken the dragon?" Morgayne asked.

The weary lines in Vadim's face settled into cynicism. "Genesis believed Jack would communicate with his mother and she could trace the dragon through him. Good logic, too. When he never returned to his mommy, we should have known he was dead."

Nods all around.

"So, Mark, do you have the real Dragon's Heart in your possession?" Zoey asked.

Mark said simply, "Yes."

For the first time, Zoey understood a little how the dragon hunters felt. Knowing Mark held the Dragon's Heart, that she might now see the legendary statue, sent a little buzz of excitement through her.

Honor glanced at her, eyes glowing. She understood. Of course she did.

"You never sold the Dragon's Heart?" Luca asked.

"No, I couldn't do that." Mark brushed that away with a whisk broom gesture.

"Isn't it priceless?" Morgayne asked. "You could have been wealthy beyond your wildest dreams!"

"I'm happy. Isn't that better?" Mark sounded and looked like a fulfilled man who had made his own way in the world. "I got a health sciences degree the usual way—scholarships, student loans, summer jobs, then added another three years in a DPT course and became a physical therapist. After working with Uncle Darrell, it was something I knew I could do well. I thought there was a chance Jack's kids were alive, and they deserved something their grandfather loved. I couldn't stand to deprive them of that. Then I would have been no better than Jack."

This time Honor mouthed, *Hero.*

Luca and Zoey nodded.

Giuseppina got to the important question. "Where is the Dragon's Heart now?"

"In the trunk of the Corvette."

Everyone stared at Mark, then out at his car, then at him again.

"In the truck of your Corvette?" Vadim repeated as if he couldn't believe it.

"There?" Zoey definitely couldn't believe it. "What if you'd been robbed? What if you'd been rear-ended?"

"Not possible. The dragon protects itself." Mark hopped off the railing and rubbed his hands in anticipation. "Do you want to see it?"

69

INITIALLY, ANGELICA LINDHOLM was displeased to discover the Gothic Garden and Flower Show wrap-up party had moved from her conservatory to Zoey Phoenix's yard and gardens, but when Marjorie told her that not only the featured Gothic gardeners would attend, but half the town intended to gate-crash, Angelica was, for the most part, relieved. After all, the day before she had returned from the hospital, and the day before that she'd been brutally attacked by her gardener, and although she hated to admit it, she had been traumatized and had not yet recovered her full strength.

Providentially, she had hired the best assistant she'd ever trained, and when Angelica had indicated her grudging approval, Marjorie swung into action. While Angelica rested, her staff boxed up the mountains of food and drink, loaded tables and chairs into her flatbed truck and transported everything down the hill. An hour later, when Marjorie drove Angelica to Zoey's, lights were strung, plates and silverware had been strategically placed and the food was ready to serve. Gothics were arriving carrying casseroles, appetizers, fruit desserts and bottles of fine California wine.

About the time Angelica realized that there weren't enough chairs, Freda Goodnight drove up in one of her pink Jeeps loaded with the Gothic Museum's folding chairs. When Freda came over to commiserate about Orvin's attack, she said, "Angelica, you could throw this party without breaking a sweat, but between the rest of us, we've got matters handled. Now sit and take it easy!"

It was true, the party had spontaneously coalesced into a sparkling tribute to the power of Gothic. For once, Angelica wasn't working. Instead she drifted through the party, observing, listening, admiring how the legendary fog had brought them lost souls, and those souls were now the backbone of the community.

Madame Rune had set up a fortune-telling station on the porch.

The Beards had provided goat milk caramels.

Sadie and Hartley's stone butterflies seemed alive in the light.

Deputy Dave had finished his shift, brought his wife to the party and found himself mobbed by Gothic citizens who wanted details about the events of the last two days.

In the living room, Mrs. Kulshan rested in the automated recliner Giuseppina had bought for herself and had had delivered late that afternoon—"Does she know she's not living with us forever?" Zoey asked Luca out of the corner of her mouth—while Mr. Kulshan sat beside Mrs. Kulshan, held her hand and described the expression on Angelica's face when she saw his beer garden.

Mrs. Kulshan beamed at him and told him he was a terrible man and she loved him and it was time they moved in together. The chances of one of them taking another fall was too great, and someone needed to be around to call for help. She already had a buyer for his house, that woman from New York, who would be a good neighbor.

He grumped a little about selling *his* house, but nothing very vigorous. Her accident had given him perspective.

When Thistle arrived, Vadim gave a shout of recognition, hurried over and shook his hand. He introduced him to Morgayne as one of his brother's guards, and Morgayne said, "You're the one sent to protect my daughter!" More reproachfully, "You didn't do a very good job."

"Wrong place, wrong time, but I was told to keep a low profile, and when the showdown occurred here, I was playing guitar on the garden tour bus." Thistle lowered his voice. "I did, however, apprehend two dragon hunters who were posing as a married couple. Clifford and Gloria, they said their names were. They took the tour, dropped out after they'd cased this place, and that made me suspicious."

"Did Deputy Dave arrest them?" Morgayne asked.

Thistle considered her as if the thought had never occurred to him.

Vadim took her arm and walked her away. "I'm sure they're in custody *somewhere*."

Three of Luca's sisters, Mina, Roxanna and Amelia, arrived to rescue Zoey from their mother's wrath and found Giuseppina giving Zoey a cooking lesson while Luca hovered in the background and dropped helpful hints like, "Use the teaspoon, not the tablespoon."

Roxanna said to Amelia, "Pretty sure it's snowing in hell right now."

Mina went out onto the far corner of the porch to join Thistle, who had settled onto a stool with his guitar, Señor Alfonso, who joined him with his bass, and Ludwig, who had set up his keyboard. They improvised jazz, rock and show tunes while Mina provided the vocals and every kid and couple in town danced on the lawn.

Set on a high shelf on the living room wall and lit by an improvised spotlight stood the guest of honor, the Dragon's Heart.

This dragon's shaped gold breastplate flashed with diamonds of exceptional color and clarity. Its grinning teeth and wicked sharp toenails gleamed with a pearly sheen of moonstone and glittered with violet amethysts. The jade scales along its spine started at its head as the richest green and faded, one by one, through red, pink, brown and ended with a black spike at the end of its tail. Rich blue sapphires had been shaped into scales and set into the silver-sheathed body—but nowhere on outer decorations of the Dragon's Heart existed a bloodred stone.

That was reserved for the perfect, mythical ruby inside its breast.

People stood beneath it and stared, hypnotized, saying many things, most of which boiled down to, "*How* much did you say it was worth?"

But there was also agreement that the dragon looked rightfully gleeful, and that his changeable cat's-eye jewels sparkled with the joy of life.

Mark Torbinson took up his station beneath the Dragon's Heart as a guard and to answer questions about the dragon's history: where it was created, where it had been and where it would go next. He was explaining to the ever-changing crowd that it was going into the private collection of the artist Mehrded until such time as the National Museum of Tajikistan could provide sufficient security to ensure its safety.

Eventually, Ripley Rath made her way over to him holding two glasses of fruit punch—no alcohol.

She wanted to compare workout programs. Before long, the dragon had acquired another dedicated guard and Mark had acquired a girlfriend.

Privately, Mark admitted to her he believed the dragon would remain safely in Mehrded's care and the care of his family, for no others would protect it with their lives.

Winifred from Mrs. Santa's Gifts and Tea Shop appeared with plates of cheese crackers and placed them in the center of Angelica's table. A swarm of Gothic residents descended and devoured them.

Winifred gloated at Angelica. She knew she now had the upper hand in the struggle for her recipe.

Morgayne and Vadim wandered around, holding hands, looking ridiculously happy and enveloping their daughters in unexpected and extended hugs. They stepped out on the porch and saw Honor pull a laughing Zoey out of the house to dance on the lawn while Luca stood at the railing, all his love shining from his face.

Vadim excused himself to Morgayne, walked over to Luca and said a few words that made Luca look very serious. When Vadim came back, Morgayne suspiciously asked, "What did you say to him?"

"I asked him about his intentions toward our daughter. He said he intended that they marry again and this time stay married. I told him tomorrow we'd discuss it, but he should take nothing for granted."

"And he said?"

"He said he could never take Zoey for granted. For him, she was magical. She makes flowers bloom."

"Good. She does have a gift. I'm glad he appreciates it." Morgayne gripped the railing and watched her daughters dance together. "Honor doesn't have any power to grow plants? Flowers? She doesn't...have a gift?"

"No. She works in Indonesia with animals, caring for them, researching... She's very talented, but..." Vadim gazed at the daughter he'd raised and loved. "She's not magical. Not the way you say Zoey is."

Morgayne put her hand over his. "The mere fact she's alive is magical, and it's all because of you."

The music stopped in the middle of a song.

Everyone turned to look.

Deputy Dave stepped up to the railing. "I got a call. Up on the north side of town, Mrs. Hummel went in to check on her two-year-old, and the child wasn't in her bed."

"Not a kidnapping." Madame Rune seemed very sure.

"No," Deputy Dave agreed. "The baby cam recording showed the little girl climbing out of her crib and out the window."

"Figures," Tamalyn said. "Trish is a handful. I've babysat her."

"I hate to have to pull anyone away from the celebration, but we need a search party." Deputy Dave gestured toward the parked cars. "If the usual group would fetch their gear, we'll meet in front of the Live Oak…"

Out on the lawn, Honor looked around as if hearing a call. She spoke to Zoey, then walked out to the edge of the lights. Zoey followed.

Morgayne watched with a frown.

At that point where the light disappeared, a dog trotted up to meet Honor.

No, not a dog. A coyote.

Honor knelt beside the mangy, ragged beast. She bent her head to its snout and appeared to listen. She nodded. She stood and walked back to Zoey, spoke to her, then continued back to the porch.

Now everyone was watching her.

Honor announced, "The coyote says there's a lost child out there, frightened and alone. She knows where the girl is. I'll follow her, you follow me, and before any of the dangerous predators find little Trish, we'll track her down. We won't let her suffer a night alone!"

★ ★ ★ ★ ★

**WOULD YOU LIKE TO ENJOY MRS. SANTA'S
AMAZING CHEESE CRACKERS?**
Find the recipe with a suggested wine pairing
on Christina's website, ChristinaDodd.com.
Search for "Mrs. Santa's cheese crackers," and be
the envy of your own Angelica Lindholm!

ACKNOWLEDGMENTS

Gothic is a fictional California town made up of memories and wishes, and The Husband drove me north on the Pacific Coast Highway (SR1) from Hearst's Castle to Monterey Bay, a marvelous adventure of a road that clings to the cliffs and swoops down to the beaches. Thank you to Scott for the planning and pleasure of traveling together.

Thank you to my editor, Michele Bidelspach, Executive Editor, HQN and Graydon House, and Susan Swinwood, HQN Editorial Director, who took over the task of guiding this book through editing while Michele took time out to be a mom. Thanks to Craig Swinwood, CEO of Harlequin and HarperCollins Canada, and Loriana Sacilotto, Executive Vice President and Publisher, Harlequin Trade Publishing: it's a pleasure to be publishing with this talented, dedicated team.

ABOUT THE AUTHOR

New York Times bestselling author Christina Dodd writes "edge-of-the-seat suspense" (Iris Johansen) with "brilliantly etched characters, polished writing, and unexpected flashes of sharp humor that are pure Dodd" (*Booklist*). Her sixty books have been called "scary, sexy, and smartly written" by *Booklist* and, much to her mother's delight, Dodd was once a clue in the *Los Angeles Times* crossword puzzle. Enter Christina's worlds and join her mailing list for humor, book sales and entertainment (yes, she's the proud author with the infamous three-armed cover) at christinadodd.com.